Memoirs of
Keladrayia

Jaxxa Rakala

Book 2 in the
Jaxxa Rakala Saga

A Novel
Bryan Caron

Memoirs of Keladrayia: Jaxxa Rakala
1st Edition
Published by Phoenix Moirai
©2015 Phoenix Moirai
publishing.phoenixmoirai.com

Text Copyright ©2015 Bryan Caron

Original Cover Art
Designed by Bryan Caron
Cover Model: Cecilia Shattuck • Photo by Susanna Shattuck
©2015 Bryan Caron

Back in 2013, when I published the second edition of *Jaxxa Rakala: The Search*, my plan was to publish the second novel in the four-part series in the summer of 2014, completely unaware of how my life was about to change. I left the job I had had for nine years and started my own business, which sucked up my time and energy like a ShamWow in a swimming pool. I watched as the deadline to complete the novel went from the summer of 2014 to late fall, to early winter 2015, to spring… all of which came and went without pause. However, through it all, I was able to carve out a few hours every few weeks to devote to getting this book completed, not only for my fans — some of whom had been waiting nearly ten years for the next chapter in the lives of Ken Brody and his family — but for myself, as the more time I spent away from writing, the more I felt I would never accomplish my ultimate goal.

Now that *Memoirs of Keladrayia* has arrived, I have several people to thank in helping me achieve success, not only in my writing, but in all of my creative endeavors.

First and foremost is my family, for whom without I wouldn't be able to write these books as quickly as I do, or pursue any of my life-long ambitions. Their support for my success is unbelievable and I cannot thank them enough for everything they've done to help me while I chase this maddening goal of becoming a successful writer, artist and filmmaker.

Secondly, I would like to send a sincere thanks to the Shattuck family. I don't know how many times I've infiltrated their home to film one of my crazy ideas, or requested the use of their film equipment for work and play. Without their incredible cooperation and dedication in helping me achieve greatness, I would not be where I am now. And I'd like to throw a special shout-out to Cecilia, who I've utilized in several of my projects to date. Thank you for continuing to be my go-to performer; you have a wonderful soul and to have you embody the character of Tracey is absolutely amazing. Keep dreaming and always seek the highest level of success in whatever you do.

Finally, and certainly not least, I would like to thank all of my terrific fans, readers and supporters. You are the blood of my craft; without you, I wouldn't be able to continue creating brand new worlds and delivering them to your anxious little hands. It's always a great feeling for any artist to know that someone out there (other than them) finds their work enjoyable, relatable and exciting.

Inspiration comes from a lot of places, but without the right kind of support, inspiration will always fade into the abyss.

Thank you all for keeping my dreams alive.

Memoirs of
Keladrayia

Jaxxa Rakala

Perils of Trynoruus

— 1 —

The sparring staff, which looked more like a wooden katana than a typical Bō staff, snapped across Jacquline's backside with the bite of a wet towel whipped across a gym shower. No amount of rubbing could polish the pain away from this or any of the other dozen or so welts Tracey had popped along the curves of her thighs.

"God, Squint," Jacquline said following an alleviating hiss. "Take it easy."

Tracey spun the staff to rest gently under her armpit and set her right foot back. She lowered her weight onto her front leg, prepping a fresh attack. "This isn't summer camp, Jacks. If you're not hurting, you're not learning."

Says you.

By Jacquline's calculations, it would be days before she'd be able to sit comfortably again. But it was well worth it. Since officially joining the *Equinox* crew, there hadn't been a lot of opportunities to do anything together. Tracey was a bit of an enigma following the battle on Xyneris, missing for hours on end, only to flutter past like a hummingbird on crack to get to her next self-appointed task. When she did take time to rest, Jacquline was either asleep or off doing something at the request of Qah-Shekel or Kahli. It was only when Jacquline learned Tracey spent a lot of time sparring with Qah-Shekel that she finally had a reason to spend time with her little sister — who wasn't all that little anymore, given her sudden growth spurt since merging (as Jacquline liked to call it) with the gem that made her appear to be a young teen—

She's still my eight-year-old sister, isn't she?

—with a slim, toned body and a gluttony of hair that pissed Jacquline off for being so perfectly wavy. Her outfit didn't help. Compiling a menagerie of accessories from Sentilla, Qah-Shekel and DovenJadden, she looked like a Disney fashionista if they allowed them to be hookers. At least she had those same magnetically periwinkle eyes that Jacquline loved so much.

Feeling her welts throb to the tune of her exhaustion (she had no idea it would be this physically strenuous, though she was aware she should have), Jacquline shook her head in defeat and squatted against the wall to catch her breath. She gripped her staff comfortably so that she could roll it up and down her thighs.

"You're too good," Jacquline said.

"Only because you allow me to be," Tracey said, never once releasing eye contact. "Slacker."

Jacquline didn't know whether to laugh or be offended, but Tracey's sly, adorable smirk was enough to fuel her determination. It was still a little uneasy wrapping her head around Tracey's alien-induced abilities (not to mention the body art that spread like vines along her entire body; at least the tattoos didn't dare rise to her face and blend with those brilliant crescents of hers), but when it came down to it, Tracey was nothing more than Jacquline's eight-year-old sister. There was no way she would be outmatched — not while Jacquline was still taller.

In one fluid motion, Jacquline jumped to her feet and spun around to give her staff the momentum needed to tattoo a nice little gift on Tracey's thigh. What she wasn't expecting (or maybe she was and only fooled herself into ignorance) was for Tracey to swing her staff into a defensive position across her body and snap Jacquline's staff so hard, it vibrated her hands to the point of numbness.

Jacquline dropped her staff and pranced around in circles attempting to swear the pain away. "Damn it, Tracey," she spit out when she could finally curl her fingers without feeling they might break off. Tracey remained statuesque as Jacquline shook the residual sting from her hand and picked her staff back up. It wasn't more than a second later that Tracey lunged forward. Without realizing, Jacquline hooked her hands around the thinly curved thorns coming off the staff in pairs about a third of the way up from either side and shielded herself from the attack. For a beginner, Jacquline was impressively agile. She sidestepped a downward thrust and somehow snapped the staff across Tracey's back to push her off balance. The smile that beamed off her lips was nothing more than genuine shock.

From that point on, Jacquline remained on the offensive, soaking in a tremendous amount of confidence matched only by Tracey's insistence on effortless defense. Every swing pushed Tracey a step back, eventually forcing her to drop to the floor so she could maneuver around Jacquline and slide back into the open arena. Coming to a stop, Tracey gently rested her fingertips on the floor and peered up at Jacquline, who took the maneuver as a sign Tracey was nearing defeat.

How wrong she was.

Jacquline spun around to whip her staff across Tracey's stomach, but wasn't planning on Tracey shifting just enough to block the blow and flip her own staff upward to knock Jacquline's hands loose. As Jacquline sought to regain her grip, Tracey planted her staff into the floor and used it to slide between Jacquline's legs. She transferred her staff from one hand to the other by wrapping it around her sister's ankle and stood. Before Jacquline could make nuts and bolts of the situation, Tracey struck the back of her knee. For a split second, Jacquline's leg went numb; she had no other recourse but to drop to the floor. As she did, Tracey pressed her staff across Jacquline's neck, resting one of the thorns along the edge of her carotid artery. The pain piercing through Jacquline's leg was nothing compared to the agony of defeat.

"What did you do wrong?" Tracey said, shoving her knee into her sister's spine.

Jacquline knew the answer but couldn't admit it.

"She was overconfident," Qah-Shekel said. He walked into the sparring hall and picked a staff from off the wall near the entry, the only part of the circular room that had even a hint of an edge or a flat surface. He examined the staff carefully. "Overconfidence is your enemy."

"The worst kind," Tracey said. She stepped toward the center of the hall where the ornamental artwork on the floor met in a circle connecting the points of a disjointed star. She never once took her eyes off Qah-Shekel, who in turn never turned his sights from his staff as he inched his way toward her. Jacquline wasn't paying much attention to any of this, having slid her way to the wall where she rubbed the unnecessary humiliation from her neck. When Qah-Shekel finally looked up to Tracey, he circled her like the vulture he was. No amount of growth could turn Tracey's frame into being anything but half the size of Qah-Shekel's. If he wanted, he could snap her in two like the brittle twig she was. But with the way the gem instantly lit up in his presence, if it came down to it, Jacquline was certain it would actually be the other way around.

Several minutes passed in silence as both opponents circled one another, matching the other's movements with eagle-eyed precision. Jacquline grew weary (and a little dizzy) watching them.

Fight already! she thought — she wasn't stupid enough to say it out loud. The second something like that left her lips, no doubt it would provoke them to turn on her instead. Jacquline's abilities were green enough against Tracey; she could only imagine the whooping she'd get if she teamed up with Qah-Shekel. So she remained quiet as a mouse, moving only slightly to stretch her muscles — an action that inadvertently caught Tracey's eye.

The distraction opened the door for Qah-Shekel. He raced forward with the snap of a dart, aiming his staff at Tracey's upper arm. Before it hit her, Tracey twisted her body and brought her staff up to meet his. The force of the blow sent her reeling backward but did nothing to break her concentration. Tracey steadied herself and found a strong footing before Qah-Shekel's follow-up attack. She remained on the defensive for a bit longer, and though Jacquline thought at first it was because Qah-Shekel had much more training —

Tracey's finally met her match!

— she knew it couldn't simply be a defense. It was a strategy.

Tracey watched every move Qah-Shekel made as he attacked, studying the intricacies of his movement. When she was confident in her ability to use his habits (and in some cases, his weaknesses) against him, Tracey knocked him slightly off-balance with a strong counterattack. It wasn't enough to disrupt his footing, but it was what she needed to start pushing her own offense. For the next several minutes, each participant took turns on the offensive, each one defending with the strategy of a master martial artist. Tracey rolled and sprinted like a playful kitten, using her agility to continually regain the upper hand; Qah-Shekel periodically changed the position of his feet, extending his fins to balance himself and using his strength to attain control of the bout.

Jacquline wasn't sure who impressed her more. Before this entire mess with alien encounters and planetary exploration, the simple act of Tracey standing up for herself was enough to amaze Jacquline. Now she wasn't only speaking in complete sentences, she was smarter than almost everyone Jacquline knew combined, exhibited skills that could rival a Jedi, and had as much confidence as George Clooney hunting for bunnies at the Playboy mansion. She knew it had everything to do with her connection to the gem. Regardless, Tracey was a completely new person Jacquline couldn't help but admire. At the same time, Qah-Shekel had grown into a very close friend. Being stuck on board the *Equinox* felt like navigating the globe in a barrel and never once finding land, so when Qah-Shekel asked her to accompany him (usually at the behest of Kahli) to an exotic world to help trade artifacts they had picked up on a couple of deserted planets in exchange for parts they needed to repair some minor systems that had been destroyed during the vermon attack on Hasten-Jackai, Jacquline didn't have to be asked twice. She felt a little insulted when she found out she was only asked because of her skills as a thief, but the exhilaration in stealing those parts right out from under that pompous alien's nose was so refreshing, Jacquline disregarded Qah-Shekel's initial motives. The point was, she proved herself capable and was asked to do the same on various other planets when the necessary goods or food rations couldn't be attained through any amount of respectable trade. Qah-Shekel trusted her to get the job done and respected her skills to the point that he once allowed her to conduct a trade on her own. How Jacquline was even able to do it, she might never know, though Kahli told her it was because of the level of vibration in her voice. Whatever the reason, her sex appeal still won over the simplicity of the hormone-fueled male anatomy, regardless of whether they even had any genitals or not. The best part was Ken never objected, which was surprising to say the least, but no less appreciated. Qah-Shekel and Jacquline had become a great team despite the verbal barrier that kept them from being able to speak to one another. They learned how to speak by other means that were far more important than words. It was very similar to the way he and Tracey spoke to each other in battle, sharing secrets in the way they danced along their strategic ballet. Jacquline was sure it wouldn't last forever; one of them would eventual find the other's Achilles heel.

And as if on cue, Tracey allowed Qah-Shekel to push her toward the wall during a relentless attack from both sides of his staff. The moment she felt her back touch the smooth, cool surface, she pushed her own staff against Qah-Shekel's and used the force of his strength to walk the wall. Her momentum (and possibly a little juice from the gem) helped her flip over Qah-Shekel and land just behind him. Before he was able to turn, Tracey sent a finishing blow to his torso — enough to drop him to his knees. Qah-Shekel was not one to concede in battle, but in this instance, he was happy to do just that with pride for his opponent. He lowered his staff to the floor and raised his arm, making sure to keep his head turned from his enemy. Upon doing so, Tracey took a few steps back and steadied herself with a defensive stance.

"Rise," she said.

Qah-Shekel did as ordered, lifting the staff along with him. As he faced her, he laid the staff across both hands and bowed, holding it out until Tracey accepted his gift — his defeat.

"Well done, young one," Qah-Shekel said.

"As to you," Tracey said, presenting him with a respectful curtsy.

Jacquline took that as her cue to applaud. "Yeah, that's my Squint. Take him down!" Qah-Shekel my have been a little upset for offering her praise to Tracey (with no accolades for him), but she threw him a wry smile in hopes of convincing him she would always respect his prowess.

"Do you know how I did it?" Tracey asked Jacquline.

"You used his strength and overconfidence against him."

"What else?"

"You used a tried and true poker trick. You bided your time until you could read all of his tells and when it was time, you struck."

"And why would I do that?"

"In this scenario? Probably because he's a freakin' beast."

"Precisely. On paper, I'm no match for him. He's bigger, he's stronger and he's had a lot more experience in combat. I should have been finished in thirty seconds."

"Probably fifteen."

"But because I remained patient," Tracey continued, ignoring Jacquline's comment, "and didn't allow my emotions to control me, it gave me time to come up with a plan that worked in my favor."

"Yeah, I get it. It doesn't matter how strong or experienced my opponent is, as long as I put my mind to it, I can accomplish anything. I know this already. What's your point?"

"My point is it goes both ways. You have to be just as patient and just as cunning when you're the stronger opponent. The moment you let your guard down is the moment you get bit."

"Never underestimate your opponent. Got it."

"And never take anything at face value. Deception can only hurt you if you let it."

"Understood, sensei." Jacquline pressed her palms together and bowed forward.

Tracey quickly snapped Jacquline's head with her staff. "Aye. Always look eye."

Jacquline broke into painful laughter. Qah-Shekel stood bemused at her mirth but remained utterly confused.

"I'll leave you," he said, which only led to more laughter. He was gone shortly after.

As Jacquline got her amusement under control and wiped the moisture from her eyes, Tracey fell to her knee. She was able to plant her hand firmly against the floor but had to drop one of the staffs to do so. Jacquline was next to her within the time it took the staff to finish its song against the floor. She pressed her hands to Tracey's back to help support her (or so she thought). "Tracey? Are you okay?"

Tracey didn't answer.

Jacquline was down on her knees now, trying her best to get Tracey to look at her. "Tracey?"

"Yeah," Tracey finally said. "Enough with the fun and games." She handed Jacquline her staff. "Time to get back to work." Tracey picked up the second staff and stepped away, deliberately hiding her face from Jacquline under her glistening hair. At first, Jacquline felt like forcing Tracey to rest; it was clear that the last few weeks had taken their toll on her. But then it occurred to her —

It's a damn test, isn't it?

Jacquline rolled her eyes. Tracey had just gone over this whole thing and here she was falling for it. Even though the pain in her thighs had become inflamed, she swung her head around in circles to crack her neck and then did a few jumps to pump herself up. "You ready, then?" she asked.

Tracey shifted her hair from her face and set her feet defensively.

I knew it, you little weasel! Game on.

Jacquline took her cue from the last challenge and waited as patiently as she could for Tracey to make the first move. After several minutes, and not one bite from Tracey, Jacquline realized that tactic wasn't going to work.

"What was all that with the staff, anyway?" she said as she gently bounced the staff in her hand, apparently gauging the weight of it.

"It's a sign of respect for when the student surpasses the master. An acknowledgment of an honorable defeat." Not one inch of movement. Not one.

"Cool."

"You can expect the same of me when I have been mastered."

"You better believe that."

Tracey nodded.

"But I can't master any of it if we don't fight, now can I?" Jacquline lowered her body, holding her staff out in front with both hands.

"I suppose not."

But Tracey didn't attack as Jacquline had expected. Instead, she relaxed her body and lowered her staff as if she had given up. Jacquline felt like doing the same, to question what was happening, but for all she knew, it was just another distraction.

Never take anything at face value.

So she stood her ground and waited.

"We'll have to pick this up later," Tracey said. "Duty calls."

Thank God, Jacquline thought, hoping against hope that she hadn't said it out loud.

— 2 —

"She's growing stronger," Qah-Shekel said as he crossed the threshold of the command center.

Sentilla sat quietly in the pilot seat, carefully monitoring the information produced by the ship's sensors as she navigated the *Equinox* through a mind-numbing stretch of dead space — a laborious task that would make even the wild beasts of Lourou grow mad with tedious fever. Traveling through a galaxy full of stars was one thing; at least then the ship was able to calculate the presence of celestial objects and reconfigure flight paths accordingly. Not so with dead space, where nothing could be seen or documented, forcing pilots of some of the most sophisticated ships to navigate manually, else find themselves lost among the void or destroyed by some rogue comet, wandering star, or a debris field of scraps leftover from the destruction of a ship and other types of trash. Sentilla would normally have Lark perform such tedious tasks for her (as her own mother had tasked her to do as a child) if she hadn't been so intent on hiding from Tracey — or more to the point, her precious gem.

"We knew she would," Sentilla said softly. She fought hard to ignore the presence of the gem, which wafted from Qah-Shekel with a light musk.

Noticing her discomfort, Qah-Shekel asked, "Is it still bothering you?"

"Like a sore in my ass," Sentilla said. "And it's getting worse."

"How so?"

"I can smell it now — it's sweet, scintillating scent. It was bad enough listening to its damn song, but now I'm hungry for it. And you're not making it any easier." Sentilla's hands shook lightly. She tried to hide it, but Qah-Shekel was far too clever for that. He took her hand and rubbed her palm with his thumb. It felt nice — relaxing.

"You can't hide from it forever. If it's growing stronger, it will eventually get the better of you. By then, it'll be too late to do anything about it."

She pulled her hand away and held it across her chest. "Don't worry. I'll figure out how to control it."

"And remain isolated in your quarters?"

"If I must."

Qah-Shekel reached out to caress Sentilla's head but was met with hostility. "You can't do that," he said, his voice now an octave lower.

"Lark" (the name of which still brought a slight dryness to her mouth) "knows the ship well enough to do what needs to be done if it comes to that."

"That's not what I meant."

Sentilla took a moment to relax her body but it was still extremely hard to look at Qah-Shekel with even the slightest of glances.

"What other choice do I have?"

"We can speak to Kahli."

"And have me put back in the chamber? No thank you."

"Sentilla, you have to try something."

"It didn't help the first time." Sentilla was now on her feet, her voice raised. "What makes you believe it'll work now?"

Qah-Shekel lowered his head and shifted his body in an attempt to calm Sentilla's raging demeanor. He would need her calm for what he was about to ask. "Have you considered Jaxxa Rakala's thoughts on the matter?"

"That I need to accept it for it to go away? Bullshit. The moment I accept it is the moment I become its slave. I am not about to allow that to happen. I am nobody's slave."

Qah-Shekel was silent. When the tension between them eased, he pulled her into a soft embrace, one she thought about fighting but accepted nonetheless.

"We'll get through this."

Sentilla nodded. She felt safe in his arms as she always has, but this time was different. This time, she felt seduced by the chill of his body. She wanted to taste him, to consume him. Gently resting her lips against his skin wasn't enough; she had to lick him and nibble his flesh like a ravenous shark. But just the touch of his skin was enough for her to realize what was happening and push him away. Resting her hand to her lips, she stepped back, fear controlling every muscle in her body. She wasn't sure what to do; she wasn't sure what to say or how to make things go back to normal.

"We're close," Sentilla said, responding to the ring in her ear. "Go. I'll be okay."

Even though Qah-Shekel wanted to help her, he knew staying would only make things worse. He left her to be at peace, but the gem's presence (even if it was just a hint) remained to agitate Sentilla to the point of shakes. She fought her tears with as much strength as she could muster — which as of right now wasn't nearly enough.

— 3 —

Joining a chain gang might have been a better sentence for Ken than the backbreaking labor he was assigned on the *Equinox*. He didn't mind when the work involved the ship's systems, such as repairing the motherboard in the Core so the lightning unit would no longer have to run off the bypass system (which would have burnt out had they traveled much farther without fixing it), but when it came to menial tasks that wouldn't even befit a janitor, Ken felt the crew may have taken the idea that he was the most expendable member of the crew a little too far. He couldn't complain, though, as doing so would make him seem petty or uncooperative, and that wasn't something Ken wanted to display no matter how much he may have felt it.

Your time will come eventually, Ken. It will.

So he kept his head down and did the work, which for now was stripping his ship for parts, cleaning up the destruction the vermon had left behind in the cargo bay, cataloging and organizing the food rations and equipment Qah-Shekel had acquired over the past few weeks — some of which weighed more than his ship (or at least felt like it) — and basically being DovenJadden's shadow, doing everything she asked, even if it felt like she was more a slave driver than a supervisor. It was obvious she had objected profusely to the whole idea when Qah-Shekel first mentioned it. Because of that, she hardly ever helped him when he was struggling, making it that much harder to prove he was worth more than an unsalted cracker. He wasn't sure if it was because Kahli had to step in and referee an argument they were having over the best way to install the new radiation regulator Ken urged Qah-Shekel to acquire so they could work inside the Core while traveling through space without fear of radiation poisoning (which Kahli eventually sided with Ken on), but DovenJadden was not about to give him any respect whatsoever.

The whole situation made him homesick. Not necessarily because he hadn't stepped foot off the *Equinox* since leaving Xyneris, but because he had very little contact with the people he trusted the most. Apart from joining Ken to clean and dispose of all the dead vermon scattered around the ship, Lark chose to spend most of her time studying Qah-Shekel's language with Kahli, which she apparently now had a decent fluency in, as evidenced by how they interacted with each other. When she wasn't with Kahli, she would be lost in her own world (or lost somewhere on the ship) or be dead asleep. The last time he spoke to her was when the ship set down on Dracmar to give Massanah a ceremonious burial. Ken tried to get her to convince Qah-Shekel to let him join them (if only to be able to get off the ship for one minute), but this would be the last time the engines would be shut down, and he was obligated to get the radiation regulator online before they were ready to leave. As for Jacquline, she had somehow formed a bond with Qah-Shekel that not even Ken thought he'd ever be able to acquire. He tried several times to sit down and talk, get her to open up about her depression, but whenever he did, she'd make an excuse to be somewhere else. And though he got some updates from Lark early on about Tracey's progress, lately it was as if she no longer existed. Judging by what the gem had apparently done to her, she no longer did — at least the shy little girl he remembered.

DovenJadden knocked Ken from his introspection with a slap to the backside of his head. His first instinct was to rip into her for even touching him, then realized why she had done it. He had started cutting into a pile of melted debris to better transport it to the compost recycler (one of the modifications Naja-Leku had added to the ship) and was slicing into the wall, which, if he wasn't careful, could sever the fiber cables regulating the holographic units throughout the ship. (Best case scenario, he only cuts a few circuit boards that operate the cargo bay's shelving compartments.)

"Sorry," he said while rubbing his fist circularly across his chest.

After a snip and a hiss, DovenJadden went back to tearing apart the engine of Ken's ship. If there was one thing Ken was proud of it was how much DovenJadden admired his design (regardless of how rudimentary it might have been). But it didn't matter much, since it was near impossible to make her see him as anything but an unintelligent nuisance. He thought maybe if there wasn't a language barrier he might have been able to convince her otherwise a long time ago; then again, with the bitterness and resentment she seemed to horde, not being able to understand each other was more than likely a good thing.

"Just imagine what might happen if we actually understood each other," he once mentioned to Lark.

"You'd be in medical twenty-four seven," Lark jokingly replied.

She wasn't far off. Even the sign language Ken created to help communicate with her gave her fits. Then again, having the ability to speak his mind and talk things through without feeling judged was actually quite liberating — and in some ways therapeutic.

"I don't know," Ken said, adjusting the blade to properly cut the rest of the scrap. "Watching Tracey mature so quickly is unsettling. I mean, I haven't seen her very often in the past couple of weeks... weeks, that's actually funny since there really is no way to know how long it's been, is there? I feel like I've only slept for two hours in the last month, but who really knows, right? But Tracey... she's blossoming into such a beautiful young woman, which is exactly why it's so bizarre. Just the word blossoming... it makes me feel a little uncomfortable. I remember when Jacquline hit puberty. I don't know what I would have done had it not been for Stacey. I wish she was here for Tracey, but I don't know. The gem seems to be taking care of whatever life cycle Tracey's going to be experiencing." Ken laughed at this. Just the thought of Tracey as an alien —

My daughter isn't even my daughter!

— was enough to send anxious chills down his spine, even after having known about it for as long as he had. "I don't think I'll ever feel comfortable about that. I mean, I love her, she's my flesh and blood, but knowing that she's so much more than that... so different... I know I shouldn't focus on that. It's no different than an interracial relationship, right? So what if she has special powers, or might be the key to destroying the universe...? She's my daughter. She may be eight years old going on fourteen, but I love her. I do."

DovenJadden carefully set one of the reactor tubes at his feet and pointed to the wall behind him. Ken smiled. She had no idea.

"And then there's Jacquline," Ken continued as he slipped the laser knife into one of the pouches of the utility belt he wore around his waist. He tapped a password into the wall (a procedure Ken was still getting used to) and opened an empty storage unit. "She's coming into her own quite nicely. I mean, she's been calling me dad, which I have to say is an awesome feeling. But I have to admit, that too is a bit unsettling. Maybe because —"

He was silenced by the call over the communication bud Kahli had implanted in his ear about a week back, just before the excursion to Dracmar. It was almost as if it was his badge of honor; having the communication bud was a sign that no matter what DovenJadden and the rest of them thought of him, he was officially part of the crew. He wouldn't ever take that for granted.

He listened intently as the message was relayed in two languages — one for his sake, the other for the rest of the crew. "I guess that means we're done for the day."

DovenJadden had left the cargo bay without Ken even realizing it. He just laughed… and followed her. It was soon after that his stomach mutated into a dozen knots. The call wasn't just some random exercise announcement; he was one step closer to having Stacey back in his arms. For all it was worth, and for all he was forced to put up with just to get by, she was still the most important part of everything.

— 4 —

Lark's knees rested gently against her chest as they always did when she hunkered down in a compartment (which she dubbed "her little clubhouse") that was hardly large enough to house a rocking chair much less a person. It wasn't the most ideal hiding place, but it was the perfect spot to escape the compression of culture shock she experienced from time to time. Although she was becoming fast friends with everyone on the *Equinox*, and had no intentions of ever returning to Earth, she still had the occasional bout of uncontrollable shaking or tearful outburst, much like she had the first couple of months at the Air Force Academy. She was eighteen with no friends to speak of, and although she had been out on her own for several years, there was something about the school's discipline and meticulousness that rubbed her the wrong way. She was fine during the day — going to classes, studying up on the different types of aircraft and history of the military (and everything else you would expect from a normal college) — but at night, she was an alley cat forced to become a house cat. She broke down quite often as she tried to study, but always made sure to bring it under control before her roommate (who broke curfew more often than she smoked a joint, but never once asked if Lark wanted to tag along — something she would have jumped at the chance to do) returned to get her requisite two hours of sleep before the next day's classes began. She eventually acclimated to the environment, as would be expected, and knew it was only a matter of time before she felt as comfortable here as she did sitting behind the cockpit of an F-22 Raptor. At least she had finally gotten used to not being able to see color thanks to Kahli, who started teaching her how to pick out a variety of colors based on their particular shade and tint.

To counter her disorientation, Lark took up cataloging every aspect of the *Equinox*, something Kahli never understood since detailed holograms and information could be accessed within seconds from any part of the ship that was assembled with holographic panels (which, as Lark would quickly find out, was basically the entire ship).

"It helps me think," Lark had said, "and it'll help me remember."

No matter how many hours she spent with Lark going over Naja-Leku's notes or teaching her Qah-Shekel's language (which she had already become nearly fluent in), Kahli could never wrap her head around what she was going through. Nonetheless, she suggested Lark try to write down all of her thoughts and feelings like Naja-Leku used to do, since that always seemed to center his mind. Lark was all for it as long as she had a secret spot where no one would be able to find her, even when they scoured the entire ship looking for her. It took Kahli all of a second to recommend a compartment unit that sat just outside her living quarters. She then gave her a paper-thin glass tablet that couldn't have been more than the size of a basic iPhone to compile information about the ship —

To keep her calm

— as well as the swarm of thoughts that caused her to feel so overwhelmed.

Lark found the device quite fascinating. Back on Earth, her thoughts were almost always traveling at the speed of light while her fingers traveled a snail's mile, which meant if she wasn't fast enough to write her thoughts down (or was busy doing something else), they would flitter off into the ether of lost ideas. With this new tablet, all she had to do was swipe her finger across the glass and every word of every thought would be transcribed into the system's memory. It wasn't quite the same as physically writing it down (or even typing it, for what it's worth), but there was still a sense of emotional release induced by the tablet, as if it wasn't only the words that were being extracted from her mind, but everything attached to them as well — the fears, the joy, the pain and the excitement. It felt good; no matter how hard it might be to get those feelings out, it always left her in a better mood than when she started.

Lark set her head against the wall and rubbed her eyes. After hours of working in the dark with nothing but the glow emanating from the edges of the tablet, her eyes always got a bit weary, regardless of what she was writing at the time (which for now were notes on a series of syntax keys to help remember certain turns in Sentilla's language). Though it could also have something to do with how hungry she was.

But whose fault is that?

Lark made the choice to limit her rations, sometimes eating hardly but every other day and only drinking when her mind felt more like a cloud than a functioning hard drive. It was worth it to make sure Jacquline — with her super sonic metabolism — and Tracey — who, despite sprouting faster than a weed, probably could have relied on the gem to survive — were able to stay healthy until the crew could reacquire the rations they had lost from the vermon attack. She could feel her stomach biting just thinking about it, but she would fight it for as long as she could, which based on the substantial gains over the past couple of weeks thanks in most part to Jacquline and her... special skills, wouldn't be that much longer.

Just then, a light started flashing. At first, Lark wasn't quite sure where it was coming from, but then realized it was her cast.

HEALING COMPLETE

"It's about god damn time," she whispered, covering the screen. She laid her head back and closed her eyes. Why was she getting so emotional about this? With all of the abuse she'd taken over her life, she often wondered how she had even survived half of it. For a while, she considered maybe she was indestructible.

"What can I say, I'm a fighter," she once mentioned to a bunkmate during a training mission that saw Lark hospitalized for a broken wrist, several broken ribs and lacerations caused by shrapnel from a rogue IED. "With what I've been through, I don't even think death could break me."

And it didn't... It didn't.

Like every other injury she's sustained, Lark's wounds would always heal — all except the deeply set internal wounds that no medicine would ever be able to cure; the ones she buried so deep, she forgot they existed; the ones that bubbled to the surface whenever a new external injury crippled her in some way, only to be suppressed once more when those injuries — her limp, her wrist and her hand included — fully healed.

"Attention all crew," Kahli said, her voice booming over the communication bud Kahli insisted all of the humans get installed, for lack of a better word. Ken wasn't sure if he'd ever get used to constantly having a voice pop up in his ear, but for Lark, it was all in a day's work. "Report to tactical immediately." The message was repeated in Qah-Shekel's language and Lark made sure to make a mental note on how it was delivered. As Lark had found out, it wasn't just the syntax that mattered; a word could mean a variety of things simply by the vocalization in her voice. Obviously, Krylexians never participated in any type of social media.

Or used Siri, for that matter.

Lark chuckled and was about to press her fingers together (as had become almost second nature), but when no one else chimed in, she decided to let the message go unanswered, even if it did feel awfully strange to do so.

She tapped the lower left corner of the tablet as she always did when she was finished transcribing, uploading the text to a private port on the ship's mainframe that only Lark had access (or so Kahli claimed) from any holoscreen on the ship. Lark was never certain when or how fast the text was uploaded, but she never waited longer than a few seconds. That was all it took to believe her life was being saved.

— 5 —

Lark was the last to enter tactical. Kahli and DovenJadden were in the middle of a heated discussion near the far corner (though with DovenJadden, everything was heated; that one was never happy) and Ken stood nearby pretending to listen. Jacquline sat across the room, red as a blood vessel, guzzling down water as if it were going out of style. Near the holostation at the center of the room, Qah-Shekel and Tracey discussed some information that Lark couldn't quite make out. When he caught sight of her, Qah-Shekel quieted the room in his exquisitely commanding voice. Lark walked to Ken as Kahli took her station next to Qah-Shekel, leaving DovenJadden seething in disgust. She must not have been happy with the outcome of their conversation.

"Where's Sentilla?" Lark whispered to Ken as Kahli danced her fingers across the holostation to replace the information the team had been examining with an image of a smoky globe.

"On the bridge, I think."

"She's not joining us?"

"Not with Tracey here."

"Right," Lark said, the word elongated for effect.

Tracey looked over at them as if she had heard them — which she probably did. Her hearing had become more powerful than Kahli's. It was hard to place her mood; she seemed frightened and disappointed at the same time. Lark smiled anxiously, hoping to lighten the tension that drifted between them.

"All right everyone," Kahli said after a lengthy conversation with Qah-Shekel. "As you may already know, the reason I have asked you here is to discuss some important matters in regards to our arrival on Trynoruus."

Lark took Ken's hand, which was understandably clammy. She didn't mind it; not one bit. In fact, she was almost expecting it, seeing as how they were that much closer to finding Stacey — in Ken's eyes anyway. Lark was a bit more pessimistic about it, saying they were closer to *learning* about Stacey, and in all honesty, that's what this was all about. Believing anything they find on Trynoruus would give them a clue to her whereabouts was about as slim as a piece of paper. But she liked that he believed it would — it gave him hope, and that's all that really mattered. What she was most excited about, along with the slight hint of a smile, was that he didn't try to let go of her hand (swearing he had gripped it even tighter).

Spreading her hands across the holostation, Kahli enhanced the size of the globe until the world became a cloudy mess of flashing blue lights that looked more like a frantic group of fireflies signaling a distress call.

Jacquline stood. "What is that?" She got as close to the hologram as she was willing, making sure (if only subconsciously) to keep a slight distance from Qah-Shekel. The closer she got, the more the lights transformed from indistinguishable dots into tiny streaks jumping across the surface. "Is there something wrong with the projector?"

"I wish it was," Tracey said. It was odd to see her so glum — and yet still radiating a level of positivity.

"What you see is a massive, global lightning storm," Kahli said. "From the readings we have gathered, the planet has become highly electrical since the war."

"What's that mean for us?" Ken said. His grip on Lark's hand had officially become tighter.

"Do not worry, Kenneth. Though the planet itself is uninhabitable, it is not impossible to explore the region."

"So long as we don't overstay our welcome," Tracey added.

"That's all well and good," Jacquline said, "but if the planet's uninhabitable, what's the point of even exploring it? It's obvious Stacey isn't there. And even if she did come back at some point, I doubt she would have stayed."

Lark rested her hand on Ken's upper arm, hoping it might calm him. All he did was pull away. For a moment, Lark wasn't sure what to do with either of her hands.

"I informed you before we set course for Trynoruus that there was only —"

"— a fraction of a chance that we'd find any evidence of her here," Ken cut in. He squeezed his arms across his chest. "I know." And then lower, with heavy disappointment,

"I know..."

"The reason we're here is to find *something* that might help us discover where she is," Tracey added in a voice so calm, it relaxed Ken. "It always has been."

"I don't know about you," Jacquline said, "but choosing to become a roasted marsh-mallow is not my idea of a good time. In my humble opinion."

Tracey opened her mouth to say something, but Jacquline cut her off. "And don't tell me the odds of getting hit by lightning are slim to none. Look at it. Why even chance it? I mean, where did everyone go after all the static electricity took over?"

"A better question would be, how could you know they went anywhere?" Tracey said.

"Tracey is correct," Kahli said. "There has been no recorded events or any physical indications that would suggest the population ever found refuge off of the planet. From what I have gathered, the storms rose quickly and unexpectedly. They may very well have killed every last survivor of the war."

"You don't think any of them might have taken refuge in a cave?" Jacquline said. "Maybe even underground?"

"It is unlikely."

"But possible."

Kahli nodded, though it seemed reluctantly. Jacquline would have felt better if the victory hadn't been infected with concession.

"If there are still inhabitants living underground, they may have the answers we're looking for," Tracey said. "Wouldn't it make sense to find out?" She turned to Ken, who may not have regained all hope, but was clearly showing signs of optimism. Tracey let her smile do the rest.

"I agree with Jacquline," Lark said.

"Thank you," Jacquline said.

"We can't risk our lives like this."

"But Lark," Ken said, "if there are survivors, and Stacey did find her way back here…"

"If, Ken. *If* is the operative word here. I know how bad you want her to be down there, but we still have no idea what actually happened after she was taken. For all we know, she's being held captive on some rock on the other side of the universe."

"That would be impossible," Kahli said. "The universe does not have edges."

Lark wanted to respond but couldn't find the words to do it. "The point is, what good is looking for Stacey if we all die doing it? We can find another way."

"But we'll never know unless we take the risk," Tracey said.

Ken was clearly conflicted. He wanted so much to find Stacey that his judgment was starting to be affected — and not necessarily in a good way.

"She's not down there, is she?" Ken asked Kahli.

"The odds are extremely remote. And if she is, the odds of her being alive are even less so."

"It is important that we learn all that we can about the planet," Qah-Shekel finally chimed in with far better English than anyone thought possible (even though each word was meticulously thought out before spoken). "We have come a long way to seek answers. We should continue to do so."

Now it was clear to Ken why they were there. "Yeah, I'm sure you're just dying to get down there for your own selfish purposes."

"Ken." Lark's voice was rough and disapproving.

Ken bit back just as hard. "What? Didn't you just say you thought it was a bad idea?"

"Well, technically," Jacquline said, and then fought Ken's cold stare with her own playful sneer.

"Yeah, I do," Lark said, "but I'm not going to belittle someone who has saved our lives on numerous occasions to prove my point."

"Why not? He brought it on himself. Can you honestly tell me that you think Qah-Shekel would risk his own life out of the goodness of his heart? He wants something, Lark, something that will help him find whatever it is he's looking for. And he's willing to put our lives at risk to do it."

"At least he's always there to save it when he does," Jacquline quipped. This time, Ken's biting eyes pushed Jacquline to back off a little.

Qah-Shekel looked to Kahli for a translation. He caught little bits and pieces of what was being said, but because of the rapid pace of the conversation, it was hard to fully comprehend. Kahli lifted her hand, signifying he didn't want to know.

"Dad," Tracey said.

When he turned to her, fear and unsettling rejection washed over his eyes. All he could do was shake his head and leave.

"Where are you going?" Kahli said. She wanted to follow but Lark stopped her.

"Let him be," she said, her eyes warm with empathy. Kahli had to trust that Lark knew more about his current state and was better left alone. She nodded agreement.

"Fine," Jacquline said, exasperated. Her eyes were set on Qah-Shekel. "If we are going to do this, I need to know exactly what we're up against. Lay it on me."

Tracey gave her big sister a little squeeze.

Kahli let the moment resonate for a second (though DovenJadden looked ready to join Ken in walking out) and then pushed in closer on a specific sector of the planet. "Based on the historical records of our time on Trynoruus, the Jistryt lived in this region here."

Tracey carefully studied every small detail of the map. The strokes of lightning flashed across her eyes with the delicate balance of a symphony. The room fell silent as she absorbed the nonexistent energy.

"Are you sure?" Jacquline said. "It doesn't look like anything is there."

"It is quite possible that the storms have vanquished all structures," Kahli said.

"Well if there's nothing left, what's the point of going down there again?"

To answer her question, Tracey let her fingers gloss across the globe, pushing the image in even tighter and focusing on a small region embedded within a cavernous area surrounded by the hands of the mountains. She didn't know why, but Tracey felt extremely familiar with it — as memorable and safe as home. "Here," she whispered, pointing to the space at the center of the mountains.

Leaning in closer, Jacquline squinted her eyes as if it would help her see it clearer. "What is it?"

"I think we need to find out," Tracey said with a gentle smirk.

Kahli didn't hesitate to pull the coordinates up into the hologram and program them into the ship's navigation. "I have sent Sentilla the coordinates. There is much to do before we arrive."

"Whoa. Slow down there, Rega," Jacquline said. "I still have a few issues to discuss before committing to this treasure hunt."

"Please state your inquiries."

"First off, according to your little hologram here, the lightning is a permanent fixture on this planet with no signs of fading. Do we have anything to deflect it, like a shield or force field or something? Or at least something to detect where each strike might hit?"

"To my knowledge, no type of device has been invented for those particular purposes," Kahli said.

"You should get on that," Jacquline said.

"But to your question, the *Equinox* should attract a majority of the electromagnetic energy."

"You're betting our entire expedition on the hope of the lighting attacking the ship?"

"Yes. It should give all of you enough of a buffer to traverse the land with ease."

"But you can't guarantee it."

"I cannot guarantee there will not be any rogue sparks of electricity along the way, but it is a risk you will have to accept."

"And what happens to the ship? If it does attract all of the electricity, wouldn't that cause a shit load of damage? I don't know about you, but I'd rather not be stranded on this planet forever."

"The hull should be able to withstand the electrical current long enough for you to thoroughly search the area," Kahli reported. "As long as I can continually update the exterior shields from inside, I do not foresee a problem."

"There are a lot of probabilities in that sentence," Lark said.

"Probability is all we have when dealing with this amount of atmospheric instability."

"Hold on. Does that mean you're not going?" Jacquline said, a little shocked.

"I am afraid that if I even step foot on Trynoruus," (she turned to Jacquline with the slightest of smiles), "I will become a roasted marshmallow."

Jacquline couldn't help match Kahli's sly smirk. "But wait. I thought you were impenetrable."

"My skin is as impenetrable as any substance in existence. But it is still quite capable of conducting electricity. One strike and my central core will expire."

"At least your skin would still look impeccably Photoshopped," Jacquline said with a wink.

Kahli cocked her head a bit and then shook it upon Qah-Shekel's request for interpretation.

"If that's the case," Jacquline said, backtracking from her failed attempt at a joke, "I think Tracey should stay here too."

"Why?" Tracey said, revealing how much of an eight-year-old she still was at heart.

"Because…" Jacquline stopped to make sure her objection came out as clearly as it sounded in her head. "Won't the gem act like a conductor as well? I mean, I love me a good barbeque, but not when my baby sister's the roasted pig."

Tracey lit up with laughter. "Jacquline, you're so cute. I love it."

"What? It's a legitimate concern."

"It is," Tracey said. She planted her hand on Jacquline's shoulder and looked directly into her eyes. "But you forget — the gem won't let me be harmed. If anything, I'll be the safest person out there. If it were up to me, I'd be the only one going."

"Yeah. That's not happening," Jacquline said.

"I never thought it would."

Jacquline smiled and pushed Tracey's head away. "So we're gonna have to wing the shit out of this, then, huh?"

"That would be an accurate assessment," Kahli said, though her expression added, *I think.*

"That's what I do best."

"Tell that to your parole officer," Tracey said.

"Oh, you think you're funny," Jacquline said, playfully punching Tracey in the shoulder. Tracey giggled frantically as Jacquline pulled her head under her arm. Kahli found a small smile as she observed their interaction. No matter how many times she saw it, she couldn't get over how loving they were together.

Lark stared at the hologram, periodically flashing a look at the girls. This is what filled the majority of stories Ken had told Lark during the four years they worked together. She loved being able to see them manifest them into reality more than she did listening to them, and she could only imagine what it was like in those five years after Stacey's abduction. She would hate it if they were forced back into that type of situation and knew if it did happen, there was no way she'd be able to live with herself.

I can't let that happen. Not to Ken. Not again.

"Count me in," Lark said.

The girls stopped their horseplay. "Are you sure?" Tracey said. She looked so cute with her hair all messed and scattered.

"Someone needs to watch out for you guys," Lark said.

"What about him?" Jacquline said, pointing at Qah-Shekel.

"No offense," Lark said to Qah-Shekel, slower than usual. "You're a mighty warrior and I would trust you with my life. But I'd feel much better watching over them with my own eyes."

Qah-Shekel gave her a nod of respect, which Lark returned graciously.

"DovenJadden will also accompany you," Kahli said —

("Does she have to?" Jacquline whispered to Tracey, who slapped her gently in the shoulder before adding her own smile.)

— "and provide protection against any unexpected contingencies."

"You mean when the zombies rise up and try to eat our brains," Jacquline said.

Once again, Kahli looked flummoxed. All Jacquline could do was let out an exasperated sigh.

"We will be landing in a matter of two quintets," Kahli continued. "I suggest everyone enjoy a meal and perhaps find a little rest before we do."

"And get a much needed cast removed," Lark said, flashing the gel screen at Kahli, who quickly grabbed it with both hands and pressed her thumbs to each side of the screen. She held them there for several seconds, producing a slight heat that warmed Lark's arm. Shortly after, the cast expanded by several millimeters, allowing Kahli to remove it from her wrist.

Lark pulled her arm close to her chest and rubbed it, flexing her wrist and fingers to reacquire their mobility. "Thanks," she said, a little surprised by the ease of its removal.

Kahli nodded. "Jacquline," she said, turning to her, "I would also like for you to join me in medical for a much needed upgrade."

"Upgrade?" Jacquline squealed. "Are you talking about installing one of those damn hearing aids?"

"I know you have objections to the communication bud, but I cannot allow you to make this expedition without one."

Jacquline rolled her eyes and huffed a short breath. Talk about a mood killer. "I've been off the ship plenty of times. Why are you so concerned about it now?"

"Those other times did not have as many unknown variables. This will allow us to protect you should anything happen."

"I knew it. You want to put a damn GPS in my head so you can keep tabs on me."

"It is for your protection," Kahli said, trying to ease the tension.

"Isn't that what they all say? Listen. I don't care what you claim it's for. It's an invasion of my privacy and I won't allow it."

"What privacy?" Tracey said. "We're in the middle of space. It's not like you're going to call Victor for a midnight hook-up."

"Tracey!" *Are you sure you're still eight?*

"What? I listen."

"Apparently a little too well."

Tracey smiled. "I don't see what the big deal is. Think of it as having a Bluetooth permanently attached to your ear."

"But that's exactly my point. I don't want everyone to know where I am at all times. What if I need to get away from all of you to cool off? Don't you ever just want to be alone? With that thing shoved into my skull, there's no way that'll happen."

"The communication bud does not work like that, Jacquline," Kahli said.

"So you say."

"Well," Tracey said softly, "the way I see it, if you ever want to be alone, you can always rip your ear off." There's that sparkle again. Jacquline couldn't be angry with her for that. "Trust me, it's not that bad," Tracey continued. "You can't even feel it."

"Make all the jokes you want, Squint. I don't want it."

Tracey's joy faded along with the glow in the gem, turning Jacquline into a guilt-ridden mess. Tracey always knew how to make her feel bad.

"Can't I just get a walkie-talkie or something like a normal person?"

"The ear bud is far more efficient."

Jacquline tried to counter, but Tracey's aura was so depressing.

"It would make me feel a whole lot better knowing you're protected… that I can call you whenever I need to, no matter where you might be."

She didn't see any, but Jacquline couldn't help but feel tears welling up inside Tracey's eyes.

How can I possibly say no?

"Fine. God. But if I find out anyone is following me or listening to me without my permission, I will rip my damn ear off. Got it?"

"Deal." The gem lit back up as if Tracey had been faking the whole thing. She hugged Jacquline and then grabbed her hand. "Come on. I'll race you."

The two shot from the room. DovenJadden followed shortly after without a word.

"Tell me the truth," Lark said. "Are we going to find anything down there?"

"It is doubtful," Kahli said.

Lark nodded. She took one last look at the location and left.

Kahli turned to Qah-Shekel. "Take care of them."

"Same to you," he said and then he, too, departed.

— 6 —

Heading back to her living quarters, Lark went through several scenarios of how to tell Ken about her decision to head out and search the planet — and if there would be any way to talk him into it. Her very own objections to wandering around a planet plagued with lightning storms were reason enough to doubt his ultimate goal. Would easing into it by explaining why soften his reluctance? Or maybe she should tell him the girls were going and they both needed to protect them? As far as she knew, just mentioning Jacquline and Tracey were going might flip him out enough to lock them away for the rest of their lives. She could just hear it now:

"You're both grounded until further notice!"

It put a welcome smile on her face. *I'd pay to see him try and lock Tracey away.*

She knew that would never happen, though — not after fighting so hard to gain their trust back. He and Jacquline were doing well building their relationship to where it was prior to the abduction; doing something so stupid might sever all of that hard work. It didn't make sense that he would go that far. Then again, Ken without Stacey could be highly unstable.

What to do... what to do...

Lark stared at the smooth glassy door of her living quarters. Finding the nerve — *the courage?* — to step through was somehow eluding her. She knew Ken was inside (or so she assumed — *making an ass out of you and me both, baby*), but she wasn't sure if she was ready to break the news to him. He was already upset with her for ditching him during some of the vermon cleanup and then forcing him to help her create a respectable wake for Naja-Leku's funeral. It wasn't that she felt he hated her for any of it (everyone graciously thanked him after Naja-Leku's body was officially jettisoned into space, where Qah-Shekel felt he belonged), but having them all piled one on top of the other, to add another bombshell — no matter how expected — might just topple it all.

She felt a little sick; lucky for her, a quiet beeping came from her pocket to distract her from having to go inside. She pulled out the tablet. The edges flashed on and off with a consistent heartbeat and a very translucent message was stamped across the screen.

SEARCH COMPLETE
One Matching Result Found

Lark's heart leapt to her chest as she read those words. She had requested to have the system search Naja-Leku's documents for any relevant information regarding Xyneris, or at the very least, his time as a prisoner. Kahli had said all of the documents from his time there were missing or hidden, but she figured it wouldn't hurt to look — just in case.

Within seconds, she had pressed her thumbs to either side of the tablet to turn the message off and slid it back into her pocket. She then rapped her fingers across the wall, bringing up a holoscreen to access her private port. A list of accessible materials appeared. Lark scrolled through them to find the one marked "Naja-Leku Ramblings."

An array of text sprayed across the wall as Lark spun the information open. She started reading (noticing quickly that most of it was stuff she already had an intimate knowledge of after hours upon hours of trying to find anything that had any relevance whatsoever to just about anything) and flipping through a series of what amounted to hundreds of pages of text until she came across a page that was brighter than the rest. It was tagged with a small symbol in the corner that glowed off and on. She isolated the page and pulled it away from the wall. At first, it didn't make a whole lot of sense and she wondered why the system would have highlighted this particular page. But as she slowed down and actually read the words, carefully examining the meaning behind them, she finally understood what the system had found.

"Following the rules of my confinement only allows for deeper — deeper, deeper — contemplation," Lark read allowed, to help absorb the words more thoroughly. "I have endured the heat of the darkness — lots of heat; lots of darkness — for long enough (too long; far too long), and have felt the passage of time weigh on my conscious — so heavy, please, please let it free me. I made a promise to the child of the jewels (damn you) and that is what I must do to protect the future, the past — the future of the past (of the future, in the past). I am sick with dementia — terribly sick, and demented. I do not know why (yes you do!); why must I be so loyal to the fate; to the song of life that tells me I must be the bearer of the words of chaos and destruction. (Why, dear child, must I be the bearer of the words — your very words — of chaos and destruction?) I must build (with what? What will I use to build?) on the foundation of the heated rock of myth — yes of course, I must — to give birth to the words (and the child) of the evil that resides. I don't want to — the child is forcing me with a promise (that I made?); war will only follow (but with reason, that is beyond the comprehension of the follower); it is necessary — without necessary there is no need (and no necessity of breath); there is no forward (or backward, because that is the way of the force that shall collapse — without prejudice, of course); the mind will cease as the stars fade — fade into the nothing of nothing; nothing I say that matters will dare recreate — with the paradox of my lie (of the truth, that is, the truth behind the lie). How I agreed — she wasted no time in recruitment (with words of love and compassion, I fell for the words of truth and lies), to beg my help to perform the dirty, dirty acts that she put into motion (so dirty — why do I feel so dirty, but yet so determined to follow my promise — that of which I should not have made so easily), and must protect to save us all, including me (and the child, and the family of the child, which she adores; and me, whom she adores for reasons beyond comprehension — which is to say, I don't know, because I don't care), the monster of the word of destiny (for which I am the keeper — the watchtower of light and dark; too much light for me to carry on my shoulders — and my conscience). It is strange — strange strange — and unusual to draw the path that he — the monster of legend (he who would burn to power the cosmos) — must follow to retain the light of the world (of worlds and worlds above, to the depths of the hands who hold it). To bear the child of the jewel a second time (a second time; along with the second piece of the puzzle, or the second of seconds, and the magic to create deception) and bring forth the fire of his darkness (the flames from which I am demented and sick — and demented because of him), by singing the praises of another into the heart of the wickedness of immorality (from which I have become the master). But I will; my will is nothing but a straw bent to the will of my master (or broken under the whim of the child), the jewel and her followers — her mind and her footsteps — loud and without malice; just love and protection (or so she claims with the song on her lips). Blazed across time and space with nothing but a whisp of air to guide her (from another dimension; another being altogether — the one that will be the goddess of us all, born to the jewels for which she has mastery). To guide the soul of the mother of us all (because of her precious voice). It was her plan (that's right — for which I followed without question — damn you); and to be here now, with the word of her voice on my lips (and only my lips; hers can be just as soft), what I will do and what I must do (must do, as opposed to choose to do) and what I have done (as opposed to what I must do), is done and shall be done (forever and in forevermore), in the name of existence (forever and in forevermore; forever). And if it is not — if I have failed (I mustn't fail — she relies on me to finish this mission) to deliver the gospel of our jewel (and sing the future into existence), then whomever shall find this must complete my task (please, oh please, complete my failed atrocity) and follow suit to bring life to us all through her song. The fire must be painted with my words (and only my words — to hide the double trouble that will come from them). Forever and in Forevermore; Forevermore."

Lark was shocked into submission as she tried to understand the implications of the message. After completing the exhaustive sentiment, Lark flipped to the next page and there they were — the pictographs from the caves of Xyneris depicting Eyrixano's capture of Stacey and the birth of Jaxxa Rakala. Eventually she found the energy to bring her thumb and forefinger together to flip on her communication bud.

"Rega, are you there?"

"Proceed."

"I found something that you need to see."

"I am nearing medical to implant a communication bud into Jacquline, and then I must make preparations for our landing. May we discuss this matter after our expedition?"

Lark tapped her foot nervously on the floor, her hand planted firmly on the wall as her fingers curled ever so slightly. She wanted to scold Kahli for even thinking this could wait, but in all honesty, no matter how important it felt, it wasn't like the premonitions from before. It could wait; not that Lark had to like it.

"Yeah, fine," she said, irritation flooding her voice. "But we need to do it soon."

"After we have departed Trynoruus, you will have my undivided attention."

"Good." Lark switched her comm off and looked back at the text. She read through it about a dozen more times until she realized all she was really doing was stalling. With this new revelation, there was no denying she had to talk to Ken — sooner rather than later. She might as well get it over with, and at the same time, let Naja-Leku's words really sink in.

— 7 —

Ken sat on the edge of his bed staring at the black void that painted the window. It was a haunting echo of his subconscious, that what he was searching for may very well be lost. Deep down he knew it would take longer than a few hours to track her down among the vastness of the universe, but he had hoped by joining this crew, finding her would be a piece of cake. In reality, all it's done is help quell his thirst to continue searching. In some ways, by putting her search on hold to help the crew restock and fix the ship, Ken felt he was distancing himself from her, pushing him back down the dark road he tried so hard to escape (and hoped he'd never have to travel again). But this time it was dulled by a force of his own making, and now...

Now he's finally given the opportunity to track her down (possibly even hold her in his arms again) and he can't even bring himself to do it. Of course it would be dangerous, and there was no guarantee that he'd find her

(*Alive*)

or even find a clue to her whereabouts, but when has that ever stopped him? Before Xyneris, Ken would have given his life to find her. He no longer felt that need — that desire — or the hope that he would find

(*Her body*)

her sitting under a flower-petaled tree next to a small pond in a sun-lit garden, waiting for him to bring her back home.

You must give it time, Ken. The whisper was like crystal, flowing past his neck in a cold drizzle of fog. Her touch was unmistakable, her kiss as lovely as ever.

"I'm trying..." Ken didn't want to turn around. The fear of knowing it was all a hallucination was too overwhelming.

You have to protect them.

"I need to protect you."

To protect me is to protect them, love.

He couldn't contain his tears. "Where are you," he said with hardly any audible recognition.

I am never far, so long as your memory remains true.

"What am I supposed to do?"

Love them, trust them and believe in them. They will guide you to where we all belong.

"I will find you."

Her response was a light kiss on his cheek, which drove him to turn around and look directly into Lark's eyes. Her smile balanced the weight of the moment with tenderness and empathy. Ken grabbed his mouth as Stacey melted into Lark's thin frame. He pushed his hand to his eyes and brushed his tears away. They were gone as fast as they had come, just as Stacey — both now and forever.

"I'm sorry," he said.

"What for?"

Ken turned back around and lowered his head. "Did they say anything?"

"Like what? Despite what you might think, this crew respects you, Ken. They aren't going to push you to do something you're not ready for."

All Ken could do was nod. The words in his head were so jumbled and incoherent.

"I decided to go with them," Lark said bluntly. Better to get it over with than to hem and haw around the issue.

"What changed your mind?"

Lark rested her hand on Ken's back and slowly moved it around in a small circle. "I thought it would be better if I kept an eye on them for you."

Ken huffed a quick breath of laughter. "You didn't have to do that. Whatever it is they're looking for is their business, not mine."

Now it was Lark's turn to chortle. "Ken, I'm not going to keep an eye on Qah-Shekel or DovenJadden. I'm going to keep an eye on the girls."

Lark had Ken's attention now. "What are you talking about?" Ken said.

"You didn't think Tracey was going to pass this up, did you?"

Yeah, I kind of did.

Ken took a deep breath. "No, I guess I figured she'd be going. And that Jacquline would follow. You didn't try to talk them out of it?"

"They're your daughters, Ken."

Ken smiled. "Yeah, I guess they are."

"Come with us."

Ken shook his head and set his hand on Lark's knee. "I wish I could, but…"

"But what?" Lark picked his hand into hers.

"There's nothing for me on Trynoruus."

"How do you know that?"

"I just… I don't know." Ken pulled his hand away and walked to the window. Small streaks of light were beginning to periodically flash by.

"What if I told you I think there's more to this than anyone really knows?"

Ken turned to Lark. "What do you mean?"

Lark joined Ken at the window. Her energy was magnetic. "I just found a piece of Naja-Leku's notes —"

Ken interrupted her with a cynical grunt and stepped away.

"What?"

"Naja-Leku? Lark, I know you want to believe that he had all of the answers, but even Qah-Shekel knew he was fifty-two cards away from a full deck. You can't read anything into what he says."

"But what about those predictions on Xyneris?"

"Coincidence."

"I don't believe that, and I'm a little shocked you would. But that's beside the point. What I read tells me that Naja-Leku is important, and that he may have known Jaxxa Rakala — on Trynoruus."

"You think Naja-Leku lived on Trynoruus?"

"I'm not sure in what capacity, but yeah, I do. And not only did he know Jaxxa Rakala, but he was an integral part of her life. I originally chose to go down there because of Tracey and Jacquline, but now I'm wondering if he might have left something behind that might help us. Even if I'm wrong, aren't you even the least bit curious to see where your wife came from?"

"More than you can imagine. But Lark… her presence is fading and it scares the piss out of me that I'm losing her… that she's…"

"That she's dead," Lark finished for him when the words failed to pass his lips. "You think you're going to find her body, don't you?"

"I just don't want to take another detour that takes us farther away from her. Do I believe there may be a chance she's dead? It kills me to say it, but yes. But if she is alive, every second we spend searching for whatever it is Qah-Shekel wants is a second we lose in saving her."

"What makes you think she needs saving?"

Ken was flabbergasted by the question.

"I've heard your side of the story," Lark said sympathetically, "but what if she left on her own? What if it was time for her to return home for a greater purpose?"

Ken shook his head through her entire theory. "That's not possible. I know what I saw."

"What you saw, or what you wanted to see?" Lark said. She could tell he was ready to throw her out the window. "Trust me, Ken. I want to believe what you saw is true, but given everything we know, you have to consider that there is more going on than what your memory is projecting."

Ken finally considered her point. He didn't like it, and would never believe it, but it didn't mean he might someday be proven wrong. "That doesn't mean I have to pander to Qah-Shekel's questionable motives."

"Do you honestly think this trip has nothing to do with Stacey?"

"For all we know, Qah-Shekel thinks he'll find some new precious gem that'll make Tracey grow ten feet tall and hold the universe in the palm of her hand."

"Ken, where the hell is all this coming from? You asked for their help. Is that not the deal we all made? Stacey could be anywhere, and out here, anywhere is literal. We've only scratched the surface of the possibilities and if you think Qah-Shekel or Rega or any of the rest of them aren't sincere about their word, perhaps we should all just go back home now and forget about all this shit."

"You're right. We should. But without Stacey, it'd all be in vain."

"And there it is, then."

"There what is?"

"We chose not to go back home because there's nothing left for us there. At least out here, we have a future, one with limitless possibilities. But God forbid it doesn't all go your way, for your own personal reasons. I've never said anything before, Ken, because I believed in your integrity, but you are the most selfish, arrogant, unstable man I have ever met."

"Then why did you stay?"

"Because I'm just like you. I'm just as selfish and arrogant and unstable as you. But if it wasn't for those attributes, neither of us would be where we are right now. If it wasn't for your unrelenting drive to find Stacey, we'd still be lost on Earth with no purpose and no future. But we have one now, and we need to follow through on that, no matter how long it takes."

"And that's exactly what scares the hell out of me. Ever since that gem embedded itself in Tracey, that drive that sustained my will has been slowly slipping away. I'm losing her, Lark. I'm losing my only purpose to live."

"I understand. Stacey was your one and only true love, but you have to stop thinking of her as your only purpose. You still have two daughters that need your love and support. Two daughters, I might add, who are just as driven to find your wife as you are. So get off of your god damn high horse and help them do that."

To protect me is to protect them, love.

"Lark, you just don't get it."

"No, I get it. That gem is a powerful little bitch. I also understand what addiction can do to a person. You're still in the middle of withdrawal and it's probably going to get worse before it gets better. But unless you fight it, you'll never get over it."

Ken took a deep breath as tears slipped down his cheeks. Lark rested her hand on his arm. He wanted to pull away, but her touch was comfortable — loving.

"Ken, listen to me." She squeezed his arm gently and didn't say anything until he found the courage to look at her. "I understand what you're going through and I hate to see it happening, but you know as well as I do that there is love on this ship. We all want to protect you; protect each other. The only way to fight this feeling and keep Stacey alive is to face those fears. We've searched maybe point one percent of what's possible out here and the odds that she returned here are minuscule at best. But those are better odds than winning Publisher's Clearing House. Come with us; regain that connection to your wife by understanding her true nature in a new light."

Ken let slip a smile. He lowered his head and covered her hand. "As far as I'm concerned, you've never been selfish or arrogant." He looked back up to connect with her in the moment. "Everything you've done has been to protect me, and I love you for that. I have to stop ignoring you."

"I don't know. If you did that, we'd never move forward, now would we?"

Ken laughed. It was well needed. "You're right about one thing. My daughters deserve more than what I've been able to give them. I learned that quite clearly on Xyneris. Tracey and I should discover Stacey's planet together. As a family."

"That's bullshit. You just don't want Tracey to see her origins without you."

"You said it yourself — I am one arrogant, selfish prick."

Ken slapped Lark's hand. His smile lit up the room, not to mention Lark's heart.

"I never said you were a prick," Lark said with a light chuckle.

The two stood together in admiration as they watched the small streaks of light pass the window, growing more numerous with each passing second.

— 8 —

"What do you think we'll find on Trynoruus?"

Jacquline sat on the medical bed, her legs flying back and forth. Waiting for Kahli was wearing on her nerves.

Tracey was examining Kahli's collection of alien organs and artifacts at the back of the room. Every time she touched an item, the gem opened her mind to information, which sometimes meant revealing entire histories, while at others meant she could barely even register a name. It was clear that whatever her mother knew about a particular item, so too would the gem, but nothing signified that Stacey had come into actual physical contact with any of them. Tracey wondered why she hadn't done this already; it was illuminating to say the least. "Your guess is as good as mine," Tracey said.

"Your mystical little gem hasn't told you?"

"Nope."

"So there is a limit to its power."

"I guess there is." Tracey hid the lightness in her eyes. It was true that she didn't know what they might find on Trynoruus, but that didn't limit the gem's power any. Having a connection to the universe, as she felt in every cell of her body, was one thing; understanding it was quite another. She had spent a countless number of hours attempting to open her mind through meditation to unlock the secret of how to fully connect to the power without becoming a slave to it, but cracking that code had become harder than expected. She wondered if it had something to do with her own selfishness; that no matter how much she might try to convince herself otherwise, her only reason for understanding how to utilize her full potential was simply to control it. To have that ability would be to know everything about everything, to see past her own present and learn to control events that she could see happen in the future — and that was dangerous. Until she could release herself of that hunger, and believe in her heart that access to the power was only for noble and honorable concerns, the gem would keep her from full comprehension. She had no doubt she would eventually learn to be altruistic; until that time, she was fine with the safety net, as just one slip into the gem's desire and Eyrixano would have his weapon.

"Where the hell is she?" Jacquline said haughtily. "I swear, if she's not here in five minutes, she can put that damn little communicator right up her gorgeous little ass."

"I appreciate your kindness as to the dexterity of my posterior, but it is certainly not an applicable place to put a communication bud." Kahli stood in front of Jacquline. How she ever got that close without her even knowing was remarkable.

Jacquline smiled. "Only when evolution dictates that we literally talk out of our own asses, I guess."

Kahli tried hard to comprehend the statement, but ultimately remained unsure as to what she was referring. Jacquline took it as her cue to help explain.

"Talking out of someone's ass is a metaphor for rambling on and saying the wrong thing and making no sense… a lot like what I'm doing now, making a complete ass out of myself. So, I'm going to shut up now and let you jack me up."

Kahli looked over to Tracey, who smiled brightly at Kahli's confusion. "Translation," Tracey said, "she's ready for the implant."

"Is that what she said?"

Tracey giggled. There's that eight-year-old again.

"Lie down on your stomach," Kahli commanded of Jacquline.

"Yes, ma'am." Jacquline lied down. Kahli moved the hair away from her ear and neck. Jacquline couldn't help but giggle.

"Hold still," Kahli said, pressing her hand firmly along Jacquline's back.

"Sorry. It just tickled."

Kahli was too busy cleaning the area behind Jacquline's ear to respond. After the cold substance turned Jacquline's skin a bright yellow, Kahli pulled a small object that resembled a microchip from the wall and rested it along the outer lining of her ear. She stared at it for a moment, adjusting it slightly, and then set the tip of a pen-like tool on top of the microchip. With a quick tap on the other end of the pen with her thumb, the microchip was rammed into the base of Jacquline's ear.

The pain was excruciating. Jacquline grabbed her ear and slid as far away from Kahli's hands as she could get without falling off the bed. "God, damn it, that hurt. You could have at least warned me." But that pain was nothing to the sensations that came next.

At first, it felt as if someone was blowing in her ear (with a little too much spit included), but that quickly turned into a pinch upon her eardrum that made her go deaf and start bleeding — at least that's what she thought, what with the oily sensation wrapping across different parts of the inner ear. Jacquline pictured snakes draping themselves around a tree attacking some small animal that dared intrude upon their claim with a bite that was like slamming her hand in a palette of needles. If she hadn't have been held in place by Kahli, she would have busted her head open on the floor.

And then, as if Kahli flipped a switch in her ear, all of the pain was gone. "What happened?" Jacquline said. She sat up and felt her ear, thinking for some reason it would somehow feel different.

Kahli removed Jacquline's hand and pushed her head sideways so she could get a better look inside. To any normal eye it was like any other ear, but to an eye capable of zooming up to three thousand times normal parameters, Kahli could see a small flashing green light hidden next to the eardrum. "Everything looks good," Kahli said and let go of Jacquline, who had to readjust her jaw.

"How do you know it worked?"

Kahli answered by jamming the pen into the forefinger of Jacquline's left hand.

Jacquline yelped and yanked her hand away, holding it tightly against her chest. "What the hell?" She sucked her finger for a few seconds and then checked it for blood. Surprisingly, there wasn't even a mark. "What was that for?"

"I had to implant the activation unit. Do you still feel pain?"

"Not really," Jacquline said, though she did feel a little hint of a pinch in her thumb. She flexed her fingers in and out of a fist.

"Do you or do you not?"

"No. Not anymore."

"Tap your thumb to your forefinger." Kahli demonstrated. Jacquline copied her and heard a small hum, much like the feedback from a speaker, inside her ear that eventually went away.

"Now what?" she asked.

"Talk."

Jacquline smiled slightly and looked to Tracey. "Hey, Tracey. What's up?"

"Hey, Jacks," Ken said, his voice as clear as if he were sitting right next to her. "You finally caved, huh?"

Oh, God. Jacquline faked a smile to hide her displeasure. "Sure did."

"Great. Now we'll always be in contact no matter what."

"Just what I've always wanted."

"Don't mind him, Jacquline," Lark said. This was starting to get weird — and a bit awkward. "He's just joking."

"Thank you for that, but no, he's not. You do know he set up a pedophile cam in my room when I was fourteen, right?"

"He what?"

"That was only because you invited that Sammy thug up to your room to do homework all the time," Ken said.

"He wasn't a thug. And his name was Danny."

"Whatever. I had to make sure there wasn't any sexual education going on."

"That's not the point," Lark said.

"Thank you," Jacquline agreed. Maybe Lark wasn't so bad after all. "Besides, what kind of sexual education did you think we'd get with my door wide open?"

"And yet you still found a way to get felt up —"

"Dad, can you not…" Jacquline's cheeks were rosier than a banished elf's. The laughter that followed echoed across multiple voices. Jacquline now had her face planted in her hands. She wasn't necessarily embarrassed about being felt up when she was fourteen (if it wasn't for the camera, she probably would have let it go a lot further); it was simply because her father said *felt up* in relation to her.

"At least you can rest assured I will no longer need the use of a nanny-cam," Ken said enthusiastically. "Now I'll be right there in your head to enjoy every minute of it."

"Dad," Jacquline said, along with Lark's, "Ken."

"Don't be so cruel," Lark continued. "She's a young woman. She deserves to have all of the experiences of a young woman without knowing her dad is just the touch of someone else's tongue in her ear away."

"God. I'm done. How do you turn this damn thing off?"

"Just tap your fingers together again."

"I know that," Jacquline said, doing just that. She could still hear Ken and Lark's conversation —

Spying is a two-way street, now, isn't it?

— and wondered if she should continue listening. Ultimately, she went with the golden rule, deciding it better she not know what everyone else says behind her back when they forget their comm buds are active. "I mean, how do you turn it all the way off."

"You can mask the communication messaging by actively telling the bud to turn all communication off."

"So, basically, I *am* the off switch."

"As a manner of speaking. Just remember, you will not be able to hear those with their communication buds on, however, there will be a constant beep that reminds you that it is off."

Before Kahli was finished, Jacquline whispered to turn the comm bud off. What she heard now was a soft hum and pop every minute or so. It was a little annoying but she figured she would get used to it over time. Anything was better than having to listen to everyone all the time.

"Any chance I can talk you into removing it?"

Kahli smiled.

Guess not.

"Come on, Squint. I'm hungry. Let's go grab a bite."

Tracey grabbed Jacquline's hand and they walked together to the nutriment hall, where Lark and Ken were having a gay old time. She sat as far away from them as possible and kept her back turned to them the entire time.

"You do know you're going to have to face him eventually," Tracey said.

"Eventually."

Tracey punched a code into the top of the table. A list appeared just above the surface and she selected several items. When she was through, she placed her hand in the center of the table. In a matter of seconds, the wall beside them opened with a plate of hot, steaming food. Tracey pulled it out and took in a breath of its sweet aroma.

Although it did smell delicious, Jacquline still hadn't gotten used to the food that the ship was able to process, which was more a plastic recreation of a copy of a blind creation of something similar to what she remembered. It didn't help that absolutely no actual food from Earth was available, since the food processors could only create food that it could first sample. Tracey was able to find a way to combine certain foodstuffs to come as close as possible to the real deal (some with great effect, others not so much), but nothing could beat a nice fat juicy filet mignon and mashed potatoes lightly sprinkled with garlic and pepper and some nice buttered asparagus right about now. Just thinking about it was far better than that kumquat thing that induced a vomit attack with nothing more than placing it on her tongue. If there was anything that would keep her from trying new things, it was that. From then on, she didn't eat unless Tracey ordered it for her.

This time, Tracey ordered a variety of vegetables inside a salad of teluse (which resembled lettuce, but was a bit sweeter than what she was used to), as well as some weird looking seafood something or other on the side. As they ate, Tracey touched the edge of the table and flipped what looked to be a holographic laptop open to examine some texts.

"Got any movies on that thing," Jacquline asked. Tracey didn't appear to hear her, but within moments, she turned the computer around to Jacquline. On it was a strange little film with some weird looking creatures that she had never seen before dancing around the screen as if part of some wild opera.

"Is that all you got?"

"Hey, this far out in space, it's hard to find anything good."

"This will have to do, I guess." And it did, as the more she watched, the more amusing it got, to the point she was all-out laughing, occasionally spitting food in Tracey's direction. "Sorry," she would say before doing it again seconds later. Only when Tracey switched the film off (which Jacquline became oddly infuriated over), did she stop her fits of laughter.

"Kahli requests our presence on command," Tracey said to try and ease her annoyance. "You'd know that if you had your comm bud on."

"What do I need the comm for," Jacquline smirked. "I have you." She winked and took Tracey's hand. As always, it was nice, something she loved, even if it was no longer the small petite hand she remembered.

— 9 —

Lightning lit up Sentilla's view screen. She frantically tapped and slid her fingers across the holopads to keep the *Equinox* balanced and on course as it descended through the thick, dense clouds of Trynoruus. "Are you sure about this, Kahli?"

Kahli stood within the confines of her holowall, sliding through readings of both the ship's integrity and the atmospheric conditions. "Keep her steady and she'll hold. I promise."

"You better be right," Sentilla growled through her teeth in a low hiss.

Although Kahli still wasn't as familiar with the word promise as her human counterparts, with only minor variances in the readings she had in front of her, she was more than ninety-nine percent sure the ship would withstand their time on the planet. Occasionally, as the heat signatures of the hull rose higher than expected, she would run her fingers across a secondary holoscreen and switch on the cooling units lined along the exterior of the ship. They helped as much as the lightning would allow, and though all of the units would eventually be extinguished, they did what Kahli needed. The ship passed atmospheric re-entry relatively unscathed.

"How are we looking?" Qah-Shekel said as he slipped into command, the humans gathering in behind him. Sentilla instantly felt Tracey's presence and had to clench her teeth to fight the urge to attack her. (Squeezing her fingers into tight little balls as she normally would to ease her tension was out of the question.) It wasn't enough. To release some of the pain that surged her body, Sentilla let out a frightening — and in some ways, hurtful — scream.

"I better go," Tracey said, her eyes fixed on Sentilla.

"What? No," Jacquline said, grabbing Tracey's shoulder. "Sentilla's gonna need to get her shit together at some point. Let her deal with it."

In a way, Jacquline was right, and no matter how awkward it might have felt, everyone seemed to agree with her. That didn't mean Tracey felt she was endangering them all if she stayed. It just meant she would need to keep a watchful eye on Sentilla to guarantee she didn't do anything stupid.

"All systems are functioning within normal parameters," Kahli said, ignoring the situation. She tapped the wall to her right and a hologram of the ship appeared just outside of her holographic boundary. There were several gaps in the image being tickled by a barrage of blue tentacles.

"Doesn't look so hot to me," Jacquline said.

"The sensors have been disabled in those sections. Do not be alarmed."

"And you're not at all worried about that constant swarm of lightning?"

"Once we land, we will power down all non-essential systems so that we have enough power to continue to attract the atmosphere but keep the damage to a minimum."

"What about liftoff?" Lark said, reiterating her argument from earlier.

Kahli pulled some new information in front of her.

Did she just ignore the question?

She double-checked the data to her right and then yelled something to Sentilla, who responded in kind. Just after, the ship maneuvered sharply to the right, causing everyone except Kahli (who didn't seem to even take notice of the abrupt turn) to jostle backward. She seemed pleased once the ship was again leveled.

"We are nearing our destination point," Kahli said. She stepped from the holopad, lowering her information wall.

"We must prepare," Qah-Shekel said in English, only to switch back into Krylexian to relay the rest of his speech. Tracey was quick to translate, though as Jacquline noted later, it was more of a summary than an accurate interpretation. "Qah-Shekel will take point with Sentilla and DovenJadden watching the rear. We have two quintets to search the grounds, after which we must return to the ship for re-assessment. If it's deemed necessary to leave the planet, anyone that has not returned will be left behind."

Keeping her back turned, Sentilla spoke — at least according to Tracey.

"Sentilla isn't coming with us," Tracey said.

"Which is probably for the best," Kahli added.

Qah-Shekel, who would have normally been upset, didn't push her. He simply squeezed her shoulder with a lover's touch and left. Kahli and DovenJadden followed without a word.

Everyone looked around, unsure.

"I guess we go," Jacquline said.

They all left. Before Tracey stepped through the watery entry, she turned back to Sentilla, who could no longer keep herself from consuming a glimpse of her. Tracey stared into her eyes as the intensity of the gem's glow rose to the point of nearly blinding her. When the light faded, Sentilla rubbed her eyes clear. Although the weight of the gem still lingered like the smell of a skunk, she was alone to land the ship comfortably without incident.

— 10 —

Tracey fell to her knees and grabbed hold of the gem. It flashed intermittently, casting rays of light to the floor with every heartbeat. Sweat dripped from her forehead as if she had just jumped out of a swimming pool. The heat was excruciating as it turned her skin a deep red, accentuating every fine line of her birthmarks. The crescent moons sizzled with a light smoke, burning their imprints into her gums. She lifted her head and screamed.

Pulling a knife from a sheath hidden under her pant cuff, Tracey set the tip on the crease between the gem and her chest. After taking in several quick breaths, she pushed the knife into her body. A scream escaped, but not from her lips. She pulled the knife back out. Her erratic breaths quickly calmed and she sat up against the wall, letting the blood seep down along her body. As the gem healed the wound, her tattoo soaked up the remaining blood and the crescents faded back to their state of inertia.

Tracey wiped her eyes, brushed the sweat from her brow and took one long, deep breath before getting up as if nothing had ever happened.

— 11 —

The normal hum of silence faded into a sonnet of nothing as all systems were shut down, engulfing the ship in darkness. It felt weird to Jacquline, who couldn't remember the last time she was in a situation that was completely silent — sans all of the movement from everyone waiting for Kahli to open the hatch. She never realized how much noise the hatch actually made until now either; hisses of air and mechanical grinding that quickly faded into loud winds ripping through her hair with an icy sting —

Thank God I brought my jacket!

— and a constant roll of rumbling thunder that sounded as if there was an endless earthquake traveling across the sky. Jacquline raised her arm to try and block the wind so she could see what she was getting herself into.

No such luck.

"You'll get used to it," Tracey said. Jacquline turned to her, unsure if she heard something or if the wind was playing tricks on her.

Tracey smiled and tapped her ear.

Jacquline nodded and pressed her fingers together. There was a series of hums and pops before she could hear Qah-Shekel talking to DovenJadden as clear as a bell.

"So weird," she whispered, only realizing everyone had heard it when DovenJadden gave her an odd sneer.

Still the newbie.

Tracey giggled. "Careful," she said with just her lips.

Jacquline rolled her eyes. Even though she couldn't feel anything, it still felt quite uncomfortable. She pressed her palm to her ear to try and shake the sensation of a foreign object hiding out inside. Tracey pulled it away and interlocked her fingers with Jacquline's as Qah-Shekel walked down the ramp with more caution than anyone could remember ever seeing from him before.

"Are you ready?" Jacquline said, attempting to speak over the wind.

"You don't have to talk so loud," Tracey said.

"Sorry," Jacquline whispered as she scanned the group. Tracey mitigated the uneasy moment by pulling Jacquline down the ramp. The air was hot and the sky was a grayish blue mess of clouds that dulled what Jacquline could only imagine were once vibrant and lavish colors. (For some reason, she liked to imagine that not all planets had solid blue or red skies, though that always seemed to be the case.) The land that wasn't covered in dirt and rock was scorched black or flourished in dry or decaying brush. For now, the lightning remained mostly at a distance, though a few bolts did strike just feet away from the ship, which forced Jacquline to pull away from Tracey and take a few steps back up the ramp.

Jacquline never did do well with lightning. One of a series of nightmares she once had as a little girl resembled much of what she was witnessing now. She would be wandering the streets looking for Gloria under a starless night. All of a sudden, the sky would open and a forest of lightning caged her within the confines of its prickly fingers as it picked her off the ground. Fear and numbness quaked through her body until she was swallowed by the sky — a dream that more often than not caused her to wet her bed and wake up screaming. Her only comfort (other than hiding under the force shield of covers) was Gloria, who would lie with her in bed for as long as she needed, even if that meant spending the night with her. Jacquline would find out later that some of those times, Gloria's motivation was more about getting away from Ken after some heated argument than it was about protecting her. Some nights when Gloria wasn't home, Jacquline would ask Ken to lie with her, but that never worked to comfort her, so she had to rely on her memory of Gloria to get past her fears. She eventually got over the nightmares, but lightning remained one of her deepest fears (no matter how much she tried to mask it — or admit it).

She jumped as Lark took a hold of her hand. Jacquline tried to pull away at first — she still disliked how Lark was trying to replace Stacey, but there was something calming about her. Eventually she gave in to the comfort Lark's touch emitted. She wasn't her mother in any sense of the word (and never would be), but for that brief moment, she did accept her as a decent surrogate. Lark smiled as Jacquline's warm appreciation resonated through her grip. Jacquline returned it with her own, but only half-heartedly. She wasn't some punk kid anymore; she was Jacquline Brody — she could face her fears without anyone's help.

This is for you, mom.

"I'm fine," she said, pulling her hand away as considerately as she could. "Let's just find out what we can and get the hell off this nightmare."

Jacquline joined Tracey once again to catch up with Qah-Shekel, who was now some fifty yards from the ship. He looked so powerful standing there holding a large staff with a spear-like tip — one that didn't attract lightning the way a typical metal would, as she learned after joking he was prepping to become a large piece of charcoal salmon

(Yeah, that didn't go over so well)

— across his chest as the storm raged among the surrounding mountains.

Jacquline wanted to push on but trusted Qah-Shekel enough to follow his lead. They waited for the rest of the group to join them before Qah-Shekel said, "Soke li pitela." Shortly after, the hatch closed and lightning surrounded the *Equinox* with a patchwork of electricity coming from all possible directions. (Jacquline could swear that one bolt shot right past her ear.) It was amazing to watch the tentacles try desperately to dig their way inside. Jacquline thought about making a sarcastic quip, but decided against it. "Let's get to it, then," she said instead, grabbing Tracey's hand. "We don't have a lot of time."

She pulled Tracey past Qah-Shekel, figuring if it wasn't the right way, he would stop her. Every time she looked behind her, he was there following them (or at the very least, leading from behind), giving Jacquline a renewed sense of pride. Then again, it may just have been because Tracey was with her. Jacquline was wholly aware of that; she was just as capable of leading them all (and probably more so) to where they needed to go. In fact, it wasn't until Tracey forced her did Jacquline have any inclination of stopping.

"What's the matter, Squint?"

Tracey knelt down and brushed a bit of dirt away. She then pressed her hand to the ground. When everyone had caught up to them, all Jacquline could do was shrug in response to their quizzical expressions.

"Tracey," Ken said. "Did you find something?"

"I don't know," she said. Her gut said something was there, but her gem wasn't being of any help.

"We should be close to the ruins, shouldn't we?" Lark said.

"Yeah, they're just up ahead, but…" Tracey closed her eyes and scrunched her brow, annoyed that she couldn't figure out why she was so attracted to this spot.

"I don't see anything."

Just then, a huge spark of lightning crashed down a few yards away, splitting the ground and sending everything collapsing into the cavern just beyond. Jacquline squealed and buried her head into Lark's arm. At the same time, Ken tightened his grip around Lark's hand and DovenJadden chirped at Qah-Shekel.

Tracey stood and took a deep breath. No one wanted to state the obvious; they simply wanted to silently agree that Tracey just saved their lives.

"We need to move," Tracey said.

The ground shook violently. "Follow me!" Tracey screamed. She ran, crevices tracking her every step. Without a second thought, Ken followed her lead with Lark pulling Jacquline quickly after them. DovenJadden froze in place to keep her balance, but on the order of Qah-Shekel, finally started running. She passed Lark, partially because Jacquline kept losing her balance, nearly taking Lark with her more often than not. Recognizing her struggle, Qah-Shekel picked Jacquline up in his arms and carried her.

A bolt of lightning struck the area they had once been standing, slicing one of the crevices open. As it widened, the land collapsed and chased the group while sending an avalanche of dirt down into the newly formed gorge. The ground finally stopped shaking as the edge of the gorge nipped at Lark's heels. If it hadn't have been for Ken turning back to help her, she wouldn't have been able to catch her balance enough to outrun it. Little good it did. Just before reaching Tracey (who by this time had stopped at a seemingly random spot), Lark collapsed. She struck her knee on a clip of sharp rocks and rolled several feet past Tracey, who stood steadfast as the expansion came to a halt at the tips of her toes.

"God damn it," Lark screamed, grabbing a hold of her knee.

Ken was the first (and only) one to help her. "Let me see," he said, but Lark refused to let go of her knee. She tried to sit up, but the sting was too great, so she remained on her back.

"I'm fine," she said through half-gritted teeth. She hissed in a breath and then calmly let it out. Her next words were much cleaner and relaxed. "I'll be okay. It's just a small cut."

Meanwhile, Jacquline walked up to Tracey (with a quick glimpse at Lark, to make sure she had adequate help) to thank her for saving their lives — *twice!* — and get a look at the massive hole. It was hard to see, what with the wind whipping dirt and hair across her face, but sitting there among the rubble, rock and dirt were the remnants of what Jacquline could only assume was a castle.

"Would you look at that?" she said, the lightning having become a distant concern.

"Home," Tracey whispered.

"What has happened?" Kahli's voice rang out over the comms. "I have readings of a massive shift in tectonic plates. Is everyone all right?"

"We're fine," Qah-Shekel said, taking consideration of Lark's injury before speaking. He stood along the edge of the hole taking in the majestic beauty of the structure below. Most of it was still buried in mounds of rock and dirt or had been obliterated by any number of reasons. Several pillars stood erect at least eighty feet high, each wrapped in carved decorations of vines and flowers. Some of them were connected with cracked or incomplete flooring and a half-buried staircase wrapped from the dirt to the uppermost floor. "We have reached our destination, but it may take more time to search the grounds."

"Understood. The *Equinox* is holding steady. I will let you know when it is time to return."

Qah-Shekel had a heated debate with DovenJadden as Tracey looked for the best path to travel downward. A few yards to her left, past Lark and Ken, she knelt down to carefully examine the edge. She then swung her feet over to rest them along the mouth of a small crevice. Jacquline was quick to grab her arm and try to pull her up. Easier said than done.

"Tracey, what are you doing?"

"We have to search the palace, Jacquline."

"It's too dangerous to go down there. How do you know we'll even be able to climb back up?"

"It's a risk I'm willing to take."

"Tracey," Ken cried out.

"I have to know."

Ken couldn't argue with her because he knew she already had her mind made up. She slid off the edge and climbed down as if she were an expert mountaineer.

"Dad, do something," Jacquline said.

He looked to Lark; she already knew what he was going to ask. She rested her hand on the back of his neck and looked directly into his worried eyes. "I'll be fine. Go discover your wife's past with your daughter." Lark ran her fingers through his hair and kissed him on the cheek. "Keep them safe," she said.

Ken smiled and nodded (if only slightly). Before Jacquline could form a coherent objection, Ken had slipped his legs over the edge and started down.

"Dad," Jacquline finally spit out. She looked around at the others for help but quickly realized she was alone in her protest. "God help me." Jacquline shifted her legs over the edge of the gorge, cautiously finding her footing (and this time, making absolutely sure her grip was solid before accepting anything — she was not about to take a tumble down this rock face). She kept her head down to keep an eye on Ken's movements so she could follow him as close as possible.

It took a while longer for Qah-Shekel to finally convince DovenJadden to stay and look after Lark, who was on the verge of telling them not to worry about her. But Qah-Shekel was adamant about DovenJadden staying behind to protect her. It was a lovely gesture that Lark hoped to repay someday.

DovenJadden let out a hiss to end the conversation and slumped down against a large rock some fifty yards away. She didn't once look at Lark. Before Qah-Shekel headed down into the gorge, he handed Lark his spear. "Protection," he said.

Lark accepted the staff with a gracious nod.

As Qah-Shekel slipped his foot over the edge, a small rock fell loose and bounced down the wall. Jacquline looked up just in time to see the rock heading straight for her head. She yelped and shifted out of the way, which caused her left foot to slip and her body to fall flat against the side of the gorge. Before she knew it, she was back in the hole on Xyneris, falling into the depths of darkness.

"Jacquline," Ken yelled, completely unable to reach out and grab her as she fell, else end up with the same fate. Lucky for her, Tracey was. She swung Jacquline upward and helped her steady herself against the side of the mountain just below her before letting go.

Cries of "Jacquline" bounced around her ear from a variety of voices. "I'm fine," she said after catching her breath and calming some of the adrenaline rushing through her heart. "I'm fine." Calmer; better.

"Don't get distracted," Tracey said. "I may not be there to catch you next time."

"Yeah. Easy for you to say."

"Nobody said this would be easy," Tracey said and waited patiently for Jacquline to start back down. They made it to the ground easily a few minutes later. As they waited for Ken to finish his descent, a lighting bolt hit one of the larger pillars of the palace, cracking it down the middle. It collapsed in a heap of dust and rubble, which immediately caused a chain reaction of cracked steps and wall mounts that forced another pillar to topple over and break into several pieces across the remaining set of stairs. At the same time, it knocked more dirt and rock loose, uncovering quite a bit more of the structure.

"Stacey lived here?" Jacquline said. "Lucky bitch. I would kill for digs like this."

"It's never too late." Tracey smirked and sent Jacquline a cute little wink.

Jacquline smiled, one that didn't last very long. "My God," she said. "This is going to take forever. How tall is that thing anyway?"

"At least five stories," Tracey discerned. "But that's after a war. Who knows how much higher the towers may have gone."

"Or how much gorgeously decorated shit they must have had." This time Jacquline winked.

Ken wrapped his arms around his daughters's shoulders. "We're not here to raid the palace," he said. "We're here for answers."

Jacquline nodded, hiding the exasperated roll of her eyes.

"No time to waste. Race you." Tracey took off running.

"Why you little cheat," Jacquline yelled as she sprinted after her.

Ken held back, choosing to walk and admire his daughters and the playful wrestling match they got into after Tracey handily beat Jacquline to the edge of the staircase. "All right, come on guys," Ken said, hating to have to break it up.

Jacquline rolled off of Tracey and helped her up. Still fighting off laughter, they started searching the palace. When Qah-Shekel finally reached the bottom of the gorge, he climbed onto one of the shattered pillars, keeping his eye on his companions while also scanning the area for anything suspicious — or significantly essential to his cause. Tracey walked up to him and pushed her fingers together. She waited for Qah-Shekel to do the same then urged him to kneel down. After checking to make sure the others weren't watching, she leaned in close.

"Are you certain you can trust DovenJadden?"

Qah-Shekel looked to the top of the gorge. After a bit of contemplation, he nodded. "She'll protect her."

Tracey wasn't sure she could believe him, but she gave him the benefit of the doubt. She trusted him, so if he trusted DovenJadden, she would take his word for it.

"What about Sentilla?"

"She told me she can sense the gem on others now."

"The pull is getting stronger."

"She's a fighter. She'll get through it."

"I'm not so sure. You saw her in command. I had to fight to keep the gem from vaporizing her. I'm afraid she's grown too dangerous."

"We can't abandon her."

"I don't want that."

"Then what do you suggest we do about it?"

"I don't know yet. But if it ever does come down to it, we may have to isolate her." Qah-Shekel nodded.

"Hey, Squint," Jacquline called out, catching Tracey's attention. "Get your scrawny ass back to work. We're not here to sight-see, you know."

Tracey waved and turned back to Qah-Shekel. "Be cautious." She pointed at him and then back up to the top of the gorge. They both nodded in acknowledgment and tapped their hands together to fire the comm buds back up. Tracey skipped her way to Jacquline's side and slapped her shoulder before returning to search the grounds — one large piece of debris at a time.

— 12 —

Sentilla rubbed her hands together as she paced restlessly in her quarters. She thought the pitch black of the room would calm her enough to take solace in sleep (as it had almost her entire life), but it seemed her last encounter with the gem, having been in such close proximity, was keeping her body from relaxing. Whenever she closed her eyes, the gem was all she could see. It sang to her, urged her to track it, take hold of it, absorb it — but always remained just out of her reach. It was infuriating. She wanted to scream —

Let it out, child

— but doing so as loud as she possibly could until her lungs wouldn't allow any more sound to leave her mouth only made her need for the gem grow that much stronger. Punching the wall in the hopes the residual, searing pain would alleviate her desire only resulted in cracking a few bones in her knuckles. The gem still teased her and taunted her with its powerful energy.

"Bist-click," she yelled out before stumbling from her quarters. She hurried down the halls, which were lit only with the slightest bit of emergency lighting that highlighted the walls in a gentle green hue — or at least green to Sentilla's eyes. Even now the gem was taunting her.

"Kahli," she said breathlessly as she entered medical. When she realized Kahli wasn't there, she called out for her several times, each one growing louder and longer until she all but collapsed to the floor. Her breath was lost, her voice sick. She had turned off her communication bud to keep her earlier breakdown a secret, but now it was the only way she could think of to find Kahli. "Kahli... I need you... in medical."

The first voice that returned was unexpected but welcome. "Sen—la—ong?" Qah-Shekel said.

"Qah-Shekel? Qah-Shekel. I need..."

"—til—you—"

"Qah-Shekel," Sentilla repeated, but didn't hear any response. She wasn't sure if it was because the communication bud had failed or because the gem was masking any type of response. Either way, she was in this alone. She lied down, dizzy and tired. The last vestige of rest she could remember having was when Tracey forced her to sleep after leaving Xyneris. This unwanted insomnia was starting to drain her soul, consequently opening her vulnerability up to the gem's sinister siren call.

I have her. Do not worry. She will be fine.

Sentilla coughed and squirmed as she was lifted off the ground. She held her bloody hand tightly to her chest, fighting the pain that now seemed inflamed beyond tolerance.

"Sentilla," Kahli said as she laid Sentilla on the medical bed. "What happened?"

"I can't take it anymore," Sentilla said. "It's too much. It hurts so much. I can't sleep."

Kahli pulled the healing gel from the wall and poured a small amount on her hand. Sentilla screamed, and though the cooling sensation eased the pain, she could still feel it biting at her muscles. Kahli then wrapped a cloth around her hand and sat her up. "Let me see," she said, opening Sentilla's eyes wide. "Your eyes are as red as can be." After typing a few notes in the holocomputer on her desk, Kahli opened a couple of compartments that held a small round piece of glass and a small needle with several wires falling off the back. She rested the glass against Sentilla's eye and scanned the information that flashed across it. "Your galleys are heated way beyond their normal measure." Wasting no time, Kahli plugged the wires of the needle into her arm. "Lie back down."

Sentilla didn't argue. Once flush on her back, Kahli rested the needle just above her left eye. She pressed a button at the top of the needle. Four small tentacles extended from its base, spreading Sentilla's eyelids open. A second button on the side of the needle sprayed a liquid into her eye, coating it in a cloudy filament. Once completed, Kahli pressed the top of the needle again, retracting the tentacles. She repeated the procedure on the second eye and then replaced the instruments back into the wall.

Sentilla sat back up as Kahli typed a few more notes into the holocomputer. "I can't see," she said, though calmer than she would have expected.

"You won't be able to see anything for several days as your eyes cool."

Sentilla felt the cold, glassy exterior of her eyes, which forced her eyelids to remain open. How this was going to help her sleep was beyond her, and remaining in complete darkness for days on end was not what she had in mind when she came to see Kahli, but then realized the gem was nowhere to be found. She could still feel its presence, as well as its magnetic pull, but its image and its excruciating call had vanished.

"Thank you," she said softly.

"I'm just glad we caught it before the heat burned a hole in your visual receptors."

Sentilla chuckled. "Yeah." She rotated her head to stretch her neck and went to rub her eyes, only to be reminded she couldn't. "Can you give me something to help me sleep?"

"Why do you need something to sleep?"

"I haven't slept since you removed me from the chamber."

"You haven't?"

Sentilla shook her head.

"Why didn't you tell me?"

"I don't know. I thought maybe it would go away, but every time I close my eyes, all I see is that child's ugly aura and her damn jewel. And it's getting worse."

"That makes sense. Your lack of rest is most likely causing your growing susceptibility to the gem. Your body hasn't been able to efficiently heal the way it should have after leaving the chamber and it's opened unintentional weaknesses in your mind. I can put you back inside to see if I can help the process along."

"Do you think that will work?"

"I can't say with all certainty, but the odds are good."

Sentilla didn't like the prospect of having to go back in the box (and neither would Qah-Shekel), but if it helped her body heal, helped her sleep and reduced her urge for the gem, she was more than willing to endure the procedure. "Okay," Sentilla said. "Put me back in."

"I'll have to place you into a coma."

"Whatever you have to do. Just make this urge go away."

"As you wish," Kahli said. "It'll take some time for me to prep the chamber."

Sentilla lied down as Kahli went to the back of the room to pull the rejuvenation chamber from the wall. She tried not to focus on the gem, but the more she tried, the more it called out for her, and she feared the longer she was forced to remain in the dark, the more it would infect her and slowly become one with her in the darkness of its soul.

This was her plan all along, wasn't it?

— 13 —

It was apparent that the portrait had been carved directly into the wall, yet it seemed to have been painted on canvas; so surreal, yet so beautiful in its realistic qualities. Stacey, no older than what Tracey appeared to be now, looked gorgeous and radiant while emitting a regal persona, exactly as Jacquline had remembered her — with the exception of the gem nestled gently against her bosom; a glaring omission that made her seem uncomfortably naked. She tried to imagine what it was like to stand and pose for such a portrait — or if she had to pose at all. For all she knew, whoever crafted this amazing work of art could have done so from memory, or even a photograph, depending on what type of technology they had. It was arrogant of her to believe they had the same exact tools used on Earth, but no matter how much she wanted to imagine some alien invention, she couldn't wrap her head around it. All she could see was Stacey standing still for hours on end in the same exact position for a craftsman to mold her likeness into the stone.

"Where do you think they did this?" Jacquline said, curious to know more about how important Stacey had been.

"I would guess somewhere in the main foray area," Tracey said.

"Or a grand ballroom," Ken added. When his girls just stared at him with their quizzical expressions, he smiled. "By the looks of the pillars and some of the flooring…" He paused to dust away some debris to reveal a sparkling wood floor, warped slightly from years of degradation. "This was more than likely a main gathering area for social events."

"I can just imagine," Jacquline said, twirling around (which wasn't easy, due to all of the rock, not to mention brick and mortar, surrounding her feet). She stopped and lifted her hand to the air, bowing as she accepted the hand of an unknown stranger. "Gathering all the nobles from across the galaxy to wish you a happy birthday, accepting the hand of the prince for his turn around the dance floor."

"What's gotten into you, Jacks?"

"Can you blame me? Look at all this stuff. It has to be worth a fortune."

"I doubt it's worth much of anything," Ken said. "Not out here."

"Are you kidding me? A life-sized portrait statue of the queen of Trynoruus is garbage?"

"She wasn't a queen," Tracey said, distracted by something in the rubble. She cautiously climbed up along the staircase.

"I thought Rega said her father was king, or whatever."

"He was, but he was still alive when she was sent to Earth, which means she never actually took the crown."

Jacquline sighed with exasperation. "Fine, she was a princess. Big deal. It still has to be worth something to someone."

"It is," Ken said. "It is." Ken pictured the portrait sitting next to the replication of Renoir's 'Two Sisters,' which Stacey talked him into buying because it reminded her most of home. If it were up to him, he wouldn't hesitate to take this with him. But despite the fact that it would be near impossible (for many reasons, the least of which would be the time it would take to tear apart the surrounding wall or the matter of being stranded if they tried), this painting was a historical relic that belonged at its birthplace. For some small part of Ken believed that if the statue remained, so too did Stacey.

"We won't need it," Tracey said. She was up on the next level, holding what appeared to be a book. The outer cover was a slick leather material and the paper was held together with a strong, heavy-duty bind. The pages, despite having been yellowed into a rich murky brown by the weathered torture of time, were surprisingly intact.

Tracey sat down at the top of the steps and let her legs dangle over the edge. Ken and Jacquline came together just below her as she flipped through the fragile pages. The ink had faded quite a bit, but Tracey could still make out the majority of what was written. She turned to a page marked with a silk strap bookmark. Upon her touch, Tracey could feel herself putting on the dress from which it was made — a deep lavender floral gown that hung gently across the frame of her shoulders and swam behind her with the curve of her hips. It was light and delicate, and showcased every detail of her body without being obvious about any of them.

"What you got there, Squint?" Jacquline said as Ken wrapped his arm across her shoulder.

"Listen to this," Tracey said and then started reading from the book:

" 'I met her that morning in the fields of ivory. When I first saw her, asleep in the jewels, she made me happy. I'm not sure why, but she emanated this aura that sang with never-ending joy and a purity like nothing I've ever seen before. I wanted to hug her instantly, and kiss her, too, which was a little odd. I've never felt the urge to kiss another female in that way before. I've kissed mother, and I've kissed Aunt Desperi, but they are family; it is my duty to give them affection. Not this girl, though she felt so much like a little sister — a twin almost. I wondered if I should wake her or call out for father. She woke before I could make that decision and grabbed my arm. I was frightened, but didn't feel like screaming. She was comfort, and pain, and she needed my help. So I brought her back here with me. Father doesn't know it yet, but I plan to tell him over dinner. Oh what fun it will be to finally have a sister.' "

"What is that?" Jacquline said.

"It's mom's journal," Tracey said matter-of-fact. "Her diary." She looked directly to Ken. His tears were left open for anyone to see.

"I can't believe it," he said. "May I see it?"

Tracey closed the book and tossed it down to him, urging him to be extremely careful. She didn't have to remind him twice, as simply touching the book was like touching Stacey and nothing in this world would ever lead him to do harm to his lovely wife. He opened the book to start reading, thinking it would miraculously turn to English simply because he touched it (or that it was already in English — a fool's hope). The disappointment was quite haunting, but quite illuminating. This was the closest he had been to Stacey in years, and with her portrait staring back at him from only a few feet away, she could have been standing right there with them, holding him in a blanket of love as she narrated her tale.

"I found another one," Tracey said after beginning her search of the upper floor once again. She picked up the book and brushed the dirt off. Jacquline had discovered a way to climb up the steps and joined Tracey. "I think I see one here," she said. As she picked it out of a pile of rock, she asked, "How many do you think there are?" She found another a few feet up the hill (inside a heap of torn column and brick) and Tracey found a pair of them even farther away.

Ken didn't hear them call out any of their new findings. It didn't matter if there were more; his concentration remained on this and only this book. So much so that he almost missed the warning that rang out in his ear.

— 14 —

"Incoming vessel," Kahli said, much more firmly than before. She stood in front of her holocomputer staring at a visualization of the unknown ship and skimming through whatever statistics the *Equinox* could provide under the limitation of power. "Everyone return to the ship."

"Do you think they heard you?" Sentilla said. She gripped the medical bed as if she'd fall off if she let go.

"I don't know," Kahli muttered. "The storms are causing too much interference." She franticly tapped her fingers along the keyboard, hoping to find a way to adjust the power of the signal. But with each new progression, the electricity seemed to pick up on the power and increase their attacks.

"If you can hear me. Get back to the ship. Now."

Sparks then jumped from the desk with force, compelling Kahli to duck away. The holocomputer disappeared under the fireworks leaving only a trace of smoke radiating off the desk.

"What was that?" Sentilla said, trying desperately to see.

"I have to go to command," Kahli said. "You stay here."

Kahli left in a flurry of footsteps. The silence she left behind was deafening.

— 15 —

"What did she say?" Jacquline said, looking down at Ken.

"I don't know," Ken reported back. He raised his arms up to Qah-Shekel and pointed to his ear. He wasn't sure if Qah-Shekel understood the gesture, but he shook his head, possibly responding to Jacquline's original question.

"Should we stay here? Keep looking?"

"I think we should get back to the ship," Tracey said. "At the very least, we can regroup."

"I agree," Qah-Shekel said.

"What about the journals?" Ken said. "There might be more out here."

"That's okay. These will do for now." Tracey smiled brightly at Ken's shocked gaze as he finally noticed the stack of books his daughters had collected. "We can always come back."

"If you say so," Jacquline said.

Just then, Qah-Shekel's staff rained down and plastered itself into the ground next to him. He looked to the top of the gorge as an explosion (which was not caused by lightning) tore across the edge. Rock and debris sprayed down onto the group. Jacquline pushed Tracey to the ground and fell on top of her (although it would have been better had it been the other way around) and Ken took cover behind one of the pillars. When the dust settled, Jacquline looked up.

"What the hell was that?"

"Lark," Ken yelled. "Lark, are you okay?"

No sound came back, not even a whimper. Either she had turned her comm bud off or something bad had happened. He wanted to run up that cliff like a roadrunner with a jet pack but he couldn't leave his daughters. He just couldn't.

"We have to go," Tracey said and scurried out from under Jacquline. "Grab the journals." They recovered the books — eight in all — and carried them as far down the steps as they could. "Dad, take these," Tracey said. With his help, Tracey finagled her way down the rest of the steps to the ground. Jacquline couldn't wait for Tracey. She jumped, rolling slightly upon landing to try and avoid breaking her legs.

"Are you okay," Ken said as he helped her to her feet.

"Yeah. Fine." Jacquline started collecting the journals when another explosion ripped through the sky, this one a little farther away.

Tracey took notice of the staff and pulled it from the ground. "I have a bad feeling about this," she said. "We have to hurry."

"Where's Qah-Shekel?" Jacquline said. She spotted him halfway up the cliff and moving fast.

"That asshole left us?" Jacquline had more words brewing under her cool demeanor but figured his departure had nothing to do with them and everything to do with Sentilla. She respected his love for her; that didn't mean she wouldn't still have plenty of words for him once they were back to safety.

"Give me your jacket," Tracey said, pulling Jacquline's jacket off before she even had a chance to oblige. She stacked all of the journals onto the jacket and hastily folded the excess material over them. She then bound them together by tying the sleeves across the top. After double looping the knot, Tracey pulled it up across her back and tied the cuffs of the sleeves together around her neck.

"Are you sure you can carry that?" Jacquline asked.

Tracey was already climbing up the cliff.

Jacquline was amazed at her sister's strength and drive. "I guess so," she muttered before following her up. Ken was right on her heels, keeping a sharp eye on her as they climbed, hoping there wouldn't be any additional explosions — and praying Lark was okay.

"Dad, hurry," Tracey cried out as she climbed over the edge of the cliff. She quickly scurried to Lark and knelt down next to her. The first thing she did was check her pulse.

"Tracey," Ken said through the comm bud. "Tracey, what's wrong?"

"It's Lark. She's alive, but her vitals are low."

"What happened?"

"I don't know. Just hurry."

Tracey discarded the jacket and placed her hand just between Lark's breasts. She closed her eyes and felt her patient's heart beat in her palm. The gem glowed slightly as she focused her energy to the rhythm of the beat until it felt healthy and steady.

Jacquline helped Ken up over the edge of the gorge. He ran to Lark without a single word of gratitude for Jacquline and nearly knocked Tracey over in the process.

"Is she alive?"

"She'll be fine," Tracey said, ignoring his boorish behavior. "We have to get back to the ship."

"What happened to Qah-Shekel?" Jacquline said as she walked up to them.

"A better question would be what the hell happened to DovenJadden?" Ken added. He had Lark in his arms now. "What good are these damn communicators if they don't even work?"

"Thank you," Jacquline said, swiping her jacket up, an act much easier said than done.

"We'll worry about all of that later," Tracey said, calming the situation. She helped Ken to his feet. "We need to go."

Before they could take another step, an explosion propelled them all backward, everyone and everything sailing in different directions.

— 16 —

Nothing about the situation made sense. The *Equinox* hadn't been followed — if Sentilla hadn't detected them while traveling through empty space, Kahli certainly would have. She thought at first Eyrixano must have placed a tracking device on the ship, but she had thoroughly checked every inch of the transport ship, as well as the *Equinox*, days after departing Xyneris, even running several diagnostics to the ship's systems to be certain. Everything had been clear. It didn't stop her from running those diagnostics once more now, but as far as she could tell, the systems were clean and there was no indication that any foreign devices had been transmitting at all. The only other thing it might be was that Jacquline's assumption of inhabitants still living underground on Trynoruus were correct and they had tracked the *Equinox* to their position as they landed.

That has to be it.

But something still didn't feel right. It wasn't because she hadn't detected any type of technology before landing; Trysians (as they liked to be classified) could easily have found a way to use the electrical storms, not to mention the planet's crust, to mask their presence. It wasn't that they were attacking without provocation, as choosing to land on the planet was enough to cause suspicion. It wasn't even because Kahli didn't recognize the ship. From the readings she had gathered, it had very similar properties to a variety of different technologies, from those used on Trynoruus to others used on her very own home planet, the two of which historically traded quite often in a variety of manners. No, it was something else, something that bit at her gut and wouldn't let go. Kahli would continue to look for the missing piece to the equation, even if it took her centuries to figure out. What else could she do, other than run through every micro unit of information? From what she could gather, the most she could do right now was continue to keep the lightning focused on the *Equinox*, giving her team a fair shot to survive the trip back. Otherwise, unless the attackers raided the ship, she was all but worthless in a fight. And maybe that was it? Perhaps Kahli was feeling guilty for not being able to help. It was an emotion she hadn't felt in a while, not ever since she decided to leave Rega-One during the genocide. She was one of the only Alpha-Nine units to fight back against the Regans when they sent out the call for all Alpha-Nines to be upgraded with some of the benefits of a Beta-One. It turned out the Beta-One unit wasn't an upgrade at all; it was a downgrade from humanity to mechanical servitude. They were being spoon-fed rhetoric about how the enhancements would protect them from electrical current, even proving as much on a Beta-One volunteer who was subject to "electrical currents" that didn't effect her in the slightest.

They all fell for it — hook, line and sinker.

Kahli didn't buy any of it. She was aware of reports from organics who complained about the Alpha-Nine units being far too human; that they were a threat because of their emotion processors. Whether the Regans wanted to remove the emotion or completely shut them down was beside the point. They were looking to destroy them and would stop at nothing to do so. Kahli tried to spread the word that the Alpha-Nines would lose their identity if they agreed to the upgrade, but most of them didn't trust her. After the first wave of "upgrades" (wherein the Regans pulled the power cores from the Alpha-Nines and discarded the bodies in a refinery that would melt them down so as to be reintegrated into the newer models), the Alpha-Nines finally started to fight back, but by then it was a pointless gesture. The Beta-One units were far superior in technical advancement. Without a moral code running their operating system, they were the greatest weapon against the Alpha-Nine uprising the Regans had.

Kahli had gone into hiding during the mass of upgrades, but when she saw the reports of casualties on both sides, she wanted so much to fight with the Alpha-Nine coalition. That also meant having to expose herself, which probably meant destruction. So she remained hidden — guilty for the inability to access any amount of courage to do what was right, angry with the Regans for lying, and glad she was able to see it coming. When the majority of the Alpha-Nines had been wiped out, the Regans sent out an urgent call to surrounding worlds to help locate and wipe out all remaining Alpha-Nines that had fled. It was then that Kahli knew she would need to leave the planet altogether. Upon departure from Rega-One, Kahli felt the need to track down the remaining Alpha-Nines, but to do so would be a suicide mission. Much good it did, as sitting on her hands killed her anyway. Finding a way to shut down that specific set of emotions, as well as all of those that caused the Regans to fear the Alpha-Nines in the first place, was the only way she would be able to cope with her weakness — her cowardice. Never again would she let someone die because she was too afraid to fight for them. It was only when she first made contact with the gem that she started to feel these emotions rise back up to the surface. She thought she had been able to counter the gem's effects, to keep them at bay, and for the most part, she had. But they were becoming unstable and she wasn't sure how they might affect her judgment. Kahli hated herself for not seeing it before now.

That's it, she thought. "I didn't see it."

She sped her fingers across the holowall to bring up information they had gathered about the bomb placed on the transport vessel. She had failed to detect that piece of machinery. What if Eyrixano had tracked them using material similar to that of the bomb? It still wouldn't confirm anything, but it would give her a better idea as to what was happening.

She examined the properties of the bomb carefully, cross-referencing every element used with similar elements on the ship, including those that they had picked up recently on other planets. It didn't matter how small it was, she was going to check it all.

In the end, there was only one match, and it turned Kahli's eyes red.

"Kayla."

— 17 —

There was only one thing on Qah-Shekel's mind as he reached the *Equinox*. He had tried to contact Sentilla via the communication bud, but either there was far too much interference or she was dead — and he was not about to believe the latter.

Kahli had already opened the hatch in anticipation for their return, however, lightning continued to cover the ship in a blanket of white and blue veins, partially blocking the entry. He watched the movement of the electricity, and though there didn't seem to be any reliable pattern, every so often the hatch would be uncovered for a matter of seconds, usually after a measure of five beats from the time a swarm of electricity flashed across it. The timing would need to be perfect.

He set his feet and watched as a series of bolts zapped across the hatch. After it disappeared, Qah-Shekel started rocking back and forth, prepping for the next flash, which came quicker than expected. He sprinted for the hatch with less time than he was hoping. As the spark dissipated, he was still a few steps from where he wanted to be, but stopping now would be fatal. He pushed his legs to move faster. When he reached the edge of the ramp, he leapt through the hatch just as a fresh array of bolts shot downward across the opening, nicking the bottom of his foot.

Qah-Shekel crashed hard against the wall. His foot burned, but that was the least of his worries. The last time he was in this position, two crew members — and friends — died. Having that happen again scared him to his marrow. He got up rather quickly, ignoring the ache in his shoulders and torso, and flew down the halls. His first instinct was to head for command, but having shut down all of the major systems, that was the last place Sentilla would be. Judging by her demeanor prior to his departure, her most likely whereabouts was her living quarters, which were closer anyway. When she didn't answer his call for entry, Qah-Shekel swiped his hand across the wall, highlighting a small holographic box. He quickly punched in a series of squares in a seemingly random order until the door slid downward into the floor. Qah-Shekel rushed in to find a small stain of blood on the wall across from him. It was then that he remembered the call she made earlier. He didn't think much of it then, but now he feared the worst. Qah-Shekel wasted no time racing to medical, hoping Sentilla wasn't lying on her deathbed.

Which is exactly what it looked like when he first entered medical. Sentilla didn't appear to be breathing as she lay on the medical bed, and the rejuvenation chamber looked to be in the early stages of preparation, both of which nearly burned his heart to ash. He was afraid to touch her, but he needed to be certain and there was no time to track down Kahli. He tore open the examination table and lit up the hologram of her internal organs. To his relief, her heart beat steadily and all readings were healthy. He fell to the floor, unable to control the shake in his body, even as he squeezed his fingers across his temples.

"Qah-Shekel?" Sentilla said softly. "Is that you? What's wrong?"

Qah-Shekel immediately hugged her, easing his anxiety. Although she wanted to push him away because of the unsettling sent of the gem, she didn't resist him.

"I thought you might be dead," Qah-Shekel said, retracting the examination table.

"I thought the same of you. What happened out there?"

"I don't know. There were a couple of explosions, but I didn't see who caused them." That's when he saw her eyes. "What happened?" he said, passing his fingers over the shells that encased them.

"The gem must have caused my eyes to start burning hotter than they should, so Kahli doused them to bring the temperature down."

"That's all?" he said, taking her hand.

"Yeah," Sentilla said, embarrassed. She pulled her hand away and massaged it. "I was being stupid."

"And the chamber?"

Sentilla let out a short chuckle. "Kahli said it might help ease my addiction for the gem if I went back in."

"You agreed to go back in? Why would you do that?"

"I need to do something. If I don't, I might snap."

"I won't let that happen," Qah-Shekel said. "Not when there's something else we can do."

"What are you suggesting?"

Qah-Shekel didn't say anything, but his intentions were clear.

"We can't do that," Sentilla said.

"Getting you as far away from that gem is the only other solution."

"I agree, but Qah-Shekel, with my eyes shut down, I need Lark to fly the ship, and none of those humans are going to allow us to leave that little urchin behind."

"Kahli can pilot the ship until you've been able to heal properly."

Sentilla took a moment to contemplate Qah-Shekel's solution. "Okay," she said.

Qah-Shekel smiled. "Where's Kahli. We're leaving right now."

"She went to command to learn more about the ship that attacked us."

"Stay here." Qah-Shekel kissed Sentilla on the forehead and sprinted from the room.

"Qah-Shekel, wait," Sentilla called out. "What about DovenJadden?"

When he didn't respond, she tapped her fingers together and tried again. Still nothing. She didn't care what happened to Tracey, her family, or that absurd gem. But Sentilla couldn't strand a friend on a planet that couldn't wait to devour her — if it hadn't already — so she slid off the bed and slowly felt her way out of the room.

— 18 —

Tracey woke abruptly.

The wind had completely died away and an exhilarating fog that bit at her skin with light electrical shocks had formed around her. Three of the books lay at varying distances from where she sat. The rest, much like Ken, Lark and Jacquline, must have been hidden by the fog.

"Dad," she called out. "Jacquline? Are you there?"

She waited patiently for an answer before rising to her feet. Oddly, she had to stretch her shoulders a bit and rub her neck. There was also a slight hint of pain in her ankle that was easily quelled with a little massaging and a few steps. She quickly looked for her family as she gathered the books. After several feet in one direction (and nothing to show for it), she got worried that maybe they had been taken — or at the very least, she had (which, when she thought about it, actually made more sense). Although it was drowned out — almost muffled by the distance in a way — the constant sound of thunder assured her that she was still on Trynoruus. Where was an entirely different matter.

Her concerns were rendered moot when she found Jacquline lying still against a large rock. "Jacquline," she screamed. She dropped the journals and ran to her. With just the touch of her fingers along Jacquline's skin, relief washed over her. It was a bittersweet moment, though, as waking her proved to be impossible.

"It is sad," a voice hissed from behind her. "The love of one child for another, unwanted and unfulfilled."

Tracey's fears shifted to controlled anger as she paced her breaths rhythmically. She didn't want it to be true, but if it was, she couldn't allow her emotions to get the better of her.

"How did you find us?" Tracey said. Her hand, as well as her eyes, remained on Jacquline.

"I find it's best to always have an ear alongside your enemies."

"You planted a tracker."

"In a manner of speaking."

"I won't let you hurt them." Her voice was hard and feral.

"Never," Eyrixano hissed. Tracey could feel his presence swarm around her. "But you're afraid. You're weakening. I can feel it."

Tracey fought the power of his words even as it grew tougher to remain composed with every one. Her birthmarks burned her cheeks.

"The power is beginning to eat you alive, isn't it? You need to release the energy that's building up inside of you."

"I am in control," Tracey said, though not even she could believe that.

"For now. But it won't be long before you lose that control and harm those most dear to you."

"No," Tracey whispered.

"Those you have fought so tirelessly to protect will be destroyed by your own hand."

"No."

"Your family, vaporized by the obstinate arrogance of a selfish young child."

"No." Tracey turned to Eyrixano. She was still several inches shorter than him, but at this moment, she felt so much taller. Without even considering the consequences, Tracey built a wall of fog and pushed it toward him, lighting him up with gnats of electrical sparks. She could now see Lark and Ken, both lying unconscious (at least she hoped) several feet in opposite directions. Several journals lay with them. It all gave Tracey the motivation she needed to bring the gem under control.

Eyrixano laughed heartily, brushing the last of the electricity from his robes. Tracey took a few deep breaths and walked toward him. Flames rose high under his hood, igniting a flurry of pain and regret within Tracey as she fought to keep Stacey from appearing within them. What she wasn't counting on were for the flames to rise up from the ground and surround her.

She smiled. The heat was bearable and hardly anything but a nuisance. She stepped right through the flames without even a scratch.

"I am not as weak as you think, Eyrixano?"

"We'll see about that." Eyrixano burst into a cloud of smoke and dissipated among the fog. The flames flashed away with him, leaving Tracey alone in silence. She could no longer feel him, even as she utilized every ounce of focus the gem would allow. When she turned to check on Ken and Lark, they too had disappeared. She ran to where she remembered them being, but they had become ghosts, as had the journals. Looking around frantically, she wondered if she had run the wrong way. But that was impossible; she would have felt it. The gem would have told her. As she tried to understand what could have happened, she started to feel dizzy and lighter than she had in a long time. She reached for the gem to balance herself, but as she pressed her hand to her chest, panic filled her veins.

The gem was gone.

— 19 —

Qah-Shekel reached command to find it as empty as the rest of the ship. He tried the communication bud once more to no effect.

"Kan se," he muttered. He interlocked his fingers behind his head and squeezed his arms together. Screaming wouldn't help the situation, so he took a few breaths to calm down, trying hard to apply the words his father told him before leaving for his trials:

Help is not always going to be there when you need it. If you ever find yourself in a position where you must fend for yourself, slow down, breathe, and consider your options. Serenity and relaxation are your only friends; they will hold your hand and guide you. But be wary; fear, anger and frustration wait patiently to divert your attention and do you harm. Believe you are capable, and you will accomplish any goal.

He let out a breath. When he was younger (and in his mind, a far cry from being ready to lead), Qah-Shekel had been in a similar predicament. Circumstances had forced him to take control of a dire situation. He had no plan, no training and nothing to guide him except the love of a friend and his desire to protect her. Like that incident, all he had to do was slow down, take his time and do what was necessary — even if that meant once again starting over with only Sentilla by his side, though part of him would miss Jacquline... a little.

"Qah-Shekel?" Sentilla said. She was inching her way through the command center's gateway. Qah-Shekel quickly took hold of her arms to help escort her into the room.

"What are you doing? I told you to stay in medical."

"I couldn't let you leave without DovenJadden," she said.

Qah-Shekel rubbed his forehead. "Yeah, about her."

Sentilla cupped her mouth with horror and shook her head.

"I'm sorry." Qah-Shekel wrapped his arms around her, knowing it was only a useless attempt to comfort her.

"How?"

"She was watching over Lark when they attacked."

Sentilla wrapped her arms around Qah-Shekel. "This can't be happening again," she said.

"I know. But we did it once, we can do it again."

"I'm not sure I can."

Qah-Shekel kissed Sentilla's temple and then loosened his grip. Just then, DovenJadden stepped through the door.

"What's happening?" she said.

Sentilla flipped around, her hand once again covering her mouth — at least until she had her arms wrapped around DovenJadden (which wasn't easy, since she had to guess where she was, though her current scent was powerful enough to track). "You're alive."

"Yeah," DovenJadden said, doing everything possible to squirm her way out of Sentilla's grip. "What the hell is going on?"

"We thought you were killed," Sentilla said.

"Yeah, well, I'm not." She shoved Sentilla off of her and set her weapons down. "I can't say the same for the humans."

"What happened?"

"After the first explosion, a couple of those bastard aliens dropped from the ship and chased after me. I was able to lose them, but when I doubled back to check on Lark, a third shot took them all out." For effect, DovenJadden snapped with the word out.

"Did you get a good look at them?" Qah-Shekel asked.

"There's no way they survived."

"I meant the aliens."

"No. They had some sort of protective suits on."

Qah-Shekel nodded. "Something happened to the comm buds. Get them back up and running and prep the ship for takeoff." He started for the door.

"Where are you going?" DovenJadden hissed.

"To find Kahli."

DovenJadden fought back the urge to stop him and looked to Sentilla.

"What the hell happened to your eyes?"

Sentilla smiled. *Good to have you back.*

— 20 —

Lark was the first to wake. She looked around groggily. When she saw Ken nearby, she crawled to him despite the immense pain in her knee that also made her feel nauseated. "Ken," she said, her throat dry. It only took a little shake to wake him —

Damn!

He sat up as if he had been shocked awake by a shot of adrenaline. "Where's Tracey?" he said.

"I don't know," Lark said. They both looked around and called out for both Tracey and Jacquline (at least Lark did), but all either of them could see were several journals thrown about in all directions.

Ken stood, frantic. "Tracey!" he continued to yell until his throat closed.

"Ken," Lark said. "They're not here."

"Well, where is she?" His voice was scratched and half spent. "Tracey!"

"Continuing to yell for them won't do anything. We should get back to the ship."

"Not until I find her."

"What if they're already there?"

Ken didn't want to admit she made sense. He clenched his teeth and gave in to her calm. "What happened?" he finally asked.

"All I remember is DovenJadden getting up from her little pity party and firing at something. Then I woke up here."

Ken shook his head and looked over the landscape. He now had a splitting headache unlike any he'd ever had before.

"Come on," Lark said as she attempted to stand. She stopped Ken from helping her; she needed to test the strength of her leg. "We need to get back to the *Equinox*. Kahli should be able to track Jacquline and Tracey from there."

"Are you going to be able to make it?"

"Yeah." Lark took a few steps in a circle, hissing with each one. "Nothing a little healing gel couldn't cure."

As Lark limped away, Ken caught sight of the journals. "Wait," he called out.

Lark stopped, a bit aggravated. "What now?" Ken was frantically picking up the journals. "Ken, we don't have time for this."

"I'm not leaving them."

"What are they?"

"Stacey's journals."

Lark took a breath. She didn't necessarily want to indulge in this crazy act of obsession but knew how important something like this was for him. He would never leave them behind, so she carefully picked up a couple of journals nearest her. She looked for more, but Ken had already gathered the rest, even though he scurried about for others.

"I think that's all," she said.

"No. There's nine of them."

"Ken, look around. If there were any more, they're gone. Maybe Tracey has them. Or Jacquline."

Lark was right (again!) but Ken still didn't want to admit it. "Fine," he said and stayed several feet in front of her (sometimes having to slow down to keep her close) as they made their way back to the *Equinox*. When they reached the ship, they caught sight of something wholly unexpected.

"Rega!" Lark screamed. She dropped the books and skip-jogged to Kahli, who was lying just off to the side of the *Equinox*, smoke fuming off of her entire body. "God damn it, Rega," she said as she knelt down next to her. She didn't know what to do — just touching her might shock her to death.

Ken remained a few feet away, fighting his frustration. "What now?" he said.

Lark sat back and shook her head. No solution came to her as she rubbed her mouth.

"Kahli, are you there?" Qah-Shekel said over the comm bud. "Come in."

Lark suddenly perked up. "Qah-Shekel."

"Lark? Where are you?"

"Ken and I are right outside the ship with Rega," she said in Qah-Shekel's tongue. "But we have…" Lark paused for a moment. She knew how to say the right word in English, but wasn't quite sure how to say it in Krylexian. "An issue," she finally coughed out, though she didn't think it was right.

Qah-Shekel didn't miss a beat. "What kind of problem?"

Lark smiled. Now at least she knew how to say it. Store that in the memory banks. "Rega's been… decommissioned." This time the word came out in English.

"I'm unfamiliar with that word."

"It means hurt, out-of-service, laid out, kaput, no longer working," Lark said hastily. "We need you to shut down the ship so we can get back in."

She could feel the cold seething anger on the other line, which didn't show up in his voice — when it eventually came.

"Shut it down." Obviously he was talking to Sentilla (or DovenJadden, if she had made her way back). It became clear when the purr ripped through her ear.

"Don't argue," Qah-Shekel said.

"What's going on?" Ken asked.

"Just wait."

Shortly after, the static covering the ship disappeared. A bolt of lightning struck the ground next to Ken. He dropped all of the journals (a couple of which flew several yards away) as he was thrown toward the ship.

Lark limped to him to check that he was okay.

"I'm fine," he muttered, though it was more a lie than anything else. He instantly started to pick up the journals.

"Lark, are you on board?" Qah-Shekel said.

"One minute," she said. "I need your help, Ken."

"I need the journals," he yelled. He already had four when he spotted the others.

Lark stopped him from running after them. "Ken, we need to get Rega to medical. She's our only chance of getting the girls back."

Ken wanted to fight her, but was he angry because she wouldn't let him get the journals or because she had been nothing but right this whole time? He let out a frustrated grunt and tossed the journals into the ship.

"Let's hurry," he said and ran to Kahli. He cautiously touched her shoulder. Though there was a smart little flick of a shock, he was able to wrap his hands under her armpits and lift her up. Lark did the same with her legs and they waddled their way onto the ship.

"We're on board." Lark said after collapsing to the ground, alleviating the searing pain in her knee.

Within seconds, the electricity wrapped around the ship as it came to life once again.

"I need you in command immediately," Qah-Shekel answered.

"What about Rega?"

"There's nothing we can do right now. You must come to command."

Lark and Ken shared a very long and important silent conversation within a matter of seconds.

"Fine. I'm on my way." Lark eased back to her feet and shifted past Ken, who immediately picked up one of the journals. But it no longer seemed to matter. All he could think about was Tracey and how scared she must be out there alone. He threw the journal against the wall and let out a much-needed scream before collapsing to the ground and taking one last look at hope lost.

— 21 —

Tracey ran until her legs burned her to her knees. If she had had the gem, nothing could stop her from running the entire planet two times over without breaking a sweat, but without it, her stamina depleted faster than she ever remembered before the gem. It made her sick. How could Eyrixano possibly have gotten the gem in the first place? She didn't remember ever feeling his hot, burning hands on her — that was a sensation she would never forget — and though she couldn't access its power, she swore the cool, electrical vibrations running through her blood were still extremely evident in her veins.

That's it!

The gem hadn't gone anywhere. Tracey had been fooled into believing it had.

Never take anything at face value.

How the gem had allowed Eyrixano to do it was beyond her, but he must have drawn her into the flames somehow. Apparently, Jacquline was right — the gem wasn't without its flaws. The only question left:

How was she going to escape the dream?

Tracey sat up on her knees and straightened her body until it was stiff. She then closed her eyes and took in several deep breaths, picturing that ever-engulfing flame. She was inside of it, around it, part of it — she allowed the heat to lick her skin. There was nothing else around but the darkness of her mind.

She then stood and stepped back. With every step, the flames burned brighter and higher in front of her. They curved around her body, licking her skin but never once burning her. The bite of heat on her spine grew weaker and weaker until the flames were reduced to dance inside the black shadow of the hood. Suddenly, a pair of eyes flashed within the scorching blaze and then everything vanished with a rash of fog and smoke. Electricity fired through the sky above her. The wind whipped past her and lit the gem with the brightness of a watchtower beacon.

Tracey's eyes ripped open as a series of lightning bolts blasted the ground in a constant flurry. She instantly grabbed her knife and pushed the tip into her skin, releasing the energy into the lightning, which popped and exploded with the hammer of rolling thunder. When the echo of her scream faded upon the rocks, Tracey took in several deep breaths and grabbed the gem, making absolutely certain that she had escaped her nightmare. She waited for the gem to heal her wound and then stood, the energy of the gem reactivating her stamina. With one last breath, Tracey bolted in the direction of the *Equinox*, which from where she was had to be several miles away and prepping to fire up. She just hoped everyone was safely on board and that she wouldn't be too late.

— 22 —

Lark hadn't even gotten her back leg through the gateway to command when Qah-Shekel grabbed her arm. He slammed her down into the pilot seat, nearly popping her wrist.

"God damn it," Lark hissed as she flexed her wrist. "What the hell?"

"You have to get us out of here," Qah-Shekel said tartly.

"Hello to you, too," she said. She shifted her body to find a more comfortable position and looked up at Sentilla, who stood just off to the side. Her eyes were wide and glossed over, looking as if she had no clue what was going on. "Are you okay?"

"Don't ask questions. Just get us out of here."

Lark trembled to her feet. "I think I deserve some answers," she said with a high, piercing authority. Qah-Shekel's stance was so imposing, it made Lark feel as small as a mouse. But she remained firm and unassailable. "Why can't Sentilla fly the ship?"

"Sentilla's been temporarily blinded," Qah-Shekel said, matching her tone without flinching.

Lark looked again to Sentilla. Yeah, that made sense now. 'Why' would have been her next question, but she guessed it probably wasn't all that important, not with the impending threats they were up against. So she bypassed it for another. "What about Rega? We need to get her back up and running."

"We can't do that. Not here."

"Why not?"

"If she was hit by any amount of electricity, her power core would have been damaged. Until we are able to acquire a new one, there is nothing we can do."

"But we need her to find Tracey and Jacquline."

"We have no time for that," Qah-Shekel said.

"Well then make time." Lark brought some extra fight to her voice that time. "They need our help. I'm not flying out of here without them."

Qah-Shekel showed much more restraint than Lark thought possible.

"You can't leave them here," Ken bellowed over the comm bud. Not that it would do anything to change his mind.

"We can't stay any longer."

"What did he say," Ken said, frantic.

"Ken, let me handle this," Lark said, piercing Qah-Shekel with daggers of contempt. "Those kids are worth more than any information you could acquire. Why can't we try to track them?"

Qah-Shekel stepped forward with just as much malice. "The electrical storms are eating at the hull. We only have a matter of quasers before it rips us apart. We have to clear the atmosphere before it does or we're all dead."

"I'd rather give my life to protect them than run away."

All of a sudden, Qah-Shekel's demeanor softened. He wrapped his hands around Lark's shoulders in a compassionate grip. "As would I, Lark. But we have no idea where they might be or if they've been captured by whoever attacked us. We're not running away; we're regrouping. We will come back for them." His eyes shifted upward to Sentilla, who caressed her elbows and lowered her head with confusion.

Who was he lying to?

"Do you promise?"

Qah-Shekel nodded ever so slightly. Lark could feel the honesty in his touch.

"We'll come back for them," she said, both to reassure herself and for Ken's benefit. A smile then washed across her lips as she realized what she was about to do.

She had been working with Sentilla for some time now (by Qah-Shekel's order) to learn everything she needed to know about piloting the ship. Kahli had generated a simulator in tactical that took Lark through the paces of the *Equinox*'s capabilities and how to access and utilize the pilot controls. Lark had yet been given the opportunity to practice her skills outside of the simulator, but just like at the Air Force Academy, at some point it's time to get behind the controls of the real deal and take your chances. At least here, she didn't have to delineate colors, as all of the information and controls were based on memory, thought and typing commands. This was going to be fun.

Lark fell back into the pilot seat, excited and more terrified than she'd ever been. She swiped her hand across the side of the chair to ignite the holopads and curled her fingers across the small touch screen, lighting up the controls. It was a weird interaction Lark wasn't sure she would ever get used to. There was nothing there — it was only a hologram after all — but there was something there. She could feel its surface, the contours of the shapes and the tickle of the light. Unable to hide her childlike glee, Lark wrapped her hand upward (as if she were scooping up her favorite snack) and then pressed her palm flat on the pad. She smiled sheepishly as the ship bounced slightly, but no one else seemed to care much. They must have expected there to be a few bumps in the road.

"Here goes nothing," she said, her stomach in the middle of her chest. She lifted her hand at the wrist and pushed it forward. It was quite bizarre, almost as if she was still in the simulator. If it weren't for the slight rock of the ship, she wouldn't have even thought they were moving. "How do I turn on the visual screen?" she said.

"We went over that," Sentilla said.

"I know, but —"

"Think. Remember."

Lark took a breath. She ran through some of the commands on the viewer, thinking that might be what it is. When she couldn't find anything, she growled, "Come on." The viewer flickered on for a split second. She blinked rapidly, trying to figure out how she did it, then realized what she had done. Swiping three fingers across the screen and then across her body, she thought, remote viewer, and then opened her palm in front of her. The screen instantly opened. All she could see was the electricity obstructing her view of the mountain landscape moving away from them in the distance.

"Whoops," she said. She spun her hand through the holographic viewer, forcing it to change to forward view. "That's better." Now she had all the confidence she needed to pull this off without a hitch.

— 23 —

As Tracey climbed up and over the rock face, the *Equinox* slid away from her at an extremely low altitude with a sluggishly steady pace. It was as if a student driver had gotten behind the wheel of a car for the first time and wasn't sure how much to apply the gas without taking their foot off the brake. But it gave her the chance she needed to get back on the ship.

"*Equinox*, come in," she said in several different languages. Only silence returned, which meant that the electrical interference was far too great. If she was going to do this, she was going to need to pump her little legs faster than ever before and hope the ship didn't lift off before she could reach it.

First things first. Tracey focused all of her energy into telekinetically grabbing hold of the hatch, which she saw ever more clearly as she continued to pull at it. The hatch fought her for quite a long time but eventually gave in and fell open, That was her cue to start moving. As she passed a couple of the abandoned journals, a bolt of lightning set one of them aflame. She felt it burn to ash, the memory of whatever was written inside gone to the memory of the universe. But she couldn't worry about that. The ship was picking up speed. Her feet burned the ground as she forced the gem to circulate her blood to match her velocity. She was at a good, comfortable pace when the hatch started to rise. This was it; once that ramp closed, the *Equinox* would be gone. But if she tried to stop it or slow it down, the lightning would devour it, and that wasn't an option. Neither was being stranded on this planet. The gem could only sustain her body for so long before the lack of nutrients, both solid and liquid, deteriorated her body beyond the gem's restorative properties.

It was now or never. She had to take her chance. Her momentum would have to carry her through.

She jumped.

Barely able to wrap her fingers around the edge of the hatch, Tracey swung forward against it. The electricity wrapped around her body, deflected easily by the gem's force field. Like picking up a feather, Tracey pulled herself up over the top of the hatch. She could see Kahli's body lying in the hallway. Residual smoke poured from her scorched suit.

Ouch, Tracey thought as she rolled into the ship, moments before the hatch hissed closed. Turning to Kahli, she smiled and grabbed a hold of the gem. Her lungs tightened in heated tenderness as she felt the pressure of the ship rise upward.

— 24 —

Ken set the journals down on the table. Lightning washed across the window as the clouds burned past. He pounded his fist on the stack of books and ran his fingers through his hair, eventually grabbing some and nearly pulling it from his skull.

Qah-Shekel had abandoned his daughters on this god-forsaken rock without even the least bit of explanation. Worse yet, Lark allowed him to do it. How could she have given in to him so easily? Why didn't she fight harder?

Maybe she was coerced; threatened by DevenJadden, or even Qah-Shekel for that matter. Unless Qah-Shekel's comm bud was active, Ken wouldn't be able to hear a word he said (not like he'd understand any of it), and listening to one side of a phone conversation told him absolutely nothing about what actually went down. He thought about going to command and threatening Qah-Shekel for answers, but that would probably result in Ken's body being shot out into space just for the fun of it. Plus, he didn't want to leave the journals. They were his only connection to Stacey — he needed to keep them safe.

Keep them safe.

Ken chuckled, wiping his watery eyes. "Keep them safe," he whispered. "You'll never be able to do that." *Not on this ship.*

I'm sorry, love, he thought as he ran his thumb across the pages of the topmost journal. *I couldn't do what you asked. I couldn't...* He plastered his hand across his mouth; he could no longer fight his sorrow.

"You look like I feel," Tracey said.

Ken turned to the door but no one was there. Which only made his anguish intensify. Now he was hallucinating.

"We need to get you to medical."

That wasn't a hallucination. Tracey's voice was far too clear. Then it came to him and he felt absolutely foolish. He tapped his fingers together. "Tracey?"

"Dad. Rega's been damaged."

Ken sucked in a breath to help control the joy and relief that wanted to leap from his voice. "I know. Are *you* okay?"

"I'm fine," Tracey said. "What was Rega doing outside?"

"I don't know. Tracey, come to the room. I have four of the journals. You need to translate them for me."

"What about Jacquline?"

Ken's silence was enough of an answer. After some time, he said, "He won't go back for her," but Tracey didn't respond. He called her name, but again, silence. He lowered his forehead into his clenched fists. If he was correct in his thinking, Tracey was headed for command to get the truth once and for all.

— 25 —

"Systems are shutting down," Qah-Shekel said, relaying DovenJadden's frantic purr to Lark.

"I'm pushing the engines as hard as I can," Lark said, whipping her fingers around the holopads. "I can't go any faster if we want to pass through the atmosphere without being torn apart."

"We're going to be torn apart if we don't," Sentilla said after another cry from DovenJadden.

"Then I guess we get torn apart." Lark looked at Sentilla, even though she knew she wouldn't notice. "You know better than anyone what this ship can handle. Should I jump to lightning one?"

Sentilla took a moment and then said, "No. If we don't get ripped apart, doing that might destroy the lightning fuselages. We can't risk it." After another pause, she finished with, "It'll hold together."

Lark let slip a smirk; she was able to understand some of that without interpretation. She switched her attention to Qah-Shekel, who nodded, giving her complete authority on getting the ship up and out.

DovenJadden purred abhorrently, something evidently no one wanted to repeat — unless, of course, they were simply distracted by Tracey's grand entrance. Sentilla was the first to notice her; even blind she knew who it was and exactly where she was. She wrapped her arms around her chest and backed away.

"What are you doing?" Tracey said, her sights on Qah-Shekel.

"Tracey!" Lark wanted to throw her arms around the child and bear hug her until the gem popped loose, but she had more important things to worry about. "I'm trying to get us out of here."

"Not you. Him."

Qah-Shekel was more annoyed than anything else. "We would have all died had we stayed. Once we regroup, we will go back for her."

Tracey wasn't sure if he was lying (which her gut told her he was), but for now, she would trust him. She had no logical reason not to.

"Do we have any idea what happened to her?"

"I'm afraid not. For all we know, she died."

"She's not dead," Tracey said confidently. "I can still feel her."

"Then she's either wandering around somewhere down there, or whoever attacked us took her prisoner."

"I think it was Eyrixano."

The room was silent. Lark was the first to break it. "Are you sure?"

"That can't be," DovenJadden purred. "Vermon didn't attack us. It was something different; something I've never seen before."

"What attacked you at the palace, Lark?" Tracey said. It wasn't that she didn't believe DovenJadden, but she had to make sure.

"I don't remember," Lark said.

Tracey looked long and hard at DovenJadden. "Fine. Then who was it?"

"As far as we can tell," Qah-Shekel said, "inhabitants of Trynoruus."

Tracey took a deep, calm breath. If it was inhabitants of Trynoruus, and they had taken Jacquline captive, at least there was a good chance she would remain protected, if not scared out of her mind.

Just then, the *Equinox* broke through the atmosphere and the clear glass of space gave Lark a chance to breathe. As she slowed the ship, the last of the electricity that peppered the view screen dissipated. "We're clear," she said happily.

"You need to go," Sentilla said to no one in particular, although it was clear who it was. "Now. Leave."

Sentilla's plea was drowned out by DovenJadden's hysterical purr. "What did she say?" Lark asked.

"The system's are still malfunctioning," Tracey translated. "What do you need me to do?"

"I need your help to isolate the malfunction. I can't do it from here." DovenJadden tapped through the holoscreen rapidly, running through several sets of diagnostics.

"I'll do what I can," Tracey said.

"No!" Sentilla screamed.

Tracey ignored Sentilla's plea and jumped to Kahli's holopad, hoping that the gem would assist her in bypassing Kahli's necessary signature. As expected, nothing happened.

Come on, she thought as she tried to figure out how to make it work. Finally, she tried the only thing that made any sense. She pressed her hand firmly on the gem and knelt down, touching the center of the pad. With a quick shot of light, the holowall lit up, surrounding Tracey in sheer beauty.

"Ha," she exclaimed as she hopped back up. "Here we go. Tell me something." She spun through the elements on the wall (nowhere near as fast as Kahli), focusing on any red flags or codes that had been damaged or manipulated.

"Is there anything I need to do?" Lark asked.

"Power down the lightning unit and any other engines. If the malfunctions are anywhere near the core, at least we can sustain the blast and keep it from funneling through the ship."

She didn't have to ask twice. Lark quickly powered down the engines, leaving the *Equinox* to float through space at their current rate of speed. "What now?"

"Keep an eye out for any objects, comets, ships or debris. If it doesn't look right, or we're headed for a collision, tell me immediately."

"You got it." Lark switched on the sensor readings but nothing made sense as she scanned through them. She had watched Sentilla do this on several occasions, but having never been officially taught, she figured she'd done something wrong. "Sentilla, I need your help."

When Sentilla didn't answer, Lark looked up at her. She was as stiff as a taxidermist's prized specimen and her eyes glowed red with heat.

"Sentilla," Lark said more forcefully.

"I can't," Sentilla whispered.

"You have to."

Sentilla stood deathly still, staring in Tracey's direction.

Fed up, Lark grabbed a hold of Sentilla's shoulders. "Sentilla, look at me. Look. At. Me." When she finally responded, Lark bore deep into the ice of her eye sockets. "I know you can't see and I know that the gem is causing you to wig out, but you need to concentrate. I need you to help me navigate."

Sentilla clenched her teeth. She knew she was facing Lark, but all she could see was a deep, dark green void, one that pulsated and grew heavier with each passing second. A soft hum sang to her with a lullaby that soaked into her mind, calling for her to do whatever it took to use it and engage with its boundless power. Lark's voice was hidden underneath it all in a cloak of silence. No matter how much she wanted to stop it, no matter how much she wanted to resist, Sentilla was weakened by its strength. She would succumb and fight to be the universe.

"I found it," Tracey announced. She pulled a window with hundreds of lines of coded information down in front of her. She scanned through them with her finger and then enlarged the one specific line that had caught her attention. "The holosystems," she whispered.

That was when Sentilla let out a deafening scream and threw Lark across the room. she slammed into Naja-Leku's cubicle and tumbled unconsciously to the floor.

"Sentilla," Qah-Shekel yelled as she let loose a bright white beam of light from the palm of her hand. Tracey stumbled backward as the gem absorbed its power. It wasn't long before Qah-Shekel raised the fins on his forearm and sliced down against the beam. As the light ricocheted back toward Sentilla, Qah-Shekel was thrown sideways, slamming into the floor.

Sentilla ducked past the ricochet and bolted toward Tracey, catching her off-guard as she tried to re-orient herself after absorbing so much energy. Sentilla shoved Tracey from the holowall (which remained active) and pounced on top of her, scratching and clawing at the gem. It didn't take much for Tracey to grab hold of Sentilla's wrist and bend it backward until it snapped. Sentilla released a shrill cry of pain as her body fell numb long enough for Tracey to knock her to the ground and stand up, unaware of the sparks bouncing from the base of the holopad. The power of the gem kept Sentilla's adrenaline racing. She reached out for Tracey, who quickly grabbed her arm, pulled her in close and sent two hard elbows to Sentilla's temple, knocking her unconscious. Tracey lowered her body to the floor to keep from inflicting any further damage and then ran to the holopad.

Just before stepping back onto it, an explosion ripped the pad apart. Tracey flew backward, and though the gem protected her from injuring herself, the damage had been done. Sparks suddenly flew from the pilot seat, leaving behind flames and smoke as it shut down completely. Tracey grabbed her gem as she felt the same happening all over the ship. Without the holosystems, the ship was dead in the water. They weren't going anywhere anytime soon.

Tracey cringed. Jacquline was on her own and would have to fight if she expected to survive.

PRISONERS OF PERCEPTION

— 1 —

The young woman couldn't possibly be Keladrayia. Her hair said otherwise, but she was far too young and her features didn't quite match the remnants of her past. The resemblance still gave Jaenice pause. If she wasn't Keladrayia, there was a good chance she was related to her. Could she be the daughter of legend? The one who would bond with the gem of Jaxxa Rakala and rule the universe?

Jaenice brushed the girl's hair back to get a better view of her face. Beautiful in shape but pockmarked with several puncture wounds lining her ears and brow that looked to still be healing. Her skin was warm as Jaenice lightly grazed her fingers across the girl's cheeks, which must have accidentally activated a sensitive point in her skin because the girl's body involuntarily curled inward on itself. Jaenice backed off slightly in response.

The girl slowly opened her eyes. When she saw Jaenice, she scurried away from her into the farthest corner of the cell. Jaenice raised her hands in a gesture of kindness and safety. The girl looked around the bare room with several erratic breaths. All she could see were a couple of pads off to the side. When her eyes landed back on Jaenice, she opened her mouth. It took a few seconds for any sound to escape.

"Where—"

All of a sudden, the girl screamed and grabbed her ear. She curled back on the floor, fighting a pain that Jaenice could only imagine. But it didn't last long. When the girl stopped screaming, Jaenice crawled to her and tried to offer her help. The girl stared at her as if she didn't know what was happening, and then passed out. Jaenice thought about touching her again, then decided it was best if she left her be. She looked so peaceful in her current state of unconsciousness. When she woke, Jaenice would be there to console her — but only if she wanted.

"Sleep well, child of Keladrayia. Sleep well."

— 2 —

Groggy and clouded, Sentilla's head felt ready to explode. She was unaware of her surroundings or how she got there. It was only when she tried to grab her head to ease the pain that her mind finally woke up.

Her hands were locked behind her back in electrical binds attached to the wall.

She could feel her fingers on her right hand, but attempting to move them only caused her wrist to throb with a dull, dense tightening. When she struggled to pull away, the bracelets burned her wrists with an excruciating pain that sent her into a convulsive mess. She let out several grunts under heavy breaths.

"You should know better than that," Tracey said. She sat straight and proper at the opposite side of the cell with her arms wrapped gently across her lap.

"You get me out of these," Sentilla said, looking in her general direction.

Tracey flashed her eyes downward and then said, "I can't."

"Get me out," Sentilla shouted, once again struggling for freedom, once again being sent to the floor with a self-inflicted seizure. She hid her tears as she calmed her nerves.

"I only want to help," Tracey said.

"Then leave the ship and never come back."

"That won't help you. The gem has dug too deep a foundation. No amount of distance will keep you from yearning for it."

"So you're just going to keep me locked up here for the rest of my life? Why not kill me now and get it over with. It's what you've wanted from the start, isn't it?"

"I never meant you any harm, Sentilla."

"Yeah. I'm sure everything you've done was to protect me."

"And the crew," Tracey said.

"Liar. You may have been able to deceive everyone else, but not me. I know what you really want."

"You do?"

"I knew from the moment you attacked me on Xyneris."

"What is it that you believe I want?"

"You want to enslave us all. Use us as pawns in your sick little game."

"Is that so?" Tracey smiled sheepishly.

"You think this is funny? I know what you are, *child*. You're a witch with nothing but dominion in your heart. I know you were never held prisoner. It was all an elaborate setup so you could infiltrate the crew and create an army of hypnotized fools."

"It's certainly a creative scenario." The light smirk remained glowing across her lips.

"You don't deny it, then? You knew you weren't going to be able to control me, so you made sure to put me down as soon as possible. Well, you aren't going to get away with it. I'm not going to allow that to happen."

"You believe you can defeat me?" Tracey said.

"Once I have the gem," Sentilla said sharply.

"And that's the only reason you need it?"

"That's right."

"Then why has it been affecting you? The gem only affects those who have a desire for its power."

"No. It's you. *It's you.*"

Tracey crawled slowly toward Sentilla. With every inch, Sentilla's head expanded with pain to the point she needed to let out a slight scream.

"Stop," she cried. "Stop."

But Tracey didn't stop, not until she was nose to nose with Sentilla, whose skin burned with a desire usually reserved for the Bestwick right before dropping a litter of babies. She tried to ignore it, but the itch was too much to bear.

"I will destroy you," Sentilla yelled. "The gem will be mine!"

Tracey playfully bit her own tongue. "I'll make a deal with you. Prove to me that the gem means nothing to you and I will lay down my body for you."

Sentilla made every attempt to turn away, but the gem glowed bright, its rays of glistening sparkles reaching out to hold her chin in place and caress her cheeks. Tracey waited until Sentilla lunged forward to bite the gem from her chest. "Give it to me! It's mine. You have no right to it." The shocks from the cuffs no longer seemed to affect her as she jostled about to attack Tracey.

"I will get you through this," Tracey whispered.

"You lie!"

"The gem is a drug, Sentilla," Tracey said with rich authority. "Once you understand that and open yourself up to accepting your addiction, we can work to wean you off of it."

"How do you expect to do that?" It didn't matter that she was still blind; Sentilla's mind manifested the gem's image, forcing her eyes to remain glued to it.

"There are only two ways to deal with an addiction. The first is to strip the source away from the addict, which, in this circumstance, isn't going to work. The gem is too far ingrained within you and will control your actions no matter how far away I might go."

"Because it's mine," Sentilla growled.

"The second," Tracey continued, "is to make you immune to its effects."

"Immune?"

"I am going to expose you to the gem until you are no longer hungry for its power."

"You can save time by giving it to me."

"Probably, but I have something much more effective in mind."

"Tracey," Qah-Shekel said over the communication bud.

She tapped her fingers together. "Yes, sir," she said. "What do you need?"

"I need you in medical right away."

"I'm on my way."

Tracey closed the communication bud and stood.

"Where are you going?" Sentilla said, feeling the gem's power fade ever so slightly.

"Qah-Shekel needs my help," Tracey said. She walked a few feet from Sentilla and then waved her hand in the air. A gold web flashed on and off. After Tracey walked through it, the web snapped back up, fading slowly into an invisible wall.

"You won't get away with this," Sentilla screamed. "Qah-Shekel will never allow you to keep me here."

"Who do you think brought you here?" Tracey said and walked away.

The sentiment didn't take long to sink in. Sentilla screamed out some nonsensical threats and again attempted to break free of her bonds. This time, she felt every snap of electricity, which sent her back into convulsive pain and a flow of tears.

— 3 —

The dream was pleasant enough that realizing it was simply a dream was disheartening, especially when the pain of reality set in. A surge of heat pinched at Lark's spine, sending a heavy amount of discomfort through every muscle in her body. But it wasn't anything Lark hadn't been through before; being able to shake it off was almost instinctive. At least her leg had finally been healed.

She stretched her shoulders and rubbed the back of her neck as she sat up. The room was awash in a purple haze. Kahli lay dead as ever on the bed next to her. It was quite unsettling to see her so still and quiet. She slid off her bed to examine the android in more detail. What was left of her uniform had been heavily scorched, and now that it had cooled, it had become very brittle to the touch. Ken had said how much she looked like a life-size Barbie doll, but she didn't believe him until now. There was a patchwork of lines that looked to have been drawn across her skin with a pen. She assumed that as the electricity coursed through her body, it burned the skin from the inside, leaving behind a branding stamp for each of the different components that made up the inner workings of her body. It was remarkable to imagine the intricacy of what was hidden beneath the complexity of the top-most accessories. She knew it was wrong, but deep down, she couldn't wait to open her up and see it all first hand. Reaching Kahli's unaffected face (except for the burns and scars that traced her eye sockets and around the corners of her mouth), Lark rested her hand upon her cheek to take in the honest beauty of her design. It felt incredibly similar to plastic — silkier than human skin, but clearly an organic compound that reacted to her touch, turning a light pink with the subtle weight of her fingers. To see if the entire body reacted the same way, Lark traced her fingers up and down her torso, the pink contrail disappearing like that of a meteor streaking across the night sky.

"Fascinating," she whispered. She was so engrossed in Kahli that she didn't hear Qah-Shekel enter. When she finally took notice of him standing directly across the bed from her, she squeaked in fear and jumped back slightly.

"God," she said, pasting her hand to her chest.

"How are you feeling?" Qah-Shekel said.

It took a moment for Lark to register the question. "Yeah, I'm fine. I'll be fine. Is Sentilla okay?"

"We've placed her into solitary for the time being." Qah-Shekel was doing a good job at staying strong but he was clearly remorseful.

"She'll be okay," Lark said with a soft, comforting touch across his arm.

"I know."

Lark smiled. "I'm not sure I can say the same for her." She looked down at Kahli.

"There's only one way to know for sure," Qah-Shekel said. "Help me turn her over."

Lark found Kahli to be much heavier than she thought, though she should have expected it — she was an android after all. But she could hardly lift her, even with Qah-Shekel doing most of the grunt work. It made her wonder if this is what dead weight felt like.

"Clear the debris," Qah-Shekel said.

Lark did as she was asked, though it felt odd and discomforting. As she did, Qah-Shekel lifted a small container bound with a metal casing from the floor and placed it next to Kahli's head. After shifting her hair away from her neck, he pulled up a portion of Kahli's skin and inserted a cable attached to the container into the exposed port. He then slid his hand downward across the container. It started to glow lightly with a soothing, musical hum.

Finding Lark's task to be sufficiently completed, Qah-Shekel set both hands on Kahli's back, one flat between her shoulder blades, the other at a slight angle against the base of her spine, his middle finger pressing uncomfortably close to the top of Kahli's posterior. He pressed firmly down, using as much of his weight as he could and held this position for some time before letting up. After taking a short pause, he double checked the cable's connection and then pressed back down on her back. Once again, nothing happened, so Qah-Shekel pumped his hands with quick bursts of strength, apparently trying to activate something.

"Can I help?" Lark asked. She counted at least eight pumps before a small click sounded, jump-starting whatever it was Qah-Shekel was trying to activate. As he lifted his hands, Kahli's entire back opened. It was no more than a half an inch, but it was enough for the smell to force Lark into a retch of dry heaves for several seconds before gaining control of her involuntary impulses.

"What the hell is that smell?" Lark covered her nose with her shirt and held it tight. She could hardly breathe, but anything was better than having to endure that smell.

"The liquid from the power core," Qah-Shekel said, completely unaffected. He tried to slide his fingers inside the gap, but it was impossible. "I need you to unlatch the panel." He waved for Lark to join him on his side of the bed. She was reluctant, but knew she couldn't refuse. "Slide your fingers underneath and feel for the latches, here and here." Qah-Shekel pointed to two points on her back spaced some eight inches apart. It was clear she was going to have to use both hands to do this, so she was also going to have to deal with the smell of rotten oysters mixed with gasoline and vomit.

She sucked in a deep breath before letting go of her shirt. It didn't help much, as the smell permeated her nostrils. At least it was greatly subdued. She quickly placed her fingers under Kahli's back and slid them across to the points Qah-Shekel had mentioned. She wasn't sure what she was looking for until her fingers brushed against a hard, round object connecting Kahli's back to the rest of her body. Figuring out how to unlatch them was another thing altogether. Placing her forefinger at the top of the cylinder and her thumb at the bottom, Lark twisted her fingers around, spinning the ball bearing until the friction would no longer allow her. With a quick hit from the butt of her palms, Kahli's back lifted up enough for Qah-Shekel to take hold of it. Lark backed away and let her breath out, fighting to keep her nausea under control. Meanwhile, Qah-Shekel unlatched a couple of hooks on the other side of Kahli's body and removed the panel.

Regardless of the smell, Lark had to get a peek inside. As Qah-Shekel reached into Kahli's body, Lark inched around the bed to get a closer look (and keep from bothering Qah-Shekel). At first sight, it looked very much like lifting the hood to the engine of a fifty-year-old fighter jet with a dozen leaks. Everything was doused in a dark, oil-like liquid, and the parts that weren't, or where the liquid had been thinned, were painted with black scorch marks. Despite all of that, she recognized — or was at least familiar with — a lot of the pieces that went into building the internal working organs. Suddenly, the smell was no longer a factor. She was so interested in getting to know the working parts of the android and how they interacted when humming along with power that the odor became more of a nuisance than an overpowering hindrance.

By now, Qah-Shekel had grabbed something and was slowly sliding his hand back and forth. He would add a little pressure and then stop and pull, repeating the cycle over and over until he pulled out a black cylinder that seemed to be crumbling inside his hands before he even got it out of her. Just the slightest squeeze caused it to fall into a pile of ash on the floor. "Kan se."

"What was that?" Lark asked.

"The power core." Qah-Shekel reached back into her body and started scooping out ash and grease from inside.

"What does that mean?"

"If the power cell was still intact, we might have been able to recharge it, at least for a limited time."

"Can we do anything without it?"

Qah-Shekel grunted and pulled his hand from the body. He rubbed his finger with his thumb for a moment and then let some saliva drip onto the wound. "Not with what we have here," he said. "Until we can collect a new power core, Kahli's as good as dead."

"Well, where can we get one?"

"Rega-One."

"Is it far?"

"No," Qah-Shekel said a bit too quietly for Lark's liking. "All of the moons of Rega used to be strong trading partners with Trynoruus."

"Then what are we waiting for?"

"We aren't going anywhere until we fix the holosystems."

"Why? What happened?"

"Sentilla caused them to malfunction when she attacked Jaxxa Rakala."

"How do we get them back up and running?"

"I'm afraid you can't help with that."

"Why?"

"Because it relies on a space walk."

"Great. Suit me up," Lark said.

"That's impossible. We have nothing to fit your needs."

"I'm basically the same size and height as Sentilla —"

"Sentilla has never walked in space."

"Well, who has?"

"No one. We've never had to make repairs when we're incapable of landing first."

"Do you not have a back-up plan in place?"

Qah-Shekel motioned toward Kahli.

Lark felt foolish. "Then how are you planning to fix this?"

"He's going to send me," Tracey said as she walked into medical.

"How are you supposed to —" Lark didn't have to finish the question. The answer was probably sitting in the back of her mind the whole time, but her childhood dream of one day exploring space in anti-gravitational situations — and having that opportunity given to an eight-year-old mutant — clouded her thoughts from the reality of the situation. "Right," she finally uttered, though a bit more resentfully than she would have liked.

"Don't worry," Tracey said. "You'll get your chance."

Lark smiled; how could she possibly be jealous. They were a team. "Yeah, thanks."

"You need me to access the resource hatch on the ship's underbelly, yeah?"

Qah-Shekel nodded.

"What resource hatch?"

"Massanah believed that because the ship relies so heavily on the holosystems, we should have a failsafe that only two people knew the location of. That way, if there was ever any major damage to the systems, including the main repair station, we wouldn't be completely out of commission."

"Too bad you didn't think about that with Kahli," Lark mumbled. She didn't think either of them heard, but the silence said otherwise. "I'm guessing you and Massanah were the two who knew about this hatch," she said, hoping to relieve the awkward moment.

"If both Massanah and I were to die, the holosystems would eventually fail —"

"And the only thing the ship would be good for then would be spare parts." Lark smiled. "I like the way you think. And I'm guessing now that Massanah has died, Tracey's become your new second."

"You would be correct."

Now she could be jealous. At least she knew how to hide it.

"It's a shame Massanah isn't around to see us use it," Tracey said. Her memory of the little guy may not have been very favorable, but from what she had been able to learn of him, they probably would have gotten along quite well.

"You're up to the task, then?"

"I'm ready when you are," Tracey said.

"Good. Head down to the compression chamber. I'll guide you over the comms from there."

Tracey grabbed Lark's hand and gave it a quick squeeze. "I'll be okay." Then she left.

Lark wasn't sure how Tracey knew she was frightened for her, but it was nice of her to reassure her like that.

Qah-Shekel activated his communication bud. "Let me know when you've arrived."

As Lark waited with Qah-Shekel for Tracey's response, Lark's nerves started to get the better of her. And if she was this bad, she could only imagine what Ken would be going through if he knew. "I better go check on Ken," she said.

"Why?"

"You know him. He's going to go ballistic when he finds out what Tracey's doing."

Lark winked to add fuel to Qah-Shekel's smile and trotted out. Hopefully she could get to Ken before Tracey got to the chamber.

"I'm there," Tracey sang in her ear.

Damn. Too late.

"Great," Qah-Shekel said. "Let's get started."

— 4 —

Following Qah-Shekel's instructions, Tracey closed and sealed the compression chamber door by pushing several thick, brass levers inward into the floor (which would usually have been magnetically sealed had the holosystems still been functioning). Ken's frantic voice rang out over the comm bud when the last had been set in place. "Tracey. What's going on? What are you doing?"

"Ken," Lark said before Tracey had a chance to respond. "Where are you?"

"In our room."

"Stay there. We need to talk."

"What do you know, Lark?"

"Just stay there. And turn off the comm bud."

"Not until I know —"

"God damn it, Ken. Just trust me. Turn your comm bud off and I'll explain when I get there."

There was a brief moment of silence, and then, "Fine. As long as Tracey doesn't do anything until then."

"Fine," Lark said for her.

"I want to hear it from her."

"Dad, I'm fine," Tracey assured. "Trust Lark."

Again silence. Tracey waited until he finally confirmed he would turn his communication bud off before starting down the ladder into the chamber. She knew Lark would be able to calm him down and there was no time to lose. The longer they waited to fix the holosystems, the longer Jacquline would be alone. She couldn't wait, and Ken would eventually agree.

The chamber was a small hexagonal box that would have been pitch black if it wasn't for the light from the gem. It wasn't a part of the ship that was accessed often, if at all, so Tracey could only suspect that had the holosystems been functioning, the room would have been lit up in a harmonious dance of readouts and holoscreens she would have been able to use to open the outer hatch. As it was, she was going to have to do everything by hand.

Her first task, according to Qah-Shekel, was to open the main control panel in the wall next to the outer hatch, which was easy enough. She then had to reach in and extract a large handle attached to a long metal rib at the center of the column. Once it sat on the edge of the panel opening, Tracey pumped the handle several times, each one harder than the last, until she heard a click, followed quickly by a small hiss. She pushed the handle all the way back into the panel and pulled out a second handle to repeat the process. This one was harder to pump than the first, forcing her to use her entire body. She wasn't sure she was going to able to do it without accessing strength from the gem (not with her scrawny physique), but when she heard the click and hiss, she collapsed in relief.

At least she would have collapsed if it hadn't have been for the gem, which wrapped a thin coating of protection around her entire body, helping feed her the oxygen she needed after switching the generators off. She took a moment to relax before pulling a small panel from the wall (or kicked it, to be more exact). The space would have been no problem for Tracey to crawl through two weeks ago, but thanks to the gem, it was a bit of a squeeze. Thankfully, it didn't take too long to track down a set of three valves that Qah-Shekel said would shut down the atmospheric generators and depressurize the chamber. They sat against the side of the wall approximately three feet apart from each other. The first one she had to access was the farthest valve, forcing her to shimmy past the other two. Sitting against it wasn't at all comfortable as they dug into her shoulder and hip. She turned the first valve the mandated three-quarters of a rotation and a red light started flashing, which Qah-Shekel told her to ignore. She then inched her way backward to get better access to the second valve. As she did, her belt latched onto the third and rotated it. It didn't turn more than a half an inch, but it was enough to ignite the alarms and try to pull her from the ducts. She grabbed a hold of the pipes that lined the space to keep herself steady and spun the third valve back to where it should be. Nothing changed, so she decided it best to keep going with the process and hope it didn't rip the compartment right off the ship. Despite Qah-Shekel's constant twittering in her ear, Tracey focused her attention to turning the second valve three quarters of a turn. The pull on Tracey slowly gave way to weightlessness due to the lack of an atmosphere and she took that as her cue to turn the third valve, fully opening the outer airlock.

"I'm fine," Tracey said repeatedly to calm Qah-Shekel (and possibly Lark, who she suspected was still listening even though she wouldn't have admitted it — not if she was trying to keep Ken calm). "I'm heading out now."

Tracey cautiously pushed her way out of the ducts and floated to the open hatch to get her first glimpse at the magnificence of the galaxy without a filter. What caught her attention most — over the array of stars, galaxies and molecular anomalies — were the vibrating clouds surrounding Trynoruus, which, along with the planet's twin moons (and a small rock in the distance that Tracey assumed to be another planet in this particular solar system), took up most of her overall view. Although the holographic projection did represent the planet to the degree of a high definition television, nothing matched the magnitude of viewing the planet in its natural environment. Now she understood why Lark had been so jealous; to absorb this endless sea of celestial grandeur would take anyone's breath away.

"Are you there?" Qah-Shekel said, breaking Tracey from her spellbound hypnosis.

"Almost," she said, hoping the way she expressed the term would give Qah-Shekel a sense that it was a lot harder for her to walk through space than she originally may have implied — which wasn't true at all. She wrapped her way around the edge of the hatch and clung to the slippery smooth surface like a bug on a windshield. It didn't take her long at all to glide her way to the underbelly of the engine housing at the rear of the ship.

"I'm ready," Tracey said, only moments after her last response.

"Trace your hand backward from the edge of the secondary engines. There will be a section that's hotter than the rest."

"One second." Though Tracey could already detect the heat signature of the area he was mentioning, she traced her hand along the hull to make sure it was accurate (or at the very least, to give the impression that she had actually taken her time to do it). "Okay, I found it."

"Press the palm of your hand to the center of that section."

As she did, four separate areas of the hull, each about a foot in diameter and symmetrically spaced around her, became lightly transparent.

"I see four frosted squares," she said.

"Open the one farthest from the edge of the engine."

Tracey slid to the square on her left and pressed down on the edges, popping the panel upward about a half an inch. It hissed and spread open, exposing a set of inner panels of flashing lights. "Got it. What next?"

"You should see a small light board."

"Yeah."

"Figure out the pattern and then locate the panel that has the exact opposite pattern."

"Okay," she said, hiding any anxiety that might have been tickling her stomach. At least she didn't let it affect her focus as she watched the pattern with eagle-eyed precision. At first it seemed to be awfully random, spinning from flashing two lights to four, back to two and then three. It then repeated the pattern backwards, adding flashes of one light and five lights at different points each time. But the longer Tracey watched, the more it became clear that it wasn't the pattern itself she should be watching for, it was how many times it changed before repeating the pattern from the very beginning. This particular light board cycled through a pattern of ten separate flashes five times before starting over from scratch to repeat the entire set once again. With that in mind, she had to look for a light board that cycled through a pattern of five separate flashes ten times before repeating the cycle.

She jumped to the panel on her right and opened it up. After several minutes, Tracey concluded it was cycling through a six/eight pattern. The next set seemed to be what she was looking for, but to make absolutely sure, she checked the fourth to confirm it with a four/two pattern. Sliding back to the panel exactly opposite the main panel, Tracey said, "I got it. What next?"

"Are you certain it's the correct panel?"

"I am," Tracey said with feigned confidence

"Good, because if you choose the wrong one, the engines will self-destruct."

Way to make me totally second guess myself. "I'm certain."

"Do you see the latch?"

It took a second, but she eventually found it hidden in the wall on the side of the panel she was lying on. "Yeah."

"Pull it out and turn it half a turn. This should make the light board solid and bring up an independent holoscreen."

It was a little difficult to find a grip on the latch, but once she had, everything lit up as Qah-Shekel had said.

"Insert the pattern code into the holoscreen and then activate."

When Tracey touched the screen, a set of numbers appeared above it. At the same time, the light board cycled through its pattern once again. She quickly entered the numbers in accordance with each flash, keeping in mind the sets of numbers that she would have to enter. There was nothing more to do but wait when she finished. For a moment, she thought she may have done something wrong, but she was afraid to touch anything in fear of causing the explosion she was hoping to avoid. Finally, the keypad was replaced with a single bar that read 'Activate.' Her finger hovered over the button for several seconds as she cycled through a few deep breaths.

It's now or never.

She closed her eyes and pressed the button. It disappeared directly after, but Tracey wasn't willing to open her eyes until she heard a confirmation of success.

"Holosystems are back online," Qah-Shekel reported. "Good job."

Tracey let out the breath she was unconsciously holding and laid back against the hull. "Good to hear," she said. "See you back inside."

But she wasn't ready to go back — not just yet. She wanted to remain out here for as long as she could and take in every bit of the extraordinary view, one that overwhelmed the significance of a lost —and most likely terrified — older sister that Tracey wished she could share this inimitable experience.

— 5 —

The smell was completely unfamiliar to Jacquline as she lay on the course, rocky bed, unwilling to open her eyes for fear of what she would see when she did. If there was anything she could relate it to, it was as if her surroundings were plastered in some kind of manure sprayed with Lysol and then covered with a variety of scented hangars that turned your stomach one second, only to make you feel back home in your tub with a full bubble bath the next. It was only when she heard a slight rustling behind her that she decided it might be best to find out exactly where she was.

From what she could tell through the extremely limited light source, she was inside a giant pit that someone had dug into the ground, but that didn't have any perceivable access from any direction. The walls were jaded with rocks and the ceiling sat some twenty feet above her (so even if there was some sort of trap door, she would never be able to reach it) with lines of softly glowing wire coming from inside one wall and running into the opposite. On the ground in front of her were two blanket-like pads that felt familiar, though she didn't know why — not until she caught sight of the young woman curled up against the wall in the opposite corner of the pit, one leg pulled up so she could rest her arm across her knee, the other stretched out along the wall giving off the perception that, when she stood, she might just be seven feet tall. Nevertheless, the woman was very human in appearance with long black hair tied and draped across her shoulder, revealing flame-red tips. Her bangs curled over her forehead with a slight wave and hid her eyes in the shallow depths of her very pointed features. A brown cloth that looked like a muumuu made for a rocky mountain recluse was draped across her body, signifying that she had probably been here for quite some time. What made her all the more menacing was the way she sucked on what looked like a long twig, but which let out a hint of smoke from its tip.

"Welcome to hell," the woman said, the smoke wafting from her lips with every word.

"Who are you?" Jacquline said. She had to flex her jaw to try and pop her ear, which felt awfully dull and empty. She pressed her fingers to her lobes and even twirled her pinkie inside as deep as she could, but nothing helped. "What the hell?" she whispered.

"I'm not sure what happened earlier, but you seem to have had one major auditory burnout."

Jacquline looked at her cellmate with razor sharp antipathy, which only made the woman crack a haughty smile. She took a hit from her twig. "I'm Jaenice. And you are…?"

Jacquline was unsure if she was willing to answer.

"Do you have one?" Jaenice paused, and when it was clear Jacquline wasn't going to give up her name, she said, "Fine. You don't trust me. I understand. So until you do, how about I call you baby Kel?"

Jacquline furrowed her brow slightly.

Jaenice laughed. "You don't have any idea what I'm talking about, do you?"

"Keladrayia," Jacquline said, and realized her throat was dry and scratchy. Not only that, but it was clear it would take time for her to get used to being deaf in one ear.

"She speaks," Jaenice sang.

"What do you know about Keladrayia?"

"Only the bullshit rumor that she's the mother of all destruction."

Jacquline grew curious. "I thought her daughter would become —"

"Yeah," Jaenice cut in, "therefore, she's the mother —"

"— of all destruction," Jacquline said along with Jaenice. "Got it."

"You've been through a lot. I'll forgive you for the lapse in brain function."

Holding back a smirk, Jacquline said, "Why is it a bullshit rumor?"

"Because there's no truth to it. But it's *'prophetic'*, so every Tom, Dick and Harry have become mad with this delusional theory that they can become the master of the universe, when in reality, the only one who's controlling anything is the puppeteer behind the legend."

"Jaxxa Rakala."

Jaenice laughed. "Yeah, I don't think so."

"Why not?"

"Honestly, I don't think she even exists. I think the whole thing was made up to incite a countless number of wars across the galaxies in order to wipe out every species except for the puppeteer's marionettes."

Jacquline smiled a knowing smile, but held back from telling her what she knew. "So then who do you think the puppeteer is?"

"I wish I knew. At least then I'd know whose ass to kick when I get the hell out of here. But whoever it is sure did have a hard on for Trynoruus."

"Where the whole thing started."

Jaenice nodded and took another hit. "So what's your story? What got you thrown down in the dungeon?"

"I could ask you the same thing."

"I'm betting our stories would be pretty similar."

"Try me."

"They think you're Keladrayia, right? Or at the very least, a descendant?"

"Why would you think that?"

Jaenice pointed at Jacquline's hair. "The stripes, baby Kel. I can tell you, I was almost fooled the first time I saw you, too. But there's no way you could be Keladrayia. You're too young. Not to mention you're from Earth, right?"

"How would you know…?"

Jaenice laughed, this time with a hearty guffaw. "Haven't you figured it out yet?" she finally said.

"You're from Earth?"

Jaenice sucked some smoke into her lungs and pointed the twig at Jacquline. "I'm thinking you might need a hit to wrap your mind around this."

"No," Jacquline said, feeling quite dizzy. "I haven't smoked a joint in over, what? Three years?"

"Let me tell you, baby Kel. This is not your ordinary homegrown shit." Jaenice wouldn't retract her arm until she took the twig from her, which meant crawling closer than Jacquline was comfortable.

"I'm not a cannibal," Jaenice said.

Jacquline sneered slightly and then swiped the twig from Jaenice's hand. She sniffed at the smoke emanating from the tip. It was pungent to be sure, but it settled in her nose with a pleasant aroma that reminded her of freshly cut strawberries. Setting the twig on her lips, she could feel the scent creeping around her mouth with the fruit of succulence. Before she knew it, she was sucking the smoke into her lungs, providing her an instant hit of euphoria.

"Good, right?" Jaenice said.

Jacquline smiled and closed her eyes, savoring the vibrant taste in every molecule of her breath as she exhaled.

— 6 —

It didn't take Lark long to plant her butt back into the pilot seat and pop the holopads up. She spun her fingers through a variety of destinations, or so she thought. If the ship had been Krylexian, she'd have no problem reading the star charts. But because the ship was originally from Ersphina, Lark only recognized the terms Sentilla had taught her — none of which included anything but the necessary commands for piloting the ship.

"Qah-Shekel. I need you on the bridge," Lark said after switching on her comm bud.

"What for?"

"Sentilla taught me how to fly this monster but she never taught me how to locate the coordinates for a planet, much less set a course."

There was a deathly silence, which worried Lark until he finally came back with, "DovenJadden. Get to command and help Lark."

A soft, almost disgruntled purr responded. Lark was about to say something to try and help Qah-Shekel convince her to assist, but she thought better of it. She was already on DovenJadden's bad side (why, she wasn't exactly sure; maybe everyone was always on her bad side), so keeping her mouth shut and letting Qah-Shekel handle this was probably for the best.

"Don't argue," Qah-Shekel yelled. "Go help her."

A vindictive purr preceded the silence. Lark figured DovenJadden was on her way, but she had so much energy swimming through her, she needed to do something while she waited. Pacing command might make DovenJadden think she was impatient (which, on top of already thinking she was incompetent wasn't something Lark wanted), so she took to running through the texts again, even though she knew it was utterly pointless to do so. When DovenJadden finally arrived, Lark had spun through the list of planets and destinations nearly a dozen times.

"Thanks for this," Lark said as happily as she could.

DovenJadden just growled (or so it seemed) as she buzzed through the list for no more than a few seconds before shutting it down and bringing up a completely different one. Lark hid her embarrassment for being in the wrong list the entire time as best she could. After navigating through a couple of different menus, DovenJadden looked at Lark and purred.

"Uh... Rega-One?"

DovenJadden stood upright, looking quizzically at her. She then tapped her fingers together and purred anxiously.

"Rega-One," Qah-Shekel confirmed. DovenJadden argued once again but was completely overruled by Qah-Shekel, who sounded very much like he was holding his anger in check for Lark's benefit.

Don't mind me, she thought. *Give her all you got.*

DovenJadden let slip one more disgruntled purr and then went back to locating Rega-One in the database. She brought up a large view of the planet specs, typed in a bit of information into the holoscreen below it, and then shut the entire thing down, returning the pads to functioning flight pattern.

"Thank you," Lark said again.

All she got in return was a dark set of condescending eyes. DovenJadden then stormed from command without even a hint of kindness. Lark was now alone —

Good riddance!

— to get them to their destination.

You can do this, she thought as she rested her hands on the pads. *Just like flight school*. She ran her fingers over the pads as she had been taught. Indicators on the left of her holoscreen lit up green, signifying the engines had come to life, ready for ignition.

"Tracey? Are you back inside? We're ready to roll."

"Yeah. You're good to go."

Lark nodded to no one in particular and curled her middle fingers under her palms. Before she knew it, the screen in front of her went from a sprinkled black canvas to a wash of white as they entered lightning five. Hopefully DovenJadden had set the course correctly and they wouldn't encounter any debris or other rogue objects (you know, like a giant sun). Lark would be in a hell of a spot if they did. She'd do what she could, but maneuvering a jet at Mach 3 is a great deal different than maneuvering a spaceship at the speed of light. For now, though, none of that really mattered. This was still one of the coolest experiences she had ever had. She was going to embrace the moment and enjoy every second of it.

— 7 —

"What in the hell do you think you're doing?" DovenJadden stormed into medical with a flurry of disdain. Qah-Shekel whipped around and grabbed her neck before she could rip into him any further. "I've made my decision," he said in a low, deathly growl. He squinted his eyes to the point they were mere lines, glowing with all the anger of a Frassaw. "Don't you ever undermine my authority again, understood?"

DovenJadden, unable to breathe, lowered her eyes, surrendering to him with as much dignity as she could muster under the circumstances.

He gently lowered her back to the floor and turned to Kahli to continue cleaning the inside of her body.

"What good do you think this will do?" DovenJadden said, much more subdued.

"I have no choice," Qah-Shekel said. "We need to acquire a new power core for Kahli and Rega-One is the only place we can do that."

"She's going to get us killed the second we set down. I hope you realize that."

"It's a risk I'm willing to take."

"For whom? Those humans?"

Qah-Shekel remained silent.

"I can't believe you're still trusting those fools," DovenJadden said. "It wasn't that long ago that you were willing to leave them all behind."

"As I was you, DovenJadden. Don't think you hold higher regard than anyone else on this ship."

"They are retched scum and should never have been allowed on this ship. We should have left them to die with Keluwa."

"If we had, we might all be dead right now. And we would have destroyed Jaxxa Rakala."

"So what? You seem to forget, it's because of her that Sentilla's gone mad. How do we know she wasn't the one who forced Kahli outside on Trynoruus?"

"Why would she do that?"

"Maybe she wants us on Rega-One. Maybe this whole charade has been a trap."

Qah-Shekel stopped wiping Kahli's body and turned to face DovenJadden. "I can't believe that."

"Who was it that found the bomb on Xyneris?"

"Jaxxa Rakala."

"And who dismantled it?"

"Jacquline."

"Who's to say they didn't put it there themselves to gain our trust? How was it that Jaxxa Rakala was able to access Kahli's holostation? What if they aren't 'human' at all? For all we know, they're Regans seeking to acquire the gem for a new weapon."

Qah-Shekel chuckled. "Now you're reaching," he said, though without any level of confidence whatsoever. No matter how little, DovenJadden was getting to him. "They've done nothing that warrants such assumptions."

"All I'm saying is we need to be more cautious."

"Noted." Qah-Shekel and DovenJadden stood in a silent battle of power for some time before DovenJadden gave in and left medical. Qah-Shekel returned to cleaning Kahli, though with a new sense of diffidence. Though he couldn't believe that his new passengers were anything but what they said, his growing relationships with them — and Jacquline in particular — may have been affecting his decisions. Until he knew without a doubt, he would have to be cautious... but also remain skeptical to DovenJadden's biased accusations.

— 8 —

Even though he couldn't read any part of what amounted to a stew of chicken scratch, Ken could still hear Stacey's voice reading to him as he scanned the pages of the journals. He could vividly see her sitting at her desk, surrounded by elegance, the sun beaming through the window and warming her face as her hand scrawled her beautiful, succinct, carefree thoughts across the pages. He imagined heartfelt purity in those pages and didn't care if he was being completely naïve. His vision of her being at peace (as opposed to having been a part of the destruction seen on Trynoruus) was all he cared to remember, especially now that they were traveling away from her home with no real inclination to ever return. It scared him, not because he was afraid of losing Stacey once and for all (as leaving Trynoruus without any actual clue made it seem as if the search was finally over), but because he would never forgive himself for leaving Jacquline without even attempting to search for her. Then again, he could spend a lifetime on that planet and never come close to finding any clue to her whereabouts, so fixing Kahli was pretty much his only option in tracking her down. That still didn't give him any comfort. His only option was to hide in a world of serenity, imagining Jacquline to be the princess he never allowed her to be.

"Hey, dad," Tracey said as she walked into the living quarters. "You doing okay?"

On impulse, Ken went to Tracey and held her in his arms, hugging her for Jacquline and Stacey, as well as expressing his relief for her safety.

Tracey kissed Ken on his cheek. "I'm fine, dad. And so is Jacquline."

Ken pulled away, keeping his hands around her upper arms, and smiled (though he knew Tracey could see right through it). "Don't ever do that again," he said.

"I can't promise I won't," she said with a bright smile and a quick wink that gave Ken the genuine bliss he needed. She tapped his cheek and walked to the table. Catching sight of the journals, she rubbed her hand gently across the open pages.

"Do you want to know?"

"I did at first," Ken said softly, "but I can't. It would be a violation of her trust."

"Or maybe it's a story you were always meant to read."

"If she meant for me to know what was in there, she would have already told me about it."

"Not if you weren't ready to hear it."

"No," he said, shaking his head. "Not like this. Lark was right when she said I was overstepping my bounds with Jacquline. She wouldn't want me reading her diary, so how would I justify reading Stacey's most intimate thoughts?"

"You don't think you'll love her the same way if you know what's in here, do you?"

Ken averted his eyes as if he had to be ashamed of that. "I don't know what it is. No matter how much of her I feel in these books — her touch, her smell, her soul — I don't know if I'm ready to accept this part of her."

"Because it makes it real."

Ken chuckled lightly. "No, I think all of this has made it pretty real. I'm more afraid that knowing what's inside those books will turn her into someone I don't know, in a life that I…"

"You don't want it to ruin the memory of her."

"I want to remember her for who she is, not who she was. If I know this part of her life, how am I going to react when we find her?"

"And if we don't find her?

Ken sat down and rubbed his face, digging his fingers onto the bridge of his nose. Her voice echoed the sentiment in his mind.

"I don't think anything will be different at all," Tracey said, easing his pain. "Her circumstances may have changed, but she hasn't."

"How can you be so sure?"

"She was, is and always will be happy and kind," Tracey said. "Take comfort in that."

Ken smiled and dropped his hand to hers. "I do."

"Here's what we'll do. I'm going to read these journals to Sentilla."

"Sentilla? Why —"

"Don't worry about that. As I read, I'll keep my comm active. You can keep yours off for as long as you need, but when you're ready to listen, simply turn it on."

"But that means everyone else will hear them, too."

"It will, but I have a feeling they're going to want to know a lot of what's in here."

"Will it help find her?"

Tracey smiled. Ken opened his mouth wide, fighting to find a breath among the fierce urge to let his emotions run free. When he regained control, he reached out and took Tracey's hand, giving it a loving — fatherly — squeeze. "You're a great kid," he said.

"Save that for Jacquline." Tracey swept the journals into her arms. She smiled, hoping to give Ken another quick bout of bliss, and left.

Ken looked out the whitewashed window, running his hand over his mouth. He hated Tracey being so introspective —

Give me back my baby girl!

— but she was right. Jacquline was still out there and when they came back to find her, he would embrace her the way he used to when she was a bouncy little girl without much care in the world except how fast she could catch that pretty little butterfly, or the amazement of a talking stuffed animal. Those days were gone and it was his fault; he wouldn't make that mistake again. He could no longer hide the fact his entire family, not just Stacey, was everything to him, even when they infuriated him beyond belief. And now that he understood that

(*Thank you, Stacey*)

he could honestly make the amends that had fractured not only his family, but him as a person — and as a father. All he had to do now was take the necessary steps to prove that to them, if not to himself.

— 9 —

"You're far from being the first human abducted from Earth," Jaenice said. "In my time out here, I've probably run into a half a dozen humans. Some are scared out of their minds, praying to be returned home. And then there are those like me, who have embraced the idea of never going back because roaming the galaxy is far too invigorating."

"How long have you been gone?" Jacquline asked. The twig had been set aside but there was no way to extinguish it. Once it was lit, it would burn until the fuel had run its course, which by Jaenice's estimation was usually a few years, depending on how much someone actually smoked it. But given the state of her own buzz, if anyone smoked more often than what she had, they'd be in a constant state of lethargy.

"I don't even know anymore. Time isn't the same out here. It was hard to let go of the concept of hours, days and years, but once you understand that those things are only a construct we gave ourselves to understand our limited capacity of the universe, it liberates your mind. Seriously, I have never felt so free."

"Even after being trapped in this god forsaken hell hole?"

"I may physically be a prisoner, but mentally? Now that's where freedom reins."

Jacquline smiled.

"And you'd best be getting on board that train sooner rather than later because there's no telling when you'll ever get out of here."

"How were you abducted?"

It was Jaenice's turn to smile. "A rouge band of mercenaries came to Earth some time after the prophecy was released. I'm not exactly sure what they were looking for. I think maybe they heard Jaxxa Rakala was a female and they figured any female would do, like, maybe there was only one female on Earth. Ever."

"Where did they come from?"

"Hell if I know. I had just been bailed out of the pen for drag racing a few hours earlier."

"You drag race?"

"Only on weekends, and holidays... and anytime the sun goes down. I couldn't tell you if I could still do it. I haven't seen much of what would resemble a car out here. But there was this one time we stopped on this planet —"

"Wait," Jacquline interrupted. She rubbed her eyes, hoping it might help her mind focus enough to string the words she was thinking into an actual sentence. Apparently, the drug wasn't done affecting her. "Who's we?"

Jaenice's smile grew wider. "Oh, right. After the piss-ant aliens found out I wasn't

Jaxxa Rakala, they used me as trade for some weapons grade materials. From there, I was shopped around like a damn fruitcake, bouncing from one alien planet to the next."

"That sucks," Jacquline said, hoping it came off sincere.

"Tell me about it. But I did learn a lot about a lot of different things. This one group of filthy creatures had me doing all types of menial tasks, from engineering to janitorial shit. But it taught me about how things operated, and the more I learned, the more valuable I became. Before you know it, I was worth a small transport ship." Jaenice raised her eyebrows to match Jacquline's enthusiastic expression.

"That's so cool."

"Yeah, but after awhile, you get tired of being property."

"Right? My dad thinks he owns me sometimes. Kiss my ass, dad." The last sentence came out a lot louder than Jacquline realized, but she didn't care. She laughed as if it was the funniest thing in the world.

Jaenice couldn't keep from joining her. "Here here," she said, and then with a loud echoed yell, "Kiss my ass!"

The two laughed for some time — Jacquline uncontrollably, Jaenice with measured command. If she hadn't, Jacquline may well have dropped her pants to complete the image. Luckily, Jaenice kept her from going all the way.

"Finally," Jaenice continued as Jacquline found solace once again, "I figured I'd make a run for it. I knew enough to fix and fly pretty much any small vessel, so when the time was right, I snuck away from my captor and made a break for one of the ships. I didn't know they could be tracked, though, and as the little creep pursued me, I crashed on this volcanic planet where I met this alien known as Eyrixano."

Suddenly, no amount of drugs could keep Jacquline from paying attention. In fact, the name pretty much sobered her up with the snap of a finger. "Eyrixano?"

"You've heard of him?"

"The bastard tried to kill me," Jacquline said with bite. "And my sister."

"I can't believe that," Jaenice said.

"Then you're delusional."

"Far from it. The man saved my life."

"Now that I can't believe. Eyrixano is a monster."

"He's my savior," Jaenice said with vile fervor. "He protected me and gave me the freedom I deserved. I abhor anyone that says any different."

"Then how do you explain him strapping my sister to a wall and nearly choking her to death?"

"He did what?"

Jacquline nodded, her eyes bright with her own passionate animosity.

"Are we talking about the same Eyrixano?"

"Black cloak. Flames for a face?"

Jaenice sat back a little. "I don't understand. What did your sister do to him to make him want to do such a thing?"

"Nothing," Jacquline said. "He attacked us."

"Why?"

"Maybe because he thought my sister was Jaxxa Rakala."

"Your sister is Jaxxa Rakala?"

"Honestly, I don't know. But Eyrixano freakin' embedded a damn rock in her chest that made her…" Jacquline was hard pressed to find the right word, and the more she thought about it, the more Jaenice's claim actually started to make sense. "Better," she finally said. "I don't know. It's weird."

"A rock made her better? How?"

"She's more alive, I guess. She started talking again, she's way smarter than I am… and she has this spirit about her. It's hard to explain."

"And Eyrixano did that for her?"

Jacquline was so confused. She had spent so much time believing that what Eyrixano had done was a bad thing, but now…

"Don't you think that all Eyrixano was trying to do was help her become what she was meant to be and you took it the wrong way because of some pre-conceived notion about who he was and what he was after?"

"He wants to use her to take over the universe."

"Or perhaps he was liberating her from anyone else gaining control. Did it ever occur to you that your sister might have been controlling him the whole time?"

"That's impossible. She protected us from him."

"Did she?"

Jacquline looked at Jaenice as if she were crazy, though a part of her couldn't help but feel she might be right. But how could she be right? Tracey didn't want any of this, and even if she had, how could she have known what was going to happen? Then again, she was half alien. For all Jacquline knew, Tracey could have been planning everything from the time she decided to stow away on the ship, just so she could track down the gem and gain access to the power she so desperately wanted.

But that was insane. She couldn't believe that her little sister could have that much influence. Not Tracey; not her sweet, innocent sister. No.

No.

Are you sure? She was expelled for ripping the face off a young kid. Could that have been a deliberate act?

"It might have," Jacquline whispered to herself, unknowingly.

"I don't know your sister," Jaenice said, hoping Jacquline wouldn't bite her head off, "but if she is Jaxxa Rakala, there's a lot you'll never understand."

"I thought you said Jaxxa Rakala was bullshit."

"I did, and I do. At least until I have solid proof otherwise. That doesn't mean it's not true."

Jacquline curled her chin to the top of her knees.

"Look, I didn't mean to make you doubt what you saw or make you afraid of your little sister."

"I'm not afraid of her," Jacquline bellowed. *At least, I don't want to be.*

"I just want you to consider that perhaps Eyrixano isn't the monster you first made him out to be. I know him; I lived with him for a long time. We've hunted together, we've been partners. He doesn't want to rule the universe as much as he wants to help it succeed and grow and flourish."

"Yeah," Jacquline said, agreeing for the sake of argument. "Fine."

Jaenice smiled slightly, knowing she was only acquiescing to change the topic. "How about a peace offering?" she said.

"What kind of peace offering?"

Jaenice reached into her tunic and pulled out Jacquline's leather jacket. "It's yours, isn't it?" She tossed it to Jacquline, who looked at it as if she'd never seen it before.

"They brought it in with you. I was going to keep it, but if I'm going to earn your trust, I'd better be as honest with you as I can."

Jacquline pulled the jacket to her chest and turned around. It couldn't be clear, but there was a good chance her sudden change of mood wasn't because of the thoughts Jaenice had planted into her head. It was possible that the effects of the drug were finally wearing thin, causing her to hit a low that only one thing could help correct.

She took a hit from the twig with no regrets.

— 10 —

After the web shot back into place, Tracey took a seat at the opposite side of the cell from Sentilla. She set the journals down next to her and crossed her legs together, resting her hands in her lap. Her back was as straight as an arrow and her chin was raised just slightly higher than it normally would.

"How are you feeling?" she asked.

Sentilla rolled her head back against the wall. The piercing gaze of her eyes through the meshed canvas said everything Tracey needed to know. They weren't just blood-shot; they were dark and encrusted. Tracey relaxed a bit, allowing her shoulders to roll forward a little and her head to bounce lightly against them.

"Where are we going?" Sentilla said. Her throat was as dry as her eyes, but also soft — calm.

"Rega-One," Tracey said, just as relaxed.

Sentilla shifted her head to the side and chuckled softly, infecting Tracey with her own curious smile.

"What's so funny?"

"Oh, you'll find out soon enough," Sentilla said, followed by a soft moan. Tracey took a moment to read Sentilla's body language and then walked up to her. Sentilla tried her best to turn away, but the gem was still too strong. She just didn't have the wherewithal to do much else but allow Tracey to remove the crust and gunk that had been built up around her eye sockets. Though it was hard to admit, the sensation of having the pressure removed from her eyes was more than relaxing — it was exactly what she needed.

Tracey returned to her spot next to the journals. "Should we not be setting foot on Rega-One?"

Sentilla smiled brightly. "Not if the Regans have anything to say about it."

"Why's that?"

"The minute we're detected in orbit, they'll know that a Xyla-Alpha-Nine is on board. It's only a matter of time before we're all killed just for having her."

"How will they know she's on board if she's powered down? Does she have some kind of tracking device?"

"You could say that."

"Can we disable it?"

"Not unless we burn the body. Whether or not Kahli is powered up, her skin produces a unique emissions signature that the Betas were programmed to track. Trust me. They will know she's here. And even if they didn't, the Regans aren't ones to passively allow newcomers to roam their planet."

"Why? What secrets are they hiding?"

"I have no idea, and I've never had the desire to find out."

"Why's that?"

"It's none of my business. Why should I go poking around for something that doesn't concern me?"

"And what if it did? Wouldn't you want the chance to stop it before it happened?"

"Stop what? Rega-One is full of narcissistic fools who almost destroyed themselves with their own arrogance. They thought they could live forever by creating androids that had similar brain chemistries, only to find out that when push came to shove, the androids were smarter than they were. And with an unlimited amount of brain capacity and a set of emotions, they were indestructible. It was only a matter of time before they figured out they could control the world, so the Regans destroyed them all, only to replace them with drones that would willingly follow the Regans. At least that's the bedtime story my mother used to tell me."

"Your mother told you that as a bedtime story?"

"It was meant to be a morality tale to remind me to respect one another, how emotions are necessary if we wish to live happily, and that trying to control others can only lead to evil."

"Interesting tale."

"Suffice it to say, I don't think I've come across a Regan since I was a child. Ever since they used their Betas to wipe out the Alpha-Nines, they've lived in seclusion. The bastards are highly territorial and don't want anything or anyone attempting a takeover of the way they do things on their blissful little planet. If it was up to me, Kahli would never have been allowed aboard this ship."

"I know the feeling," Tracey said with a bit of a smirk that may not have registered correctly in her voice.

"I keep thinking I may have been able to talk him out of it had I not been on a separate expedition when he first met her."

"What was it about Kahli that had you so angry at her without even knowing her?"

"Weren't you listening? She was an Alpha-Nine android. Any respectable being at the time knew the Regans were hunting them down. She was a huge asset who, if not dealt with, could have gotten us all killed. Qah-Shekel believed she deserved to live and was adamant that I not destroy her the moment I first laid eyes on her. I had to trust he knew what he was doing. As my mother always said, 'Respect other's opinions and you'll have a friend for the ages.'"

"Spoken like someone who's hiding from the truth."

Sentilla didn't say anything, though she wanted to. Yelling would only force the gem to continue to push her anger over the edge until she lost all control. She couldn't let that happen. Waiting for Tracey to return had at least taught her that.

"I'm sure Qah-Shekel has already taken all of that into consideration and will figure out how to be as cautious as possible."

"I hope you're right." Sentilla coughed, a rough and phlegmy hack that felt like it ripped part of her throat.

"How about I talk for a little while so you can rest," Tracey said. She picked up one of the journals and opened it to the first page. "Father doesn't understand," she read with a deliberately sweet tone. "My new friend, whom I've dubbed Jaxxa Rakala, is the sweetest thing in the whole world."

"Wait," Sentilla interrupted. "Are you reading something?"

"My mother's journal."

"Keladrayia's journal?"

"We found them on Trynoruus. I thought you might like to hear some of them."

"Why would you think that?"

"No matter what your mother may have told you, sometimes it's better to know someone's secret before it hurts the ones you love. And besides, I have to be in here anyway to wean you off the gem. This will give us a chance to find out who my mother was and give us something to do together."

It took a while for Sentilla to say anything, but when she did, it was a simple, "All right." Although Sentilla didn't seem at all happy about it, Tracey felt good about her progression. She smiled and turned her eyes down to the book to once again recite her mother's story.

— 11 —

Father doesn't understand.

Jaxxa Rakala is the sweetest thing in the whole world. She is kind to me, helps me when I am in trouble, and gives me comfort when I am sad. Father says that a pet will do the same, but she is not a pet; she is a Trysian. I don't care that she arrived here like no other before, but he does, probably because her arrival represents a loss of control. It is clear to me that he does not fear her as a child; he fears her as a threat to the way things have been, are and should forever be. But I don't see her in that way. Jaxxa Rakala, the daughter of the gems, is my love, and I am hers.

Our stately ball is occurring under the light of the new moon two days hence, and I have asked my sweet Jaxxa Rakala to accompany me, though it is uncertain whether father will allow her to attend. He has forbidden her to leave her domicile for any purpose except to share a meal, and even then the palace curtains are drawn to keep the light from shining upon her. But she is not a prisoner. She doesn't seem to mind, showing a kindly amount of respect and honor for the wishes of my father, for which the servants hold for her in return. In their hearts, they revere her as they do our gracious, loving Father of the higher realm. It's as if she is His daughter; her mere presence elicits deference to her protection. They must always be mindful of her, give her all that she wishes, and never confront her or even look her in the eye, lest they be shot down in the middle of life and sent to the far reaches of devastation.

All I see is a child. A friend.

So I will present her to my people as my guest, as my partner. She will dance with me. She will enjoy the fruits we have to offer the people of our land and the labor of our love. We will treat her as an equal. Not atop a pedestal, not below our stature.

She shall be an equal measured for her beauty and grace as much as her background and her life.

Father will understand.

* * *

I am so furious. I have never been this angry before in all of my days on this land. Father has refused to allow Jaxxa Rakala to accompany me to the dance. He refuses; he will not even listen to my words. He just infuriates me so. What shall I do now? Shall I run away and bring Jaxxa Rakala with me, to live our life by our own rules? Shall I disobey his word and have her escort me anyway, to prove to him that she is not unlike any other, that she is a Trysian and should be respected as such. I don't know. I have already promised Jaxxa Rakala the chance to leave her domicile, so to obey father would force me to go back on my word, which would, in essence, make me no better than he. If I do not obey, I will be seen as callous and disrespectful to the Father, and may be buried to the depths of devastation for my insubordination and my candor. But then, perhaps our servant is correct — by helping Jaxxa Rakala, I will be seen as glorious among the eyes of our beloved creator and be given father's crown in His honor. Is it worth the risk? Is she worth the risk?

I believe she is.

* * *

What do I do? Where do I go? Father has embarrassed me and turned my people against me. Have I entered devastation? Jaxxa Rakala has been locked away in the dungeons. She is now a prisoner. Her insubordination — my insubordination — has led her to this, and I am no better than she. So why have I remained in the highest regard only to watch her die among thieves?

She didn't want to go to the ball; she felt it best that she give my father time. But I wouldn't listen. I forced her into one of my gowns, beautiful and elegant. She looked so flattering in the light of the moon — that of the flower blossoming like no other before her. Her grace and posture was regal in all of its creation. If I hadn't witnessed her arrival myself, I would have believed she had been a queen of a generation gone by. My people are gracious and kind, or at least, so they appear. They did not detest her; they did not shun her in any way. They honored Jaxxa Rakala with the kindest of words and the purest of hearts, curious to know of her origins. That is until my father commanded them otherwise.

When he saw her in my arms, spinning among our gracious onlookers in a dance of the lovely sprite, his blood boiled with rage. He ripped her from me and brought her to his throne to degrade her before his people. I begged him to stop but he turned his words against me and devoured my reputation in one word:

Disgraceful.

I was in tears when he declared her to be a criminal; that she would pay for her crimes. Everyone agreed that she should be convicted, even though she had done nothing wrong except exist among us. Where did she come from? What was her name? Who was she? What was her crime? All valid questions left ignored and unmasked. They did not have the wherewithal to demand he reconsider, to go against his wishes. And so, he condemned her to a life of chains and wallow, to see the light of our beloved Father only when meals are presented and to be given no comfort beyond what she makes for herself. And then to me — I would not be allowed to ever see her again, forcing my punishment upon me with a stern hand and voice of disappointment.

I cannot let it be; she is too precious to me. I will not see her rot without the hand of a friend, even if it means that I must, too, wallow until I am no more than a skeletal mass on the edge of forever.

* * *

I feel good on this day of rest. I thought my secret excursions to visit Jaxxa Rakala while my father is away might have met their end when our servant caught me slipping into the dungeon. Praise to the Father of the higher realm, he smiled and gave me his blessing to continue, promising to keep his lips sealed. He allowed me to bring her food and juice, and I was able to remain longer than I ever have; talk until the day had gone and I had to perform my diligence in the absence of father.

But that is not the only reason today was special. Along with my company, I presented Jaxxa Rakala with a gift. It was a small green jewel from which my mother had once worn; from which she handed down to me on the day of her death and asked me to keep safe until such time that I, too, could pass it along to a deserving love. The jewel, she said, was a rare stone, one that held the mightiest of powers. In the right hands, it would wield the best of luck. In the wrong hands, it could ease destruction among us. She made it clear that I was only to give the jewel to someone I felt was worthy of forgiveness, honor and grace, as she considered me to hold all of those qualities and would be able to see them in others. I had never met anyone I felt held all of those qualities until the day I met Jaxxa Rakala in her bed of gems. It was a sign that the most powerful breed would one day be entrusted to her.

And so I graced it upon her.

The kindness and warmth she displayed was enough to make the coldest heart melt. There must be a way I can convince father to let her go, to reconsider his punishment without revealing my transgression. If I cannot, I still must get her out of there. I asked once for her to run away, to find a home that could give her what she needed. But she only reminded me that she had everything she ever would need in me and refused to escape. That alone should be reason enough to set her free.

*   *   *

This has been the happiest day of my young life. Father returned home today and before I could say a word to him of Jaxxa Rakala, he ordered our servant to fetch her for him. He lowered her to her knees and asked of her intentions. From the honesty of her answers, father gave her pardon and allowed her to stay with the freedom of a daughter.

I am not sure what changed his mind, or how he came to terms with her, but I do not care. He has given me the greatest gift of all and now she and I may be the best of friends for the rest of time. Praise to the Father of the higher realm, for he is good to us in all that he has given in his name.

— 12 —

Ken wasn't sure how long he'd been asleep, or if he had even slept at all. He thought he may have dozed off, but his thoughts were so random, there wasn't any way of knowing if any of them had been turned into fully realized dreams or if they were just snapshots of his mind's eye as he tried to imagine what might be in those journals. Of course, doing so only led to memories of him and Stacey, or of the fanciful bedtime stories she told Tracey, which now seemed as if they may not have been as fictionalized as he originally thought. There was a good chance that all of the fairy tales Ken had tried to get Stacey to publish, like the one about the woman who fought the tiger to win the packs respect, or the one about the king forcing his daughters to write a hymn that extolled the virtues of their character to decide who should win the hand of a neighboring kingdom, were events that actually happened, if not simple morality tales her father once told her. For all he knew, every page of those journals could be full of such tales, having nothing to do with Stacey herself. Perhaps they were full of notes on political issues, helping her understand how to rule a country —

or a planet

— and the structure of her father's laws. But no matter how much he wanted to find out, he fought the temptation to turn on his communication bud. It wasn't just about betraying Stacey by reading her diary; he didn't want to hear Stacey's words through Tracey's voice. Stacey's past should be delivered through Stacey's own luscious soliloquy, and he would wait for as long as was necessary for that to happen.

Despite whether he had gotten any sleep, Ken was no longer tired, and lying on his bed only made his curiosity and desire to learn Stacey's past that much stronger. He had to do something to keep his mind occupied. So he left his room and headed straight for medical.

Lying on the table in the haze of purple was a lifeless mannequin with her back removed. *In my wildest dreams*, he sang in his head as he chuckled, imagining Stacey suddenly bringing Kahli to life as a real human only he could see.

Wouldn't that be something?

He had to rub his eyes after believing he actually did see Kahli move her arm, answering the question of whether he had gotten any sleep. After checking to see if anyone else was there (as if they might have been able to corroborate his delusion), Ken walked up to Kahli to get a better look inside. Placing his hand inside to feel the smooth, glassy texture of the components was almost like ripping open his old Apple II computer to see how it operated. Man, did his parents have a fit when they found him sprawled on the floor with the guts of his expensive birthday present surrounding him. He was grounded for two weeks and had to pay for half the cost to get it fixed, but it was worth it, giving him his first insight into what engineering and robotics was all about. From then on, there was no stopping him, even if there were a few sidetracks thrown in for responsibilities sake. Having to take care of a wife and daughter so early in life wasn't how he had pictured his life as a kid, but it was no less special. For a long time, making sure they were happy and taken care of was all that mattered, even if it meant taking a desk job to put food on the table. Staring at Kahli's components now, with all of the knowledge he had accumulated over the years, Ken wondered if he would have been able to design such a masterpiece. After all, without hardly any cash flow, he was able to build an entire shuttle that remained in one piece even past the point of light speed; and what he considered his greatest accomplishment would never be known to anyone that mattered. Or at least, anyone that mattered in his head, since the only ones who should ever really matter were with him already — or in the very least, should be.

"You'll be okay," he said. And with nothing much else to do, he left medical.

Traveling the ship gave him enough time to clear his reddening eyes before reaching command, where he assumed Lark would be since Tracey was reading Sentilla her bedtime stories in the brig. He had to tell her how much she meant to him. Even if it might not be exactly how she felt of him, she was, and would forever be, part of his family. She probably knew it already, but saying it out loud would mean so much more — to both of them. For all she had done for him over the last four years, it was only right he finally acknowledge his appreciation the way she deserved.

Lark was indeed in command — as was DovenJadden. Not the reunion he was hoping for. But what he had to say couldn't wait, and though he wanted to talk to Lark alone, he knew the private matter would remain private, regardless of Doven-Jadden's presence.

"Lark, we need to talk," he said, kneeling down next to her so that she blocked his view of DovenJadden. It was just easier for him if he could at least hide the fact that she was staring at them.

"Not now," Lark said. "According to this, we're closing in on Rega-One."

"Already?" Ken smiled slightly. He hadn't realized he'd be able to get this ship turned around and back to Trynoruus so quickly.

"Yep. I'm betting you don't want me to crash right into it."

"Huh, yeah. That wouldn't be good."

Lark turned to him, the soft smile Ken had grown to love gracing her lips. "Can it wait until after we get what we need to fix Rega?"

Ken returned her smile. "Yeah." *What's another few hours?*

DovenJadden broke the moment when she bounded toward them, crying in a rapid purr. Ken stepped back as she scorned Lark for failing to notice a flashing light on the holopad.

"Oh shit," Lark whispered and spun her forefinger in a circle twice, followed by a double tap on the holopad. She then slid the middle finger of both hands upward from the palm out. The white view screen instantly became a blanket of stars with a giant gas bubble looming over them like a feral beast. She quickly slid her palms across the holopads, shifting the *Equinox* to the side, then tapped a few keys to ignite the engines in a concession of short bursts that kept them from getting caught in the planet's gravitational pull.

"Sorry," Ken said, a bit sheepish.

Lark huffed a short laugh, keeping her attention on the flight path of the *Equinox*. As they swung around the parameter of the gaseous planet, they got their first glimpse of at least three moons. The first looked heavily petrified; another looked to be more gaseous — a smaller version of its parent body. The third, well, that was a sight to see.

"Would you look at that," Lark said, admiring the clouds that hovered above the mix of water and land.

"It looks exactly like Earth," Ken marveled.

They were so awestruck, they didn't even notice DovenJadden purring in their ears. By the time they realized she had said anything, Qah-Shekel had entered command, muttering something Ken didn't understand.

Lark answered him and then turned to Ken.

"Ready to do some sight seeing?"

Ken matched her smile. He was one step closer to getting Jacquline back and was more than ready to do anything to speed up that process.

"One small step," he said, squeezing Lark's shoulder.

— 13 —

"We've arrived," Sentilla said.

With the sudden rock in the ship's movement, something more must have happened, and Tracey thought it interesting that Sentilla chose not to acknowledge it. "A little less smooth than I would of thought."

"What do you expect from rookie pilots?"

"You don't seem phased."

Sentilla couldn't help but chuff a little. "It happened to me a couple of times when I first took the reigns, but I've been trained since birth to remain calm in situations like that."

"You've been trained since birth?"

Tracey's curiosity was evident in her silence, if not by the way she sat with her eyes glued to Sentilla like a kid waiting to hear how the prince would save the princess from the fat, smelly ogre. Sentilla had no reason not to regale her with her story.

"I'm not sure if you know this, but I was born on this ship. I was part of this crew even before Qah-Shekel."

"Wow," Tracey said with honest fascination. "So you probably know this ship better than anyone."

"I used to," Sentilla said after a soft chuckle, "before Kahli and DovenJadden showed up. Now it's like I hardly know the ship at all."

"Did they make alterations?"

"No, they just know more about the guts of the ship than I do. You know, a lot of her secrets. But, if you want to know what mood she's in, there's no one better than me."

"The ship has moods?"

"Oh yeah. She can be quite temperamental, a real bitch sometimes. But I know how to listen to her needs and comfort her."

"How?"

"My mom taught me to feel the subtle nuances in her movement, to hear the subtleness in her speech patterns, to know when she's sick and how to use her to the best of her advantage. In a way, the *Equinox* is an extension of myself, so whenever something happens to her, I can feel it in the way she moves, the way she talks, the way she breathes. Like right now. I know she's in pain."

"How can you tell?"

"The lightning unit is being tasked too hard because so many manual overrides have been put in place. She's beginning to stutter and there's a faint whimper in her hum, which means we may need to repair her secondary units soon. But that's arbitrary, really. With the slight vibration in the floors, she's frightened, too. Lark isn't doing anything for her disposition."

"You talk about her as if she were a child."

"She is my child. My baby."

"Your love above all else."

Sentilla turned her head downward slightly. Don't think Tracey didn't take notice.

"Not above all else," she said. "Qah-Shekel ranks higher, doesn't he?"

Sentilla licked her lips.

"Why is that?"

It was clear Sentilla didn't want to discuss it, but the continued silence pushed her into finally saying through a closed throat, "We saved each other's lives."

"How so?"

Sentilla took a deep breath. She might as well just let it all out. "He was the first to pay attention to me beyond my parents. But at the same time, he had just lost his. I was his rock, in a way."

"You gave each other the strength you needed to move forward."

"I guess you can say that." Sentilla sat quiet for a moment. Tracey remained just as quiet, unwilling to break Sentilla's fond memory. "He was pretty destructive at the time, always looking to do anything dangerous, sometimes even doing things that would have otherwise gotten anyone else killed."

"Like what?"

"Like running into the engine room during a space jump, or surfing the hatch of a vessel during liftoff. He was fearless, come to think of it."

"How'd you ever get him to stop?"

"One day we were on a routine bartering run and the ship was attacked by a team of silkwood pirates. At the time, he and I were together" (Tracey assumed she meant as a couple and didn't press the matter) "and we heard several explosions hit the ship. When he went to check on what was happening, like the curious little bug I was, I chased after him. I caught up with him just in time to watch them kill —"

Sentilla was nearly in tears. Tracey took a deep breath, wanting to hug her — to comfort her — but she knew Sentilla wasn't ready for her to get that close. The room was silent for some time as Sentilla composed herself. When she had, she continued without any need for a prompt.

"Qah-Shekel protected me by hiding with me until the initial fight was over. I didn't know if I'd ever be able to stop crying, but he relaxed me enough by simply letting me. I'm not sure how long we were hidden, but eventually, Qah-Shekel made up his mind to do something about what happened. There was a fire in him that couldn't be denied. For a long time, I was afraid something might have happened to him, but then he came back, covered in blood. It was hard for me to accept his hand, scared of what might happen. He insisted everything would be okay. He walked me to command and told me to fly anywhere I wanted. Whether that was a specific spot or a continuous circle, it didn't matter. He just wanted me to fly."

"Is that what you did?"

"I don't even remember, not that it matters. He only did it to distract me so he could clean up the ship and take the bodies to the compression chamber for ejection. From that day on, he never once tried anything dangerous again unless it meant protecting me or members of his crew."

"What happened with your mother?"

"I don't know. Her body was never recovered. But we traveled to one of her favorite spots on Luna Grasty and set up a memorial there for her."

"It sounds beautiful."

"It was."

Tracey nodded. After a bit of silent reminiscing, she said, "Back to reading, then?"

"I think I'd like that."

"Good." Tracey opened the book. "Mother had always been the doting type. She never turned away a peasant, never sought to degrade another for their insolence or seek retribution for a crime. That was father's job. She supported him in any decision he made because she was his wife, but her heart —"

Tracey stopped short and looked down to the floor.

"What is it? Why did you stop?"

"The crew is meeting in tactical. I should be there. I'm sorry." Tracey set the journal on top of the others and hurried from the cell.

Sentilla still felt Tracey's presence, and the need for her remained strong. But compared to earlier, it seemed as if she had grown more accepting — not to mention quite fond of the little girl.

— 14 —

The plan was sound. Upon landing, the crew would meet an escort who would take them on a tour of the Capitol city (one of the only ones left standing after what had been dubbed "the android wars"). Once they reached the manufacturing plant at the far side of the city, Lark and Ken would draw the guards away, allowing Qah-Shekel to drop inside and steal the power core. Meanwhile, Ken and Lark would get back to the ship and have it ready for takeoff by the time Qah-Shekel arrived. If it all went smoothly, they would be in and out without hardly any reason for the Regans to know they were there. But like any well-intentioned plan, there was always going to be a flaw, and that flaw was revealed through Tracey's lips.

"It won't work," she said as they finished explaining the details to her.

"Why not? What's wrong with it?" Ken looked a bit agitated. After all, it was mostly his brilliant plan she was tearing down.

"Two reasons. The first is Rega's tracking signature."

"What tracking signature?"

"All android units were designed with a unique radiation signature," Qah-Shekel said. "The ship has been masking that signature ever since she became a part of this crew."

"Are you sure?" Tracey asked. "Sentilla tends to think the androids will know she's here when we're detected in orbit."

"Why would she think that?"

"I'm not sure, but she seemed very confident in that fact."

Qah-Shekel took a moment to speak with DovenJadden. He nodded.

"I concur," Tracey said.

"What did she say?" Lark asked.

"It's possible that the androids have learned to detect the mask that would hide an Alpha-Nine. Just by having it in place could signify we're hiding one."

"And if they do," Lark said, "we're in deep shit."

Tracey nodded.

"So what do we do about that?" Ken said.

"What if we put her in the rejuvenation chamber?" Lark said. "Would that be enough to cover the smell?"

Qah-Shekel looked at Lark oddly, then realized what she meant. "Yes, I do believe that is a very perceptive observation."

"Great, so we have no other issues," Ken said.

"Except for the fact that the minute you cause your... *distraction*, the Regans, not to mention their full force of loyal Beta units, will be crawling all over this ship."

Ken wanted to kick something, but chose to wipe his mouth instead.

"We must arrive in stealth," Tracey said.

"How are we supposed to do that?" Ken bellowed. "Throw an invisibility cloak over the whole damn ship?"

"That's not a bad idea," Lark said, her brain spinning a mile a minute as she looked over the hologram of the moon. "Check this out. If we break the atmosphere on the opposite side of the planet, we can coast along the rim as close to the ground as possible until we reach this desert oasis, here." Lark mapped her plan out along the hologram with her finger. "If we can find a way to match the temperature of the desert, and keep only essential units on, it would make it appear as if we were cloaked."

"Is that even possible?" Ken said.

Qah-Shekel was already discussing the possibilities with DovenJadden, who left the room shortly after without even a modicum of objection — in fact, she looked almost gleeful as she skipped away.

"DovenJadden will match the ship's radiation signature with that of the desert."

"Perfect." Ken looked back to Tracey. "Any more holes you want to poke in my plan?"

"Only one," Tracey said with just as much ire. "Now that we're going in secretly, there will be a ton of androids itching to kill you for even thinking about wandering around that planet without an escort."

Ken curled his lips around, tightening them to keep from exploding. He knew she was right. As Qah-Shekel had explained it, the Regans did not like foreign bodies walking around their planet alone for fear they might uncover some top-secret something-or-other. It was supposed to be so simple.

"We've checked the schematics," Lark said to calm Ken's temper. "The amount of androids is minimal. We can avoid them."

"I don't know," Tracey said. "If the androids are capable of deciphering between different radiation signatures, who's to say they won't be able to detect us the same way.

The possibility that we share the same signature as the Regans is slim to none. The way I see it, there is no way any of you are getting anywhere near that manufacturing facility."

"Is there any way we can mask our signatures?"

Qah-Shekel thought a moment. "None that I am aware."

Ken shook his head. "Then what are we supposed to do?"

"I'll do it," Tracey said softly.

"No," Ken barked. "I'm not about to let you wander around that planet alone."

"That's not what I'm suggesting. There may be a way for me to track the radiation signature of the Regans and focus that aura onto you."

"Are you sure?" Lark asked. "That sounds like it would be extremely taxing."

"It will be, but I think I can hold the mask up long enough for you guys to reach the manufacturing plant."

"Then what?"

"Then you're on your own. I mean, what better distraction could there be than to suddenly be recognized as impostors."

Ken had to smile. "Then it's set."

"Wait," Lark said, causing Ken to fall back to his well of annoyed frustration. "What about Qah-Shekel? He's going to stick out like a sore thumb, regardless of whether his signature is masked."

"I will be shrouded by my cloak," Qah-Shekel said.

"Yeah, like that won't look suspicious," Ken said.

"Without an escort, your original plan is shot anyway," Tracey said. She reached up and expanded the view of the hologram to focus on the city "I suggest you two head for the center of the city, here at the main plaza. Remain there until the sirens go off."

"And then?"

"Run like hell."

"Where will Qah-Shekel be?"

"He'll use your original escape route to make his way to the manufacturing plant."

Ken took a deep breath. It wasn't his, but the plan was sound. "So the only thing we need to figure out, then, is our new escape route."

"Let's get to it." Lark enlarged the hologram to get a more precise view of every nook and cranny of the city. As she studied it, looking for every possible issue — such as dead-ends, condensed concentrations of androids, and openness of space — Ken peered over at Tracey, who tried to remain optimistic. But Ken knew her better than she thought and could see right into the heart of his frightened little girl.

"What's wrong?"

"I'll be fine," she said.

"Are you sure?"

"Not really, but it's the only way to save both Rega and Jacquline. I'll find a way." Her smile infected Ken with warmth.

"Come here," he said and collected her in his arms. "I guess you could say, if we weren't all scared about what might happen, it wouldn't be what we're supposed to do, now would it?"

"Okay, now you're just speaking gibberish," Lark said and gave Ken a sly grin.

"You just do your job and I know we'll get out of this unscathed."

Tracey accepted his confidence, even if she remained skeptical. "I better get back to Sentilla," she said. As soon as she was out of the room, she grabbed a hold of the gem and closed her eyes, praying that her body would be able to take the punishment she was about to inflict upon herself.

— 15 —

The cell was as cold and icy as the tension between Jacquline and Jaenice, but thanks to Jaenice, Jacquline could hardly feel the frigidity of either one. Having put her jacket back on, only the tips of her nose and ears were affected by the climate, and the twig had done the rest, keeping her in a sweet lull of contemplation as some awfully crazy thoughts — mostly about her family — ransacked her mind, the most prominent one being, *was her family even looking for her?* Tracey might be, but in her experience, Jacquline was a forgettable figure in the scheme of her father's life. If he was still pining over Stacey the way he had been over the past few years, there was a very slim chance that he would take the time to come looking for her. Over time, she would become but a mere memory, much as a friend turns into a mere acquaintance, or a loved one eventually fades away after death. But how could that be possible? Ken may treat her like an old dog, but even then, when the dog goes missing, you're bound to at least pin up posters around town. Ken may have been ready to leave her behind on Earth, but that was when he knew she could take care of herself. Without knowing what happened to her, he had to feel the need to find her, didn't he? It gave her at least some hope. Then again, she could easily be anywhere in the universe right now. The odds of her still being on Trynoruus were high, but even if she was, the quest to find her might take hundreds of years. Ken would die in his defeat; Lark would be long gone from exasperation and exhaustion; and Tracey might lose all hope. Though she wouldn't stop looking, it would no longer be a priority.

As Jacquline continued to cycle through all of the likely scenarios, it became clear that she was on her own. If she wanted to live any sort of life, she was going to have to break herself out, and with no noticeable doors or windows, that was going to be much harder than she initially thought. She figured there had to be some kind of lever or holographic mechanism that activated some door hidden behind its own wall of holograms (man, she felt so geeky right now), but for her to know for sure, she would have to wait until someone actually came in to feed her, or drag her off for some experiments... or with any luck, take her for some exercise and fresh air, none of which were likely as of right now, though Jaenice remained healthy enough.

"Do they ever feed us in this rat hole?" Jacquline spit out finally, turning her head just enough to catch Jaenice's frame in her peripheral view.

"Sometimes. It's not routine."

"How does it work?"

"Not sure I get what you're asking."

"How do they get it in here?"

"Beats me. I'm never awake when they deliver it."

"They put you to sleep?" Jacquline had rotated her upper body so she could see Jaenice without obstruction.

"Possibly. I've never really thought about it."

"Bastards."

Jaenice smiled, holding back a laugh. Jacquline turned slightly around, finding a more comfortable position.

"So how do you think they get it in here?"

"You mean, how can we find a way out?"

Jacquline smirked and glanced up at Jaenice as if she had guessed a secret Jacquline had been hiding for a century.

"Trust me, baby Kel, I have thought about this for as long as you've been alive. There is no way out... except..." Jaenice pointed upward, keeping her hand tucked in close to her body as if someone was watching and would punish her if they knew she knew their dastardly secret. "Maybe up."

Jacquline sighed. "Damn it."

"Yeah." Jaenice ran her fingers through her hair. "If there was any other way out, don't you think I would have found it already?"

Jacquline rubbed her eyes. Fatigue was setting in and no hit off of the twig was going to fix it. She sat back against the wall and rubbed her forehead. For a moment, she thought about bellowing out a scream, maybe even call for someone to give her answers, but doing so would be a waste of time. If Jaenice hadn't already done the same, her captor more than likely wouldn't have any idea what she was saying.

"Get used to it, kid."

Jacquline looked at Jaenice, exasperated. At least she wasn't completely alone. "You never did tell me how you wound up here."

Jaenice looked to Jacquline and smiled. "I'm not so sure you want to hear it."

"Tell me," Jacquline said quickly, "even if it involves Eyrixano."

"Okay." Jaenice sat up and held out her hand. Jacquline reached out and Jaenice playfully slapped her hand away. "The twig, baby Kel."

Jacquline expressed her stupidity and handed her the twig. Jaenice took a long hit and sat back, letting her legs stretch out. They nearly touched Jacquline's thigh (and would on occasion as she relayed her story). After releasing a seemingly never-ending trail of smoke that rose to the roof and dissipated like mist, Jaenice said,

"Eyrixano and I had spent a lot of time looking for the gem, tracking it across several galaxies, even coming within feet of it in the swamps of Lorai. I was so close; I could feel it pulling me toward it. But a swarm of hivers jumped us before we were able to secure it. I got stung as we fought them off and needed to get to a nearby planet for medical attention. When I woke up, Eyrixano was gone. I assumed he went back to the hivers, thinking that maybe the gem had killed them all off by pitting them against each other, or in the very least, urged one of them to run away with it. I waited for three days, which on Yolmeni, was probably twice as long as a day on Earth.

"During that time, I started hearing rumors that a lot of hunters were heading to Trynoruus to find evidence as to Keladrayia's whereabouts and the possibility of finding out what she actually looked like. The problem was everyone trying to hunt down the Trystet's palace had died due to the chemical storms that had laced the land uninhabitable. But if the rumors were true…"

Jaenice took another hit from the twig. "For all I knew, Eyrixano went down into the hive maze on Lorai and was gone, and I wasn't about to wait around forever just so someone else could get a jump start on tracking her down. I hijacked a short-range vessel and tweaked its power cores to get to Trynoruus. If I had known how bad the planet really was, I probably wouldn't have risked it. The second I hit the atmosphere my ship was lit up, like, crazy electrocuted. I must have crashed because the next thing I knew, I was here."

"Do you think Eyrixano looked for you?"

"Until you said you knew him, I thought he was dead. He probably thought the same of me."

Jacquline tucked her chin into her arms. "You weren't completely wrong," she said. "There is a statue of Stacey… I mean, Keladrayia, in the Trystet's castle."

Jaenice curled the tips of her lips upwards. "Stacey?"

It made Jacquline giggle. "That's what she called herself on Earth. I guess she figured Keladrayia might raise some red flags."

"So you really did know her, then?"

"She married my dad. My step-mother really was an alien."

Jaenice smiled, shaking the twig in Jacquline's direction, acknowledging the reference. "That must have been a little awkward."

"It might have been, if I knew she was one at the time. She had us all fooled for years. Hell, I didn't consider the idea even after she was taken."

"Do you know who took her?"

"I have no clue. To be honest, I didn't even believe she had been abducted. It wasn't until I found out that Tracey was this damn Jaxxa Rakala that it finally sunk in. I thought she just ran away like my mom."

"Your mom ran away?"

Jacquline lowered her eyes and sunk them into her arms.

Jaenice looked her over carefully. "There's something that doesn't make sense," she said, obviously changing the subject. "If your sister was alive when Keladrayia was abducted, why wasn't she taken, too. I mean, it wouldn't matter much to have Keladrayia if the child of legend had already been born."

"Your guess is as good as mine," Jacquline said.

"Maybe they did."

Jacquline looked up, utterly confused. "But she wasn't. She was there that morning."

"That's not what I meant. Maybe they tried to take her but she got away somehow."

It took Jacquline a second to register what Jaenice was getting at, but then, "She did act strange that morning. It was like a switch turned off her spirit. I thought it was just the beginning of her gradual degradation, but now that you bring it up, she was always like that."

"They took something from her."

"The gem."

Jaenice nodded. "There was no way she was going to stay away from that gem for long. She was going to find a way to get back to it, whatever it took."

"No," Jacquline said. "I can't believe that. Tracey... she was too demure."

"Biding her time."

"It doesn't make any sense. My dad built the spaceship to find Stacey. It was his idea to go search for them."

"Was it? Even without the gem, Jaxxa Rakala would have had access to some power, whether she was conscious of it or not."

"You're trying to tell me that Tracey was manipulating my dad into building the ship?" Jacquline was not amused.

"All I'm saying is you have to consider it a possibility."

"No. I can't."

"That gem was meant to be with Jaxxa Rakala. No matter where it was in the universe, she was going to track it down."

Jacquline huffed her disapproval. "It doesn't make sense, then. If they knew Tracey was alive, why didn't they come back for her?"

"Maybe they didn't realize who she was. There's a chance that whomever abducted Keladrayia tried and failed to birth Jaxxa Rakala and thought they once again must have had the wrong person."

"But Stacey had the gem," Jacquline said.

"I guess we'll never know for sure. But if we ever do get out of here, just remember to keep your eye on that sister of yours. If she is one with the gem, there's no telling what she'll do."

"She's not evil."

"So you said."

Jacquline shook her head, completely flabbergasted. "She's done nothing to harm anyone."

She tore some kid's face off!

"She left you here, yes?"

"There could be a million reasons why she left."

"The point is she left you."

Jacquline's eyes said everything Jaenice needed to know.

"Jaxxa Rakala is a manipulative, evil soul. Everything she has done, and will do, is predetermined and for a purpose. She left you because she needs you out of the way. And if I'm right, your dad is still under her control."

"Shut up," Jacquline screamed. "Just, shut up. It's not true."

Jaenice lay back against the wall and sucked on the twig. She stared at Jacquline, who shook slightly as she wiped away fresh tears. The longer she sat in silence, the more Jaenice's theories infected her thoughts, adding to the fuel that had already been burning.

"I don't mean to upset you," Jaenice said in a sweet, passive voice. "You may be right. Jaxxa Rakala may love you so much, there's no possible way she would ever harm you. I just want to make sure you're able to see past all of the bias and the bullshit and look at all of this with clear eyes."

As Jacquline looked up to Jaenice, wondering if what she was saying could be true, she grew extremely lightheaded. She watched Jaenice cover her own eyes and drop the twig to the floor, and then bent her head back against the wall, hoping to ease the dizzy spell that was coming on. It wasn't clear what was happening, but for a split second, she thought perhaps it was time to eat. She had to stay diligent, had to remain alert so she might see how the Trysians entered the cell. After rubbing her eyes graciously, she opened them to find the food had already been delivered.

She looked around, yelling for anyone to come back. It was futile. She crawled to the corner, as far away from the plate of shrimp, potatoes and gravy as she could get, wanting to have nothing to do with it. But the food smelled so delicious, her stomach ached for it. In no time flat, Jacquline swallowed it down like a duck. As she enjoyed the ecstasy of her meal — which actually tasted better than she had remembered on Earth — she looked to Jaenice and called for her to wake up. When she didn't move, Jacquline shifted closer, only to realize that something was different.

The body in front of her wasn't Jaenice.

She could tell it was a woman from the wet hair sprawled out across the floor and the breasts that played peek-a-boo with her outer garment. At first she thought maybe Lark had been captured as well, that her family may be closer to finding her than she thought. But that wasn't it. The body was fatter than Lark would ever be in her life.

No, this was someone — *or something* — else.

Cautiously, Jacquline moved the hair away from the woman's face. The woman shifted slightly at her touch. Jacquline slid away on her knees until she was a fair distance from the body.

The woman let out a hearty cough full of phlegm and possibly blood. Who knows what the Trysians had done to her. Jacquline tried hard to get a good glimpse of the woman, but no angle helped. She leaned a little further back as the woman finally calmed and turned to her, the wet strands of hair dangling like satanic snakes across her eyes. She stared at Jacquline as if she was readying to pounce and enjoy a good meal.

Was this the end?

"Jacquline?" The woman's voice was familiar, soft yet deep. Jacquline tried to place it, but it felt somehow foreign to her. So she responded the only way she knew she could.

"How do you know my name?"

"Jacquline..." this time, relief washed through the woman's voice, and as she brushed her hair away, Jacquline's heart burst with fear, confusion and love.

"Mom?"

— 16 —

Mother had always been the doting type. She never turned away a peasant, never sought to degrade another for their insolence or seek retribution for a crime. That was father's job. She supported him in any decision he made because she was his wife, but her heart was incapable of doing anything that would cause harm, pity, prejudice or unkindly manners to anyone under her kingdom. I have to believe that even from the grave, she had some influence in father's decision to allow Jaxxa Rakala her freedom.

And I couldn't be happier.

We spent the day together, Jaxxa Rakala and I, along the Salotuious River. We bared our skivers and waded into the water to fish and hunt and play until the light of our star spoke bright among the land. We then ate and told stories, hiked and ran like the free birds we were until our star gave way to all of his brothers and sisters. It was one of the best days I have had in my life, and I am sure one of the best days Jaxxa Rakala has had in many past lives.

Her smile is so radiant, it is a sight unto itself. Like the majestic colored bow that strikes across the sky in the tears of the Father of the higher realm, I could look into them forever. They sparkle with such life, even when she is being ridiculed or is caught within a cell, they never cease to radiate joy and compassion, love or acceptance. She is perfect in every way possible — so much so that I want to emulate her as much as I can. I do not want to be her, or be one with her, but I wish to follow her ways and give to others the way she so delicately does. Between her and mother, they are a pair of genuine loving souls that prove that perfection of the universe can be attained through any means, if only you can believe that nothing will harm you, that all is good and just, and that the hand of the Father of the higher realm is always with you and will protect you. He has granted all of our lives, and He will always do unto us as we do unto Him.

* * *

It is my fiftieth year of life today. I am so happy. Especially because I get to share it with such a wonderful friend, one I almost didn't have. It makes the day even brighter that I not only get to share it with her, but with the people who have finally accepted her as my sister. Some even believe she is my biological sister, born to mother through means of a deceitful deed. I'm not quite sure how the rumor of mother lying with a man other than father got started, but it grew quickly, like the flames through the life of mount Grecian. Anyone who knew mother wouldn't believe she would have done such a thing, and no other man would be bold enough, or stupid enough, to force my mother to lay with him. Nonetheless, that is the prevailing idea behind why father was so reluctant to accept Jaxxa Rakala in the first place. She was hidden out of the shame and ridicule of his wife having been spoiled by another, and it all became an accepted idea. And so, too, have I accepted it. I know that she is not mother's daughter, and that she holds not one blood tie to me at all, but I like that she is considered such, and will give my life to protect hers as I would my mother, my father, and my sister.

It has been agreed that she will accompany me to my Quincekilera. I would have asked her to be my partner regardless of my emotion, but I am frightened of what the day may bring, for tonight, I will meet the men of my favor and I shall choose he who will become my love for eternity. I am certain that having Jaxxa Rakala along my arm this day will help soften those fears and give me the strength and courage to choose with my heart, not with the influence of so many others who may push me into a disastrous affair of sickening platitudes.

May the Father of the higher realm hold me close this day and bring me the fruit of my heart to bear witness of my decisions.

*   *   *

Well, I've done it. I've destroyed my family and our legacy. I'm not sure if I, or they, will ever recover, but I couldn't honor the decision as my family wanted. I tried to follow my heart and choose he who made the most sense, but whenever I felt one of them was to be chosen, something inside burned with doubt. These are the suitors of my hand, and they are whom I must choose from, but it has became clear to me that none of these men will suffice. I know it is because of Jaxxa Rakala that I was unable to choose, but I have to believe that she has my best interest at heart. She must have felt something in them that I couldn't see — or chose not to see — and helped me from making the mistakes of a life unsatisfied. There is also the possibility that she only stopped me because of her own jealous tendencies, or because she had once had a past with any one of them, or would like to lay upon their beds as her own and defile our Father's will. In any such case, I must confront her about it, regardless of how it might make her feel. Otherwise, I will always wonder and believe that the manipulation of this day was for selfish reasons, to which point, I would no longer be able to call Jaxxa Rakala my sister, but my enemy.

Of the men who bowed to my hand, there were three that from the manner of their appearance and the language of their body were struck from my list automatically.

There would never be a way for me to condone their inhibitions (or lay by their side and not find sickness among their breath). That left six others who I was to decide from, and each one had their advantages.

Prelyte, a missionary from the realm of the Killiad, was of good voice and kind heart, and his feet were light among the dance. Ophel, prince of Teluse, was kind and gentle, favoring my hand with the kiss of a loving soul. Mestephel, lord of the Gulf region of Keluwa, delighted in his own amusement, but was indeed intelligent in his speech and knowledge of all things. Yusphelou, a delightful little creature from the Reseir galaxy, who came quite a long way to honor me, was fun and delightful, but didn't seem to be the best suited for my kind father — though he would be excellent in leadership and compassion. Malastar came from the woodland hills of Hester, and his knightly presence and command was very intoxicating, as too, were his deep-set eyes and luscious lips (my heart flutters just a bit more thinking of him so regal and fair). Finally, a man from a realm I have yet to hear of, grown and stoic in his presence, yet reticent to the touch, came about in an odd, unfamiliar way. He did not take my hand and kiss it, as all others did, nor did he make reference to my beauty, nor my position. I would say he was brutish in his approach. But that was what was so alluring about him. He was unorthodox, unwilling to give in to the nature of the beast, and instead, took hold of his own definition of life. To be in his arms felt like being a world away, capable of creating ones own timeline; he was my most difficult choice, for to do so would be to go against all of what I was taught. Not to would keep me from exploring my own goals and dreams, and squelch the desires of life. He was also the one man for whom Jaxxa Rakala seemed the most reticent. She was almost frightened of him, to the extent that she believed him evil. I do not know how she could believe such a thing, but when someone can remove the brightness from someone's eyes so easily, caution must be appointed.

The others didn't have that much of an effect on her, though with each one came a light tightness to my hand and a song of resistance to her eyes, which forced me to move on. When the announcement that I had to have more time escaped my lips, the gasp that silenced the room was heart shattering. I couldn't look at anyone's face. Not even Jaxxa Rakala could settle my nerves. I had to be alone. So here I stand, my future unknown, and the dreams of my father broken in one frightened little girl.

— 17 —

"That's appalling."

Tracey looked up. She was sitting closer to Sentilla, who looked so much healthier than before. "What?"

"Forcing a young girl to choose a suitor like that; it's abhorrent."

"Your planet doesn't have a history of arranged marriages?"

"I don't know. I've never been to my planet. Why? Does yours?"

Tracey smiled. "There are several cultures that support arranged marriages on Earth. In fact, in most cases, the suitor was chosen for them, sometimes as early as birth. And whether you liked it or not, that was who you would be with for the rest of your life."

"Deplorable." Sentilla looked away.

"I agree," Tracey said. "I would hate it if my dad decided who I was going to marry. But no matter what we think about it, we have to respect the culture. At least Keladrayia had a choice, and it's not like he asked for them to come. They chose to come."

"Yeah, like that helps. I mean, what are their motivations? It seems to me all they really wanted was the power of the Trystet's crown."

"You're probably right."

"So she should have been able to choose from anyone at anytime, not just those specific individuals."

"I agree," Tracey said again.

Sentilla wasn't sure if she believed her, though the sincerity in her voice was unmistakable.

"But I will say," Tracey continued, "it does seem to me your own situation is very much like Keladrayia's."

"Why would you say that? My mother would never have pushed me into a relationship I didn't want to be a part of."

"I know, and I'm not trying to disparage your family in any way. But you do realize that by keeping you on this ship, your options were very limited, and because of that, you were more prone to find someone on this crew than anyone else."

"What are you saying? That my affection for Qah-Shekel only stems from being in close quarters with him?"

"I'm saying that if you weren't born on this ship and only met Qah-Shekel randomly on some other planet for a brief moment, would that affection be as strong as it is right now? You said yourself, he saved your life; he protected you. So is your affection for him because of those circumstances, or does it go beyond that?"

"Look, child. My love and my relationships are none of your concern."

"Don't deflect the issue."

"I'm not deflecting."

"You are. Do you know how I know that? Because I've had to ask that same question about my own father. Would he have loved my mother the same way had it not been for this gem?"

Sentilla was silent, though still angry.

"Had the gem not pulled him to her, and had he not gotten drunk on the juice of its power, would he still have been this determined to find her? Would his love have been no match for it?"

"You think without the gem, he wouldn't have had the same amount of fervor to find her?"

"I'm very curious to find out." Tracey waited, watching Sentilla closely.

"Okay, I'll submit. If I hadn't been so close to Qah-Shekel for so long, perhaps maybe I wouldn't have the same feelings for him. But that's not the point. Circumstance may have brought us together, but it's our feelings for each other that will keep us together."

Tracey smiled. "I agree. If love can find its way beyond the circumstances, then the love is true. And because you understand that, you can understand how to overcome the circumstances and find the will to conquer the urges and feelings you have no control over. Your desire to acquire this gem far outweighs your ability to control it. But once you learn that the power is nothing more than a circumstance of proximity can you understand that it is you who has the power already, and that the gem is only a symptom of your own weaknesses."

"And what weaknesses are those?"

"You tell me."

Sentilla laughed and swore under her breath, choosing not to say anymore about it.

— 18 —

Kahli's skin felt like plastic that had been left in a perpetual block of ice, and the weight of her body made it seem as if she was. Qah-Shekel didn't struggle near as much as Ken, whose face was a steady red as they carried her to the rejuvenation bed. It was a relief just to make it without dropping her. For a few seconds after setting her legs into the chamber, Ken thought he was floating (most likely because of the lightheadedness that came with his heavy breaths). As he flexed his arms to reignite circulation —

Good thing Lark wasn't around to see that ugly display!

— Qah-Shekel closed the rejuvenation bed. Shortly after, it filled with a light fog swarming Kahli, but at no point covering her entire body.

"You think this will actually hide her?" Ken said.

"As long as the smoke remains."

Ken nodded, accepting his answer. What else was he supposed to do? He felt quite awkward as Qah-Shekel watched the swirl of the mist. "I should try to get some rest," he finally said. When Qah-Shekel didn't respond, Ken hesitantly turned and left medical, occasionally turning back to see if Qah-Shekel would notice his departure.

He didn't. Qah-Shekel's focus was entirely on the smoke swarming Kahli's —

Sentilla's

— soft features inside the chamber. He could still feel the pain she couldn't, comforted only by the warmth of Lark's hand against his. Sentilla's fear and confusion as he pulled her from the chamber and cradled her in his arms still weighed heavily on his mind, and only added to the helplessness of not being able to help her fight the gem's magnetic power. Qah-Shekel couldn't understand how she could be so susceptible, but when he himself was all but immune from its effects, how could he? He felt guilty for his utter lack of empathy and for failing to do more as she clung her arms around his neck, looking for nothing but answers; he felt even more so now that he once again had no answers to give. But there was still one thing he could provide that she desperately needed, if only as a symbolic gesture.

Qah-Shekel left medical with resolute steps.

— 19 —

Lark felt right at home sliding the ship across the ground, hovering mere inches above the freshly flourishing brush that covered the majority of a once scorched land. She had made a career out of doing this with new military aircraft —

Getting high, riding low

— and though the mass of the ship made it feel more like a cruise liner in the middle of an ocean than a sonic jet weaving and flipping through the crevice of a mountain, at least she felt safe from any harm. Then again, what was the fun in that? The adrenaline that came with the danger of imminent death was the best part.

She hadn't noticed that she had started dozing until DovenJadden purred frantically in her ear. She shot to attention and noticed right away the landscape had become a sweeping desert. Above the view screen was a hologram of Rega-One, complete with a small 'X' (Ken's idea) marking her destination. At her current velocity, the ship would be ready to set down in a matter of minutes; it was time to slow the ship and prep for landing. DovenJadden kept a watchful eye on every little thing Lark did (probably hoping Lark would screw up so she could bitch and moan to Qah-Shekel), but she was as cool as a cucumber, sliding the *Equinox* into position and setting it down as gently as any other aircraft she'd ever flown. After performing a quick diagnostic as Sentilla had shown her a dozen times in the simulator, Lark powered down the pilot station. The arrogant smile directed at DovenJadden couldn't have been more deliciously satisfying.

DovenJadden rolled her eyes and purred under her breath before pounding back to her station. Lark laughed to herself and then tapped her fingers together.

"Landing successful," she said.

"We'll meet you at the main hatch," Qah-Shekel replied.

"Ten four," Lark said gleefully before switching off the comm bud. Taking one last look over at DovenJadden, who was angrily shutting down the engines and other minor systems, Lark sat back and took a moment to enjoy her (small) victory.

— 20 —

Tracey sat still and quiet with her legs crossed in the corner of the cell. Sentilla beamed with delight near the barrier as she talked with Qah-Shekel, at least up until the point he had to leave. She urged him to stay, but knew it was futile, doing nothing except fuel his guilt. She finally conceded, acknowledging the importance of his mission and bidding him luck and a safe journey. He set his hand up as close to the barrier as he could, knowing she couldn't see him do it.

"Are you ready?" Qah-Shekel asked Tracey.

Tracey nodded.

Qah-Shekel said nothing more as he left. Sentilla sat down and lowered her head to her knees. It was a melancholy moment for Tracey, one she was going to have to reluctantly expound on.

"I'm going to need your help," she said.

Sentilla looked in her general direction. "With what?"

Without an answer, Tracey pulled a small magnetic strip from her pocket and crawled to Sentilla, who had to turn away as her body cramped up tight in response to the vicinity of the gem.

"What are you doing?" Sentilla said, each word a struggle.

Tracey forced Sentilla to sit forward and lowered the magnet to Sentilla's shackles. The instant it touched the edge of the cuffs, there was a light spark and they fell to the floor. Sentilla quickly curled against the wall to massage her wrists, even though her freedom was enough to soothe any pain away.

"Thank you," she said sheepishly.

"Don't thank me just yet," Tracey said and pulled the knife from her ankle sheath. She inched her way back to Sentilla, who immediately felt as if the walls were closing in on her. It still didn't stop Tracey from pressing her body flush with Sentilla's. "Here," she said, taking hold of Sentilla's wrist and pressing the butt of the knife firmly in her palm.

"What's this?" Sentilla asked.

"Take it."

"What am I supposed to do with it?"

"Just take it."

All of Sentilla's muscles were so tight, she wasn't sure she would be able to. But with Tracey's help, she curled her fingers along the butt of the knife. Tracey then stepped back, allowing Sentilla to crawl to the back wall, the knife sticking prominently out of the huddled mass she had become. Tracey, meanwhile turned to the barrier and stared out at the wall, doubts swimming through her head that not even the gem could cover up.

"I'm about to do something that very well might kill me," Tracey said bluntly. She bent her head down slightly. "I'm going to need you to keep that from happening."

"How?"

"It's not going to be easy. The gem is going to try and consume you. You have to find the courage to fight it and do what needs to be done."

"Which is?"

"In just a few quasers, you will no longer feel the effects of the gem." Now she had Sentilla's interest. She sat straight and listened more intently. "I don't know how long it will be, but eventually, its effects will hit you with an immeasurable force. When that happens, you're going to need to locate my body."

"Where will your body be?"

"Honestly, I'm not sure. Just know that it will be somewhere close. Find me and stab that knife into my chest against the edge of the gem."

"You want me to what?" Sentilla felt the knife grow heavy in her hand, compelling her to drop it. "I don't know if I can do that."

"If you don't, we'll both die."

"Why? What'll happen if I don't do it?"

"A blast comparable to a supernova."

Sentilla's silence told Tracey she understood. "You're the only one that can do this," she whispered.

Sentilla shook her head. "Who came up with this damn plan?"

Tracey smiled, a gesture that didn't last long.

"We're in position," Qah-Shekel chirped in her ear.

Tracey took a deep breath. "Hold on." She stared out at the wall, not once blinking as she drew the power of the gem into her mind, opening it up enough to track the radiation signatures within a hundred miles of where she stood. Most of them were inconsequential, representing the fruits of the land, so pinpointing the inhabitants of Rega-One, both organic and otherwise, wasn't difficult. It was deciphering which one was which that caused her fits of annoyance. That is until she noticed several variances in one of the patterns that wasn't evident in the other, signifying an organic presence. It was all she had to go by; it would have to suffice. She then quickly located Ken, Lark and Qah-Shekel waiting patiently near the outer hatch and recorded their signatures into her mind. Once she had them locked and ready, she raised her hands up so that her palms were within millimeters of the barrier. She could feel its warmth and the light spark of electricity just waiting to bite. Closing her eyes, she took in a long deep breath, and then, "Go. Now."

Using all of her strength to lay the Regan signature over her companions, Tracey pushed her palms into the barrier. She clenched her teeth together to keep from screaming as the gem washed the entire cell in a green hue. Sentilla heard the crackle of electricity, and even though Tracey wasn't making a sound other than a few small whimpers, she knew Tracey had ignited the barrier and was holding on for dear life. The funny thing was, the longer she listened, the more it became a soft, soothing hum.

Better yet, a weight had been lifted. It was as if Sentilla had never encountered the gem — which scared the living daylights out of her. If Tracey was right about this, she could only imagine the pain she was about to endure.

— 21 —

The hardest part of speaking when in total shock is piecing any semblance of a coherent sentence together. Jacquline wanted to say so much, ask so many things, but all that escaped her lips were small beats of unusual noises. It was only when Gloria spoke that she found the resolve to slow her mind and find her words.

"What's going on? Where am I?" Gloria said, a bit frantic.

"A better question would be, 'Where'd you come from?'"

"I don't... the last thing I remember..." Gloria grabbed the back of her head and hissed a bit in pain. "Someone must have cold-cocked me." She pressed the butt of her palm to her forehead.

Jacquline wanted so much to grab hold of Gloria and never let go, but she couldn't bring herself to actually do anything. She had been thinking and dreaming about this moment for so long, now that it was here, she wasn't sure if she was ready to accept her mother back into her life. Besides, what happened to Jaenice? Did they somehow give her a facelift to look exactly like Gloria?

(*Anything was possible nowadays.*)

If Jacquline didn't know any better, this whole thing was probably a trick — some elaborate hallucination — generated by the Trysians to make her feel more comfortable and complacent. "That doesn't make any sense."

"You think I'm lying?" Gloria said, exasperated.

"Well, it wouldn't be the first time," Jacquline said with just as much ire.

"What are you saying?"

Jacquline fired a set of piercing eyes at her mother. Gloria was more than ready to fire back, but chose to let it go. She slid backward to lie against the wall. Jacquline did the same, crossing her arms across her chest, waiting for Gloria to apologize — for everything.

"I'm sorry," Gloria said.

Jacquline shook her head, avoiding eye contact.

Despite Jacquline's resentment, Gloria was awestruck. She never once thought she would ever see her daughter again, and for a long time, she wondered how she could ever have left in the first place. No matter how long she stared, Gloria couldn't believe how beautiful her baby girl had become. Even the white stripes in her hair represented a maturity she never thought possible. Jacquline had become a woman; she deserved the answers Gloria couldn't give her before.

"You're probably wondering why I left," she said with as much of a motherly voice as she could muster. It had been a while.

"Not really," Jacquline said. An obvious lie.

"I couldn't take the pressure anymore," Gloria said anyway. "I know it's a piss-poor excuse —"

"You can say that again."

"Look, Jacquline. Leaving had nothing to do with you. I was a mess."

"That's not news. I know you ditched me for your own selfish reasons, but why do it without even saying goodbye? Not even one word. Do you know how that felt? To suddenly have no mother?"

"I know," Gloria said sheepishly. "You don't know how sorry I am for leaving you alone with him. But I had to make a choice, one that would allow me the happiness I was desperate to get back."

"And your happiness was leaving me behind?"

"Jacquline —"

"No, mom. I get it. You were drowning and I was part of that weight. Fine. It's history. Moving on."

"I don't think you do get it, Jackie. I know it sounds horrible and selfish, but I needed my freedom. I needed to find my place outside of you and Ken."

"Then you talk about it, tell us you're unhappy and need a break. Get a divorce even. Yeah, it would have hurt like hell, but at least I would have known where you were. You just vanished. How was I supposed to take that?"

"What would you have done if Ken and I had gotten divorced? What would have been your choice?"

"Honestly? I would have chosen to stay with you."

"Exactly. Then I would have had to have said no."

"Which only proves how chicken-shit you really are. You may have needed to find yourself, but I needed you. I. Needed. You. And you weren't there for me. You weren't there and I never thought I'd see you again."

"Jackie, you have to believe me. I always planned to come back."

Jacquline grunted and turned away, refusing to look at Gloria (and to hide her growing vulnerability).

"Jackie, please." When Jacquline didn't even move a muscle, Gloria said, "Look. From where I sit, we're going to be locked in this shithole for a while, so we might as well put all of our shit behind us and find a way through this, don't you?"

Jacquline waved her hand, acknowledging her when she knew she shouldn't.

Gloria set her head back against the wall (taking in a sharp breath with the scorching pain of her wound) and sat silent for some time. Finally, as she felt the tension between them diminishing (if ever so slightly), she said, "How's Stacey?"

Jacquline didn't want to look at Gloria, but curiosity got the best of her. "How do you know Stacey?"

"You don't think I kept tabs on the woman taking care of my baby?" Gloria said.

"You were spying on us?"

"Hardly. When I found out Ken had remarried, I did some research, asked around about her."

Jacquline chuffed. "Didn't find much, did you?"

"No, I didn't. And I couldn't have been happier. As far as I was concerned, she was exactly the role model you needed."

"Because she had no history whatsoever? Seriously? That didn't raise any red flags?"

"I never thought of it that way."

"Yeah, wonderful parenting. I don't even know why that surprises me."

"You're still alive."

"No thanks to you."

"What's that supposed to mean?"

"You got lucky, mom" Jacquline said. "When you left, you stole the most important pieces of me — *my* happiness; *my* joy; *my* spirit. You killed me by leaving the way you did."

"I know, baby, and I'm sorry," Gloria said. Both girls were flirting with tears but fighting to let them go.

"No, you don't know. I would have died had it not been for Stacey. I was ready to kill myself, mom. I was ready... Stacey *literally* saved my life."

Gloria couldn't fight her tears any longer. And she couldn't keep from holding her daughter. Jacquline tried to refuse the embrace, but Gloria was too strong for her. That or it was exactly what Jacquline needed — what she wanted — from her mother.

"Stacey was there for me," Jacquline squeaked out. "She protected me... but it wasn't the same. It always felt like a replica. I needed the real thing. I needed you."

Gloria held her daughter tighter, showing her pain and regret in the power of her hug. "I'm so sorry, Jackie. I am. Can you ever forgive me?"

A moment later, Jacquline was embracing her just as tightly. If this was an allusion, it was an extremely good one. Her smell was just as Jacquline remembered, as was her warm and generous touch. Gloria took Jacquline's reciprocation as a possibility of forgiveness and they remained in each other's arms for some time, listening to the beats of their hearts and welcoming this first step to reconciliation.

— 22 —

It was nearly a three-mile trek from the ship to the city, but in these conditions it felt like thirty. The wind remained silent as the immense heat pricked at Ken's skin like needles. He hadn't gotten but two steps from the ship when his mouth went as dry as the air. Compared to this, Xyneris felt like a vacation, leading him to wonder aloud about how it might feel running through the desert at midday if it was already this hot at the crack of dawn.

"It's really no worse than any desert on Earth," Lark mused, hiding her own dry throat as best she could.

Ken was sure she was right; it still didn't make it any less scorching, and he couldn't imagine how Qah-Shekel was getting along. His skin cracked worse than a parched plateau the moment he exited the ship to make his way around the parameter of the city. Whether the amphibious alien would even make it to the manufacturing plant was a gamble Ken wasn't sure he'd put money on. The only relief came when they could see the towers of the city rise above the horizon. The closer they got, the more moisture returned to the air, cooling the temperature tremendously. So much so, Ken no longer had to keep forcing Lark to take breaks for water (which he claimed were for her benefit). As they approached a set of rocks that formed a quasi-natural border around the outer rim of the city (where the desert started to flourish with exotic brush and greenery), they instantly took notice of the eerie silence that blanketed the streets.

"Is there some sort of curfew?" Lark asked.

"I don't know," Ken said as he peered cautiously above the rocks. "But if there is, we're screwed."

"Should we chance it?"

Ken shrugged and shook his head. Though he knew it didn't really matter where they were when Tracey dropped the curtain (the androids would detect them no matter what), if they were too far outside the city when it happened, they wouldn't be able to draw the amount of ruckus they needed to open the window for Qah-Shekel's infiltration. On the other hand, if they were caught doing something out of the ordinary before Qah-Shekel was even in place, the entire plan could find itself in jeopardy. Given the choice, it was better to choose the former.

Just then, a delicate chime spread across the city three times, prompting several battalions of androids to begin roaming the streets. The curvatures of their bodies were on glorious display with help from the soft glow of the sun piercing past the buildings. What was even more striking was the radiance of their eyes. They looked like hundreds of pairs of fireflies, twinkling in unison as if they were hypnotized.

"Would you look at all of the Roxanas?" Ken said.

Lark almost lost it. She had never thought of using that term before, but it worked — if the androids were Alpha-Nines. But no matter how close they appeared to resemble Kahli, there was something about them that gave them a far superior air about them (and that wasn't counting the deep red tips of their short black locks).

"I actually think those are the Beta units," she said.

"So Roxboas, then?"

Lark giggled uncontrollably.

"Yeah, doesn't seem to have the same ring to it, does it?" Ken said, enjoying Lark's infectious laugh.

Her spirits grew even higher when she saw a few Regans weave through the dispersing Beta units. "There," she said with a cracked voice. "Look. It's go time."

Ken and Lark slid over the rocks with ease and grace, landing on the opposite side of the barrier in a crouched position. Lark pulled the glass tablet from her pocket and swiped her fingers along the entirety of its edge. A hologram of the city lit up above it for a few seconds before she shut it back down. She nodded and led Ken briskly into the city where they strolled along as if they had lived there their whole lives.

Can't look conspicuous, now can we?

The city was quite large and for the most part, other than some wildly overgrown plant life and odd, but fascinating architecture (one building in particular that Ken found quite amusing looked like a jelly doughnut stabbed with a knife and then left to decay on the kitchen counter), the city looked like New York without vehicles. The outer edges seemed to contain the majority of homes and condo-type apartments, while the business district, with its variety of high-rises, restaurants and mom-and-pop shops, was concentrated within the inner hubs.

"How much you want to bet we find a Starbucks," Ken said, receiving a good-natured slap from Lark. He wasn't far off, as they saw a dozen or so Regans entering and exiting an establishment shaped like a glass that looked to be about eight feet high. It included a bulbous base that weaved into a bar of tall spouts from which the patrons would suckle from like a baby bottle. It was an odd thing to watch, really, but the refreshment left an aroma that smelled absolutely amazing. If they had gone with the original plan and had used the escort, Ken probably would have demanded they stop to try it.

Although they got some odd looks from a few of the locals (who clearly didn't rec-ognize them, but apparently weren't willing to say anything), for the most part, they were ignored. They just hoped they could continue the ruse now that they were in the central plaza at the center of the city. It was at least a half a mile in diameter and lined with tall, bronzed totems, hand-crafted to signify, as Lark assumed, the history of the planet's civilization. The ground was covered in all types of plant life, separated by a set of walkways lined in a specific pattern that if Lark had to guess, held a strong, significant meaning. The surrounding buildings were decorated in a variety of colors and shapes that each held their own possible meaning, while working together to create a masterful work of art. The curves, the angles — it took Lark's breath away, prompting Ken to give her a generous elbow to the gut to keep her from gawking like some over-caffeinated tourist. She curled her lips in embarrassed concern, then took hold of Ken's hand and leaned in close. He wasn't sure why, but then noticed a few other couples roaming the plaza in the same manner. It was a romantic area, to be sure, and Ken realized if they were going to pull this off for as long as they had to, this would definitely give them the best shot. So he wrapped his arm around her waist and walked her to one of the ironclad benches. They sat to take in the scenery — and their sweet, simulated love.

— 23 —

It took Qah-Shekel a lot longer to traverse the terrain than he had initially hoped. It was clear, from the formation of the rocks, the density of the scattered ash and crater-like indentions that this had been a location for several recent battles. With it being so close to the manufacturing areas of the city, it made sense. Taking control of the livelihood of the citizens was one way to seize control, especially when it involved the manufacturing of the most lethal weapons the Regans had at their disposal.

After being forced to travel about a quarter-mile out of the way due to some man-made trenches that still held a cavalcade of rocks sharpened into deadly spikes (and at least one possible explosive device half-hidden under some dirt), Qah-Shekel found his way to the rear of the city, which, as the hologram had indicated, had been barricaded by an immense concrete wall. He scanned the parameter for sentries who may be guarding the gateway the team was initially going to use to escape. After about a mile walk along the edge of the wall, two Beta units stood locked against it, each armed with a thin, staff-like weapon. Qah-Shekel knew if he attacked — or if they saw him for that matter — a swarm of androids would be on him in seconds. So he remained low inside a nearby crater and tapped his fingers together.

"I'm in position," he said.

— 24 —

"Here we go," Lark said, squeezing Ken's hand tightly.

The alarms came a lot quicker and were far louder than they anticipated. It reminded Ken of a raid siren if it was gurgling water. The time it took them to adjust to the level of noise was just enough time for the Beta units to nearly surround the plaza. Lark was quick to her feet, though she couldn't see any escape route, not with the Betas advancing toward them from every walkway in two-by-two formation. As they closed in, Lark realized they weren't willing to use their weapons (or else, she assumed, they would already be dead) or step foot on the greenery. She used that to her advantage, dragging Ken through the grassy cutaways as fast as his legs could bear. Once clear of the plaza, they raced through the streets, shifting and weaving through whatever new alley or road a new horde of Betas forced them down. The burn in their legs grew harder to ignore, as did the squeeze in their chests. It wasn't until they jetted through the lobby of a high-rise that seemed to be under construction and maneuvering out into a dank alley that was Beta free (for the time being) that Lark and Ken were finally able to stop and catch their breath. Lark took the break to pull the tablet out and bring the hologram of the city back up.

"God damn it, Tracey," Lark hissed as she studied the hologram as quickly as she could. Not only were the Betas swarming the building, but the two of them were way off their originally planned escape route. "A little help would go a long way right now."

The Betas continued to move in from all possible directions. Ken took Lark's hand and closed his eyes, repeating "Come on" with every new breath. Lark hardly noticed, as her attention remained focused on the tablet. That is until she lowered it to her side as the Betas rushed into the alley.

"What is your purpose here?" one of the Betas said. It was Kahli's voice, but lacked any emotion whatsoever, making it as robotic as it could without sounding like a computerized telemarketing message. What shocked Lark was that she could even understand her. It then suddenly occurred to her that they had no intention of harming them. If anything, they were as confused as she was.

"I saw the intruders running through the hestenia and thought we could help," Lark said, surprised she'd even know how to respond.

"Where did they go?"

"I don't know. When we got out here, they were gone."

The Beta looked them over carefully (nearly taking Ken's massive amount of sweat as a sign of deception) and then said, "Be on your way."

Lark let slip a surprised smile and then nodded. She pulled Ken back into the building and together walked slowly, but briskly back to the main street. Tracey had just pulled off another stellar little magic trick and Ken was all too aware of that fact.

— 25 —

The sirens didn't phase the sentries one bit, but Qah-Shekel didn't expect any different. By now, the majority of androids in the city were in hot pursuit of Lark and Ken, so once he got past these two, he'd be free to infiltrate the manufacturing plant with ease. The key to doing so would be to force them into hand-to-hand combat, so Qah-Shekel didn't have to think twice about slicing his thumb laser across the torso of each android. Along with leaving a large cut along their required jumpsuit (and exposing a bit of their unscathed skin), the shot cut their staffs in half.

The laser was still burning hot when the androids charged him. His reaction time was fierce, spinning and slicing his right fin across the first androids back as he slapped a tiny round button onto her shoulder blade. He used his momentum to sweep the second androids legs, pasting a similar button near her thigh. There was no time to breathe, though, as the first android was back on her feet before the other had face planted into the rock. She struck Qah-Shekel in the back with her knuckles, nearly breaking his spine, and then threw him as if he was a weightless rag doll. Had the wall not stopped his flight, he may have traveled for miles on end. The android hovered over him before he was able to get his bearings. She grabbed his throat and pulled him up to her chest. The second android had returned to her feet, but remained back as her counterpart dug her fingers into Qah-Shekel's temples. He fought the unrelenting urge to pass out, somehow finding a way to press his wrists together as if he was preparing to be detained in Eutherian cuffs. He could feel his death upon him as he swiped his wrists in opposite directions, keeping his skin pressed as firmly together as possible — a task that took much longer than it actually felt. The androids were suddenly stricken stiff. Qah-Shekel felt the noose on his neck tighten greatly before he finally found his breath again. He made sure to bend along with his attacker so her grip wouldn't tear out his throat as she fell to the ground.

God damn it, Tracey, he heard, if only faintly. *A little help would go a long way right now.* Though he knew Lark's voice was being transmitted through the comm bud, for the life of him, it felt as if she was nearby, screaming out at the top of her lungs. But even if she were right on the other side of the wall, he was of no use to them right now — not where he was physically, in all manner of the word.

His head was spinning. After using twice as much strength than he was accustomed to fully remove the android's fingers from his throat, he fell backward against the wall to catch his breath. It was only when he felt his strength return and could once again make sense of what was happening that he realized the sirens had stopped. Either Ken and Lark had been captured or Tracey had returned their cloaks. Whatever the case, the androids would be returning to their normal posts soon enough. If he was going to get inside the manufacturing plant, he would have to move fast.

He took a moment to balance himself after standing, then pulled the android to the entry without any further complications. On its face, it appeared to be just another part of the wall, but upon closer inspection, Qah-Shekel could make out indentations that couldn't have been more than a fraction off from the rest of the wall. He set the androids palm to the center of that specific area. It quickly lit up in a soft red hue and then slowly receded, giving him the access he needed.

Just beyond the wall was his target — a large, windowless steel structure at least three stories tall and a half-mile wide. A dozen pipes extended from the base of the building and stretched parallel up to the wall, where they then branched out and buried themselves into the ground at various intervals.

Qah-Shekel inched across the pipes, taking care not to slip into one of the fine gaps or cut his feet on the sharp edges that formed the outer rim construction of each individual pipe. The ground stopped a few yards from the edge of the manufacturing plant, forming a suitable (though somewhat dangerous) walkway. Though some of the pipes continued on a level plane into the building, the majority of them turned downward into the waterless moat before either turning into the building or lining the floor some eight feet below. It gave Qah-Shekel the perfect ladder to weave his way downward to the cold steel floor, where he maneuvered his way to a heavy steel door protected by a scanning device. He wasn't sure how much time he would have to search the premises, so tracking down some random android that may not even have the necessary access permissions would do him absolutely no good. The only way in was to jam his fin into the door and cut a hole that would allow him to fit through without setting off the building's alarms. Once through (and relieved that for the moment, he was still an undetected phantom), Qah-Shekel remained fleet-footed as he raced through the darkened tunnels.

— 26 —

The sweat dripping from Tracey's body had formed a small puddle at her feet. Her eyes were soaked with heat and her breaths had stopped for some time. Her concentration was waning as the grip along the edges of her brain felt as if her skull was looking to squash it like a rotten grape. Scorch marks leaked out from all around the gem like veins, wrapping up and around her neck. Her body tattoo was lit up to the point that if Sentilla wasn't still blind, she'd be able to see the physical attributes of the mark as if Tracey wasn't wearing any clothes. She had no idea how much longer she'd be able to hold on; how much longer she'd be able to protect her family. She'd soon find out.

As Qah-Shekel dropped into the shadows of the alley alongside the manufacturing plant, her skull cracked, thrusting a piece of bone into her brain. The gem's focus immediately switched to protect that precious organ, causing the tapestry of the barrier to explode at the base of her palms. Tracey flew backward, cracking the uppermost vertebrae of her neck against the wall a few feet from Sentilla. She lay lifeless as the gem steadily grew white hot.

At the same time, Sentilla received a jolt of excruciating pain. She vomited before letting out a scream that overshadowed the oscillating hum generated by the gem. She could see it floating and spinning wildly inside her mind, digging its electrical fingers into every inch of her body. She was trapped, hurt, and devoutly submissive to its call.

— 27 —

The sirens wailed once again.

"Damn it," Lark said and sprinted down the crowded street. Ken had to dodge several Regans to keep up with her.

Letting the tablet guide her through the streets to avoid new formations of Betas, Lark hurried down an alley, helped Ken scale a small barrier, then turned down another main roadway that led to a smaller residential street, which allowed them to maneuver through a gateway of housing (and subsequently attracting two groups of Betas together). Ken and Lark were eventually forced down a back road of small shops and businesses that compelled them into another cold, dank alley — and a dead end. Four teams of Betas were now heading their way. Their only recourse was up.

"Go," Lark said hoarsely. She wasn't quite as drained as Ken, who looked about ready to pass out if he didn't rest. His legs were a rubbery mess and he wasn't sure his arms would be any better. He shook his head, unable to get any words out.

"We have to, Ken. Unless you'd like to become Beta road kill, get your ass moving." She pushed him to the piping that lined the outside of one of the buildings. Pressing his feet along the perpendicular wall, he quickly found he had much more strength than he first thought. Lark followed behind as the Betas made their way into the alley.

"Stop, intruders," one of the Betas announced, "or you will be eliminated."

Go ahead and take your best shot, Lark thought. And she did, leaping to grab Lark's leg and missing by mere centimeters (if Lark didn't know any better, she would have sworn she felt the air whip past her leg). By this time Ken had reached the top of the building and reached down to pull Lark up. Some of the Betas chose to break away and head around to the other side of the building, but those who stayed climbed the pipe, their speed matched only by their tenacity.

After Lark pulled her way onto the roof, she spun around and sent a boot to the lead Beta's head. It slowed her upward momentum, but unless Lark could find some way to cause enough damage to shut her down, it wasn't going to stop her from reaching the top. So Lark continued to kick the Beta's head backward until there was a loud pop. The Beta immediately started twitching, her head shifted slightly to the right. She tried to operate her arms and legs but failed to move them more than a millimeter at a time before they reset back to their original position. Unable to maneuver around her, the rest of the Betas had to stop climbing.

"Gotta love robotics," Lark said with a bright smile. She grabbed Ken's hand. "Come on, before they spider over her."

Ken was stabilizing, but still nowhere near ready to continue. Not that it mattered. Lark briskly pulled him across several rooftops (some of which had gaps he didn't think he'd ever be able to make if it wasn't for the rush of adrenaline that kept his legs from completely failing him). After several minutes, they finally reached the top of a building that had an access ladder and wasn't surrounded by Betas. It felt a little too convenient for Ken, but they were nearing the edge of the city and the desert was just out of reach. This could be their last chance.

As Lark set foot down on the street, she studied the area with the tablet. She hadn't realized it before, but the Betas had stopped tracking them because the sirens had been shut down. Had Tracey returned their shield? Every call to find out was returned with silence.

"I don't like this," she said as Ken tumbled to the ground. He tried, but he was unable to get back up.

"Tracey must have raised the cloak again," Ken said, fighting the urge to vomit. "We're clear."

"I don't know. She's not responding. Besides, why would she have even dropped it again? It doesn't make sense."

Ken grabbed his sweat-laced forehead and rubbed his eyes.

Just then, a group of heavily armed Regans came rushing toward them from both sides of the roadway. Ken dipped into his reserve tank and stood. "Go," he said to Lark. "I'll hold them off. Get back to the ship."

Lark's first instinct was to ignore him and fight the Regans alongside him. Either that or pull him with her into the desert. But what would that do exactly? No matter what may happen to one of them, the other had to get back to the ship. Given Ken's place among the crew, that person had to be her. She was the only one who could fly the *Equinox* off of this godforsaken rock. She just had to pray the Regans wouldn't kill Ken and that she would get a chance to rescue him — eventually. So Lark ran toward the desert as fast as her thin little legs could carry her. A couple of Regans followed her to the edge of the desert before giving up. The majority, though, stayed to subdue Ken. He put up a good fight, but in the end was relegated to an unconscious heap of meat.

— 28 —

Sentilla's muscles had seized, constraining her body to lie flat and stiff on the ground, her hands in fists that turned her skin an iridescent yellow — all of which was in contradiction to what her mind was experiencing. She was nearly numb to all pain now that the gem had become her heartbeat. The touch of its fingers made her feel warm and loved. Giving into the gem's importance and its cry for her flesh was growing far easier, and her reluctance had been diminished to the whimper of her will. She craved it more than ever, could taste the spirit of its core and see the future of its intentions.

No!

Sentilla heard the cry from deep within the shadows of her memory. She wasn't sure if it was real or simply remnants of her past dying into the mist. Ignoring it was her best option.

You mustn't give in, the voice cried out. It was still soft and distant, but it felt more real this time. *You must fight the temptation. Listen to me. You must fight it.*

 She felt the gem desperately trying to suppress the voice, but it couldn't continue pulling her into its breast and push the voice away. It grew louder —

You're stronger than this, Sentilla.

— and louder —

Look past the temptation. You can fight this. I have faith in you.

— and louder —

Find me, Sentilla. Hear my words. I am your hope. I am your savior. Fight this. Find your way back.

— until finally, Sentilla saw the bright flash of Tracey staring back at her through the light of the gem. It didn't last long, but it gave Sentilla the strength to locate her again. Tracey's eyes were a piercing periwinkle with turquoise veins, highlighted by the green flesh of the crescent moons that pulled the gem away, breaking Sentilla free of its grip. Suddenly, Sentilla could feel the sharp sting of her muscles gripping her to the floor. The more she focused on those eyes —

You can do this. Fight it. Don't give in. Finish the task. Make this right. Give us both our freedom.

— the more she was able to relax her body enough to regain control. She curled up first, opening her hands ever so slightly to make absolutely sure she was in control and then sat up. The gem fought her every step of the way, but she pushed back just as hard, maybe even a little harder.

With Tracey's voice continually urging her to continue to fight, Sentilla searched for the knife, which she found in less time than it took her to actually pick it up. Once she had a good grip on it, she used Tracey's voice to crawl to her body. She carefully felt for the gem's physical frame and then traced her finger along the gem's smooth, crystalline structure. She had to take a breath to build her courage, but with one last message —

Set us free!

— Sentilla jammed the knife into the fire of Tracey's skin.

She didn't feel the blood pour across her fingers because the pain from the light that erupted from Tracey's chest pushed her against the wall. Sentilla's scream matched Tracey's. She could see a bright white blur that lasted for what felt like a dozen lifetimes. When the darkness finally enveloped the light, the searing pain faded along with it and Sentilla felt curiously refreshed. Not one muscle was tight, not one breath was errant. She was a newborn child emerging from the womb, ready to explore the world. What she hadn't expected, and what filled every pore with a rush of excitement and relief, was the colors that came when she opened her eyes.

— 29 —

The laughter was much needed. Hearing some of the stories Gloria had to tell were so familiar and so strangely like her own, Jacquline couldn't help but feel connected to her in a much deeper way than she ever thought possible.

"And so, I'm sneaking around this house, getting pricked by a dozen thorn bushes, trying to keep from being seen by both the cops and the crazy asshole wielding the fire poker that slashed my damn hand. When I thought I was in the clear and was about to make a break for it, this dog started yapping its jaw, leading the cops directly to me. Now I had no choice. I bolted like the Flash to get the hell out of there. I'm not sure if one of the cops hopped in a unit or not, but lucky for me, the pig on my tail was just that. There wasn't any way he was going to keep up with me, not unless I was dragging a Twinkie and a roasted hoagie behind me. About a mile in, I heard the guy puke chives, so I hopped a couple of fences and ran into a nearby house that left their garage door open. When the sirens finally faded, I just moseyed my way on back outside."

"And lifted a few souvenirs while you were at it," Jacquline said with a wink.

"Of course. I don't even think the owners ever woke up."

"Ah, I wish I could have been there for that. What happened with the blood?"

"Knowing the police, they probably didn't even check for any. And even if they had, I'm not in the system, so I was in the clear."

"God, I wish I could say that."

"Why? What happened to you?"

"I was stupid enough to take a job from this damn slut and her pathetic pimp of a boyfriend."

"Now what did I tell you about that?"

"Yeah, I know. I'm well aware I shouldn't have done it. But the score was too good to pass up."

"What happened?" Gloria was extremely intrigued.

"After getting inside — which was no easy feat, what with having the suckle-fun twins distracting me the whole time — I thought I had taken out the security system, but I must have set off a silent alarm because before I knew it, the cops were there. I tried to get away in this sweet, beautiful 'Vette — oh my god, such a precious little gem of a car. But it wasn't enough. I flipped when the damn cop shot out the tires. I couldn't believe it. I mean, it's the first time I've ever had the cops arrive at a job."

"I remember the first time they showed up at one of my jobs. This was way before you and Ken. I did have a partner then, too, and he was a dumb shit if there ever was one. But I thought I loved the guy and it was our first job together… let's just say he got a little too greedy, I got a little too into the whole thing and we ended up getting our nasty on inside the house. While the owners were there, mind you."

"No, you didn't."

"Right on their kitchen table to boot."

Jacquline had her mouth covered, shocked and utterly thrilled by the whole thing.

"Before we were finished, the owner had a gun on our asses. He made us get on our knees, but I wasn't about to go to jail. I was only a junior in high school and having this on my record wouldn't just end it for me with my parents, it would end my reputation. So I did the only sensible thing I could."

"You left the poor schmuck hanging in the wind."

"I was out the back door like a leopard. The asshole actually fired at me, but he must not have ever fired a gun before because the bullet hit the window. It's possible some of it may have been sent into my partner's back or something, because he screamed like a little bitch. But the guy didn't come after me. I think he was happy enough to have at least one of us. And nothing was stolen. But here I was, forced to make my way back home buck naked, looking over my shoulder for any signs of the cops. It was scary as shit, but damn sexy and very cold. I'll never forget it."

"Seems to me that's a great reason to use a partner. When the shit hits the fan, you can leave them holding the bag."

"But the shit hardly ever hits the fan when you're alone, and if it does —"

"You only have yourself to blame," Jacquline finished as if she had just won a million dollar prize on a game show. Gloria pointed with a nod.

"So this douchebag of yours was your last partner, then?"

"Actually, no. I did use another partner for a few other jobs, but that went south because the jackass double crossed me and stole a bunch of my money. You can't trust anyone in this world, Jackie, except yourself. Remember that."

Jacquline nodded. She still wanted to believe that her family had protected her, but there were still some lingering doubts as to whether Jaenice had been right about Tracey and Ken, and that they had left her behind on purpose. Something inside her kept telling her the trust she thought she earned was fake, a ruse to finally get rid of her once and for all. No one was out there waiting for her; no one was out there looking for her; no one was out there listening to her —

Tracey!

"God damn," Jacquline hissed. "Why didn't I think of this before?"

"What?" Gloria propped herself up as she looked for a possible threat.

"No, it's nothing..." Jacquline couldn't think straight enough to speak and do what she needed at the same time. She took a breath and concentrated.

Communicator on.

She couldn't hear anything, which, when she thought about it, was to be expected. So she pressed her hand against her ear, hoping it might help with the sound — nothing.

"Damn it," she whispered.

"What is it?"

Jacquline looked at Gloria a bit defeated. "I have this communicator thing embedded in my ear but I have no idea if it's working or not because I can't hear a damn thing in this ear anymore."

"Do you think you might still get a message out?"

"I don't know. It's possible, unless the communicator was what shredded my eardrum."

"Might as well give it the old college try."

"I guess," Jacquline said and tapped her fingers together. "Tracey, can you hear me? Lark? Ken? Anyone come in. Are you there? I need help."

She sat still, hoping she might hear something come back. But it was all for naught. She shook her head and slumped back.

"It was worth a shot. Maybe it went out and you just can't hear them. You never know."

Jacquline didn't count on it. Jaenice was right. She was going to be there for the long haul and there wasn't anything she could do about it.

— 30 —

As the city was but a thimble in the distance, Lark stopped to lie down and catch her breath. It didn't sit well with her that no one had pursued her (or that she left Ken to be captured), and though she was less than a mile from the *Equinox*, they couldn't leave until Qah-Shekel returned anyway, so she had time to give in to the temptation of rest. She wouldn't be much help in saving Jacquline if she collapsed and died of heat stroke and exhaustion, now would she?

Lark had only been lying under the burning sun for a matter of minutes when a call came through, blasting her body to full alertness with a rush of adrenaline. She tapped her fingers together. "Jackie, is that you? Jackie?"

No one answered. She tried again, but still nothing. Lark started to wonder if Jacquline had really made the call or if it was a hallucination brought on by the heat. Whatever the case, she needed to find out.

"Qah-Shekel. Tracey. Did you hear that?"

No answer.

"Qah-Shekel. Tracey. DovenJadden. Anybody. Talk to me."

Now she was getting worried. *What the hell is going on?*

There was only one way to find out. She ran as the sun baked the back of her neck.

— 31 —

The bowels of the manufacturing plant were just that — empty, cold, and crawling with several species of rodent that fed on the accumulation of bio toxins on the walls and the floor. Ventilation units lining the top of the walls pumped contaminants into the corridors and made them reek with the bio-liquid that fueled the power cores. Lucky for Qah-Shekel, his skin filtered the toxins out and allowed him to walk through the uninhabitable tunnels with the ease of an android.

The end of the corridor was about a half a mile walk inward. There was a large steel door with a pressurized seal locking it shut. To the right was an authorization pad. It sat blank as it slept, but awoke brightly when Qah-Shekel touched the center of it. The outside was lined in a deep red and a series of codes started printing across the gel screen, disappearing off the top as they continued downward. When the text finally came to a stop, it held steady for several seconds before the screen went blank again (though it was much brighter, with a wash of opaqueness). A few seconds later, another set of text popped up with a voice-activated response that said, "Authorization code."

Qah-Shekel was amused that the voice repeating her chant several times sounded so much like Kahli. It was ironic, too, with what he was going to be doing to supply his access code. Qah-Shekel pulled another button used to disable the androids out of his pouch and placed it onto the center of the gel screen.

"Foreign object detected," the voice said. "Please remove foreign —"

Qah-Shekel swiped his wrists together before the voice finished its command. A quick spark and a flash of light caused the screen to crack and go dark. Seconds later, a dull hiss was followed by a thump and the seal on the door broke. Qah-Shekel slowly pulled it open, checking to make sure no one was waiting for him on the other side and then stole his way into the holding chamber. At first glance, there were at least a dozen android units sitting in hibernation on the walls inside the access room, but as he walked to the windows overlooking the main room, he could see hundreds of units in varying degrees of production. In the center of the circular chamber was a computer tower from which all of the units were connected.

Qah-Shekel swiftly worked his way through the maze like hallway toward the tower. Accessing the computers was a lot easier than expected, and though he couldn't read the language, he didn't have to. Much like the voice operated access panel, the tower had the capability of speech, and he understood the language enough to navigate the tower's main systems. He found a map of the facility and located where the power cores were stored before being inserted into the androids. There would be a limited amount of time from retrieving the cores to finding his way back out, so he mapped out a secondary route in case leaving the way he came turned out to be ineffective.

As he went to switch the tower back to stasis mode, the voice announced, "Trace amounts of Krylox detected. Please transport material to unit D for liquefying."

Curious, Qah-Shekel quickly brought up a hologram of unit D. It was a larger chamber with massive metal boxes and tubing that led into the adjoining room. That didn't help much, so he navigated through the system manifest for unit D until he found a source that was in some way Krylox related. The computer suddenly went into a speech that nearly pushed Qah-Shekel to his knees. Trying his best to keep himself composed, he stammered along the catwalks to the ladder that would lead to the upper testing and engineering labs, fighting the pain and the anger that was now coursing every vein in his body.

— 32 —

The halls were dark and musky, though Tracey walked through them with confidence. She didn't know where she was, or why she felt so at home, all she knew (or at least thought she knew) was that she was meant to be there. She had been searching for something at the end of the hall. The culmination of her seemingly endless quest fueled her determination to reach the unattainable goal.

Without warning, movement became possible. It wasn't a wall, not a solid one anyway, but Tracey couldn't move forward any further. Choosing to return from where she had come —

Where did she come from?

— wasn't an option, not even if she wanted to. There wasn't any way her body would respond to doing such a cruel thing. Her objective — her life —was here. If she left, there would be no coming back; there would be no second chances.

She tried to call out, but her voice was vacant, and the longer she tried, the harder it became. Exhaustion sunk in deep within her entire body, forcing her to her knees. But she didn't give up. She continued to call out for her savior, fighting hard enough to overcome the fear of breaking her knees and standing. Her lungs roasted to a brittle charcoal within her chest and her eyes pinched with searing tenderness that might have traumatized anyone else into a crippling puddle of bubbling sludge.

Anyone else... without the gem.

Green flashes slowly pulsed in the room in front of her, matching the deadening beat of Tracey's heart. But with it came the reason for her travel — the reason for her strength. Standing feet away, producing the enigmatic light, was Jacquline.

"Tracey, can you hear me?" Jacquline's voice was so hollow, it was hard to recognize. But the muffled reverberation made it clear. "Lark? Ken? Anyone come in. Are you there? I need help."

Tracey tried to call back, but the sound that came from her mouth was not her own. "Jackie, is that you? Jackie?" It gave her a warm feeling, even if she didn't recognize it. However, she wasn't willing to repeat it. Instead, she pressed her hands against the invisible barrier, prompting Jacquline to reach out for her. Jacquline's voice continued to bounce around her ears, over and over, the words overlapping to make it sound as if she was a collection of hundreds of young women calling for help at the same time. She covered her ears to try to make it stop, but that only made it worse. The voices grew louder and quickened in pace until it was no longer a series of voices, but one incredibly piercing howl. Tracey looked up to Jacquline, who stood with her mouth agape, and pounded at the wall for her to stop. She closed her eyes as the cry grew louder.

Louder. Louder...

The wall suddenly shattered. Tracey fell forward and everything went silent. She opened her eyes. The light was gone. She looked around, but with every movement, no sound was heard.

Am I deaf?

She stood. Jacquline's eyes broke through the darkness.

"I just want to sleep." The whisper pushed Tracey down the corridor and then —

— 33 —

Sentilla looked up. "Tracey?"

Tracey moaned and shifted slightly. Sentilla cautiously crawled over to her, unsure of what kind of hold the gem may still have over her. She could feel its presence — its siren call — but it was nowhere near as strong as it had been. In fact, if she wasn't mistaken, it continued to fade the closer she got to it. She felt stronger and more at peace.

"Tracey? Are you okay?"

She was about to touch her shoulder when Tracey opened her eyes. Upon acknowledging Sentilla, she took a deep breath and pressed the palm of her hand to her forehead. She quickly noticed the knife dangling from her chest and pulled it out. The wound healed fast enough, but much slower than it had before. Tracey dropped the knife and smiled graciously at Sentilla.

"Thank you."

Sentilla let out a relieved sigh and returned the smile.

Tracey shook her head. She felt she had forgotten something.

"What's wrong?" Sentilla asked.

"I don't know," Tracey whispered. "I just feel like..." She flashed a smile. "Never mind. It's probably just the effects of the gem. How are you?" Tracey's tone instantly shifted to curious whimsy with that question.

Sentilla smiled softly. "Better," she said. "Much better, actually."

Tracey nodded, her smile fixed to her face.

"How did you know?"

"I didn't." Tracey crawled back to the journals. "But we're not through. You still need more time to become fully immune."

"Why are you so adamant about helping me?" Sentilla said after a short pause.

"Weaknesses are only as strong as the weakest will. You've proven you have the strength to fight your weaknesses, now you need to follow through and conquer them."

"That doesn't really answer my question."

Tracey didn't skip a beat. "Back on Earth, I was weak because I let myself be weak. Even though I had all of this inherent power, I never knew I had it because I saw myself as a victim. After my mother disappeared, my dad fell into the depths of his own fantasies and Jacquline spiraled out of control. I felt so lost and utterly worthless. No one loved me, not the way I needed. I was on my own — alone. For a long time, I thought I was the reason for their problems, the reason my mom left. So to punish myself for that, I let others walk all over me. It got to the point where I had no control over the anger and the fear that was festering within me, so when I hit my ultimate tipping point, I had no way of controlling that anger; that power. Had I realized that it wasn't me who was driving everyone away or causing them pain, I might have been able to make friends; I might have been able to have fun and give myself a chance to explore what made me tick — to find my happiness.

"When I first met you on that transport ship, I automatically knew you were just like me. There was something inside you that you were covering up, that you were hiding from. The gem was going to tap into that core of anger and regret, and use it to seduce you. Whatever it is that you are suppressing, that something that you're not allowing yourself to accept, is fueling your fundamental weakness. But once you're able to identify that weakness and let go of it, only then will you be able to fully overcome it. Why am I adamant in helping you? Because I was just like you, Sentilla, and I don't want what happened to me to happen to you."

Sentilla took some time to let Tracey's words sink in. "What exactly happened to you?" she finally said.

"I killed someone," Tracey said. "At least, that's what I keep telling myself. I'm not sure if either one of them died, but they were seriously injured. Either way, I saw the monster I could become and there is no way I would wish that on anyone, not so long as I can help it."

"But what will becoming immune to the gem do? Even if I become desensitized to its call, I'm still going to have that so-called 'deep anger' bubbling inside me, right?"

"Until you understand what you're hiding from and deal with it, yes, of course. But by understanding how to control your weaknesses, it opens up the possibility of discovering what that is, and one day, when those feelings do finally bubble to the surface, you'll know exactly what it is and how to mend the wounds it's already made."

Sentilla chuckled and shook her head.

"What's funny?" Tracey said, also amused.

"I never thought I'd be taking advice from a kid."

"A smarter than your average kid," Tracey corrected with a wink.

"I do have to wonder if you'd be this smart without that little piece of jewelry."

Tracey contemplated the question, and then with a little bit of sarcasm, "Yeah, I think I would." This was followed by an uncontrolled laugh.

"I'm not so sure," Sentilla said, taking the answer a little too seriously. "I think you'd just be another run-of-the-mill average being with nothing special about her."

"Except for being the daughter of an alien species that no one on Earth knows about."

"Which you never would have found out about if your mother wouldn't have been taken."

"Maybe, maybe not. I'm sure she would have told us all about it someday."

"Trust me, telling someone you love that you've been lying to them their whole lives is hard to do without the circumstances that call for it."

"It's much harder to live with the lie," Tracey said.

"Maybe, but in my experience, she would have died with that secret."

"That's a confident statement."

Sentilla shrugged. "It's honest."

"That it is," Tracey said. "But it begs the question for why you would think that."

"Let's just say that I've had my share of secrets I never knew about until death opened his lips."

"You're getting closer to finding your truth."

"What truth?"

"Think about it." Tracey picked up one of the books.

Sentilla bit her lip. As she tried to understand Tracey's hidden message, the relentless tickle in her stomach beat alongside her heart as a friend, albeit, one who was doing her wrong, even as she went along with everything it asked of her. What she didn't know (or completely understand) was that with every bite of need Sentilla endured, Tracey could feel every part of it at the same time.

— 34 —

Xynia came to my domicile tonight. I hadn't left all morning, though Jaxxa Rakala did come to bring my sustenance and talk about what happened. We discussed each of the suitors and when I asked her who she felt was the best, she reminded me that it was always my choice, and that my heart would tell me who was right. I didn't like that answer, so she told me that the one who goes out of their way to seek my hand is the one I should pay attention to. At no time did I ever think it would be Xynia.

His curtsy was quite regal. He swept my hand into his, kissed it gently and offered to take a walk with me along the berrazza. I was blushed, unable to speak. Jaxxa Rakala looked quite uneasy about him, but it was not her decision, as I clearly reminded her. She agreed and did not fight my decision to accept his offer.

I'm so very happy I did. I could not have had a better conversation with anyone in the lands of the Father of the higher realm. He was generous with his thoughts as well as his ear, and he gave me all of the courtesy I could ever ask for. As it turns out, Xynia is an orphan, abandoned by his parents when he was just an infant. Without supervision, he learned quickly how to fend for himself. He was near death when a pack of Rethyens found him on an expedition to mine some type of ore that they were bound to use in mechanizations on their own planet. He was fed, given a bed and clothed. He remained with them over the course of several mining expeditions, where he assisted in extracting various minerals from distant planets before returning to Rethyen. From there, he was given a home and looked out for — protected.

I told him that Jaxxa Rakala was very much like him. That she was not my sister, but in fact was found and brought into the family with love and admiration. He was very curious about her, eager to learn about someone who had experienced life as he once had. He wished to speak with her, but I didn't want to share him. I asked for his hand in a dance around the berrazzo and we danced as graceful as any other. We then lay in each other's arms to watch the lights of the night fade into sleep. I woke in my domicile, his presence gone, but not the memory of the night, from which I had the sweetest of dreams.

* * *

Jaxxa Rakala has been wary to speak with Xynia. I tried to explain his experience, but she was adamant against seeing him. Only when I told her I was going to ask his hand in union did she finally succumb to my persistence and agree to speak with him. I was so excited; I wasted no time. I knocked upon his door, but he was gone. I searched the grounds twice over, and yet, no one could claim of his whereabouts. Why would he disappear on me? For the first time, I felt the mistake was mine, and that if I could make such a false choice with him, what is to keep me from making yet another?

I cried in Jaxxa Rakala's arms until I was so tired, my eyelids fell and would no longer lift. She stayed with me until I woke and then agreed to retrieve us breakfast. What am I to do?

* * *

Xynia returned to me last night. I thought it was a dream, but his touch was far too real. He said he retrieved a call over the night's past and had to return home to help his family. He was sorry for not telling me, but it was an emergency. When I asked if they were all right, he said his parents — those that raised him, as it were — had passed. My tears were strong enough for the both of us. He says he would like me to accompany him to their burial, which is why he returned so quickly. Jaxxa Rakala is against me going, but I think she's wrong. I have to do this; I need to understand his past, which can only strengthen the resolve of my decisions.

* * *

I have returned from the burial of Xynia's parents. It was a quiet, peaceful event in the lovely, serene mountains of his home. After the ceremony, we ate and reflected on their life and the influence they made on him. His love for them was evident. That he would care for someone so passionately was so alluring; I knew then that I could not find a better suitor to lead my land in honor. I had no other choice.

I laid with Xynia in union.

It was quite intoxicating and felt more ethereal than anything I had ever felt before. I didn't want to leave his side, but I had to return home. He did not fight it; he escorted me back. I have yet to inform father of my decision and have yet to reveal my secret to Jaxxa Rakala. I'm actually a bit frightened as to what they may say, or whether they will ridicule my decision and find disappoint in me. Father should find my decision favorable; after all, Xynia is one of the suitors he had agreed to accept into my hand. It is Jaxxa Rakala's wrath I fear the most, and an approval I don't think I could move forward without.

* * *

I haven't the nerve to tell Jaxxa Rakala what happened. I've informed father of my decision and he has planned an elegant party in my honor to announce it to our people under the ever-watchful eye of the Father of the higher realm. It should be an exciting moment for me, but it is the moment I most dread. I do not want to lose Jaxxa

Rakala as a friend, or as a sister. She has been my support for such a long time that if I don't have her favor, I am afraid I may not be able to live in happiness any longer. But when I am in Xynia's arms, I am safe; I am happy. There is no amount of thought that could pull me away from him, so if Jaxxa Rakala does not approve, I may have to severe that tie. She was right when she said it wasn't her choice to make, as it is my life that I must live. I don't want it to happen, and my tears will be evident if she chooses to abandon me, but if she cannot be happy for me, that is her choice. I will learn the outcome tonight when all is revealed.

*   *   *

My fears came true this night, a night of chaos and destruction. I haven't stopped crying since the ball, where my honor and my voice were silenced by a magic I never thought possible and the death of a friend I thought would be forever more.

Jaxxa Rakala knew an announcement was going to take place and she warned me that if it was to name Xynia as my suitor that she would have to step in and stop it by any means necessary. I tried to convince her of my love, but she couldn't accept it. She left my side for the conclusion of the day, and when the stars awoke, the ball had commenced. I thought perhaps that Jaxxa Rakala had left, had decided to seek out a new home because the sight of me and my decision were too much to bear. It hurt me greatly, but there was more pressing issues to deal with in the moment.

The event began as any other, and when the patrons had had their meal, and were thoroughly full of vibrancy and conversation, sustenance and goilus, my father stepped to his perch and brought me upon the stage. His hand in mine, he announced that I had made my decision for a suitor. Before I could say his name, Jaxxa Rakala yelled from the back of the crowd that she objected to the union and could not let it happen. Xynia stepped up to the perch and called her out, asking for the unfavorable to step forward and show herself. When she did, Xynia asked why she objected so. Jaxxa Rakala answered that she did not trust him and that his entire presence there made her weak, causing a pain in her gut reserved for the most hated of creatures. He denied this to be true, claiming that she did not know him. She quickly refuted his claim, revealing that she did, in fact, know who he was and what a madness he carried with him. Xynia instantly ordered the guards to arrest her for the blasphemous words she spoke. She could not allow such a thing and before the guards could wrap their bounds around her, they were thrown away like papyrus in the wind.

Everyone screamed in fright and scattered. Except for Jaxxa Rakala, who stood her ground. Father rushed me from the area, so I did not see much else of what transpired, but the noise and the screams and the fear that remained behind me was excruciating. I haven't left my domicile since that time. Whether either of my loves is still alive is unknown, and something I can't bear to find out. All I can think about is what Jaxxa Rakala said about Xynia, and I can't help but wonder if any of it is true. If it is, I don't know if I can ever forgive myself for falling for him with my heart. If it is not, my love of Jaxxa Rakala has been shattered beyond repair.

I am so alone.

— 35 —

The pristine glass walls hid nothing of the dozen or so laboratories and clean rooms that, when paired in conjunction, would be used as research and development facilities, testing new and improved methods for manufacturing and the production of their bounty of androids. The facility directly to Qah-Shekel's left was the only one hidden by opaque walls and could only be entered through a thick metal door with a large symbol labeling it 'Unit D'. A rectangular red light rested just above the door, signifying that it had been sealed because operations had commenced. Qah-Shekel didn't dare try and break in, even though what was inside was of utmost importance to him. He feared that if he did, he wouldn't be able to control his emotions and everything he and his crew had done to this point would be for not. No. There would be a time for retribution; this wasn't it.

He carefully examined each laboratory as he walked the cascade of hallways. Several labs were stockpiled with individual parts. Metallic skulls with lifeless eyes hung on the walls when they weren't held in testing clamps; arms and legs swung from the ceilings, while several others lay on conveyor belts and testing tables waiting for the various robotic engineers to dive in and test, repair or complete the mechanisms; chests and torsos were spread at length like an army battalion waiting for orders; piles of hair graced the majority of the space for several machines with spiked arms that wove and colored the wigs that would adorn each of the android's heads; and possibly the creepiest of them all, jars full of nails and teeth filling dozens of shelves like some serial killer's trophy room. A few other labs were dedicated to the biological testing and growth of organs, as evidenced by the tubes that encompassed a variety of fetuses, hearts, brains and kidneys. There was still no sign of the power cores.

Thinking the cores might be hidden somewhere in the walls or masked shelving units, Qah-Shekel stepped into one lab that seemed incredibly empty. The entire space came to life the moment he reached the center of the room. Holographic (and incredibly detailed) diagrams of different androids in different phases of development swarmed him. Curious, he shifted through some of the models until he came across a diagram that had two figures lying next to one another. One looked to be android while the other was organic. He pulled the image forward and a voice rang out.

"Current data insufficient for brainwave transfer. How do you wish to proceed?"

The holograms vanished as Qah-Shekel left the room. He stood absolutely still for some time as he considered the ramifications of what he had just heard. It was against nature to think such technology was possible, but here it was. It was abhorrent; nothing should live forever, especially those with emotions that can be easily corrupted. He considered what he might be able to do to stop it, but it was best he kept moving before Ken and Lark's distraction ended and everything went back to normal. He shifted his focus back to the task at hand. It didn't take much longer to find the room he was looking for. It was the only other one shielded by steel walls and an access pad. He immediately ripped the panel off the wall. After the sparks stopped flying, the door opened — *click-CHUNK.*

Qah-Shekel could hardly see through the fog generated by the extreme cold that covered almost every inch of the massive production area. He was thankful the burning cold reduced the retching smell to a minimum so he could fight the urge to escape back into the halls to thaw. On either side of him were two large vats, both with rotating spindles attached to three curved blades that kept the silvery-blue liquid from solidifying. Along the side of the vats was a hollow steel box that housed two clamps. Just above was a spindle peeking down just past the top of the box. Several long tables made of glass and steel sat in the center of the room, each one with a variety of tools, clamps, computer devices and torches. Drawers and cabinets along the edges stored pieces of metal, solder, wires and thick glass. Encased underneath in temperature-controlled cases were pairs of tanks with the necessary accelerant. A few unfinished power casings lay in stacked holders with curved legs to help house the cylindrical casings.

Toward the back of the room was where the prize was kept. Stored inside individual cooling units that fit the cylinders like a glove, separated only by thin lines of sheet metal for stabilization, were stacks of completed power cores. On each side of the glass casing was a metal attachment with several icicle-like drops touching the shimmering liquid. On the outside of the caps were eight misaligned prongs surrounded by vents that would help alleviate the heat generated by the liquid. One would be enough, but should something happen like this again, he wanted to have at least one backup. He decided four would be enough (mostly because that was what he could fit in his pack).

Before leaving the lab, Qah-Shekel opened the valves to both vats, allowing the liquid to spill out over the housing and onto the floor. It solidified almost instantly, forming a solid mass of frozen liquid that would be nearly impossible to clean without first exposing the entire room to normal temperatures. God how he wished he could be there to watch what would happen. As he slid back into the hallway, a quick glance through the glass walls ended his good mood.

He must have set off a silent alarm when tearing through the access panel (or Tracey was no longer masking him, which was a very likely option) because several androids marched through the hallways on a mission. He quickly scurried into a nearby lab that housed a variety of plant life and other organic utilities, which he figured were used to explore the capabilities of producing the organic organs he saw earlier — for that more natural feel. Then again, it could have been a way to test nutrients and medicinal properties for an extended faculty of life. Whatever the case, it gave him the cover he needed to contact his crew (a futile endeavor) and contemplate his next course of action before the androids arrived. Which wasn't long at all.

Each one held the same type of weapon as the guards he encountered at the gate and he wasn't really in the mood to find out what it did. Aiming the thumb laser at the lead android, he waited until they had all collected inside the room to fire. The weapons were sliced in half and shards from the front most android's uniforms were torn away.

"Stop! Unauthorized intruder." With a wave from the lead android's fist, the rest of the faction charged in his direction. But Qah-Shekel was too cunning for them, slinking about the vegetation like a snake in a garden. As they all clambered to detect his whereabouts, Qah-Shekel rose up and pulled the lead android's head down into the nearest plant, which immediately wrapped its vines around her and tried to sink its thick thorns into her body. It failed to do so, but was still strong enough to fight against the android's attempt at escape. Because of this, the rest of the androids flanked his position. It was only a matter of time before he would have nowhere else to run. This was his last chance. He quickly took stock of where each of the androids was and found a gap that led to the door where one of the androids still held her ground, complete with a functional weapon. Without any further hesitation, Qah-Shekel sprinted as fast as he could toward the door. The android fired a small, round puck within seconds of his exposure. Qah-Shekel deflected it with his fin and grabbed a hold of the android before she had a chance to fire another. The android remained on her feet but struggled to keep control as Qah-Shekel squeezed her hands tightly around the weapon, firing off several more pucks. One of them struck an android near the back of the greenroom. Upon contact, it lit up bright, exposed a tier of teeth that latched to her outfit and then sent a fierce electrical shock to her body. She was on the floor smoking within seconds.

Feeling his grip slipping, Qah-Shekel sliced the androids uniform with his thumb laser and popped the back plate open, tearing it off of her like a moist, juicy piece of meat from a bone. He then jammed his fin into the casing as hard as he could, cracking it just enough to start a growing web before he was thrown across the hall. He smashed through the wall on the opposite end and slid a few feet, coming to a stop at the edge of a desk. For a second, he was worried that he may have shattered the power cores in his pack, but there was no time to check. The androids returned to lockstep formation and moved forward as a collective unit. Qah-Shekel needed to run, but his legs had other plans. Getting up was not an option. Before the lead android had stepped two feet into the hall, the greenroom ignited, sending a massive shockwave throughout the facility. Fire blossomed, glass shattered, and the androids were thrown as far as the blast's intensity would allow. Qah-Shekel might have been torched to a blackened crisp had one of the android's bodies not have been thrown on top of him, soaking up the majority of the shockwave.

He pushed the body off of him and collected himself, taking a good, hard look at the wreckage. The android stirred as it rebooted its programs. Qah-Shekel didn't know what had happened, but he was not in the mood for another go-round with the surviving Betas, so he swept her weapon up and took off. Every few yards, he'd fire a puck down to the floor, lighting it up with an electrical current. When he reached the ladder leading back down into the hive bed, he tossed the weapon across the hall, shredded it with the thumb laser for good measure, and then took one last satisfying look at his destructive wake.

— 36 —

Someone tossed Ken into a large chair where his body slumped as if he were a doll with no cotton to keep its shape. Blood streaked across his face and neck like a poorly striped war paint. His wrists were quickly strapped to the arms of the chair with thin, razor-sharp wires that wanted to cut into his skin with even the slightest of movements. Not like he moved all that much, since he could barely feel his heavily bruised body.

After strapping his ankles to the legs of the chair with the same wire, a very petite hand with slick skin pulled his head back against the top of the chair. He tried to open his eyes, but one had been swollen shut and the other hung heavy. The only images he could gather were dark and blurred, flashes of softened color with hardly any definition to them. He was dizzy and wanted to pass out, but he couldn't; he wouldn't allow himself to do that — to be that weak.

"What do you want with me?" he choked out, though for him it sounded more like, "Wha-ou wahh wii ee."

A hand combed his wet hair back along his skull and a pair of lips pressed gently along the outer rim of his ear. A woman's voice said something he didn't understand (though he did recognize the voice) and then he felt a sharp pinch in the back of his ear. The pain grew increasingly excruciating as whatever pricked his ear expanded into the size of a baseball. He spit out a scream that only faded when the baseball was ripped away, taking a bit of skin with it (or so he thought). He lay back and let the tears smear the blood on his face. "Stop," he moaned with the softness of a man who had been tortured for over a year. He had no strength left to keep fighting.

"Don't worry, father," the woman said. "It's almost over." Ken's heart sank. Not only had he been able to understand her now, but her voice echoed through his mind; the lost daughter of a life unlived.

"Jacquline?" He didn't want to believe it, but he had to know.

The woman pet his cheek. "Shh, shh…" she said. "I just have a few questions to ask you. Are you here with the Tracey?"

With that one simple definite article, he was certain it couldn't be her. But he had to give it to the Beta unit for her extremely clever impersonation.

"You can stop the ruse," Ken said.

The Beta laughed softly. "Very well," she said. "I only thought it might help bring you comfort."

"The only thing that will bring me comfort is letting me go." Each word was a struggle, but he fought through his severe discomfort.

"Tell me what I want to know, and I promise you won't get hurt." The Beta slid her fingers down the side of his face as she walked around him. "Are you here with the Tracey?"

Ken rolled his head to the side. The pain in his ear was beginning to squeeze his temple, but any effort to ease the tenderness only caused the straps to prick deeper into his wrists, eventually breaking the skin. Ken hissed and brought in a breath that scratched at his throat. A line of blood dripped down the back of his hand, leaping off of the tip of his middle finger.

"Ken, you are only hurting yourself by not answering. I'll give you one last chance. Are you here with the Tracey?"

Ken remained silent, even after the cold steel of a blade gently touched his throat.

"Very well," the Beta said.

The blade sliced through his skin. He held his scream in check the best he could as blood oozed onto his shoulder. When the blade reached the center of his throat, he squeaked out, "Yes." Saliva dripped from his lips as the slick metal was pulled away. "Yes," he said softer, almost in tears. "Tracey is here."

"Is she on your ship?"

The scratch in the back of his throat was too hot to speak over if he didn't have to. Ken nodded.

"I'm sorry, Ken, but you will have to speak to answer the next question." The Beta lifted his chin up. "What is your purpose here?"

Ken took in several deep breaths and then swallowed dryly, hoping he could force the burn in his throat away. The Beta waited patiently. Finally, Ken found his voice.

"The cores," he said with little more than a breath.

"What cores?"

"The power cores," he said. "For the androids."

"What is your purpose with the power cores?"

"We need…. need to repair Rega." Ken felt like passing out. Maybe then he'd be able to forgo snitching any longer. For some reason, he couldn't.

"Thank you, Ken. You did the right thing."

"What are you going to do?" Ken said.

The Beta snickered. "It's not what I'm going to do to you, Ken. It's what you're going to do for me."

Suddenly, a loud, heavy rumble echoed from a distance. The Beta moved back. Her silence was haunting.

"What was that?" Ken said. His answer came in the form of a prick in his arm that finally sent him into the sleep he had been hoping for just minutes before.

— 37 —

Lark's lungs were on fire and her throat felt like sandpaper when she finally got back to the *Equinox*. She collapsed through the hatch to soak in the refreshing coolness, all but ready to pass out. It didn't do much to help her throat, but at least her body temperature would soon be down to a reasonable level.

When her legs finally got enough strength back, Lark closed the hatch and made her way to the nutriment hall, where she popped in the code for water and guzzled about a gallon of it before taking a breath. It didn't matter one iota if it made her sick; it was far too refreshing. She then poured some over her body — which shook uncontrollably and felt like rubber — to wash away the sweat. A twenty-mile run didn't even make her as sticky as she felt right now. It wasn't until she could no longer feel the beat in her chest that she developed strength enough to head for command.

Halfway there, DovenJadden came barreling around one of the corridors. Along with her normal gun, she carried two smaller pistol-type weapons on her legs and a large knife across her back.

"DovenJadden," Lark chirped. She grabbed DovenJadden's arm and pulled her back when she didn't stop. "Where are you going?"

DovenJadden purred furiously, but Lark wouldn't let go of her. Finally, she brought her hands together in fists and then spread them apart as she opened her fingers.

"I don't... was there an explosion?" Lark said.

This time, DovenJadden ripped Lark's hand away and pushed her back. She purred and pointed, and then ran away.

Lark stood, contemplating whether she should run after her. In the end, it was best if she left her alone. She wouldn't get any answers out of her anyway. There was one other person who would be able to tell her what the hell was going on. She just hoped she was still alive.

— 38 —

It's the day I've been dreading.

Jaxxa Rakala warned me that I might have to one day leave my home, my father and my people to venture off into hiding. I didn't believe her at the time, but now it seems she was right. I wish I would have believed her. It would have given me more time to cherish that which I would inevitably have to leave. Instead, I've taken my loved ones for granted and it's far too late to make amends for some of the things I might have said or done to those I will never again see. It breaks my heart.

Especially in regards to father. He has been crushed by the idea of having to send me away. But with all that has happened in the last cycle, it's a necessary action. It's the only thing that will keep me protected. Jaxxa Rakala's power has been realized in the gem she gifted me, and according to her, if it were to fall into the wrong hands, the entire universe might fall into chaos. Trying to hide it would do no good, so the only thing I can do is find a home for which has no connection to our world, or any other, within the galaxy of Dominion. I must seek out another world, a quiet world, developed, but blind to the war; blind to the universe around them; blind to the knowledge that there is life outside of their own. If I can find such a world, I will happily live there for the rest of my life, so long as it doesn't take a lifetime to find it. Loneliness may find its way into my heart, but what else am I to do? I may have been a fool to promise my sister that I would protect this beautiful piece of jewelry for her, but I am not about to break my word. Not after all she has done for me.

I can feel her in the gem. I know this may sound weird, but her presence is still very much alive within it, and it warms my heart to the most extreme blessing. Sometimes I feel that if I did go against my word, the gem would strike me dead without hesitation, and then somehow hide itself from any prying eyes who wish to acquire it. Maybe it's the gem filling my head with such thoughts, as whenever I remove it, I become rather ill and can barely breathe. The moment I put it on, the gem became connected to me in ways I could never understand, but there is a love and a charm and an affection with it that is infectious. It's a drug that I, nor anyone else it seems, will ever be able to let go of.

Since first putting it on, there have been several individuals looking to cut my throat. It's why I have locked myself away in the cells, to keep myself and the gem safe until the launch. It's actually been a blessing in disguise. It's given me a chance to become familiar with being alone, even though I know, somehow, that will never be the case, for even though it may only be an object, the gem — my sister — will always be there to keep me company. She will keep my mind active and free of mindless ravings, and protect me from the evils of dark space.

All I can do now is wait. The launch will occur at the peak of the night sky to keep from adding any focus to my destination. It is to be a coordinated launch, sending me along in the trail of a passing comet that, once clear of the planet, will guide me along a course through all of space and beyond. It still rather frightens me to think of the pod and its body forming mechanics, but with access to a holographic system from which I can navigate and discern between the plethora of new homes, at the very least, I will be able to occupy my mind, though it has always felt to be an impossible task. I'll be looking for worlds not currently in the universal databank, which means that it's either so far out that I never reach it, or those who have discovered them in the past died before they were able to register its coordinates and galactic quadrants (or they decided it full of riches they wished to keep hidden, and might just kill whomever decides to encroach on their bounty). How far must I travel before I locate an unregistered planet that is both habitable and worth exploring without danger? How far must I travel before I reach farther than anyone else has gone? I am not afraid of running out of fuel or energy, not after having acquired two Darsinnian cells from Rega-One; my fear lies in not having the means of returning, should Jaxxa Rakala one day wish to retrieve her precious cargo. If that day would ever come, and I am free to return to her and my people, without an interstellar hyper unit, I will be stranded.

But that is also what has excited me so. There are so many questions with very little answers and to be able to travel through the unknown like this is something I have dreamed about in secret, and something I never felt would ever be possible. And now it is. And now, I can see the future.

* * *

This will be my final entry. With it, I would like to say how much I will miss my home and all of those who have loved me over my time on this planet. For all of my friends, I wish upon you the deepest wishes of companionship and achievement. It is in these that you will find life, and with it, respect and honor. Do not squander these things, as they are rare and need to be nourished if the hand from our Father of the higher realm is to gift you with his heart. Make certain that you give more than you receive and always remember to be honest with yourself and never forget me. I may never come back, but I am always here so long as you hold me close.

But especially to father, who has shed more than enough tears already over my departure. I want that you should let your last tear fall and heed these words: I may be gone, but I am not dead. You are my rock and my voice, and I will never forget you. With my departure comes a new reason for life and the chance to make things right. Give your people the love you have reserved for me, and use that to choose your successor wisely, honestly and respectfully. Do not let any man take advantage of your kindness, but do not show greed among them. Your word is strong, and you will always be, so long as it is conducted with honor, respect and the command of faith. I trust that you are doing what's best for me, so trust too, that I am doing the best for you. By leaving, I am giving you and our land the chance it deserves to flourish. Trust that the Father of the higher realm has chosen me for a much grander plan, and that he will protect you as he is protecting me.

This isn't the end. It is the beginning of a life unknown.

Farewell, dear father. I will miss you as I have missed mother.

Love is our path; life is our destiny.

— 39 —

Tracey set the book down. Sentilla sat next to her with her head rolled back against the wall, as quiet and calm as a child getting ready to take a nap. After a moment, she rested her hand on Tracey's leg. "Your mother sounds like a wonderful creature."

"She was rare," Tracey said.

"I always felt the same about my mother." Sentilla swept the medallion dangling around her neck into her hand and peered at it with longing.

"Tell me about her."

Sentilla smiled. "I wish I could. What I remember of her is quite foggy."

"Please try," Tracey urged, sliding a little closer.

"This was hers," she said as she handed Tracey the medallion. Tracey had always been aware of it but never had the chance to ever see it up close. The centerpiece looked like a raven, or some other similar exotic bird resting on the bud of a flower wrapped in the fingers of the vines that formed the outer edge. Laced across the topmost portion, just above the head of the raven, was a string of tiny beads that fell loosely across the centerpiece, forming a home at the bottom. On the sides were two curved spikes that accentuated the fierce, warrior appeal of the raven, but were etched with a lovely floral pattern highlighting the serenity of the bud.

"It's beautiful." Tracey handed the medallion back to Sentilla, who briefly admired it once more.

"She gave it to me as a gift the day she said she had nothing left to teach me about piloting the *Equinox*. She said it was a symbol of elegant victory, that when worn, represented the strength of mind to think in the moment, the tranquility of peace to stay calm in the face of fear, and the tenacity to do what was needed. It's a reminder of who my mother was and what I will always strive to be."

"That's really sweet."

Sentilla chuckled. "She could be quite the stern hand as well. I remember this one time we were on an expedition on Hasten-Jackai, before it was stripped of all its minerals. I remained on the ship as my mother went out to scout the parameter, and as per usual, she remained close as the scouting party went out in search of some minerals that could be used in several different space flight and weaponized acid technologies. I didn't much care for any of that; I was just looking to have some fun. So even though we weren't supposed to, some of us kids started running around the ship. We eventually found our way to command, and though it was against the rules for us to step foot inside without an aged individual, one of my friends dared me to anyway. We were having so much fun, I didn't think it would do much harm. I had been in command plenty with my mother, so I knew what the rules were, you know, what I could touch, what was dangerous, that kind of thing. But no one else had ever had a chance to see it, so I said I'd do it if they came with me. I didn't have to ask them twice. I felt so much like the queen of all things important explaining everything to them and I got a little too carried away in my need to impress them. So when they refused to believe I knew anything about flying the ship, I had to prove them wrong."

Tracey was smiling brightly. "I can imagine what happened next," she said.

"You and me both. I jumped in that pilot chair and lit up the holocontrols like a seasoned pro. Before I knew it, though, I had accidentally switched on the outer engines. The ship took off like a rocket, tearing across that planet like nothing you've ever seen before. Let me tell you, by the time I got it stopped, I'd made my mark, both on the planet and the ship, which I pretty much destroyed after striking a mountain. Not enough to keep it from flying, but enough that we would eventually have to use up the majority of our mineral find to repair.

"My friends left command faster than lightning seven and eventually ratted me out as the instigator of the whole thing. It was their word against mine, and since I was the only one who actually knew how to ignite the engines, I took the heat. My mother was so upset I grew some three inches before I was even allowed in command again. I also received a nice red whooping and I had to tell the captain what I had done, apologize, help in the repairs and clean the entire ship from top to bottom three times. It was excruciating."

"She sounds like a good parent," Tracey said.

"She was. It still didn't keep me from hating her for a long time afterward. It kills me that I wasn't able to reconcile sooner; I was only starting to forgive her when she died."

"You shouldn't be so hard on yourself. You were just a kid."

"I know, and in retrospect, the punishment wasn't really a punishment at all. It felt like one as a kid, but what it really did was give me the opportunity to learn every aspect of the ship. I learned more in that time than I could ever have learned otherwise, and it really did help me understand how to control the ship with the delicacy it deserved. It was a lesson she felt I needed, and I respect that punishment more every day."

"If only you could have said that to her."

Sentilla nodded, trying to hide her tears with a smile.

"You don't have to hide your tears from me," Tracey said, leaning in to wipe her thumb across Sentilla's cheek. "They're a symbol of your love. You should never feel guilty for that."

Sentilla hugged Tracey, completely unaware that the gem was touching her skin. When she let go, she felt more connected to Tracey than she did to her jewelry.

"It's rather quite amazing," Sentilla said.

"What is?"

"That something so powerfully attracted to an individual's deepest fears and aggressions could also emit so much love."

Tracey smiled brightly. "The gem only attracts that which is dominant in the soul. You are starting to find your forgiveness. So is the gem."

Sentilla huffed a laugh.

"It's a very sweet sentiment," Lark said. Both Sentilla and Tracey looked to her.

Tracey stood. "You're back. Where's my dad?"

Lark looked away, afraid to tell her what happened. But what was the point? Tracey probably already knew. "The Regans took him."

"What about Qah-Shekel?" Sentilla asked.

"I don't know. I wasn't able to raise him on the comms after the Betas stopped chasing us."

"The Betas stopped chasing you?" Tracey said, highly inquisitively. "When?"

"I don't know... just before the Regans came after us, I guess."

Tracey turned her head down, her brain going a mile a minute. She whispered Lark's answer to herself.

"That's not why I'm here. I need to know what kind of range these comm buds have."

Tracey looked back to Lark oddly. "Not far. Maybe a few thousand kilometers."

"I thought so." Lark looked disappointed and a bit worried. "So there would be no way I could have heard Jacquline if she called out for help?"

Tracey giggled. "No. Not unless she was..." Tracey's eyes were wide with excitement.

"On the planet," Lark and Tracey said in unison.

"Do you even think that's possible?" Lark continued.

Tracey bit her upper lip. Again, her thoughts were spinning faster than a dreidel at hyper speed.

"How long ago did you hear her?"

"Not long. I thought maybe it was the heat playing games with me. Why else would I be the only one that heard it?"

"There's quite a few reasons for that. If she's here, we need to find her."

"What about the Beta units?" Sentilla said.

"Apparently, they're not much of a threat anymore. If they were they would have already swarmed the ship. Someone is keeping them from attacking and I think I know who it is." Tracey brought down the cell's shield.

"Where are you going?" Sentilla said.

"To talk to DovenJadden."

"You can't," Lark said. "She's gone."

Tracey stopped cold. "Where did she go?"

"To help Qah-Shekel, I suppose. She mentioned some kind of explosion."

Tracey pursed her lips together so tight, they turned white. "DovenJadden," she finally said. "Come in. Talk to me."

"I can't hear you," Lark said.

Tracey closed her eyes. A soft glow from the gem slowly pulsated. When it stopped, Tracey tapped her fingers together. "DovenJadden, respond."

Lark was shocked, a little amused and a bit weirded out. *Did the gem just repair her damn comm bud?*

Tracey growled slightly when DovenJadden once again failed to respond.

"Jaxxa Rakala, what's wrong?" Both Tracey and Lark sighed a bit in relief at Qah-Shekel's voice.

"Qah-Shekel, what happened?" Tracey said. "Lark said there was an explosion?"

"Nothing to worry about. I'll be back to the ship shortly."

"Keep an eye out for DovenJadden. She went to go find you but isn't answering her comm."

"I will. Has Lark prepped the ship for takeoff?"

"We can't leave," Lark said sharply. "Ken was taken and we believe Jacquline may be on the planet."

There was silence. Lark figured he was contemplating his next move, but with the way the comms had been operating as of late…

"The Regans are keeping the Betas at bay," Tracey said. "We should be fine for now."

Another long silence, and then, "Prep the ship."

"But Qah-Shekel —"

"We'll wake Kahli before going anywhere. But I want to make sure we're ready if and when the karlic begins to fly."

Lark cracked a smile. She was still getting used to hearing him swear.

"You heard him," Tracey said.

"I want to help," Sentilla said.

"You're not ready."

"To hell I'm not. I haven't tried to kill you since you woke up. I'm fine."

"Really? How many fingers am I holding up?" (Lark huffed slightly when she noticed Tracey wasn't holding any fingers up.)

Sentilla growled slightly. "What does that matter? I can fly this baby blindfolded. You can't keep me prisoner on my own damn ship."

Tracey took a breath to fight the discomfort of the gem reacting to her growing anger.

"No. You aren't ready. We need more time."

Sentilla took in a few deep and angry breaths of her own, desperately wanting to wrap her hands around Tracey's throat. But she could feel the gem eating away at her progress. Tracey was right; she wasn't quite ready. She planted her head in her arms and slowly steadied her breathing, focusing on resisting the gem's tightening grasp.

"Get the ship prepped and let me know when Qah-Shekel returns," Tracey said to Lark, who was about to claim that she needed Sentilla to make sure she was doing everything correctly. But Tracey would be able to see right through that lie, so she nodded her agreement. Tracey accepted and walked back into the cell. She retrieved a journal before sitting next to Sentilla so that their shoulders almost touched.

Lark admired how close they had gotten in such a short amount of time, especially after what had happened between them. As much as she tried, she couldn't fathom ever having reconciled with her father in that way. All she could see was him sitting in front of her, ready to slap her if she even blinked — and probably even if she didn't, just for the fun of it. To forgive him would be as likely as moving a mountain, but to see Sentilla smile as Tracey read a passage from the journal gave her hope that even if it might not be in person, perhaps one day she would in fact be able to finally say,

"I forgive you."

— 40 —

Qah-Shekel sprinted up to the *Equinox* and stopped just before entering the hatch. He peered out at the desert, searching, thinking... wondering.

"Lark. I've returned. Meet me in medical."

It was another few heartbeats before Qah-Shekel stole his way into the ship.

— 41 —

Lark was in medical without even realizing she had run the entire course of the ship. She hadn't even realized she was breathing hard until she opened her mouth and was only able to push out incoherent syllables under puffs of air. She rested her hands on the medical bed and held her chin to her chest as she focused on slowing her breaths. Qah-Shekel was busy shutting down the rejuvenation chamber anyway, which gave her the time she needed to regain her ability to speak. "You got them?"

Qah-Shekel pointed to the pack on the floor at her feet. She reached in and removed one of the cores, fascinated by the intricacy of the craftsmanship. It never ceased to amaze her how much she continued to be amazed.

"Help me," Qah-Shekel said as the glass cover retracted into the bed. The smoke that wafted from within dissipated quickly against the touch of the air.

Lark set the power core at the edge of the bed and grabbed Kahli's legs. "What about DovenJadden?" she said, struggling to carry Kahli across the room. It seemed to take more out of her than running through the desert. "Is she back on the ship?"

Qah-Shekel didn't answer as they laid Kahli on the table. He set her back plate on the desk. For the most part, the rejuvenation chamber had concealed the smell, but it was slowly becoming prominent again. Qah-Shekel didn't seem to notice as he opened a compartment in the wall that looked like a linen closet. He grabbed a couple of smaller rags and tossed them to Lark. "Clean her."

At first, Lark wasn't sure how the cloths would do any good. They were silky smooth without even as much as a visible fiber. But the second she lowered the cloth to the oil, it soaked up the liquid and, for lack of a better word, cleansed the fabric; there weren't any remnants of the oil left on the cloth when she examined it. *Good thing Jacks isn't here*, she thought with a smile. *She'd want to sell this shit on eBay.*

It didn't take long at all for Lark to finish her task, which included removing all scorch mark residue. With all of the pieces looking good as new, it gave her a chance to examine them in more detail. They shimmered in a coat of silver that looked on the face to be some type of steal (or a metal in close relation to such), but which sparkled like glittered puff paint. Nothing looked to be connected by any type of wire, though she did notice some thin string that felt like extra-strength fishing wire — and gave her a small paper cut with just the lightest of touches — looped around several pieces with small, screw-like grooves that were interconnected to some of the larger mechanics. The spine was also incredibly detailed, looking much like silver-plated bone fragments, all connected with some type of polyelixer. There were no screws or bolts or washers or rivets or anything of the sort anywhere she could see.

What excited her most, though, was the anatomy of the organs. They looked as real as she could tell, but they had to have been synthesized; how else would they be functioning without having to actually function. Then again, unless there was some sort of liquid inside the lining of the organs that helped break down the elements and dissolve them, Lark wasn't sure if they even actually did anything, since there was no way of extracting waste as far as she could tell. That was going to have to be a conversation she and Kahli would need to have when the android was back to full functioning parameters.

During Lark's mini-examination, Qah-Shekel had been conducting his own inspection on the compartment that would eventually hold Kahli's new power core. He had retrieved a small square device with a couple of wires dangling off the top, clipped at the end with a brass hook. He tapped the hooks to the top of the compartment, causing a series of sparks to jump off the ends. Lark flinched like a little girl the first time it happened, but she was so engrossed in Kahli's mechanics she didn't notice that the same test on the bottom of the device didn't produce the same results — not until Qah-Shekel swore lightly under his breath and handed her the device.

"Hold this. I need to fix the containment." Qah-Shekel grabbed another square tool, this one with four long tacks on each corner. He attached the box to the bottom of the compartment and then hit the center of the square. The edges immediately glowed a light blue and projected a hologram above it, magnifying the container's mechanics by at least a hundred times. It was like looking at a diode reduced to two hundred times its normal size. She could now see the requisite parts — transistors, resisters, oscillators and capacitors mixed with some components she wasn't familiar with — all packaged on a circuit board the size of a molecule.

"There," she said, pointing to one of the terminals of a transistor that had been blackened and cut from the solder. Qah-Shekel pulled the focus on the hologram to the transistor and then swung his hand upward from the bottom of the hologram, bringing up a board of information. After typing in a series of commands, a thin laser that Lark couldn't see with the naked eye but was clearly visible in the hologram fired at the transistor from the center of the square. It stayed focused on one spot for quite some time, slowly melting the solder before splitting into several different beams and reconstructing the terminal. Once completed, the laser re-soldered it into place. Qah-Shekel shut the whole thing down with a touch to the center of the box. He removed it from the power core and hooked the electrical test cables to the container.

Spark.

With that, Qah-Shekel grabbed the power core from the table and gently set the bottom half into the compartment. With even more caution, he set the top edge of the power core on the other side and waited until the top of the compartment contracted slightly, allowing the edge to slide in easily. Once the mechanisms had been fully embedded in place, the compartment secured the core and Kahli's entire body lit up, the fishing lines spilling across her body like a blue river of electricity.

"We have life," Lark mused.

Qah-Shekel ignored her comment as he covered the glory with Kahli's back panel. "Push," he said and together, he and Lark held each end of the panel down as it locked itself in place. Qah-Shekel then easily turned Kahli onto her back.

"She isn't awake," Lark said, surprised that she hadn't already jumped off the table to begin work on rescuing Ken and Jacquline.

"It will take time for her systems to fully charge," Qah-Shekel said.

"How much time?"

Qah-Shekel looked at Lark. He was just as concerned as she was.

— 42 —

Bear with me; this is my first entry. It feels silly to be doing this, but a friend seemed quite adamant in keeping me honest and true to myself. It's not that I haven't kept a journal before, but that was simply dictating my thoughts to the framework and storing them in the city's memorybots. It's easy and reliable, however, my friend insists that I place my thoughts down this way instead. She claims we can't rely on the framework to keep such crucial information protected. The framework, after all, is only a machine; if it were to fail, all of our history would be lost. Personally, I don't ever see that happening; the framework is the most sophisticated piece of intelligence I have ever encountered. But my friend won't shut up about it, so I will oblige, if only to get her off my back. Besides, this could be fun. I've already learned an archaic method of crafting the tool to put letter to papyrus as well as turning the papyrus into a tomb of knowledge, bound by the reliten plant for safe harbor. Not only was it fun, but it gave me a chance to get to know her better and learn more about her. She is such a nice, dear child; I have grown quite fond of her.

I guess I should begin with her. I have already dictated this portion of my thoughts to the framework, but I feel it best to reiterate here in case she is correct and the framework does one day fail. At least then the information about why she is so incredibly special will remain intact in at least one form for future generations to discover. Not because she is different in any way, or because she comes from a different planet than ours (which I mistakenly thought was one of our neighbors, Rega-One, which it has been well documented is where we ourselves have been descended), but because she appeared one day like a gift from the Father of the higher realm. As far as I know, she wasn't born at all. She appeared from the light cast of the star's influence over the garden of the jewels. One second, all was normal; the next, she was there, like a sprite from the netherworld of magic and mystery. Which is why I have dubbed her Jaxxa Rakala, or as it has been translated, "Daughter of the Gems."

No one believed me when I told them what I saw, not even father. He claimed that I told wild stories, and that I should simply keep my dreams to myself. After that, I didn't tell anyone about what I know I saw, all the while tending to my new friend, who remained sick with fever. Occasionally, someone would ask about my story, and I would say it was just that — a young girl's imagination run wild. They would laugh and spread the tall-tale to anyone who would listen, including young children as they turned in for rest, presenting it as an allegory for a variety of different lessons. The one I liked most was the one where the child came to me to grant me three wishes, of which I would spoil two and find redemption in the third by granting the child love.

It started to become a habit to tell anyone who visited that she was a sick friend from Rega-One who needed our tending because it was unsafe to travel until she was once again well. But she isn't ordinary in the least, which is what I love about her the most. There is something about her — the way she smells, the way she breaths, the way she sleeps — that signifies she will change everything for us; change the way we understand the world, and ourselves. Father says she's dangerous, but I don't see it; all I see is a love that is willing to help us when real danger arises. When that might be, I don't know, but she is not against us as he so adamantly believes.

That idea was reinforced when she finally woke up. She wasn't afraid of me at all. She embraced me with open arms and even cried for me. When I asked her why, she was hesitant to answer, but I will eventually learn the truth. When that might be, I am unaware, but it's her story to tell, and when she is ready, I am certain she will be honest and free in her words. Privacy is key to freedom; I will not take that away from her.

Father, on the other hand, wishes to find out who she is immediately. I have stalled him as much as I can, but he is ready to lynch her if he doesn't learn the truth soon. I continue to try and explain to him that she is a friend, and that she does not wish us any harm, but he is so stone-headed, he cannot see beyond his own ideas. He cannot believe that the Father of the higher realm would ever send a messenger, let alone one to me. He only believes that the Father himself will return to save us all from destruction, not some silly girl. If this were a sign of things to come, then it is in the evil of the Rhinehearted that she has been sent, and unless she can convince him otherwise, with the powers of the Father and the higher realm, she will be killed for her blasphemy. I will do everything in my power to make sure that does not come to pass, but it will be a hard fought road. Even if that means sacrificing myself, the last heir of our Father's land. Father will not allow that under any circumstances, so Jaxxa Rakala, for the time being, will remain safe.

I just hope I'm right, and that I'm not leading us down the road to our own destruction.

— 43 —

Sentilla smiled. "That's always the hardest part."

"Sacrificing yourself for what you believe in?" Tracey said.

"No. Doing what you think is right when everyone else believes it's wrong, and not knowing if the whole thing will eventually blow up in your face."

Tracey nodded. "Have you ever been in a situation like that?"

"Not that I can recall. But I know Qah-Shekel has."

"It's what makes him a strong leader."

"I suppose. But I've seen what making the wrong decision has done to him. I don't know if I'd ever be strong enough to keep fighting after a choice I made went so horribly wrong, with as much death as he's had to endure."

"You have to believe it's ultimately not your fault. All of your choices affect everyone around you whether you realize it or not. Sometimes, they don't work out the way you expect, but that's the nature of the universe."

Sentilla chuckled lightly. "Yeah, you're probably right."

"All we can do when something doesn't go according to plan is find a way to make it right."

"That's what my mother would have said."

"Mine, too." Tracey rubbed Sentilla's knee. "And it's especially true about yourself. Guilt will eventually kill you if you let it fester for too long. Only when you can let it go can you truly be free."

The two remained silent for some time, soaking in their company.

"I was the one who did it," Sentilla said softly, breaking the silence. "I killed her."

Tracey took a moment to let the words sink in before asking, "Who did you kill?" — even though she already knew the answer.

"The crew had just collected a bunch of specimens from this planet a few hundred light years from Trynoruus that had never been explored, and the things they were bringing back were some exotic shit. Qah-Shekel and I wanted to take a closer look, but everything had been locked up in medical, for which we were forbidden, of course, since we were still pretty young. But we had to see some of the stuff up close, so after we landed on Trynoruus and the majority of the crew had gone to sow their oats, we snuck our way into medical. It was so wild and scary and exciting. My hands shook like crazy. Qah-Shekel was so composed, he kept trying to calm me down. A lot of the specimens were in jars and I became mesmerized by this one in particular. It almost glowed sitting there in the purple haze. I can still remember that magic yellow color with that little stick dashing about the liquid. I couldn't help but reach up and bring it in close, feel its presence against my skin. Qah-Shekel told me to put it back, but I was so lost in this thing, I didn't hear him. When he grabbed my shoulder to get my attention, I got startled and dropped the jar. It shattered with the sharpest of breaks. We tried to find something to clean it up, but the energy bleeder soaked its way into the floor before we even realized it was anything but a liquid. It infiltrated the systems so fast, we barely got back to our chambers before the entire ship shut down. It took the crew forever to clean every last bit of the bleeder from the systems, even with the Trysian's help, which at the time was pretty limited. I didn't know it was because of the war that was raging between worlds, and because of me, we were caught right in the middle of it with no way out. Before the ship was fully functional, a band of Jeshikes raided the ship and killed —" Sentilla had to stop. The lump in her throat was too big.

"You didn't do anything wrong," Tracey said.

"I keep thinking if I had just said something, if I had just told my mother what I had done, that we could have avoided the whole thing."

"It wasn't your fault there was a war going on."

"But it was my decision to go to medical. It was my fault we were stranded in the first place. It was *my* fault."

Tracey set her hand on Sentilla's shoulder and looked her directly in the eye. "Listen to me. What happened was an accident. You had no control over the events that happened because of it. Nothing you could have done would have changed anything."

"I should have followed the rules."

"It's only out of curiosity that change happens. Without it, life would cease to evolve."

Sentilla wouldn't allow her grief to get the best of her.

"Where would we be now if you hadn't been curious?"

"With my mother. My friends."

"And what would you have missed out on in the process?"

Now Sentilla couldn't resist. She pressed her hand to her mouth and let her emotions flow.

Tracey smiled as the gem filled her with liberation. She set her hand to Sentilla's cheek and kissed her temple, then ran to the barrier and flashed it off. Sentilla wasn't sure if she should get up and make a run for it or stay where she was. For some reason, she almost feared leaving. She sucked in a few scattered breaths, wiped her eyes and looked to Tracey, who brought up a holographic window on the wall just outside of the cell to run through a series of programs.

"What are you doing?"

"What do you know about DovenJadden?"

"Not a whole lot. I mean, except for her ability with weapons and her occasional temper, she's pretty reserved and quiet. Why?"

Tracey continued her search. Finally, she said, "Qah-Shekel. Lark. I need to see you at the cells."

"Why? What's wrong? Did something happen —"

"No questions. Come. Now."

Tracey buzzed through a few different systems and then brought up a second screen to start scanning through it as well. Sentilla stood to get a closer (and much clearer) look at what she was doing.

"What is that?" Sentilla asked.

"Something's been bothering me ever since Lark got back. I'm cross-checking some of the systems to see if I can find..." Tracey stopped running her hands across the screen and enlarged one of the boxes of text to fill it. She scrolled through the information the box contained, flipped open a fresh window on the second screen and tossed the info from one to the other. A series of codes started running across the text. Tracey watched intently as symbols and letters flashed through one another.

"Sentilla," Qah-Shekel said with relief. "You're okay."

Upon seeing Qah-Shekel, Sentilla embraced him without even realizing it. When they finally let go, their eyes said everything they needed to hear.

"Does this mean she's cured?" Lark said.

Tracey flashed a look at Lark with the slightest of grins.

"What's all this?"

"We all need to turn off our communication buds."

"What for?" Qah-Shekel said. His arms never left Sentilla.

"I've been thinking about what you said," Tracey said. "About the Betas and the Regans. It didn't make sense to me that they would stop their pursuit unless someone specifically gave them an order. Then that whole thing with DovenJadden…"

"You think DovenJadden had something to do with that?"

"I wasn't sure, so I ran some diagnostics and found this series of coded messages sent recently to someone on the planet. I'm looking for additional messages that include the same pattern, but if I'm right —"

"Then that bitch has been spying on us this whole time?" Lark snapped.

"Easy now," Qah-Shekel said. "We don't know anything."

"But if I'm right," Tracey said, "we can't risk keeping her in our heads."

"Which is why we need to turn off the comms," Lark said.

Tracey nodded, her attention glued to the translation key and running through other messaging programs.

"But wait," Sentilla said. "If DovenJadden was working with someone on the planet, presumably to kill us all, why would she keep the Betas from attacking?"

"She wants to draw me out." Tracey pointed to one of the messages that had been translated:

The child is on board but has locked herself away.

Will figure out a way to get her to you.

"Son of a bitch," Lark said under her breath. She turned to Qah-Shekel, and though it was clear he didn't want to give up his only source of communication — or give up on DovenJadden so quickly — the evidence was enough to warrant precaution. He nodded, and they both shut their communications down.

"I think I should go after her."

"You can't," Lark said. "That's exactly what she wants."

"I know. But as long as I'm out there, presumably she won't attack the rest of you."

"No." Lark was adamant. "I don't care what she wants. I won't let her add you to her collection. If we're going to go after her, we do it as a team." She looked at everyone. "All of us."

"I agree," Qah-Shekel said and then turned to Sentilla. "But you need rest. You've been through a lot."

"I'm ready."

"I don't care. Kahli will be up and running soon. When she is, Lark and I will go after everyone."

"Including Ken?" Lark said.

"And Jacquline," Tracey added.

"If time permits," Qah-Shekel said. "You and Jaxxa Rakala will guard the ship in case the Regans change their minds."

Sentilla was clearly upset. Qah-Shekel took her face in his hands. "I will feel better if you were here with her. Please do this. For me."

She didn't want to, but she agreed by squeezing his hand and kissing him gently.

Qah-Shekel rested his forehead on hers. "Thank you." He then turned back to Lark. "Everyone should get some rest."

"I'm going to stay here and see if I can't decipher more of these messages," Tracey said, "Maybe I can find out who she's been sending them to."

Lark squeezed her shoulder and nodded at Qah-Shekel before leaving. Qah-Shekel and Sentilla followed shortly after, hand-in-hand, shoulder-to-shoulder, heart-to-heart.

— 44 —

Gloria was the first thing Jacquline saw when she woke up and she was happy it was. She rubbed her eyes and stretched her neck. Sleeping on this floor wasn't doing anything for her body.

"Have a nice nap?" Gloria said with a delicate smile.

Jacquline sat against the wall. "As good as you might expect." That was when she finally noticed the extra body in the room. She perked up a bit, recognizing him almost immediately. "Dad?"

She crawled to him, repeatedly calling out for him. Gloria was quick to stop her. The struggle to get past her was fierce. Jacquline's forehead struck Gloria in the jaw, cutting them both.

"Jacquline, calm down," Gloria said.

"Let go of me. I want to see him."

"Not like this," Gloria insisted and sunk her nails into the back of Jacquline's neck (which she would always do to calm Jacquline down when she was a kid).

Jacquline let out a whimpered scream and slid back. She felt blood dripping down her neck. "What the hell, mom?"

"Your dad's been severely beaten, Jackie, and he's been sedated."

"So what? You have no right to keep me from him." Jacquline moved forward slightly, but Gloria was insistent about keeping her distance.

"Knowing your dad, he may be quite aggressive when he wakes up. I'd rather you not be sitting right next to him when that happens."

Jacquline saw the concern on Gloria's face. And though seeing Ken once again enhanced her hope for a possible rescue, thinking back on it, Gloria was probably right. She slid against the wall but kept her eyes glued to her father. She pressed her hand to her forehead, finally recognizing the pain.

Gloria, satisfied that Jacquline accepted her premise, spit out a bit of blood and checked for the gash on the inside of her lower lip. "That's one mighty head-butt you got there."

Jacquline didn't want to, but she chortled anyway. "Sorry," she said.

Gloria smiled and leaned back. For some reason, she couldn't help but laugh. Neither could Jacquline. The moment was just ripe for a good release of tension. When the two finally brought their emotion under control, Gloria stared at Ken. From what Jacquline could tell, there still seemed to be an inkling of love there, hidden by a lot of pain and torture.

"What happened between you two?" Jacquline asked.

Without turning away from him, Gloria said, "We drifted apart."

"Don't give me that bullshit response, mom. Something else happened. I'm not some kid anymore. Tell me the truth."

Gloria looked at Jacquline. It was time. "Your father did a lot of terrible things, Jacquline. Never in front of you, of course. He could never hurt his little girl. But with me..." Gloria's eyes glazed over with moisture.

"What happened?" Jacquline insisted.

"Your father was a narcissistic, wandering bastard."

Those words struck Jacquline hard.

"I'm sorry," Gloria said.

Jacquline shook her head. "No, you're right. He may not have ever wanted to hurt his little girl, but he sure as hell couldn't care less about his juvenile delinquent."

"Did he hurt you?"

"Not physically," Jacquline said, and that all but ended that part of the conversation.

Gloria nodded slightly. "Ken was always more concerned about his life, his job, his ideas. He never took anyone else's feelings into consideration. It was all about control for him. That and his need to be recognized, to be liked — to be appreciated."

"To be loved," Jacquline added.

Gloria chuckled. "He absolutely loved to be loved," she said. "It's probably what started our decline."

"What do you mean?"

"He had a lot of mistresses on the side that he would dance with when I shut him out. Of course, the reason I shut him out in the first place was because of the mistresses, so I guess the whole thing was a lose-lose for me. It's when I started confronting him about it that it started getting really bad."

"How so?"

"He thought I should be a loyal wife — a doting wife. One who lets her man do whatever it is he wants and then continue to love him and cherish him and be submissive to him. I asked him once what he would do if I cheated on him. You know what he said?"

Jacquline shook her head. It was hard to hear this, but funnily enough, it made a lot of sense.

"He said he'd teach me how to be a better wife and make sure I never did anything like that again. I looked him straight in the eye and said, 'How about I make sure you never do it again,' and squeezed his balls so tight, I swear one of them popped."

Jacquline cupped her mouth in amused shock. "Mom," she said.

Gloria smiled brazenly.

"Did you ever confront any of the mistresses?" Jacquline said after a moment.

"I couldn't tell you how many he actually had, but I do know of one that I guess was far more precious to him than any other."

"Lark?" Jacquline squeaked out as if it was the only obvious answer.

"Stacey," Gloria said.

"Wait." Jacquline had to shift her body to find the words her mind was now cluttered with. "Dad was having an affair with Stacey before you even left?"

"Yeah, a pretty heated one, if I'm not mistaken. She's the reason I left, Jackie. I could see it in him. He absolutely loved her far more than me and there was no turning back from that. He threatened the shit out of me, telling me he'd kill me if I even thought about leaving him. But I didn't care. I had to. I had to get out. He never saw me as a human being. I was just a piece of meat — a piece of his estate. I had to get away from that."

Had I only known, Jacquline thought. She crawled to Gloria and hugged her, without spite — without anger. And it was so full of affection. After letting go, she looked back to Ken and something lit the proverbial light bulb.

"How did he get in here?"

"I wish I knew. After you dozed off, they must have put me to sleep too, because the next thing I know, he was here. I haven't met an alien yet who didn't manipulate me in some way."

"What exactly happened there?" Jacquline said, sitting back, ready for a story. "How did you get here?"

"Oh, Jackie, that is a long story, one that involves a lot of prison, a lot of torture and a lot of bartering. I left Ken because I didn't like the thought of being property, only to be abducted by assholes who actually made me property. I can't remember exactly when I was first abducted, or even why —"

"I know why," Jacquline said.

"Oh, you do?"

"They were looking for Stacey."

"Even better," Gloria said before the two erupted in laughter. "Is that why you're here? They think you were Stacey, too?"

"That might be a reason, but I wasn't abducted. Not from Earth anyway." She pointed to Ken. "This asshole built his very own bucket of bolts to track Stacey after *she* was abducted. I was just a stowaway."

"That's when you met the pirates?"

"Yeah, and joined the crew. We came here to find out what we could about Stacey's past when we were ambushed. Up until now, I just suspected they had all abandoned me. Or were all killed."

"So you're telling me Stacey is an alien, and it's because of her that we're all here?"

Jacquline thought about it for a second and then said, "Yeah. I guess you could say that."

"That bitch." More laughter.

"It's actually ironic because I'm only in this hell-hole with you because of an ambush. My current slaveholders were getting ready to sell me away for the fifth time when things just started exploding all around us. It was insane."

"What was it exactly that made you trade bait? Your amazing personality?"

"What else? I mean, who wouldn't want to get rid of that?"

A heavy moaning interrupted their laughter. Both Jacquline and Gloria looked to Ken, who shifted slightly in pain.

"Dad?" Jacquline said.

Ken quickly registered her voice and turned to her with the biggest smile she'd ever seen from him. "Jacquline," he whispered and found a way to overcome the scream of torture in his muscles to embrace her. "I'm so happy to see you."

"Me, too. And I'm not the only one."

Jacquline motioned to Gloria.

His smile faded, leaving a sickening taste in his mouth. "Gloria," he said with a contemptible tone. He instantly grabbed her throat and squeezed as hard as his grip could bear.

Jacquline tried everything she could to pull his arm away. "Dad, let her go. What are doing? Stop!"

But no amount of yelling or pressure or scratching could keep Ken from wringing the last breath from Gloria's lungs. Even after she fell limp against the wall, Ken wouldn't let go, piercing her skin with his nails until her cold blood dripped across his fingers.

"Dad," Jacquline screamed, flush with tears. "What have you done?"

He finally looked at her without one ounce of remorse. Gloria's body slumped to the floor as he finally let go. Jacquline covered her, hoping she would find the slightest hint of life, but knowing that would forever remain a wish. "What did you do? What did you do?"

"I did what I had to," he said.

Jacquline started hitting Ken as hard as she could. "You didn't have to kill her, you bastard," she screamed. Ken let her do what she had to do. When she grew weak with fatigue, he grabbed her wrists and pulled her in close.

"No," she screamed, trying to push away. "Let me go."

But Ken held her strong against his chest until she calmed down.

"Why would you do that?" she said, quieter and with hardly any clarity. "Why?"

"She deserved it," Ken said. "Same as you."

Jacquline suddenly felt Ken's hand on the back of her head, smothering her against his chest. Her lungs began to constrict as she searched for air. She struggled to call out for help or scream for him to stop. Her mind slowly grew foggy; she could see the end of the road nearing.

Suddenly, she dropped to the floor after a slight shock burned against her cheek. She sucked in as much air as she could before Ken fell to the floor in a constant fit of convulsions. Smoke dripped from his skin as it burned away, the smell of which was repugnant enough to force Jacquline to gag several times. By the time his body stopped shaking, his skin had all but melted from his bones, leaving behind a pool of organs and blood. The sight was as excruciating to look at as it was to smell. Jacquline was able to hold her nausea in check — but not the flow of sorrow that found its way dripping from her cheeks.

"Baby Kel. Are you okay?" Jaenice wrapped her arms around her friend.

"Jaenice, thank god," Jacquline whispered. "Thank…" She caught a glimpse of Gloria and then buried her head into Jaenice's shoulder to hide from it, as if it would make all of it disappear.

"It's okay, baby Kel," Jaenice said. "It's okay. You're okay."

Suddenly Jacquline realized something and looked up to Jaenice, who appeared as a fuzzy blob through the lens of Jacquline's puffy eyes. "Where did you come from?"

Jaenice smiled and nodded to her right. Jacquline was not prepared for what she saw.

"Eyrixano?" Her first instinct was to back away as far as she could, but then she noticed the staff he held in his hand as he lorded over Ken's remains.

"It's okay. He came to rescue us."

Jacquline was as confused as all get out. But she didn't have any reason to disbelieve her. Not now.

"Come with us. There's nothing but death left for you here."

Jacquline took a moment to ponder her request. She didn't want to go with Eyrixano, not after what he had done, but in the end, it was really her only option.

Victims of Circumstance

— 1 —

Lark found sleep eluding her. Her mind was frantic with thoughts of Ken being tortured, beaten and God knows what else — not to mention the constant scenarios of Betas storming the ship with guns blazing, killing everyone on board in one gruesome way or another. Sometimes she would see Tracey using the gem to wipe them all out, having to sacrifice her and the crew in the process. Jacquline also remained a focus when she thought of her returning with great glee, only to be betrayed and killed because the Betas compelled her to do their bidding. She knew it was all figments of her wild imagination, but as she rolled around in bed, she was lost.

The only thing she could think to do to calm her mind was continue learning Sentilla's language. She didn't want to bother Sentilla with such arbitrary lessons (not after what she had just gone through), so she returned to medical to keep an eye on Kahli's progress at the same time. It wasn't quite as nice as her usual hiding spot, but the hum of Kahli's internal mechanics eased her mind. It felt very much like she was back in the college library's computer lab, where the hustle and bustle of people pretending to be quiet gave her the comfort of knowing she couldn't be harmed. The smell of the librarian's mocha cappuccino and the hundreds of books that filled the shelves were a complete contradiction to the smell of booze her father would drown her in. And though there were instances when the soothing sound of Kahli spinning through her startup processes seduced her into closing her eyes with a yawn, her dreams would betray her with images of Ken. At one point, after her body was shocked awake as if realizing she had fallen asleep when she wasn't supposed to, Lark took a moment to regain the recognition of her surroundings and noticed Kahli was no longer lying on the table. She stood at attention and looked around, finding nothing more than an empty room.

God damn it, she thought as she remembered (just in time) that she couldn't use the communicator to inform Qah-Shekel of her disappearance. She would have to track him down and hope nothing happened to Kahli in the meantime. Before she reached the door, Lark heard movement in the shadows near the specimen area. Her heart bounced a few beats too many as she considered whether to find out who it might be (the odds of it being Kahli were very high, but who knows how long she might have been asleep) or go find Qah-Shekel and let him take point on this whole mess. If she did that, though, whoever it might be could do irreparable damage if left alone.

"Rega?" she said, going with her best judgment call.

It took several prolonged seconds for anything to happen, and when Kahli finally did step into the soft haze of light, Lark calmed considerably and swiped her hand against the wall to bring up the room's full lighting. Kahli took it as a sign of aggression. She lunged at Lark and swung her up against the wall. Lark didn't register it, not with Kahli's eyes searing into hers, but her toes weren't touching the floor.

Kahli said something in some oddly mixed language. It didn't take her long to figure out Lark didn't understand, or restate her message in a variety of languages. "Who are you?" she finally queried correctly.

"Rega, it's me. Lark."

"How did you get into the factory?" Her voice was more robotic than usual. "What is your access code?"

"Factory? Rega, we're on the ship."

"We are on a ship?"

"Yes. Our ship. The *Equinox*."

"Why have you removed me from my brethren?"

"Rega, please. What's wrong?"

"Kahli," Qah-Shekel said with biting authority.

With her eyes squeezing into small slits, Kahli threw Lark at Qah-Shekel. He caught her as best he could (though Lark could swear he deliberately tried to break a couple of her ribs in the process) and set her down gently.

"State your name and purpose," Kahli said.

Qah-Shekel stepped to Kahli, pushing his chest against hers.

"I said state your name and purpose. Why have you removed me from my brethren?" Kahli used English, most likely believing that everyone on the ship spoke the same as Lark. And though Qah-Shekel did understand her (for the most part), he made it seem as if he didn't. For now, it was better if he stayed silent; saying anything would only reveal what language to speak. Unable to acquire an answer, Kahli held her arm against Qah-Shekel's chest and stepped back slightly. "I demand to know why I have been removed from my brethren."

Qah-Shekel still refused to answer.

"So be it." Kahli drew her arm back and then, as if it had just been loaded into a slingshot, pushed it into his chest. Qah-Shekel stumbled backward but remained on his feet. Before Kahli was allowed another shot, Qah-Shekel had his fins erect and blocked her attack. He quickly countered with his own sharp punch to the head, which did absolutely nothing. Kahli lifted Qah-Shekel off the ground by his fins and whipped him into the display at the back of the room.

Lark was still in a lot of pain, but had stabilized. "Rega, stop this. We're friends. Allies."

"My brethren are my only allies."

"Your brethren have all been destroyed," Lark said boldly.

"You destroyed them?" Kahli stormed toward Lark, the intent to kill filling every step.

"No. It was your creators. They destroyed them. We rescued you." Lark didn't want to show any weakness, but she couldn't help push her chin to her chest and close her eyes, waiting for her father to punch a hole through her face.

It never came. When she opened her eyes, Kahli was staring into them with cold hollowness.

"Why would my creators destroy us?" Kahli said.

"You were too human," Lark said honestly. "Your brains processed far too many emotions to control. They feared you, so they destroyed you."

"Do you have proof of this accusation?"

Lark shifted her body, cautiously keeping her eyes on Kahli. Qah-Shekel had stood and was slinking across the walls to find a better position for an attack. Lark thought she might wait for him, but figured any attempt at stopping her would be a waste of time. Honesty was working for now; that was her best course of action if she hoped to survive. "I can't. Not yet."

"Then you are my enemy."

"But she's not your enemy." Tracey walked up behind Lark and helped her to her feet. "Go," she whispered to Lark, who stumbled past Kahli to the medical bed. Kahli didn't seem to notice; the gem had absorbed all of her attention. It was so beautiful, so magnificent; so powerful. "She is your friend," Tracey said, feeling the gem heating up with rage. "As am I."

"You are not a friend. You have removed me from my brethren and are deceiving me with the power from the gem of Jaxxa Rakala."

"We haven't deceived you," Tracey said before Lark could. (Then again, nothing seemed to escape Lark's lips when she tried.) "If you don't believe me, take it. Then you will know all. You will be... all." Tracey held out her arms, the gem glowing brightly upon her chest.

Kahli didn't hesitate. "Gladly."

Lark squeezed her shoulders together slightly, digging her chin into her neck in anticipation for an explosion of mass proportions — or something even worse. Whatever it might be, it wasn't going to be pleasant.

As Kahli's hand touched the gem, she screamed with excruciating madness. She tried to pull away, but the gem was unwilling to let go. The pain eventually forced Kahli to her knees, giving Tracey the chance to look directly into her eyes.

"Kill me if you must," Kahli said.

"I'm not going to kill you," Tracey said. Several bursts of electric shocks thrust into Kahli's hand, and with each one, Kahli bounced with convulsions. She fell to the floor when the gem finally let go.

"What did you do?" Lark asked Tracey, unwilling to move.

"Replacing her power core must have rebooted her entire system. I activated her backup memory files and reinstalled them into her primary system cache. With any luck, when she wakes up, she'll be back to her old self."

"With any luck?" Lark said.

Tracey smiled and gave Lark a trusting wink.

Lark chuckled her anxiety away as Qah-Shekel moved Kahli to the bed.

— 2 —

The dryness of Jacquline's eyes burned to the point of being unable to blink. She carried herself with a stiff upper body as she followed Eyrixano through the hallowed dungeons below Trynoruus. The palm of her hand remained pressed against the walls as if she were waiting to hear a heartbeat come to life —

Her heartbeat?

The world around her had all but dissolved into the black hole that she remembered most from when she was young. But this time, she knew Gloria wasn't coming back; this time, she would never see her again. And now that she knew the truth about Ken

— that he, too, felt she was more of a burden than anything else — what was left for her? There was no guarantee that Tracey would come looking for her (after what Ken tried to do, Tracey could have been conspiring against her the entire time; it would explain why she hardly ever saw her on the ship), so Jacquline was as alone now as she always thought she was. The loneliness was her only true, real friend.

Because Jacquline was so caught in the depths of her mind, she didn't feel the sickness upon her until it was too late. She vomited on a cascade of rocks and quickly lost the battle with the weakness in her knees. Covering her mouth, Jacquline desperately forced herself from erupting into a sobbing mess. She hadn't noticed the only reason she remained upright was because of Jaenice, who was quick to steady her before she tumbled all the way to the floor.

"Steady, girl," she said. "That's it." Her words sounded so distant and soft — nothing more than a faint whisper in the fog of soundless air. "Relax, baby Kel. Relax."

This time, Jacquline registered enough to rest her head against Jaenice's chest. The weight of her eyelids was hard to fight. She slumped down as deep within herself as her body would allow, all the while finding comfort in Jaenice's warmth.

"What are you feeling, baby Kel?" Jaenice said.

"I'm tired of all this shit." Jacquline's voice cracked with every word.

"I can understand that. It's scary to know those you once loved don't love you back. But believe me, I want to help. *We* want to help. Eyrixano found me when I was at my weakest. He nurtured me, became more than just a friend. We are family, baby Kel. We trust each other, support each other and defend each other when no one else will. Don't you want that? A family that will always be proud of you no matter what happens, or what flaws you may have."

"I thought…"

"You thought you could trust them, right? I get it. They're blood. Believing they'll always be on your side is just common sense. But it doesn't always work out that way. In my experience, it never works out that way. There are only a handful of people you can ever trust to keep their word, but the most important one of them is you."

"So, what? I should only trust myself?"

"Until you feel comfortable trusting someone else. One act of kindness doesn't create a lifetime of love. It's an ongoing struggle, and from what I've seen and heard from you, your family never loved you."

Jacquline's tears kept her from speaking.

"It's a lesson we all have to learn at some point in our lives, baby Kel. Don't feel ashamed that you had to learn it the hard way."

"I'm not ashamed. I feel stupid."

"Because you were deceived?"

"Because I let it happen. I always knew in my gut they were all liars; that I couldn't trust them. But I continued to pretend I was imagining things. I bought into the idea that someday it would change. But I had to protect my little sister. I had to."

"Why?"

"Because she..."

"She didn't need protecting," Jaenice said.

"I know that now," Jacquline screamed. "But she was so quiet, so innocent, so helpless back then. I didn't want her to end up like me. It kills me to know it was all some damn charade."

"Our emotions can stop us from seeing the truth."

"I should have just run away when I had the chance."

"Run away?"

"Yeah," Jacquline said. "When my dad had his psychotic break."

"After Keladrayia was taken."

"Apparently, the only thing keeping him in check was that damn gem of hers. I never considered it before, but now... I have to wonder — if it wasn't for that damn ship, how long would it have been before he took all of his aggression out on me?"

"Because you were a burden?"

"Because I reminded him of my mom."

Jaenice rubbed Jacquline's shoulder tightly to try and calm her down.

"Where would you have gone?" Jaenice asked. "Had you run away?"

"I don't know. To find my mom. Or just hit the road and see where it took me. Anything would have been better than ending up here."

"Even death?"

Jacquline looked at her wrists. "If I was smart, I would have done it myself a long time ago."

"Sometimes it's the only way."

Jacquline walked a few feet from Jaenice, holding her arms tightly across her chest. "Sometimes, I guess it is," she whispered.

"Eyrixano and I want to give you the life you deserve," Jaenice said. "The one you've always dreamed of. Let us do that."

"I thought you said I couldn't trust anyone but myself."

Jaenice rubbed Jacquline's shoulders gently. She then rested her chin on Jacquline's shoulder and said, "We're here for you. Always."

Jacquline again covered her mouth to keep from tearing up. Jaenice walked back to Eyrixano, who was still waiting patiently for them to resolve their female issues. Jacquline peered over at them, assessing whether she should believe them. Right now, they were her best chance of getting off Trynoruus. At the very least, she had to give them the benefit of the doubt — for now.

She nodded and slid over to join Jaenice, who wrapped her arm around her shoulder with a great big smile. "You won't regret this, baby Kel." Jaenice planted a nice big kiss on her cheek and then confidently followed Eyrixano.

You can't trust anyone, Jacquline kept repeating to herself. *Not anymore.*

— 3 —

To keep her mind busy, Sentilla convinced Qah-Shekel to let her get back to command and check on the systems so as to figure out what was causing the symptoms she heard earlier in the cell. She sat in her pilot seat for quite awhile. As much as she respected his concern, she quickly grew a bit smothered by the way Qah-Shekel hovered over her. He must have felt it, too. Instead of having to ask him, he left on his own to check on Kahli. And though his departure did give Sentilla a chance to breathe, it also caused her thoughts to wander much more freely. She mechanically ran through several forms of diagnostics but didn't register any of the information. There could have been a complete meltdown and she wouldn't have noticed. It got so bad that even though her vision was still relegated to blurry colors, she had to get up and walk around to clear her head.

She spent the next hour wandering the ship, checking systems here and there, correcting any parameters that had become slightly off due to her absence. None of that mattered; it was just a distraction to keep her from dwelling on the past and the remorse that continued to fill her soul. Tracey was right; speaking about it was a huge step in letting go, but it was only the first. She was afraid of what the effects of moving forward might do to the memory she so desperately longed to hold onto. Would letting go of her guilt cause her to forget her mother? Would accepting that it wasn't her fault give her a reason to neglect the path her mother started her on? Would putting her mother's death in the past cause her future to become one that her mother would be ashamed of? Should she even care if it did? Her life was her own, wasn't it? This was no longer her mother's life, and until she embraced that fact, would she ever be able to live the life she was meant for? Would she ever be able to rise to her full capabilities? It was all so aggravating that it nearly pushed her into madness. She needed answers; she needed to get all of this out of her system; she needed to talk to someone she knew wouldn't ever judge her or the fears and concerns she had — the one person who wouldn't accuse her of being childish or foolish in any way. It took her a long time to actually step into the room, believing she should have to figure this out on her own or else feel the weight of her own failure. But Tracey was the only one who could guide her to the right answer, so she had to get past her anxiety and just do it.

Tracey was sitting in the cell with a journal in her lap. She didn't look up or acknowledge Sentilla in any way. It wasn't clear if she was asleep or just immersed so deeply in the journal that she had blinders on, making Sentilla feel a bit awkward. It was only when Tracey didn't move a muscle for several minutes (not even to turn the pages of the journal) that Sentilla realized she was asleep. She considered going back to her living quarters and attempt to do the same, but she felt comfortable with Tracey. Her mind was clear and she figured it was because of the gem. She knew she was going to have to confront her feelings sooner or later, but until she could get Tracey's advice on the matter, she felt it better to remain as close to her as possible. So she silently sat just outside of the cell with her legs up against her chest and kept her eyes glued to the little rock in the center of Tracey's chest.

— 4 —

Qah-Shekel was pacing a hole into the floor, which kept a smile locked on Lark's lips. She knew very well why he was pacing and found it quite endearing. Telling him to stop would only lead to an angry scowl and possibly some resentment, so she kept her mouth shut and sat in the corner farthest from the door to catalog her thoughts on the most recent events. The only thing that would put him to rest would be Kahli's resurrection, and though Tracey assured them she would wake up (and be back to normal operating parameters), when that would happen was completely unknown, even to little miss gem. Waiting was all they had left to do.

Lark was in the middle of a thought about where DovenJadden had gone

(*If there really is a God, she was captured by the Betas and is being probed up her hairy little ass*)

when Kahli suddenly sat straight up. Qah-Shekel stopped cold and raised his fins in preparation for another attack. Kahli sat so still, it irked Lark a bit. She wondered if there was some other malfunction Tracey didn't detect at the time of the surge. The room was still as Lark (her lungs closed for business) and Qah-Shekel (his eyes pierced tightly in firm vigilance) waited. Finally, Kahli robotically shifted her head to Qah-Shekel, stared at him for several frozen seconds, and then said, "Qah-Shekel."

Though Qah-Shekel kept his guard up (unwilling to except a perfect reboot), Kahli's acknowledgment of who he was did relax his nerves — if only slightly. Lark was a little more forgiving. "Rega?"

Kahli whipped her head around like a possessed owl and adjusted her pupils to focus on Lark, who sat with her hands in front of her in a sign of peace. "Lark. Is everything okay?" Her voice remained extremely robotic and somewhat staticky.

"Are you okay?" Lark asked. She set the tablet on the floor and stood up as cautiously as she could. "You took a pretty good shock earlier."

Kahli, unsure of Lark's answer, turned back to Qah-Shekel. "What has happened? Has there been an error?"

Qah-Shekel finally retracted his fins and stood upright. "A lightning strike back on Trynoruus destroyed your power core."

"Yeah, and it caused your entire system to go batshit crazy. You would have killed us both if it weren't for Tracey."

Kahli still seemed confused. "How am I in operation?"

"We replaced your power core," Lark said.

"Replacing my power core would require us to travel to Rega-One." She looked Qah-Shekel over carefully. "You would not risk such a thing for me."

"He would," Lark said brightly. "And he did."

"Why would you do that?"

"Because we need your help to find Jacquline. Or at least, we thought we did."

Kahli turned to Lark. "I do not comprehend."

"We thought we lost Jacquline on Trynoruus and you were the only one who had the means to track her down. But now, we think she might be here. On Rega-One."

"We are still on Rega-One?"

"Yeah."

"No. We must go. Now." Kahli went to her computer terminal and brought up the main engine displays.

"Wait, Rega. We're not in danger. At least not yet."

"Every moment we spend here puts us further at risk."

"I believe you. But the Betas aren't after us. Someone has ordered them to stand down."

Kahli looked back and forth from Lark to Qah-Shekel, believing in some part that Qah-Shekel would never condone such a theory. How wrong she was. "Someone has ordered the Beta units to stand down?"

Lark nodded, mouthing her acknowledgment.

"Is everyone else unharmed?"

Lark paused a moment, taking her cue from Qah-Shekel. "Not really. Sentilla's been locked away with Tracey to try and kill her addiction to the gem and Ken was taken prisoner by the Regans."

Kahli sat stiff for a few moments, running diagnostics on her own systems. It was kind of creepy to watch, as her eyes were so deathly hollow. When the light returned to them, she looked more frightened than either Lark or Qah-Shekel had ever seen her. She flew through several screens on the holocomputer, flashing by them so fast, Lark wasn't even sure she was looking at actual text. When she finally stopped her scan, she pounded the table with enough force to crack it in half.

"Kan se," she yelled.

"What is it?" Qah-Shekel said.

"Where's DovenJadden?"

"She's gone missing," Lark said. "Tracey thinks she may have had something to do with this whole mess."

"Yeah," Kahli said and burst from the room.

"Rega," Lark cried out as she pursued her. Qah-Shekel didn't remain far behind. They followed her all the way to command, where she stood in what looked like shock.

"What's wrong?" Lark said.

"What has happened to my holopad?"

"Long story. Let's just say, we're lucky no one got seriously injured."

Kahli didn't like the answer but she didn't have time to complain. In no time flat, she had commandeered DovenJadden's station and was spinning through dozens of system checks.

"I have deactivated all of our communication buds," she said. Her voice was back to normal, as was her spirit. "We cannot risk using them."

"Tracey already made that assumption."

"Good."

Lark tried, but it was impossible to keep up with the speed of Kahli's movements. "What are you doing now?"

"I am attempting to overwrite DovenJadden's firewall."

"Why? What did she do now?"

"I noticed you are using the ship's heat signature to mask the *Equinox*. DovenJadden has set a timer to deactivate it. When that happens —"

"All hell breaks loose," Lark said. "Can you stop it?"

"I do not believe I can. DovenJadden set up a sophisticated network of commands. We may not be able to gain access without her."

"So we're screwed?"

"Not yet. There may still be one option."

Kahli left command without another word. This was becoming exasperating. Lark and Qah-Shekel followed behind nonetheless and were led to the cells. Lark, completely out of breath, rested against the wall, jealous of Qah-Shekel's unmitigated stamina.

Sentilla perked up quickly when she saw Kahli dash past her. "Kahli."

Kahli ignored her completely. "Jaxxa Rakala. I need DovenJadden's communication records." When Tracey didn't respond, Kahli repeated her request.

Sentilla was now standing, her hand resting gently on Qah-Shekel's back.

"Tracey," Kahli said, hoping to get a response with a more personal approach. When it didn't work, she reached down to grab her shoulder.

Her hand went right through her.

Kahli took a step back. She tried again, this time swiping her hand through Tracey's head. Tracey's image shimmered and then disappeared.

"It is a deception," Kahli said. "A hologram."

Kahli marched back to Lark and grabbed her chin. "Where is Tracey?"

— 5 —

Tracey stood just outside the outskirts of the city. A scarf she stole from Sentilla's quarters was wrapped around her neck, covering the gem. Now that her ruse had been exposed, she considered returning to the ship, or at the very least, waiting for them to track her down. Either one would put everyone in danger, and because she no longer had to focus energy to produce her holographic doppelgänger, it would be much easier to walk the streets of the city without detection. It was a no-brainer.

She skirted across the outer ridge separating the desert from the outlying vegetation and hurried into the city. It was odd at first watching the packs of Beta units monitor each and every Regan like authorized gangs just waiting for them to break a law, which, judging by the fact that there weren't any children, might very well be here any second. She tried her best to keep from acting like a random tourist, but from the shimmering metallic designs decorating the lampposts to the unorthodox curvature of some of the buildings, Tracey was mesmerized by how the technology had developed so far yet retained such a primitive state of stagnation. A few Betas did give her the stink eye as she walked stringently through the main commerce district, though none of them acted on her presence, so whatever she was doing to blend in seemed to be working. Not even the Regans displayed much concern for her presence — if they even took notice of her at all. It helped that she had the gem to guide her. As long as no one stopped her on account of being unfamiliar —

And just as the thought crossed her mind, that's exactly what happened.

A young woman, attractive in the eyes but portly and a little grotesque everywhere else, grabbed her arm as she passed by one of the patios of a restaurant where several Regans had gathered to enjoy the near perfect weather. It startled her, but not enough to cause her to do anything that might trigger a Beta warning.

"Excuse me," the woman said. "What are you doing?"

"Pardon?" Tracey said as nonchalantly as possible.

"Shouldn't you be in acadia?"

"Acadia?" Tracey said.

"I thought the explosion locked that sector down."

Based on the word and the context, Tracey figured the woman meant she should be in some type of school. Uncertain, she deflected. "Why was the sector locked down?"

"If you were in acadia, you'd know why."

"I do apologize," Tracey said. "I was ill this morning, so my mother contacted the acadia to report my absence on my behalf."

"Lucky for you. But if you're sick, why are you wandering the streets alone?"

"I have an appointment with the physician. And you're making me late."

"You shouldn't be going to the physician without supervision, child."

"I do have supervision." She looked down the road and pointed to a very frail woman with a slow step. The woman looked much too elderly to have a child so young, but Tracey figured she could be a caretaker. "There," she said.

The woman didn't take a second glance. "Then hurry to her," she said. "And feel better. Stay safe."

"Yes, of course," Tracey said with a gentle curtsy. "Thank you."

The woman was taken aback by this unorthodox gesture, so Tracey scurried off before she had time to ask any more questions. As she reached the old woman, she heard the portly one report her suspicious behavior to a Beta. But Tracey had already sprinted her way through a few alleyways, up and over a couple of obnoxious barriers and across a small barren park before they even reached the old woman. Taking into account the possibility that the information came from the ramblings of a woman who may have been infected by small amounts of radiation due to the explosion, Tracey figured it would take quite a while before they were able to locate her (if they even pursued it), so she was in the clear — for now.

A crowd had gathered outside the perimeter of the sector that had been locked down, leaving a lot of the nearby buildings vacant. Tracey used this to her advantage, sneaking into the building that would offer her the best vantage point. She used the stairwell to reach the third level, then climbed up into the ducts and squirreled her way to one of the ceiling vents. Popping it was easier than she would have expected, as was climbing out onto the relatively flat roof. One misstep and she'd fly right off the slick surface, but the risk was worth it. Beta units were lined shoulder-to-shoulder, acting as a barrier to keep any unauthorized individuals from entering or exiting the area, which, despite housing several buildings, weren't as large as she suspected (including what she believed to be the acadia, what with the giant medallion that hovered above the entry with words that translated to "Learning Is Life" etched into the bottom of two triangles that were layered at a forty-five degree angle over one another, making each appear as if they were on the top). About a mile from the acadia was the manufacturing plant, a relatively flat, steel building that stretched for a mile in all directions. There was still a light hint of smoke drifting from various parts of the structure and dozens of Beta units swarmed around it. But what was most important — and what she was looking for all along — was DovenJadden, who Tracey caught sight of walking toward the boundary with a half-dozen Betas flanking her.

Tracey didn't budge from her perch until DovenJadden was allowed to leave the lockdown area with her posse and head toward a section that was nowhere near as glamorous as any other part of the city. If she had to guess, it was Rega-One's version of the slums, which Tracey figured would be the best place to hide someone.

"Hang in there, Jacks," Tracey whispered. "I'm coming for you."

There was no time to work her way back through the building, so Tracey lowered herself as far as she could at the edge of the roof and let go. Using as little power from the gem as she could, Tracey rolled a few feet to break her fall and then quickly tracked DovenJadden through the shadows of the favela.

— 6 —

Walking through the tunnels was like walking through a house at night after a power outage. If it weren't for the light from the flame burning underneath Eyrixano's cloak, there would have been absolutely no way of knowing where they were going, and Jacquline might have broken a leg by now instead of having only procured several cuts on her shins and arms (and possibly a broken toe to boot). At least she wasn't the only one to become friends with a fair amount of bruising; Jaenice had her fair share of yelps from stubbing a toe or clipping a stalagmite with her forehead. If there were a silver lining to the whole adventure, at least they would know in advance if someone were coming, giving them plenty of time to hide.

"Not necessarily," Jaenice had said. "These people have been living underground for so long, they've probably adapted to the environment."

"Like bats?" Jacquline said.

"It's possible. We're at a disadvantage regardless. They must know these tunnels inside and out by now."

"They're gonna know we've escaped sooner rather than later. What happens then?"

"We run like hell."

Yeah. It's that simple.

It turns out, it wasn't much more complicated than that. Having spent most of his life on Xyneris, Eyrixano was used to environments like this. He had grown instinctual toward listening for noises that were out of the ordinary, so when he stopped cold after keeping such a steady pace (but no less cautious), it didn't take a lot of persuasion to keep Jacquline quiet — even if she herself didn't hear anything other than her own heart.

Something suddenly hit the wall above Jacquline, dropping pieces of rock and dust down on top of her. She inadvertently chirped in fright, the echo of which was met with more attacks. Eyrixano hissed out a cry of defense and slid backward, pushing Jacquline and Jaenice with him. It was hard for Jacquline to find a good footing, causing her to fall more than once, but Eyrixano never pushed harder or faster than she was comfortable. The shots that chased them were sporadic. Most of them hit the cavern walls, some burning hot next to Jacquline's face while others were close enough to make her flinch, but not enough to feel threatened. She wasn't sure if the Trysians were just bad shots, if they really couldn't see that well in the dark, or if shots were being deflected off of Eyrixano —

Could he really do that?

— but she knew (or at the very least, feared) that eventually they would catch up to them — and that would be the end of that.

Luckily, they were able to slip into an adjacent tunnel and do as planned. Jaenice took the lead, and though she used Eyrixano's flame as her guide, it wasn't enough to keep her from slamming into the wall at the dead-end. She fell back hard, and for a moment, looked as if she might not get back up. Eyrixano didn't stop to check on her; he went directly to the wall to examine it for a possible way out. It fell on Jacquline to see if Jaenice was okay. She was stunned but alert. However, Jacquline wasn't prepared to move her right away (not like it mattered at the moment — not with a wall on one side and a group of blood thirsty Trysians on the other).

"What now?" Jacquline said, knowing full well that Eyrixano, despite turning to her, had no idea what she was saying. So she kept her attention on making certain Jaenice remained comfortable — that is until Eyrixano wrapped himself around Jacquline. She followed suit and huddled down to protect Jaenice as a few shots hit Eyrixano's back. His body turned white hot as he somehow absorbed the attacks and then turned super cool. Jacquline peeked up with just her eyes to see Eyrixano waving his arms, deflecting the shots back into the tunnel. Eventually, the entire thing grew far too unstable and collapsed down in front of them.

When the dust settled, and Jacquline could breathe again without coughing, she leaned against the wall and covered her eyes. Jaenice finally found her faculties and joined Jacquline in silence. It wasn't until Jaenice pulled Jacquline's hand away from her face and held it did Jacquline fully comprehend her safety. She hugged Jaenice with gratitude, but kept her eyes on Eyrixano, who sat nursing his own wounds across from them.

"He saved us," Jacquline whispered.

Jaenice smiled and grabbed the back of Jacquline's head. "He knows a thing or two about abandonment."

"What happened to him?"

"I don't know all the details. All I know is that as a child, he was left for dead on Xyneris. You've been there; you can imagine what it was like for a baby."

"How did he even survive that?"

"He would never tell me, but I have my theories. Xyneris has plenty of secrets that might have helped him survive, and out of desperation, I'm sure they revealed themselves graciously. Either that or there used to be life on the planet in some form or another. They could have found him, nurtured him and when the time was right... he ate them."

Jacquline felt sick to her stomach until Jaenice couldn't hold back her smile any longer. "You bitch," Jacquline said, sending a love bug to her upper arm.

"I had you going there," Jaenice said, rubbing her arm gently. "No, Eyrixano is a survivor. I wouldn't have been able to handle it by myself, that's for damn sure. But he recognized my pain and chose to help me. If it weren't for him, I would have died a long time ago. He sees the same in you. He knows what you're going through; he just wants to protect you from anyone who would do you harm."

"But why? I tried to kill him."

Jaenice smiled. "So did I."

Jacquline sat back and stared at Eyrixano, who made her feel both uncomfortable and protected. This wasn't the monster she remembered on Xyneris, and perhaps...

"Perhaps someone was manipulating you into seeing something that wasn't there," Jaenice said.

"Tracey," Jacquline whispered. The idea that Tracey could be so devious was hard to believe, but the more she thought about the events of what happened that day — how she found her, the force field, seeing her mother, the cuffs — it could have all been designed to make her believe Eyrixano was dangerous when in fact, Tracey was the evil behind the events. It must have been true; how else could she explain him rescuing her when Tracey could easily have tracked her down by now? There was a possibility that she had died, but that was minute at best. She simply didn't care because she has her own agenda, one that would include Jacquline if she towed the line, but which made her expendable if she didn't. Tracey had her fooled.

Never again.

"So how do we get out of this shithole?" Jacquline said, standing.

Jaenice rose with a great big smile and turned to Eyrixano, whose haunting red eyes burned with pleasure behind the flame.

— 7 —

"We can't leave them here," Lark barked as she followed Kahli into command. Qah-Shekel and Sentilla, tired and still a little weak, followed them. "They'll all be killed."

"I will not allow liars to remain on this ship," Kahli said. She slipped into the pilot seat and brought up the holocontrols.

"I agree, but —"

"I fought to keep all of you here," Kahli said as she ran through several codes. "I defended you when everyone else wanted to let you die. And how do you repay me for that? By conspiring with DovenJadden."

"Are you fucking kidding me?" Lark didn't necessarily like using that word, but she had to put a stamp on her outrage. "What makes you think we conspired with DovenJadden? She despises us."

"So you would have us believe."

"Qah-Shekel," Lark said, almost pleading. "Tell her."

Sentilla spoke for him. "I don't believe any of them have conspired with DovenJadden."

Lark didn't catch all of it, but from what she was able to translate, she knew Sentilla was defending her. "Thank you."

"What makes you believe that?"

"Tracey was as upset as you when she learned DovenJadden had been sending communications to someone."

"Then why did she hide them?"

"I don't know," Sentilla said softly, defeated.

Kahli nodded and went back to her duties.

"She's trying to help Jacquline," Lark said. "And Ken. That's all."

"And how can you be so certain that they are not also in on this conspiracy? That everything that has happened has been planned from the beginning?"

Lark opened her mouth to say something, but nothing escaped; she didn't know how to defend them. Everything she's said so far had been turned around to make it appear as if they had an ulterior motive. To continue to do so would only make her sound weak and foolish.

"Ken left both of his daughters to help you," she finally spit out. "The least you can do is offer them the same damn courtesy. DovenJadden is the poison pill in this scenario and we all know it. Hell, I don't even know why I keep trying." Lark stormed for the door.

"Where are you going?" Sentilla said. This, Lark did understand.

"My friends are out there. If I die trying to get them back, so be it."

"Wait," Qah-Shekel said. "I will help you."

Kahli stood. "What are you doing?"

"Allowing DovenJadden on this ship was my call."

"And look how that turned out."

"I admit I made the wrong decision. But bringing the humans aboard this ship was yours."

"And you put their fate in my hands," Kahli said adamantly. "I may have given them the benefit of the doubt, but they have proved to be bearers of deception. I do not want them on this ship any longer."

"That's no longer your call." Qah-Shekel turned to Lark. "Let us depart."

"I want to help," Sentilla said.

Lark smiled; she finally felt accepted. "It's funny," she said. "The one person who claims to give everyone the benefit of the doubt is the only one who can't trust those she calls friend." She led the way out of command. Qah-Shekel and Sentilla followed without looking back.

Kahli's rage boiled deep within her systems. Was she really the villain in all of this? She couldn't sit down, she was so angry... so angry...

Angry.

A light bulb shot on inside of her. She quickly hummed through a diagnostic of her emotion chips and found they had all been reset to their original programming parameters. Guilt chilled her systems as she tried to figure out how she hadn't realized it before. The programmers would have wanted a complete system reboot had any of the Alphas gotten too far out of line. What she feared was having to rewrite all of the code she spent so long creating, but on further inspection, she quickly found a back door to a software program hidden deep within her memory system that allowed her to revert back to the last known operating capacities. The only person she knew who would be capable of such a thing was the one person she just accused of conspiring against her.

Kahli hurried to DovenJadden's station and brought up all relative files. The moment she opened them, Tracey's face appeared. Just below it were a series of codes that were no doubt access ports to the necessary programs. She located the required drives and entered the codes. Kahli froze for about a minute and then returned to life as if nothing had ever happened. She felt right; she felt at ease.

"Rega," Tracey's visage said. "If you're listening to this, you have been able to revert back to the state of operations before the electrocution. I'm sorry I couldn't do it for you, but it was a necessary step for you to come to terms with what I have done. You are probably aware of DovenJadden's virus, which will cause the *Equinox* to shut down in a matter of quintets. I have gone after her to try and get the necessary deactivation codes and in the hope she'll lead me to Jacquline. I apologize for deceiving everyone, but what I am doing is very dangerous and I did not want to put any more of your lives at risk. If I do not return before the virus is activated, leave and do not look back. Take care of Lark and make sure Sentilla knows that it is not her fault. Do not let anyone come after me. I cannot protect them. Thank you for saving me and my family. Our lives will forever be in your debt. Oh, and about DovenJadden's communication files. I wasn't sure when you would wake or when you might find the access codes, so I hid them, as well as some other important files, in a locked drive impenetrable to the virus. Should we succeed, and I am unable to return, the access codes have been given to someone I know I can trust. I must go now, but believe me when I say — you are my family and I will miss you dearly."

Static covered Tracey's head before it vanished, giving way to the system's normal functionality. But Kahli didn't care about that; she had been wrong about everything and needed to make it right. She burst from command and raced to tactical, where she hoped to find the rest of her crew. Lucky for her, that's exactly where they were.

"Wait," she said. "We can't go. Tracey doesn't want us to."

"What do you mean?" Lark said, thinking it was just another ploy to stop them.

"Tracey left a message for me in the holosystem. I believe you now that you had nothing to do with DovenJadden's deception. But Tracey made it explicitly clear not to follow her."

"I don't care," Lark said. "I'm going to find Ken and Jacquline with or without your help."

Kahli saw her unrelenting determination and knew right then there was no way to convince her otherwise. Tracey may have wanted to protect them, but this pack of humans was one stubborn bunch. "Fine. But if we do this, we do it smart." Kahli urged Lark out of the way and brought up a series of schematics just above the map of the city that Qah-Shekel and Lark had been looking at.

"This is the sewer system that runs underneath the city. The Alpha-Nine units reinforced them with cloaking fields so as to hide from the Beta units during the war. It is your best way in without being detected."

"I wish we would have known about those earlier," Lark said with a wry smile.

"From what I recall, the Regans used to use this area, here," Kahli continued, zooming in closer on a portion of the city that looked dilapidated compared to the rest, "to hold Alpha-Nine units for information purposes. If Ken and Jacquline are being held captive, that's most likely where they'll be."

"What's this," Lark said, pointing to a large structure that looked a lot like a canopy of some kind.

"That's one of the old docking ports," Kahli said. "It was used to transport supplies, but it was decommissioned several years before the extermination."

"I'm betting that's where we need to hit."

"You'll need to hit," Qah-Shekel said.

"You're not coming with me?"

"I have more pressing matters to attend to."

"Like what?"

"Destroying this race once and for all."

Kahli was not at all happy about that. "That is unacceptable."

"No. It is just."

"How can you conclude such a thing?"

"The Regans killed my people," Qah-Shekel said, defiant.

Lark was aghast. "What?"

Qah-Shekel raised one of his fins. "They harvested my people for their skin. It's what makes you invincible."

Kahli wasn't ready to believe him. "How can that be true?"

"I discovered it when I was in the manufacturing plant. The only way they could create the material for you was to wipe out my entire species. My family. And now, it's time I return the favor."

"If that is true," Kahli said, still unconvinced. "then the Regans deserve punishment. But no race deserves to be eradicated."

"I don't care."

"I have to agree with Rega," Lark said, a bit sheepishly. "Genocide is not an ethical recourse. I mean, you'd be no better than them."

"If your entire family was murdered, you wouldn't seek revenge?" Qah-Shekel said.

"Fair question. Of course I'd want revenge, but morally, there are far better ways to seek justice. Retribution won't bring your family back."

"And what about their plans to transfer someone's mind to another?"

"What?" Lark and Kahli said simultaneously.

"They've been working on a way to transfer one conscious mind to another body. Is that ethical? Is that… moral?"

"Why would they want to do something like that?" Lark said.

"Immortality," Kahli answered under her breath.

Lark nodded. It made sense.

"Okay," Kahli said. "You two find the crew. I will go to the manufacturing plant and check out this story."

Qah-Shekel was about to object but stopped when Kahli placed her hand on his chest. "Let me take care of this."

He backed down without showing any weakness.

"Go get our people." Kahli said, staring deep into his eyes. He nodded.

Lark hugged Kahli tightly and left with Qah-Shekel.

"What should I do?" Sentilla said.

"Get some rest. We will need you at full capacity to get us out of here."

Sentilla looked disappointed, but understood. There was no telling what might happen out there, and the way she was feeling, rest was the right call. She nodded.

Kahli remained in tactical for a little while longer, attempting to find any way into the Regan command system so as not to have to break into the manufacturing plant. With no luck whatsoever, she prepared herself for a return to a home she never thought she'd ever have to see again.

— 8 —

By the time DovenJadden stopped at a dilapidated building on the edge of the eastern desert plateau, Tracey could hardly keep up with her, almost tripping over herself a few times in the process. Taking cover behind a run-down structure that looked to be what was left of a demolished building, Tracey fought hard to breathe regularly. There were higher levels of radiation among the seemingly endless smoke that billowed from several torn down pyres nearby and it reeked of hydrochloric acid. She pressed her hand firmly against the gem and closed her eyes, focusing all of her power into her chest, which eased the pressure on her lungs but caused her nose to bleed. It dripped past her lips onto the gem, where it burned and evaporated.

As her body relaxed, Tracey brushed her hand across her nose and took a final, soothing breath of cool air (mixed with sulfur and iron). She could still hear DovenJadden rustling nearby. Betas had taken perimeter watch over the structure. Tracey could make out part of DovenJadden's body as she waited impatiently at the wall. Suddenly, smoke spilled from the bottom corners of a hidden entry, which lifted six feet along a set of extremely noisy tracks. Tracey didn't know why DovenJadden didn't move until she caught sight of that menacing black cloak and familiar, sickening hiss.

"What happened?"

"Qah-Shekel ignited one of the power cores and blew up some of the labs. Nothing critical was destroyed."

"And what of Qah-Shekel?"

"He made it back to the *Equinox*, as did that dreadful human."

"You said you had this under control."

"If you would have taken control over that child on Xyneris —"

Eyrixano wrapped his hand around DovenJadden's throat, digging his sharp nails into the back of her neck. DovenJadden didn't panic one bit. "I need that child."

"And you shall have her. When it comes to her family, she is vulnerable."

"You had better be right." Eyrixano removed his nails from DovenJadden's neck. She felt relief, even though blood soaked the fur covering her back. "Kahli must be back up and running by now. Do they have a plan in place?"

"They stopped using their communication buds. I'm in the dark."

Eyrixano stood stone cold. Even though Tracey couldn't see inside that cloak, she knew he wasn't happy. "I'm going to the plant to salvage what I can. Jacquline's close to completing her trials. Once finished, take her to my ship along with that thorn of a father of hers."

"Yes, sir," DovenJadden said, bowing her head slightly. She purred commands to the Betas and stole inside the building. The door closed fiercely behind her.

Eyrixano took no time to leave the stationary Betas. Tracey, still a bit weak, curved around the edge of the wall as he passed by. Before he was completely out of sight, he turned back and carefully examined the area in her direction, even taking a step toward her. Tracey held the gem tightly, hoping it wouldn't draw him any closer. An enormous sigh of relief followed as the gem's weight lightened. She inched her head around the edge of the brick to make sure he was completely gone, then settled in and waited. A week ago, she wouldn't have hesitated to attack the Betas and tear her way into the building, but though she was confident it wouldn't be a problem to do just that, to try now might knock her out before she was able to reach Jacquline. From the sound of it, she had little time before they moved Jacquline from whatever torture they were currently subjecting her to, so she had to be at her very best to guarantee her safety. If she was going to take on the big dogs with the scorching bite, she had to allow the gem to reenergize her abilities.

Tracey found turning off her perception filters worked best for regaining the majority of her energy. She wouldn't be able to tell where anyone was, or rely on intuitive sensations about what might be happening to them, but it was a sacrifice she needed to make in order to keep the gem from enveloping the last pieces of who she was. It's not like the gem allowed her to do it freely anyway.

She curled around the brick to gain a complete assessment of the scene at hand. Three Beta units stood in between her and the compound. Opening the door wouldn't be much of an issue, but she was going to have to find a way to get past the Betas without relying too heavily on the gem. She imagined sprinting from her hiding spot, crushing one of their knees and sending the others flying backward. When they came after her again (which was inevitable), she would swing one around with the speed of a propeller until it ripped in half, then slam her hand into the other and tear her electrical guts out. It was a fun idea but would expend too much power. She had to think more creatively than that.

Focusing her attention on the outlying rubble, Tracey expelled her image to each of the Betas in a different location.

"Halt, intruder," the Betas commanded simultaneously. They each darted after their respective artifice, which all disappeared behind nearby obstructions. Tracey waited for several seconds and then was up and running toward the compound. Without much time to waste, she ripped open the box on the wall and grabbed the lever that sat just inches above the bottom. It wasn't easy (not without pulling strength from the gem), but she managed to turn the lever to the right and pull it up. The door hissed and started to rise.

"Halt, intruder!"

Judging by the intensity of the sound, it would take the Beta approximately ten seconds to reach her, so she reset the mechanism and pushed the box back into the wall. The door was only a few inches off the ground when it started to close, but it was plenty for her to roll under, dodging a couple of pucks that ignited on the door before it locked shut.

— 9 —

The feeling in Ken's legs returned as they dragged across the smooth, crystalline floor. He tried to lift his head to get an idea as to where he was being taken (and possibly collect mental images for his escape), but it was hard enough just to open his eyes. From what he could tell, he was most likely being taken to a holding cell until the imitator was ready to continue her interrogation — then again, it wasn't clear how long he had been out. Perhaps now that he was regaining consciousness, he was being brought back from the holding cell. If that was the case, he wasn't sure if he was ready for more torturous tactics. Just the thought of it watered his eyes.

They had broken him. He was ashamed.

A hiss from the door in front of him was followed by the passage into a pitch-dark room that smelled of amber and rust. It was a lot hotter than any other place he could remember and his captors left rather quickly. His mind wandered into a dozen different scenarios. The one he liked best was where he was taken to a sauna to heal and have a slew of apologies thrown his way over an ice-cold daiquiri; the one he feared the most was one in which he was being dragged to the furnace for his final burial. The latter of which could very well have been true as he was plucked from the ground and strapped into a similar chair as before. This time, though, his arms were tied to what felt like the wings of a metallic eagle while his head was pulled back to a pike for which his head might soon be sitting if he didn't give them exactly what they wanted. The cold touch of a woman's petite hands was a relief to the building heat of the room. When she let go, Ken finally managed to open his eyes. Though there wasn't any light, he could see himself staring back at him. He looked like Rocky after spending fifteen rounds fighting the tag-team of Apollo Creed and Mr. T. When he laughed at the thought, every muscle in his face hurt. He couldn't help but add in little grunts of pain in hopes of relieving them.

"Welcome, Kenneth." The words were soft, a bit delicate, and to Ken's surprise, friendly. He wanted nothing to do with it. "I am very sorry for what we had to put you through earlier. I do hope you may one day forgive us for our boisterousness."

"Boisterousness?" Ken said through a pained laugh. "Go screw a goat."

"Now, now, Kenneth. There's no need to be tempered. I am a friend."

Ken still couldn't stop laughing, even though every muscle tightened the longer he did. When his fit of amusement finally calmed, he said, "A friend wouldn't keep me locked away in some hell hole. Why am I here?"

"That is precisely the question I am seeking an answer for myself. You were very stubborn earlier, but I was hoping you have come to your senses and will be more receptive to the kindness I am offering."

Ken chuckled, groaning as he did so.

"You find my kindness amusing?"

"Yeah... yeah I do."

"Why is that?"

Ken tried to see where the voice was coming from but could only see himself. "I've been beaten and tortured, I can barely move any part of my body, and yet you still feel the need to tie me up? How am I supposed to trust you when you keep treating me like a prisoner?"

It took a while for the voice to reply back. "You are right," she said. "I was afraid that you would try to run or cause me harm in some way, but that fear may have been misplaced. Honesty and trust must go both ways, however, so if I were to remove you from your binds, can I trust that you will do no harm to me?"

"Yeah, sure." His response was quick — perhaps a little too fast. She might not believe him.

"If you turn on your word, Kenneth, I will be forced to place you back in confinement and return you to those who will do you harm."

"Right," Ken said. "I got it. I screw you, you screw me."

"I would not have been as vulgar, but very well." The delicate caress that followed was soothing. Ken didn't move much as he waited for her to fully release him from his confines. As she lifted the final binding from his left hand, Ken darted from the chair and nearly collapsed. He caught himself against the mirror and rubbed his wrist cautiously. Looking back her way, he caught a glimpse of her frame, which was just as perfectly shaped as Kahli's.

"Who are you?" he asked.

"My name is Jaenice," the voice said. Her body hardly moved an inch.

"Are you an android?"

He couldn't see it, but somehow he felt a smile rise to her lips — although the tone in her response would remind him otherwise. "My designation is of a Rega-One-Beta-Option-Two."

Now a smile did rise to Ken's lips. "So, literally, a Robot."

"I am unsure as to your inquiry."

"It doesn't matter. The point is you're a second generation of a second unit design."

"The original android units were flawed in many ways, and as technology expands, our systems are constantly updated, yes. But I am much more than simply an android, Kenneth."

"Oh, yeah? Why's that?"

"My body may be synthetic, but my soul is far from it."

Ken wasn't quite sure how to answer that. "You have a soul?"

"As much as anyone can have a soul."

"But you remain emotionless," Ken said.

"That is still being tested," Jaenice said, "but I would say that we have the ability to adjust and refine emotion to better suit our needs. By doing so, we are able to see everything without judgment or bias."

"So you're saying you're the perfect evolutionary system."

"We are." There was no hesitation.

Ken looked to the mirror. "I can see how you'd think that. Black and white is always easier to deal with than gray."

"Right and wrong is not a source of debate. Whatever is in the best interest of our survival is right. Anything else is wrong."

"And who decides what's best for your people?"

"The preservation of life."

Ken turned back to Jaenice. "Am I a threat to your preservation of life, then?"

Jaenice chuckled. "No, Kenneth. Quite the opposite."

A bright light washed across the glass, blinding Ken. He covered his eyes and backed away. As he blinked through the wash of spots from his good eye, he focused his sights onto the walls of the room.

"What is that?" he asked.

"Take a closer look," Jaenice said. "And heed your promise."

His heart sank to the depths of his stomach when he turned to look at the glass. "Jacquline!"

She sat in a similar metal chair to the one next to him. Her face was bright pink and flushed, covered in sweat and tears, and spittle dripped from the tips of her wide-open mouth. Two thin needles attached to wires that wrapped around her head and down to a small canister at the butt of the chair were pressed into her temples. Positioned at the base of her neck was an object that appeared to be a porcelain egg, which most likely caused the vibrancy of the veins painted along the edges of her neck, shoulders and ridge of her face. She scratched at the air in front of her as if she thought she was digging her way out of something.

Ken pounded his fists against the glass and screamed her name several times at the top of his lungs to no avail. Jacquline didn't move one muscle in response. What these monsters —

That's right, they were monsters!

— have been doing to her scared him to death. He couldn't contain his anger any longer. Before he knew what was happening, he had picked Jaenice up (she was unbelievably light, at least with the adrenaline pumping through his body) and tossed her to the wall. He held her there, raised slightly up above him.

She didn't move — didn't really react at all.

"What have you done to her?"

"Set me down, Kenneth, and I shall tell you."

"I want to see her."

Jaenice sat as still as an inanimate object. The light from Jacquline's room flashed past her body, giving her the extreme elegance of an angel. It didn't matter; he still thought of her as the devil. Even then he knew no amount of force or threat was going to get her to do what he wanted. The only way he would get answers was to set her down and back away.

"That is a warning, Kenneth," Jaenice said.

Ken didn't like what this breed of robots were programmed to believe, but he couldn't be the poster child for why they thought the way they did. He had to be better than that, no matter what they said. "Tell me." he replied cautiously.

"All we are doing is opening her mind to the truth."

Ken was rightly confused. "What truth?"

"Whatever truth she believes she has suppressed over time."

"Or the truth you want her to believe," Ken barked.

"You can believe as you will, but nothing she is going through right now is controlled by us. It is all coming from a place deep within her. It is up to her to make her own decisions."

Ken curled his fingers into a fist but didn't take his eyes off of Jacquline.

"What have you done?" he whispered.

"The right thing."

Ken wanted so much to rip Jaenice's head off and use it to break through the glass, but knew that would only get him another beating, if not death. He took a few deep breaths, closed his eyes (and in the back of his mind, counted to ten) and then said, "I want to see her."

"I cannot allow that," Jaenice said in that irritating robotic monotone.

"Why not?"

"Because she believes you are dead."

Ken lowered his head and curled his fingers through his hair. As he stretched his neck and looked up to the ceiling — avoiding his daughter — he was able to eek out, "What do you want with us?"

"We do not want either of you," Jaenice said.

It was obvious what the answer would be to his next question, so Ken decided to ask, "Why do you want Tracey?"

Jaenice rested her hand on the back of Ken's head so that her palm rested just above the nape of his neck. He was ready to knock her hand away but didn't have the strength (or the will) to do so. "You see, Kenneth. The consciousness is merely a series of electrical impulses that function in a very specific way, a formula that is unique to each individual. Once you are capable of finding that unique characteristic, are able to map how each part of the brain works with the rest, and how the electrical synapses are delivered throughout, you can rewire it in order to deliver a different series of pathways."

Ken turned to Jaenice now. "You're talking about changing someone's personality."

"More like building a new soul."

"You want to alter Tracey's mind… to what? So she'll be submissive? Obey you like a mindless sheep?"

"No, Kenneth. We want to alter her brain chemistry so that she becomes someone else."

Ken shook his head. "That's impossible. There are too many other variables involved. Even if you were able to remap the brain, they wouldn't be an exact copy."

"Not unless the brainwaves were altered with the other subject's memories and full array of experiences," Jaenice said.

"Fine. Let's say that's possible. Who exactly is she supposed to become?"

Jaenice pinched Ken's neck, forcing him to turn his head toward the door. His eyes grew wide as DovenJadden entered.

She wasn't bound. She wasn't frightened.

She was one of them.

"No," he repeated over and over in soft whispers.

DovenJadden purred to Jaenice, who responded quickly and a little harshly. DovenJadden grabbed Ken just the same.

"Let go of me you traitor," he screamed.

Jaenice purred some calmer response and then said, "Don't struggle, Kenneth. It will only make it worse."

Ken wasn't having any of it, but when he considered the alternatives, it was better if he obliged. At least he'd be alive.

DovenJadden purred another few commands and then escorted a willing Ken from the room. Jaenice remained still until they had disappeared into the darkness of the hall and then turned to Jacquline. She rested the tips of her fingers lightly on the window — and waited.

— 10 —

The weakness in Sentilla's body didn't stem from her confinement but from the loss of her spiritual connectivity. She hadn't realized how mentally drained she actually was until she reached her living quarters. Walking in was like entering a dream, one that she could never escape. Was she still even here or was this a continued manifestation of the gem's power trying to hide the fact that she was still hungry for it? Until she could think clearly and rationally about everything that Tracey had done for her, she had to continue to believe it was real — but remain cautious just the same — because with the gem, she couldn't be absolutely certain of anything. She would need to slow down and give everything a second look, if only to make sure it wasn't the gem whispering her back.

Sentilla nearly passed out as she lay down on her resting space, which consisted of nothing more than an extremely thick blanket that regulated the heat of her body so as to rest comfortably no matter the situation, and a large, round tubing from inside the wall that conformed to her head with pressure. But for whatever the reason, rest continued to elude her. She rolled to her side and stared at the confines of her quarters. Though everything was still relatively blurry, she could make out the possessions stacked just above the foot of her resting space as if they were crystal clear. These weren't simply treasures she had found on one expedition or another, these were items her mother had given her when she was a child — a mix of memorabilia from days long past, each with their very own fantastic story that only a few would ever know. Some of them might be worth a lot to some traders, yet others, like a particular outfit or a piece of her hair, held no other value than Sentilla's sentimentality. Regardless of their worth, all of them reminded her of her mother's smell, her features, and events that unleashed a plethora of emotions.

The most prized of these possessions was the holographic tablet her mother was never without. Small and crescent-shaped with three tiny thorns extruding from each side of the smoothly rounded cylinder, it held her mother's most treasured thoughts. Holding it, she could activate any memory she liked and watch it play out as if it was happening at that moment. Whether it was her mother's face as Sentilla ran in for a hug, or watching her play with Qah-Shekel through the bowels of the ship, it was her only way to relive those moments without ever having to worry about the sound of a voice or the smell of a good cut of Hylo Frestuni fading into the mist of memory. Sentilla's mouth watered watching her bite into one. She hadn't had it since her mother passed, as no simulator could recreate the aroma and the electric flavors that her mother was able to produce, but the memory still made her hungry for even a second-hand version.

She scanned through a few more memories before resting it down across her legs. She looked away to recall some of her own memories and had to wipe away tears as the few she did recall were missing so much of the detail she was hoping for. As she peered back to the tablet, a perfectly focused explosion erupted across the hologram, stopping Sentilla's heart. She dropped it to the floor and caught her breath as she focused hard on what was happening. For as many times as she had viewed the memories of her mother, not once had she recalled viewing anything like this. Warring aliens of all types diverged on a landscape that Sentilla didn't recognize. After retrieving the tablet, she tried to bring the memory back to the forefront, but the hologram only flickered off and on as if the memory wasn't really there. Had she manufactured the destruction as a way to cope with her mother's death, or was the gem masking the memory because it meant something more than it was willing to give her? Perhaps it was a combination of both, something her mother had tried to suppress but that the gem was attempting to give back to her. Whatever it was, she could feel emotions pounding through her body that were foreign to her. Love mixed with fear and admiration; an odd need to help fight no matter the cost and an eagerness to destroy everything; a desire to flee and stay alive filled with guilt for even thinking it. But what was she fighting for? How was she involved, and where was everyone she had ever known?

Mind games from the gem?

A strong possibility, no doubt. The gem could be feeding her reactions to an event that Jaxxa Rakala, or even Keladrayia, had been witness to. Was that what this was? One of Keladrayia's memories? It was as good a reason as any and answered why it didn't seem to be real but still produced the sensations that came along with it. Perhaps the gem was attempting to show her something she needed to see, something that had been lost among the journals that only Sentilla could accept. If that were the case, should she let her defenses down and allow the gem to take her over?

She set the tablet down, cleared her mind of everything she possibly could and relaxed her entire body. Soon after, a bright flash shot across her mind, opening Sentilla's eyes to the world of Trynoruus at the height of war and the image of a warrior she recognized as Keladrayia.

— 11 —

"We have to get you to safety," Sentilla said as she pulled Keladrayia through the abusively decorated hallways of the castle. Several explosions, some closer than others, caused the structure to destabilize, cracking and crumbling in various places.

"I need to find father," Keladrayia said desperately.

"There is no time." Sentilla ducked away from a statue of the Trystet as it smashed against the floor. "If we don't get you to your ship now, it will all be lost." She pulled her to the wall nearest the east window of the castle that overlooked the war happening below them. Several nations from all over the galaxy had converged to fight for what they believed was theirs for the taking — a young, beautiful girl who embodied the power to bring ultimate destruction to the universe with the birth of her first child.

"It's all my fault," Keladrayia said. Her emotions ran free as she collapsed to her knees. "If I were brave enough, I would end my life now to stop this futile war."

"No," Sentilla said. "No, you cannot think like that. This is not your fault. The only way to bring an end to this war is to protect yourself."

"What's the use if I must always live in hiding?"

"Your future is more important than you realize, Keladrayia. You need to trust me. Your death will have far greater ramifications than you could possibly imagine."

Keladrayia's eyes were red with fear and pain, but Sentilla stood strong and resilient, unwilling to let her own emotions get the best of her — for Keladrayia's sake.

Seeing Sentilla's tenacity was enough to give Keladrayia what she needed to remain as courageous as her father — and Jaxxa Rakala — would expect of her. "I do trust you," she said.

"Then we must go."

Keladrayia suddenly caught sight of her father move in to spar a cloaked figure. Ignoring every plea and warning from Sentilla, she watched as a nearby explosion forced the Trystet to lose his footing, leading to what would be a devastating blow to his chest. As he dropped his weapon, the cloaked figure wrapped his meaty hands around his neck and squeezed until it was nothing more than a gel of liquid seeping *through its fingers.*

Keladrayia screamed.

The cloaked figure looked up. There was no pain that could kill Keladrayia more sharply than that searing flame.

"We have to go," Sentilla yelled, pulling her across the hall just as a series of fireballs shattered the glass. They raced down a large spiral stairwell of rusted iron and glass. Bursts of flames burned across the tower walls, causing the iron to become unstable. A ruckus of grunts and squeals echoed above them, but neither looked up. They had only one goal and nothing would keep them from completing it. Upon reaching the ground floor, Sentilla entered an access code into the panel on the wall. When the chime of acceptance rang out, she shoved the door open and entered the steel-plated chamber, which if she wasn't mistaken, was the size of the entire castle itself. She slammed the door shut behind Keladrayia and then shot her thumb laser into the operating computer, melting the controls on both sides of the door.

"That should keep them out," Sentilla said. She raced to a circle of lights on the floor in the center of the chamber and dropped to her knees. As she tapped the lights in succession, each one lit up and played a sweet, lovely chime. The panels surrounding the outside of the circle opened after lighting the final one and numerous computer stations rose from underneath. Before they had all locked in place, Sentilla found her way to the largest of the stations. The hum was loud but soothing as she powered them all on, lighting the chamber up as if she had just turned on the sun. She quickly worked her fingers across several flat keyboards, sending trillions of bits of data into the system every second. "Disrobe and get in," Sentilla said.

Keladrayia stripped away all of her clothing except for the green gem that dangled around her neck. Bright streaks of green light swam across the floor inside the circle as she cautiously stepped past the lights to stand at the very center of them.

The sound of fists striking the door was barely recognizable under the pressure of the sounds coming from the machines. Keladrayia wrapped her arms across her body, a little embarrassed and a wee bit frightened. A series of flickering purple rings flew up from the ground along Keladrayia's body, dissipating as they passed over her head. One after the other flew by, each one collecting a different piece of data that Sentilla combined together on her machine to develop a computerized replica of Keladrayia's body — one layer of cells at a time. Once the process had been completed, Sentilla ran a few diagnostic checks until the lights above her screen turned green, acknowledging acceptance of the subject's health, weight and dimensions.

"Ready to fly," she quipped.

Sentilla skipped into the circle and hugged Keladrayia tightly. "You are the only good left in this world," she said. "Always remember that." She then kissed Keladrayia lightly on the corner of her mouth and went back to the console.

"I love you," Keladrayia said.

Without a reply, Sentilla tapped the "Execute" key. Beams of electricity shot between each of the lights, surrounding Keladrayia in an electric barrier. Within moments, fingers of light slowly crawled their way to her and wrapped themselves around her body, chilling her through and through. Keladrayia grabbed hold of the gem, which gave her an incredible sense of comfort by counteracting the pressure of the light. By the time the beams made their way up to her chest, she was more than ready to accept her fate. She closed her eyes and waited patiently for the light to engulf the rest of her body. It stayed stagnant for some time, pulsating like a breathing cocoon, and then finally shot straight up into the top of the room.

Sentilla kept a close eye on the monitors, checking to make sure the light's alignment remained in sync with the glass structure absorbing it above her head. One misplaced molecule and the light would swallow Keladrayia whole, and all they worked so hard to protect would be for naught. A tear dropped from Sentilla's eye as the glass reached maximum capacity and blasted the light into infinity.

Sentilla said, "Goodbye, dear friend."

A cursor flashed on the display next to the words:

Execute another order?

Sentilla ignored the request by shutting down the entire system and sending it back to its slumber underneath the floor. Once the panels had returned to their original position, Sentilla stepped into the center of the darkened circle of dead lights, sat down on her knees and took hold of the jewel she wore around her neck.

"Be safe, my child," she said just as the door was blasted away.

The sewers didn't smell as bad as Lark originally thought they would. In fact, after slicing open the grate on the north side of the city (where Kahli departed), Lark took note of how they didn't even feel like a sewer at all. It was more in line with an underground bunker or subway tunnel. The walls were heavily fortified with scores of decrepit electrical wiring linking several lighting mechanisms (some of which still worked through the haze of muck and dust) that lined the uppermost crevices. Graffiti of all sorts (everything from maps and battle strategies to what she could only assume were anti-Alpha propaganda messages) covered stretches of pathways, and whole sections were nearly inaccessible due to how badly they had been scorched. According to the holographic map Kahli had uploaded to Lark's tablet, there was only one tunnel that led to where they needed to go. The Alpha opposition must have known that, as the debris that blocked their way was immeasurably thick and dense. Lucky for Lark and Qah-Shekel, someone had already attempted to find a way through, leaving behind a trail only a worm could love. Lark made it through well-enough (with only minor scratches along her arms), but Qah-Shekel was forced to do a little extra work, chopping away at various parts of the tunnel to allow his body to fit.

"How are you doing?" Lark said as they navigated through the tail end of the system. They had a few miles left to travel, most of which were long stretches of darker, danker passages, and Lark needed to get her mind off of it all.

"I am not sure I understand your inquiry," Qah-Shekel said robotically.

"With Sentilla," Lark clarified. "I know it must be hard for you to see her this way and not be able to do anything to help."

Qah-Shekel remained silent.

"When my mother was dying, I used to pray every night for the ability to heal her. Every day after school, I would go to the hospital, thinking this time will be different; this time when I hold her hand, everything will go back to normal. And every damn day, I'd be disappointed. But my mother remained optimistic, believing death to be the final miracle, and part of me wants to believe it, too. It's hard because her death caused me so much pain, both physically and mentally…" Lark had to stop; she didn't want to appear too vulnerable in front of Qah-Shekel, even though she knew she could.

Qah-Shekel rested his hand on her shoulder. She flashed a smile as she took a hold of it, silently thanking him for his kindness. "Then again," she finally said, "her death helped me become the person I am today, which led me here… so maybe she was right."

"Everything is connected," Qah-Shekel said. "Every choice we make will have infinite effects on the future. Depending on an individual's history, some may appear good, some will appear bad, but all are as meaningful and important as the next. We only have to change our perspective to see the truth."

"Is that why you chose to help me?" Lark said softly.

"Ken, Jacquline and Tracey are where they are because of choices I have made. Leaving them all behind is an easy fix, but doing so would only lead to more death and destruction. If I am going to make things right, and achieve retribution for the extinction of my people, it has to be now."

"Wiping out an entire race isn't retribution," Lark said. She could feel Qah-Shekel's resentment burn through the air. She turned to him and took his hand. "I know how hard all of this must be for you," Lark said with multiple layers of compassion. "There was nothing I wanted more than to strangle whatever god thought it a good idea to leave me in hell with the monster of a father. But if you resort to your enemy's level, you'll only become what you hate the most, and whatever hole you're trying to fill will remain empty and wanting."

"You sound very much like my father," Qah-Shekel said after a short pause that eased the tension surrounding them. "War isn't about retaliation or vengeance; it's about honor and principal. True victory is built on a solid foundation of honesty and integrity. Without that, you'll always be on the losing side of history."

"Very astute."

Qah-Shekel looked away. This time it was he who didn't want to appear vulnerable. "He was very peaceful, my father, but he wasn't afraid of doing what was necessary."

"For the right reasons," Lark added.

Qah-Shekel looked back to Lark. *Was that a smile?*

"I think your father and I would have gotten along pretty well." Lark slapped Qah-Shekel on the shoulder. "Listen," she continued as she headed back down the tunnel. "I don't know everything about the Regans, or the Betas, or whether any of them deserve to live or die. I'm neutral on everything until I know more of the facts, which I'm sure Kahli will get for us. But I'm no prude, and these bastards are holding our friends captive with no provocation. So regardless of what I think, or what your father believed, I give you permission to kill anyone who gets in the way of our mission. And if that includes one devious bitch of a cat, so be it."

She smiled, hoping Qah-Shekel understood to whom she was referring. He must have, because he quickly returned her earlier shoulder slap, the force of which nearly knocked her over.

— 13 —

Two squads made up of three Beta units each systematically patrolled the area outside of the manufacturing plant's main wall. Two of them flanked the entry gate while the other four — two close to the wall a few yards away on each side of the gate, two others approximately twenty yards away from the wall — scoured their designated areas in a very controlled pattern, seeking any signs of possible intrusion. The odd thing was not one of them had detected Kahli, who was positioned behind a rock formation some two hundred yards away. Her first thought was that Lark had been correct in assuming, for whatever reason, the dogs had been called off. Why the Beta units would be reprogrammed so quickly to stop recognizing her threatening scent didn't make one iota of logical sense. It could be that whatever happened with Qah-Shekel inside the factory had disengaged their sensor arrays, but that was highly unlikely. The only other explanation she could come up with was that DovenJadden was so confident that whatever she was planning would come together with unadulterated efficiency, her arrogance had undermined her commonsense — which still didn't answer the alteration of code hardwired into the Beta's programming. Someone would have had to have specifically altered and then uploaded a new set of parameters to the mainframe in order to have it filtered throughout the entirety of units, which Kahli figured DovenJadden might have been able to do from the ship — but why risk it? She knew the team was going after the power core —

The power core.

How could Kahli not have seen it before? The most effective way to change the radiation signature of the Betas would have been to alter the formula of the power core to emit a new signature. Kahli wasn't invisible to the Betas because DovenJadden had reprogrammed them; she herself had been inadvertently reprogrammed.

Kahli hit the back of her head against the face of the rock.

If only I had known.

Dwelling on what might have been a more effective plan did Kahli no good whatsoever. Her best course of action now that she had the upper hand was to adjust the current plan accordingly. Kahli crawled her way into position behind a large wall of shale and then knowingly stumbled into view before collapsing to the ground. The Beta's were quick to stand at the ready with their weapons raised.

Kahli extended her hand. "Do not — fire," she said, altering her voice to make it sound more mechanical and layered in various degrees of static. She waited a few seconds and then lifted her head. Upon seeing her, the Betas lowered their weapons.

"You are not assigned to be here," said the Beta closest to Kahli.

"Yes — I know. I was — patrol — patrolling the outer parameter of the — Tesla Desert when the intruders — intruders — intruders attacked me. They were — shielded — shielded from my — my — my — detection, and before I knew — it, they had eclipsed me of my weapon — my weapon — and used it against — me — me." Kahli twitched slightly. "I am — malfunc — malfunc — malfunctioning. I need immediate — immediate repair." She twitched again.

The front most Beta instantly pulled Kahli to her feet and cradled her in her arms as she carried her past the wall and around the building. A second followed just behind, as was protocol, leaving the other four to remain guarding the gate. Once the door had closed, Kahli used the shadows of the alley to make her move. She grabbed the back of the Beta's neck and squeezed until the unit's spinal chord had snapped. Before the Beta fell to the ground, Kahli seized her weapon and spun to her feet. The second Beta had no chance. Each shot enveloped her in electrical current until she was no longer functioning properly. She dropped to her knees, her body shaking in several locations. Kahli sent the butt of the staff into the Beta's forehead, pushing her entire head backward, rendering the unit immobilized.

Kahli thought she might feel some remorse for her actions, but was surprised to find no emotional quandary whatsoever for the damage she had caused. Wasting no more time, she retreated back to the rear of the building and slid down the piping like a snake covered in grease. Once on the ground, Kahli remained cautiously swift as she navigated her way through Qah-Shekel's improvised destruction to reach the hibernation chamber, a place she never thought she would ever have to see again. Traversing the maze to reach the tower was easy enough; what wasn't so easy was examining some of the units being held in the staging area along the bottom of the chamber. Many of them had a nameplate attached to their sleeping station. Never before had the Regans needed to label the units with anything but their designation.

What changed?

Kahli had no issue breaking through the glass wall encasing the tower and climbing down to the lower levels to investigate further. The units that had an assigned name engraved on the plates above their model designation —

Omega-Two Synthetic

— were also granted unique molds that separated them from the mass-produced Beta-One models. Not only that, but each had distinct structures, including hair, facial features and body shape that would keep them from even being recognized as an android.

"What are you planning?" Kahli whispered. Usually each station had a diagnostic display to assess the functionality of the unit before authorizing its deployment, but that display told her nothing about the reason for the upgrades. She was determined to find a secondary display that would give her answers, thoroughly checking every inch of the station for something more. It wasn't until she accidentally ran her hand across the nameplate did she uncover a hidden holographic screen displaying relevant information on a Regan with the identical name and appearance to the android unit. It revealed the height, weight and personal characteristics (such as birthmarks and altered body parts), as well as life expectancy and other health related issues. This particular woman was going to be dying very soon and her transplant order had been approved, pending the complete functionality of her android counterpart.

Kahli didn't attempt to shut the hologram off before darting up the tower bridge. Her feet were swift as she flew through the maze to reach the tower in less time it took her to spin her fingers across the control boards to locate all information related to Krylex — a search that led to a material the Regans identified as Krylox. She wasted no time activating the recounting of the substance's history.

"Krylox is a manufactured synthetic skin impenetrable to most every known toxin, substance, chemical or emission in the universe. It is mined from the planet of Krylex in the Farrah system and was found to have been biologically engineered as a pelt along the contours of the native inhabitant's extraneous appendages, which rise up in moments of distress and combat. Doctor Pentas Olygraph, a renowned Regan biologist, spent years studying one of the specimens, leading to the discovery of using a collection of bio acidic radioactive waste to liquefy the pelts, and under the right amount of heat, manipulate them into any form that when cooled would retain its designated shape. Numerous tests were performed on different types of robotic systems as a synthetic skin to protect the machinery underneath. Once perfected, the skin was applied to its first robotic counterpart, the Rega-One Synthetic Android, or ROSA. With the success of Doctor Olygraph's creation, a full operations factory was created to manufacture these androids in bulk. Synthesizing Krylox was met with failure, making it necessary to cull the inhabitants of Krylex. With Rega-One's initial acquisition of pelts, the first android army was built to fight the Krylex resistance. The war was short-lived and the procurement of genuine pelts was lucrative. Upon their defeat, the remaining Krylexian rebels destroyed their planet and fled in an attempt to live free across various star systems. This tactic destroyed the bulk of the preliminary army, but a second wave was quickly created to hunt down the remaining Krylexians. Supply has become critical, however recent attempts at synthesizing Krylox have shown promise."

Kahli spent the majority of the history lesson examining her arms. She felt polluted with the death of millions of innocent souls. including the family of a good friend. How would she ever cope with such sickening knowledge? She could always wipe the memory from her database, but then she'd be living in denial of the atrocities it took to develop her and her invincibility. No, she would make sure she remembered every word — for Qah-Shekel.

She had to suppress those feelings for the time being, though. Slaughtering an entire race was plenty reason to destroy the whole lot of android units — including herself — but that was only the tip of the iceberg when it came to the audacity of what she suspected the Regans of planning. It didn't take long for Kahli to track down a set of classified files on a secure drive and break through the layered firewalls. She read through several documents and reviewed a great deal of diagrams and simulations that clearly showed the Regans had found a way to manipulate brainwave activity by replicating synaptic connections and altering the delivery of information. Testing had been finalized with the success of configuring a synthetic brain to match the organic's electrical synapses, thus duplicating its neural functionality. From there, it was just a matter of isolating the neural network responsible for the storage and retrieval of long-term memory and adapt it to the pocket of the synthetic's cortex. With that, an organic being could now become synthetic, and in essence, immortal. But it was the long-term testing that frightened Kahli the most. With the success of this experiment, Regan scientists tested whether they could do the same from one organic species to another, eventually succeeding in transferring the mind of a Krylexian into that of a rodent. As would be expected, the full capacity of the Krylexian's mind wouldn't take due to the lack of mobility and speech capabilities, and the subject eventually died. But the Regans concluded, and rightfully so, that they could successfully transfer the consciousness of a Regan to a similar species (or within their own species, for that matter) without flaw, the development of which not only helped capture the remaining Krylexians in hiding, but led to the breeding of additional Krylexians to be butchered when they come of age for the continued manufacturing of androids that, according to the files, would be used to infiltrate every last corner of the galaxy and secure the most illusive power there is — Jaxxa Rakala.

Genocide aside, Kahli could not let that happen.

Her fingers blasted across the screens, creating thousands of lines of code that would ignite a surge in the power core of every android in the hibernation chamber, burning them from the inside out and eventually sending an electrical impulse to shut down the remaining units still in operation. Destroying the androids would certainly put her team in greater risk, so she added a timer to give her team ample time to get back to the *Equinox*. She then buried the code within a cypher that would jump randomly across systems every few seconds to keep the Regans from shutting it down. "Lasa bey," Kahli said and initiated the countdown.

After a moment of sudden remorse, she gripped the side of the tower and lowered her head. Though they were only an army of androids — a product of man's need to be the creator rather than the creation — it still felt as if she was wiping out an entire species. But having their pride and egos torn down into a heap of scrap just may very well teach the Regans a lesson in the consequences of omnipotent power — that when genocide is used to create wealth, one day it will all come crashing down — and wake them up to the atrocities of their past. It was the right thing to do; it was the rational thing to do. She sat down to live out her final moments in peaceful reflection.

The laugh that interrupted her was more chilling than Eyrixano emerging from around the tower.

Kahli stood slowly with fervent authority. "How long have you been manipulating these people to do your bidding?"

"How long is irrelevant," Eyrixano hissed, "because I've reached my desired destination."

"Universal genocide?"

"No, dear android. I'm not pleased about the destruction of Krylex, but it was a necessary evil to accomplish what I desired most."

"You'll never get her," Kahli said, confident. "She's much too smart for you. Much too powerful."

"Perhaps, but she holds many secrets, the worst of which will be her undoing. You see, your friend may be harboring the power of the gem but she isn't accepting it; she isn't allowing it to become a part of her, which makes her as volatile a weapon as any other."

"That may be true, but I suspect she's only stopping the completion of the process because to do so would land her under your complete control."

"Very astute. However, her resistance comes with a cost. Either she succumbs to my control or she will destroy the universe."

"I can't believe that. Jaxxa Rakala would not risk destroying everything."

Eyrixano secreted a subtle laugh. Kahli narrowed her eyes, unsure of what it meant.

"She knows what she's doing. She will find a way to stop it."

"And I intend to have her in my possession when that time comes."

Kahli's confidence had waned slightly, but not quite as much as when the alarms started to wail. Several red lights flashed on the tower. Pulsating on several screens was the message

DESTRUCTION OF PLANETARY CORE IMMINENT

"What did you do?" she said, but Eyrixano had vanished. Digging a little deeper into the message, she noticed that the time remaining until the planet was destroyed correlated exactly with the amount of time remaining on the execution of the code she wrote.

How is that possible?

She scanned several layers of information on a myriad of topics, none of which explained why the destruction of the androids would cause the planet core to be destroyed. That is until she caught sight of the development of the new formula for the android power core. According to the statistics, each vile, when exposed to air, had the capacity to destroy a city block. Setting a thousand off at the same time would accelerate that power exponentially.

"Kan se," Kahli shouted. Sparks jumped wildly from the console after she nearly put her hands through it. It could take her a century to track her code through the system, which meant there was no way to stop it. She would be the reason for the extinction of an entire race, all because she was hasty in her righteousness. But not everyone had to die. There was still time to guarantee her friends would make it off this rock. It wasn't the most comforting thought, but it was enough to get her feet moving.

— 14 —

The building had been a lot easier to navigate than Tracey was originally expecting. She wasn't sure if it was because Eyrixano felt protected by the amateurish security at the door, or if it was because the majority of forces had been redirected to the meltdown of the factory, but so far, every inch of the place was unguarded and empty. Not that there was much to guard in the first place — a lot of dark hallways and dusty rooms were pretty much the norm. If it weren't for the gem, which Tracey kept doused as low as she could without extinguishing it completely, she would have been walking blind.

After a slew of dead-ends in her search for Jacquline, Tracey finally heard the Betas closing in and took solace in a dilapidated room, which didn't look to have been in a functioning state for a while now. The walls had been stripped of any drywall and insulation (or whatever it was Regans used to build their structures), exposing several rusted pipes and frayed electrical. It presented Tracey with an unexpected advantage. She wrapped her hands tightly around one of the pipes and pressed her ear to it, focusing as much energy as she was willing to expend on listening to the vibrations sing throughout. With the pipes as dead as they were, it would allow for better reverberation and insight into where she might have to go. At first, she didn't hear anything, so she forced the gem to go dark and accessed that energy to heighten her senses. Immediately after doing so, a flurry of sounds flooded the pipe like traffic on a busy highway. Most of what she heard were light squeaks of some animals that sounded like rats but had to be much larger, like that of a possum or a ferret. It gave her chills just thinking about what it might look like; it didn't help that there were several variations of the squeals, forming a family of ferret rats. She tried to filter them out, but because there were so many, Tracey considered giving up and going back to blindly wandering the building. That's when she heard what she had been looking for.

"It's impossible. We're never getting out of here."

It was really faint and hardly audible above the noise of the ferret rats, but at least now she had a focal point, one that would allow her to push the rodents to the background and turn the volume up on Jacquline's one-sided conversation.

"I know," Jacquline said. There was a bit of a pause, and then, "But why do I have to suffer through this shit? If I would have just let her be, I would finally have been able to be on my own, do things on my terms." After another brief pause, Jacquline found something funny. "Thank you," she said with a light chuckle. "What's it like?"

This pause was a lot longer, and for a minute, Tracey thought she had moved away from whatever pipe she was nearest — either that or something else had happened to her. Based on the frequency of the vibrations, Tracey figured she must be a couple of stories below her and possibly fifty to a hundred yards away. A little more conversation would help pinpoint it even closer.

"I'm not going to sit back and do nothing," Jacquline said just before Tracey was about to leave. "If I'm with you, I'm all in. I'll do whatever's needed to get the job done. What you said sounds like a blast, but I want to be an equal partner. No getting sidelined because you don't think I can handle it."

Another brief pause.

"Good. Sorry about what I said earlier. I don't think I ever want to go back home. Not when there's so much treasure to get my grubby little hands on out here. Hell, now that I don't need to take care of that asshole and his little darling daughter, I'm free and clear to start my life over again… if Eyrixano can get our asses out of this mess he put us in."

Tracey wasn't quite sure what to make of any of that, but it didn't matter. She had a much better idea now about where Jacquline was being held. And by the sound of it, she needed to hurry. She transferred her energy back to illuminating the gem, double –checked that the Betas had moved on, and left the room with one specific destination in mind: a stairwell.

She finally found one at the far end of the building. Creeping in through the door, the structure was far more open, but no less decrepit. Tracey half expected a vampire to step from the shadows and devour her dry. But she knew she was in the right place, as she heard several Betas marching across the metal grates that lined the floors. The stairwell spiraled down further than two stories and the only accessible door she could find as she scurried down was at a level equivalent to four stories. Unless there was some secret access somewhere above her, this was her only option, which meant there was either another door that accessed the levels above her, or she miscalculated the distance in the pipes. As she opened the door (letting out a magnifying series of squeaks and squawks), she prayed it was the latter, though the long hallway of emptiness — no doors, no windows; nothing but endless metal — didn't encourage hope. The thing is, she couldn't help feel something was amiss. Though littered with doubt, her gut told her there had to be some type of shield masking the doors.

Footsteps from the Betas grew louder and quicker. They were definitely on their way. It was either fight or surrender, and Tracey wasn't about to give up, not when she was this close. But she had to be smart about how she handled the Betas, else be caught off-guard and out-gunned. She knelt down a few steps from the door and let the gem go dark. As the Betas wrapped around the staircase just outside, Tracey interlocked her fingers around the back of her head.

"Halt, intruder," one of the Betas shouted with a much more metallic voice pattern than Tracey was used to.

"I surrender," Tracey said. It seemed to stun the Betas a little, but two of them instantly pulled her to her feet. The third wrapped her way around her, and as she examined the crescents on her cheeks with a hint of curiosity, the gem lit up as bright as it could, burning the Beta's retinas. Tracey pulled her arms together across her chest and smashed the other two together, the force of which was enough to snap one of their spinal chords on contact. Tracey manually snapped the other one by taking hold of the Beta's neck and flipping it in the opposite direction. Meanwhile, the blind Beta inadvertently ran into a wall and dropped to her knees. Tracey squirmed her way in close as the Beta flailed her arms in a vain attempt to strike her, eventually grabbing Tracey around the waist. The pain was no more agonizing than a light pinch and allowed Tracey to press her lips gently against the Beta's ear. "Where is the female captive?"

"I will not tell you anything."

"Suit yourself." Tracey grabbed hold of the Beta's neck, and just as she did to the first, shattered the spinal chord in half with the snap of her fingers. She quickly tore the Beta's hands off of her waist and took a step away.

"Just a robot," she said and then dropped to one knee. Dousing the gem's light, she took a few moments to collect her bearings. The incident had drained her far more than she thought it would. She just hoped she'd have enough juice left to do what she had to do to find Jacquline. At least she no longer had to worry about getting caught. Or so she prayed.

She felt a bit lightheaded when she finally stood back up, but it was nothing she couldn't handle. To test her earlier theory, Tracey pressed her hands to the wall and walked the hall, hoping to find some indication of a transition from rigid to pliable. But the farther she went, the more despondent she became. Her gut may still be telling her something was there, but her eyes told a completely different story. There was only one way to be absolutely sure. Turning back the way she had come, she let the gem's power flow through her fingertips to identify variances in heat and material that she otherwise wouldn't have felt. Halfway down the hall, she finally felt a strong heat signature emanating beyond the wall. It had to be Jacquline.

It had to be.

Now it was only a matter of getting through the force field. The source of the shield could be anywhere and would take time she didn't have to find, so she was going to need to deactivate it from where she was, which meant overloading the system. Her best option would be to us the android's power core, but without a directed response, the explosion wouldn't do anything to diffuse the force field. Her only choice — one she dreaded — was to press her hands to the center of the heat source and push every ounce of energy into her hands. Sparks jumped from between her fingers as tentacles of electricity crept from her hands in all directions, seeking out the force field generators. Minutes passed as Tracey continued to pump her soul into the wall, which finally started to become fragile — at least where her hands were concerned. And because the integrity was failing, she continued to push, even as the gem glowed white hot, the crescents on her cheeks burning the inside of her jaw. Sweat dripped from every pore in her body and her legs shook. Her head pounded as if her brain had swelled three sizes to big, and if she clenched her teeth any harder, they would shatter.

Her body moved forward slightly; it was coming apart. If the force field didn't shatter soon, she would either explode (and possibly destroy the planet along with her) or she would have to succumb to the gem's unity —

Neither was a viable choice.

She had to stay strong —

Fight it!

She was almost there — just one more minute.

Without realizing what happened, Tracey fell to the ground and rolled forward. She immediately grabbed her knife and stabbed her chest to relieve all of the strain from the gem, which she was afraid would never stop. She had pushed herself to hard; she no longer had control over the gem. This was the end.

Then she exhaled and vomited a combination of water, bodily fluid and light. She pulled the bloody knife from her chest and dropped her hands to the floor. Breathing had become a chore as she shook uncontrollably, shivering in a heat-soaked sweat. The gem had returned to its brilliant green color and the heat melting her mouth had dissipated. She wasn't sure if she had fallen asleep (she hoped she hadn't — doing so in this state was far too dangerous), but she could no longer feel Eyrixano's presence in her mind. She would be okay...

She would be okay.

Stand up.

Tracey forced herself to her feet, still chilled with an occasional shiver. Blood melted into her clothing and ran down her stomach. The wound hadn't healed yet; it would take a lot more time to do so. It was inconsequential to completing her goal, which from the looks of it, was not what she had expected. Her eyes were out of focus (for now), but what she could make out was an open room with an array of pathways interlinked across several holes that went down an additional two stories.

Damn it. She was too high up.

No point in dwelling on that now. Going back was out of the question since the force field had solidified behind her. Another exertion of energy like that and there was no question she'd explode. Besides, Jacquline had to be somewhere below her. And jumping was easy enough.

Of all of the possible rooms Jacquline could be in, there was only one space among the nonexistent floor that had any indication of light. Tracey couldn't risk using the gem to see in the dark, so if that wasn't where Jacquline was being held, Tracey was lost. She cautiously walked across the beams. The relief she felt when she reached the room was so overwhelming, she nearly fainted. Tracey had to kneel down and grab hold of the beam to catch herself from falling. But it was worth it, as just below her, strapped to a chair with wires and tubes inserted into her body, was her big sister.

— 15 —

The rock crumbled away with ease as Jacquline and Eyrixano tore away at the wall. Upon breaking through the barrier, Jacquline's adrenaline pumped rapidly. In her boisterous fervor, she wrapped her arms around Eyrixano.

"Thank God."

Eyrixano didn't take much notice. Jacquline ran to Jaenice, who had been resting, and pulled her to her feet. "Come on, girl. We are finally out of this hell hole."

Jaenice smiled with relief and Jacquline joined in helping Eyrixano strip away the rest of the hole, which would allow them all to climb back into the corridors. Jacquline took a deep breath. It still smelled extremely horrid, but it felt so freeing — so refreshing. All of her teeth were on display as she smiled at Jaenice, slapping her shoulder and giving her a quick massage. She then offered her hand to Eyrixano. "What do you say we get the hell back to your ship."

The flames within Eyrixano's hood glowed bright with pleasure as he took her hand. Upon his touch, the ground dramatically shook. Jacquline and Jaenice fell to their knees for balance.

"What is that?" Jacquline yelled. "What's happening?"

Jaenice didn't get a chance to answer before the ground broke away. Jacquline lost her grip on Eyrixano and fell into one of the massive holes. Jaenice was quick to grab her wrist. She tried desperately to pull her up, but couldn't find a strong enough footing.

"Help!" Jacquline screamed. She looked down into the black abyss. "Jaenice."

"I'm trying," Jaenice said. But she sounded like Ken. When Jacquline looked back up, it was Ken straining to pull her out. She tried to grab a hold of his wrist, but it was of no use.

"I'm slipping," Jacquline said.

"I'm not letting you go," Ken assured her. He yelled as he strained to pull her up, but for some reason, Jacquline felt it was simply a ploy to make it seem as if he was trying to appease his own ego. "I love you," he said.

Nothing escaped Jacquline's lips in return. And as the sweat from the heat and the fear melted away any friction they may have had, Jacquline closed her eyes, ready to take the plunge. Suddenly, she felt something pull at her legs. "What the hell?"

"It feels like your stuck," Jaenice said.

The grip on Jacquline's wrist was like a vice. "Get me the hell out already."

"I wish I could."

Jacquline felt as if she were being stretched and no amount of movement was going to keep the void from pulling her down, even if it meant breaking her arm.

"It's pulling me in," Jaenice said. "I'm sorry." And with that, she let go.

Jaenice shrank to the point of non-existence, at which point Jacquline wasn't sure she was even falling any longer. She felt weightless and direction had become indecipherable. There was really nothing left for her to do but close her eyes and let the void do to her as it pleased. She dug her nails into her chest as her lungs started to compress, but nothing would stop the pressure. It was clear to her —

She was dying.

Then her lungs filled with air. She coughed dramatically as she sat forward in the chair. Unable to control it, Jacquline fell to the ground. She felt a pair of hands run across the back of her neck. They lifted her up.

"Jacquline, are you okay?" the soft voice said.

Jacquline wheezed in a few breaths, then said, "Jaenice."

"No, Jacquline. It's me, Tracey. Your sister."

Upon hearing her voice, Jacquline slowly looked up. It took a moment for her eyes to focus, but once they had, she screamed and pushed Tracey away. "You bitch," she said, her voice a mix of fear and anger. "You are not my sister. You are not my sister." Jacquline scurried to the wall and curled into a tight ball.

"Jacquline," Tracey said, attempting to calm her by extending her arms out in kindness.

"No!" Jacquline screamed. "You're dead. You're a ghost. You're nothing but smoke. And I hate you. *I hate you!*"

Tracey didn't let Jacquline's rant affect her. She knew Jacquline had been drugged or manipulated in some way; that didn't mean she shouldn't tread lightly. "I'm not here to hurt you," she said softly with a hint of how Jacquline used to talk to her. "I'm here to bring you home."

"Home. *Home.* Home is a lie. It's nothing more than a delivery of hatred and pain and death. It's nothing but an illusion of any mind. I have no home."

"I'm only here to help you," Tracey said again.

"You lie. You all *lie.*"

Tracey lowered her head. She wasn't sure how she was going to circumvent the noise Jacquline had absorbed. Having looked as deeply as she could into Jacquline's eyes, she didn't see any remnants of her big sister. They were cold and soulless. The only thing she thought she could do to help her was to knock her unconscious and carry her back to the ship. But to do so would almost certainly force her to succumb fully to the gem. She had to keep trying to reason with her, even if it was impossible.

As she slowly shifted closer to Jacquline, she heard a series of soft mumblings under her tears. "Kill me if you must. End my misery. Just do it. Now. Kill me if you must."

Tracey wanted to cry with her. "I don't want to kill you, Jacks," she said in the sweetest voice Jacquline had ever heard. "I want to save you."

Jacquline stopped chanting and curled her eyes upward to catch a glimpse of Tracey, who raised her hand up as slowly and cautiously as she could. "Come back with me," she said, hoping she had somehow broken through the dark skin of Jacquline's indoc-trination. With Jacquline's slight change in body language (making it seem as if she was about to accept Tracey's help), Tracey was certain she had —

If Jaenice hadn't entered the room.

"Jaxxa Rakala," Jaenice said. Jacquline perked up at the sight of her friend, but Tracey didn't notice. Her eyes were fixed on the Beta.

"I'm taking her with me," Tracey said.

"I do not think that is up to you," Jaenice replied with just as much authority. "How about we allow Jacquline to make that decision."

"She's not in her right mind to make that kind of a decision."

"You do not believe she has the right to choose?"

Tracey backed down slightly, knowing full well she would not be able to win this argument — at least not with words. "I won't allow you to corrupt my sister."

"As I told your father. We did nothing but open her mind to the truth. What she makes of that is her own doing."

"And with what influence did you use to open her mind?"

"Only those to which she already had in place. If you want to blame anyone for her current state, I would take a long, hard look in a mirror before pointing the blame at any other."

Tracey controlled the anger the gem was eager to exploit.

"The events Jacquline has been playing out in her head are based solely on the subconscious beliefs that have developed over time. If that means she no longer trusts you, it is only because she never really did. Forcing her to go with you against her will only proves why she would think such a thing. If you truly loved her, and want her to be happy, you would let her decide what is in her own best interest." Jaenice held her hand out to Jacquline. "Come, baby Kel. We have got to run."

Jacquline didn't hesitate to join her.

"No," Tracey said, stunned. At that moment, a flash of light inadvertently jumped from the gem, pushing Jaenice up the wall and across the ceiling.

"Jaenice!" Jacquline screamed.

Tracey regained control of the gem at the sound of Jacquline's voice. Jaenice dropped to the floor, unconscious. Tracey had to grab Jacquline's arm to keep her from running to her.

"Let me go, you bitch," Jacquline cried. "Jaenice!"

"Jacquline, she's lying to you."

"No she's not. She's the only one who hasn't ever lied to me."

"She poisoned your mind," Tracey said, unaware of the tightening grip on Jacquline's arm.

"Ow. Let go. You're hurting me."

Tracey noticed honesty in the tears rolling down Jacquline's cheeks. She was so lost. There was nothing Tracey could do to help but let go.

Jacquline gently rubbed her arm and pierced Tracey's eyes with a vindictive gaze. She then dropped to her knees next to Jaenice. "You killed her," she said softly.

Tracey wasn't sure what to say. She didn't think she had killed her; the force from the gem wasn't powerful enough to do much damage to her internal systems, but if the fall did somehow break her spinal mechanics, she wasn't sorry for it. "I did what I had to do." She didn't think Jacquline heard her under the sobs of Jaenice's name. "We have to go," she said a bit louder.

Jacquline looked at Tracey with the reddest of eyes. "You killed her," she screamed before jumping to her feet. Jacquline's attack caught Tracey a little off guard, but not enough to keep her from swiveling sideways and adding momentum to Jacquline as she ran past, pushing her into the wall.

"I don't want to hurt you," Tracey said, loud and firm.

"You liar." Jacquline swiftly made her way back to Tracey, fists flying in all directions. Tracey ducked and shifted and blocked every shot, refusing to give in to Jacquline's madness with any sort of counterattack. She knew if she did, she might not be able to control the gem, which was ready to kill her if she let it (or at the very least, inadvertently use energy she couldn't afford to expend). Eventually, Jacquline would wear herself out; Tracey just needed to bide her time — or so she thought. With all of the adrenaline surging through Jacquline's body, there really was no telling how long that might be, and after a few minutes of defense, Tracey was no longer willing to find out. She let herself get pinned to the wall to see what might happen.

Jacquline quickly grabbed Tracey's throat. "I will see you pay for what you and Ken did to me," she said, full of ire.

"What did we do?" Tracey asked in a muffled whisper.

"You tried to have me killed."

"That's not true. Jacquline, you have to believe me. I would never —"

Jacquline tightened her grip and pushed Tracey up the wall several inches. "I will see you hanged for your crimes."

"So be it," Tracey said and wrapped her hands around Jacquline's arms. She burned her sister's skin as she dug her nails deep within.

Jacquline screamed and let go of Tracey, who pushed Jacquline away with both hands to the chest before her feet hit the ground. The attack only made Jacquline's resolve that much greater, but this time, Tracey wasn't going to stand idly by and watch her sister fall deeper into delusion. She knew she could end the whole thing quite easily, but along with her diminished energy level (which caused her stamina to remain near non-existent), her reluctance to risk killing either one of them remained her top priority. No matter how often either was on the offensive, neither was able to take control of the situation. Not until a quick buzz of dizziness caused Tracey to stammer backward.

Jacquline took full advantage. She threw an uppercut into Tracey's jaw, connecting just under the crescent moon on her left cheek. Tracey fell to her knee, which gave Jacquline the opportunity to send her own knee into her baby sister's forehead. Tracey fell backward, exhausted and defeated.

"Baby Kel..."

Jacquline turned to Jaenice, who tried to find some semblance of balance as she rose to her knees. "Jaenice," she whispered. Tracey didn't lie about killing Jaenice after all. Did that mean she was telling the truth about everything else, or was it simply an attempt to get on Jacquline's good side in order to manipulate her even further? She couldn't take that chance. Jaenice was her family now. She couldn't let herself doubt that, not after everything they had gone through.

"I love you," Tracey said hoarsely.

The words seemed to break through Jacquline's defenses, if ever so slightly. But it wasn't enough. "Sorry, *sister*, but we have to go." In an extraordinary amount of strength Tracey would never have thought her capable, Jacquline grabbed one of Tracey's legs and swung her through the viewing window. Tracey landed with a roll across the shattered glass and came to a stop against the base of the chair.

Jacquline waited to see if Tracey would get back up. After a few moments, it was clear she wasn't. Jacquline stumbled back, finally noticing her own incredibly rapid heartbeat and need for oxygen. Her breaths had become really heavy as she helped Jaenice to her feet. "Come on," she said in between breaths.

Jaenice wrapped her arm around her sister's neck, and though she didn't need it in the least, allowed Jacquline to escort her from the room, a slight smile slipping across her lips.

— 16 —

Four Beta units escorted Ken down a cavernous stairwell. A thick metallic chord connected the magnetic cuffs that pinched his wrists to the large collar resting gently around his neck. Two lights — one a stagnant red, the other slowly pulsing blue — were prominently placed near the center of the collar just under his chin. With every move of his head, small pins pricked his neck. He was told they would inject him with a lethal dose of liquid if he tried to break the connection between any of the thick wires that snaked their way along the edge of the collar, and he was apt to believe them — especially when they went into specific details of how the poison would force him to bleed out in seconds and kill anything that came into contact with his blood.

About three stories down, a series of dimly lit corridors eventually led to a massive landing station brimming with Beta units. Though his escorts did a good job at blocking most of his view, he did manage to catch glimpses of the bizarre hustle and bustle that surrounded him. If the Beta units weren't scurrying across the room in fervent discussion or operating loaders that carried mostly large bundled crates (which Ken believed to be cleverly disguised weapons), they were glued to the plethora of computer terminals, most likely readying the aircraft for takeoff or possibly testing the integrity of the weapon systems. Above him, lining both sides of the walls, were smaller transport vessels, much like a high-end monorail system, transporting dozens upon dozens of Regans, each arriving to a salute and a hand-shake from a stationed Beta.

In the center of it all, resting gently above the ground despite there being no indication of any sort of hover jets, was a black ship shaped like a thin, sleek teardrop. A stream of purple lights highlighted its carved features and weapons ports. It was an elegant design, to be sure, but one that sickened Ken's memory. He would never forget that ship —

The one that stole his wife from him.

The closer he got to it, the sicker he became, not only because of what the ship represented, but because he couldn't feel any sign of Stacey. He realized it was probably wishful thinking, but part of him hoped if she wasn't still on board, at least he'd still be able to recognize her presence as part of the ship.

Ken felt dizzy with rage. So much so, he could hardly breathe as two vermon (who for some reason seemed fatter than some of the rest) lumbered from the ship and grabbed him by the arms. The smell of their putrid breath mixed with the texture of their calloused hands caused him to vomit in recollection of that fateful night. The vermon didn't much care. They dragged him up the ramp. Ken's desire to break his binds and strangle these monsters was subdued by forcing his body to go limp. He hated the idea, but with no help in sight, this could very well be his best chance at finding out if Stacey was in fact still alive, so he was going to have to let this one play out, no matter the consequences.

Halfway up the ramp, a loud explosion rippled throughout the loading station. The vermon dropped Ken and jumped off the ramp, pulling their whips from one of the loops latched across the series of leather belts wrapped along their bodies. Ken used the opportunity to inch his way down the ramp and roll off the edge to his feet. He remained crouched down as he looked past the vermon to see what had happened. One of the ships near the far end of the room had been devoured in flames.

Suddenly, a second ship went up in flames, diverting all attention to it. Betas, vermon and Regans all rushed to find out what was happening. That's of course not counting the flurry of Regans whose screams of panic helped drown out the commands from Betas looking to fight the flames. No one, as it turns out, was paying any attention to Ken, who slowly backed away from Eyrixano's ship. Once in the clear, he ran as fast as he could toward the stairwell, only to be stopped by DovenJadden, who came out of nowhere to dig her claws into his chest. He wanted to fall to his knees, but DovenJadden kept him upright as she carried him back toward Eyrixano's ship. They hadn't gotten but a dozen yards when Lark rolled up from around the back of the ramp with Qah-Shekel's thumb laser pointed directly at them. She would have had no problem killing DovenJadden right then if she hadn't already curled behind Ken, but it was even less of an option as the bitch wrapped her hand around the wires of his collar.

"Let him go," Lark commanded.

DovenJadden responded with a flurry or purrs, followed by a slow, resonant hiss. She knew Lark wouldn't do anything that might hurt Ken, so all advantage was on her side, even if Lark couldn't understand one bit of what she was saying. She inched her way to the ship, ignoring a third explosion with an intense lock on Lark's eyes. In turn, Lark held firm, never once flinching as she incessantly looked for an opportunity to take her out once and for all. They both spun slowly around as DovenJadden stepped onto the ramp. Just another few feet and the ship would become her protection, with or without Ken, whom Lark feared would be killed either way. DovenJadden read that fear and smiled devilishly. But before she could do anything else, Qah-Shekel dropped down from above and sliced his fins across DovenJadden's back. With an intense cry, she ripped the wires from the collar and took a swipe at Qah-Shekel, who used his fins to form a shield in front of him.

"You betrayed me," he said.

"A means to an end," DovenJadden hissed.

Meanwhile, Ken grabbed the collar and fell to the ground. "What's happening?" Lark said. She collected him in her arms mere seconds later. The blood oozing from the puncture wounds around his neck answered for him. Lark couldn't see any mechanisms that might open the collar or stop it from shrinking. All she saw was a flashing light, which matched his gradually slowing pulse. "Don't you dare," she said. "Don't you dare die on me."

Out of the corner of her eye, she saw DovenJadden leap over Qah-Shekel. As she landed, so did his fist across her cheek. She fell to the ground only to swipe her leg up across his, bringing him down with her. In a fluid motion, DovenJadden spun back up to her feet, grabbed hold of a missile gun from the rack above her on the ship and fired. Qah-Shekel avoided the blast by flying over the edge of the ramp. Lark felt the wind from the missile as she ducked to cover Ken, then watched as it connected with one of the ships across the room, killing a few Regans and Betas along with it. As DovenJadden ducked away from a bit of flying debris, Qah-Shekel rose up from under the ramp and grabbed DovenJadden's legs, spinning her off the ship and across the room. Her back tagged the transport after plowing over a couple of Regans who were racing to leave the loading station. She tried to get up, but every move of her muscle splintered her spine.

"Fix him," Qah-Shekel said to Lark.

She nodded. With no other viable options, she pulled the laser cutter from her pocket. "Here goes nothing," she said, placing the tip of the cutter on the edge of the collar. Moving it back and forth across the metal, Lark kept a light touch so as not to cut too deep at any one point. Layer after layer, she kept her eyes as sharp and focused as possible until she was down to the thin inner loop. This is where it became extremely tricky. Too much pressure and she could slice right into his neck, but if she didn't hurry, the collar would kill him anyway. She had to suck up whatever fear was lurking in her gut and make it happen. A light trickle of blood dripped across his neck as she shifted across the top — was it her, or the collar? Unwilling to take the chance, she lightened the pressure just a bit and carefully stripped away the final layer. By the time she was able to pull the collar away, Ken's heartbeat barely registered upon her touch. His head rolled to the side, limp as licorice.

"God damn it, Ken. Wake up." Unsure if he had stopped breathing, Lark leaned in and blew a good amount of air into his mouth. Ken immediately pulled away with a rough cough. Lark was relieved by his reaction, but uneasy about having enjoyed it as much as she had. Given the situation, it was far from a real kiss, but she couldn't help but wish it hadn't have been simply a life-saving act. "Are you okay?" she said, hiding her discomfort.

Ken sucked in a pound of air and coughed as he grabbed his neck. It was wet and cold. He cautiously removed his hands to see blood soaked across them. "What did you do?" he said to Lark.

"You're lucky I didn't cut your throat wide open. Come on. We have to get out of here." Lark helped balance him as she pulled him off the ramp. As they met Qah-Shekel, who hadn't once turned from watching DovenJadden, several more ships burst into a cloud of smoke and flame.

"Ready to leave this party?" Lark said.

Qah-Shekel didn't answer verbally. He just ran toward the back of the loading station. Lark and Ken limped slowly behind him, ending up on the wrong side of the shockwave from another explosion, which blew them backward a few feet. Lark rolled across Ken's body, knocking the wind out of him. He got to his knees and desperately tried to draw in air. It didn't take long, so he sat back on his legs as he waited for Lark to gather her own composure. It was then he saw Jacquline heading toward Eyrixano's ship carrying a hurt (damaged?) Jaenice.

"Jacquline!" Ken screamed.

Lark followed Ken's eye line to Jacquline. The young woman was staring back at them but her eyes were as hollow as a carved out pumpkin, barely registering them before hauling her friend into the ship without even a second thought.

It took him some time (and several attempts) to stand and stammer toward her, but Lark was quick to stop him.

"Let go," he said, pushing her off him.

Lark was stubborn as hell, holding firm to her conviction. She pulled him into her and held him close. "We don't have time. We need to let her go."

"No." Ken struggled to get free, though he could easily have done so if he really wanted to. It was hard, but knew it was true — he couldn't save Jacquline. Not now. Not yet. "I can't leave her again," he whispered in one last-ditch effort to sway her.

A few yards away, DovenJadden had finally gotten back to her feet. She was still rather weak and clearly in pain, which was enough to keep Lark calm. "We need to get the hell out of here Ken, or we're all dead."

Ken dropped his head into her shoulder. Lark, her eyes fixed on DovenJadden's progress, grabbed Ken's hand. "Can you run?"

He nodded and jogged alongside Lark as fast as he could through the now empty loading station. DovenJadden watched as they descended into the sewer system along with Qah-Shekel. But they no longer mattered. Jacquline's conversion had evidently been complete. Eyrixano had what he needed for the time being.

It would have to be enough.

— 17 —

Sentilla didn't feel she had woken up. She was simply awake, as if she had just come into existence. For a minute, she had no idea who she was, where she was or even, for that matter, what she was. She had no concept of life or death, or even being, and that state of euphoria and confusion shocked her system into petrification. Then, as if a switch had been flipped in her head, she was aware, brought to life by the electric impulse of her brain. Everything wasn't and then was; to describe it was impossible.

What shocked her system most was her ability to see as clearly as ever. She was in medical, that was certain, but how she had gotten there was beyond her. The last thing she remembered was looking into the hologram and letting the gem —

The gem.

The gem which...

Which, oddly enough, was just an object. A rock that had only been given power because she had let it, because she was told it had power and she believed it. Not anymore. There was no such thing as power — only the concept of fear and belief. She understood now that when you believe in what you fear, fear will control your actions and give power to those who choose to exploit it. She gave others power; there was nothing more to it than that.

It's all an illusion, Sentilla whispered without knowing.

"What was that?" Kahli said. She stood behind Sentilla at her computer. How long had she been there? It didn't matter, really. The point is, she was there and Sentilla felt comfortable with that.

She smiled, which Kahli returned with warm confusion.

"Am I dying?" Sentilla asked.

"On the contrary," Kahli said. "From what I've gathered, you seem healthier than ever."

"How is that possible?"

"That is a very good question, and one I look forward to finding out." Kahli typed in a few more thoughts and pulled the chord from the back of her neck. She then walked up to Sentilla. "Don't blink," she said as she studied Sentilla's eyes carefully, looking deep within the wells of every single fiber.

"You are no longer afraid," Kahli said, impressed. "Are you?"

Sentilla shook her head. "I don't know. But I do feel different. What did Jaxxa Rakala do to me?"

Kahli smiled. "She healed your soul."

And she did it without doing anything but sit with her, giving her the chance to fight the demons that had dug their claws deep within and break their torturous bonds.

"Where's Qah-Shekel?" Sentilla quickly said, sliding from the table. She felt as light as air and capable of anything.

"He hasn't returned yet."

"How long has he been gone?"

"Too long. And we don't have much time left."

"What do you mean?"

"The Beta units have been set to self-destruct."

"So what? We're not anywhere near —"

"It's much more than that. A city can be rebuilt; a moon cannot."

Sentilla's eyes grew wide. "Kahli, what did you do?"

"The Regans altered the formula to the power core after I left. It's much more potent than it was when the Alpha-Nine units were created. I didn't take that into consideration when I activated the destruction of all inactive Beta units housed at the manufacturing plant. When they shut down, the cumulative blast from all of the power cores going off at once will be the equivalent to the force of a white star supernova."

"How could you be so careless?"

Kahli had no answer, though she tried to justify her actions. "I only wanted to stop the Regans from becoming invincible immortals, and was prepared to be destroyed along with them for what they represented; what *I* represented."

Sentilla bowed her head. In a way, she understood, but it still felt wrong. "This is your home," she said.

"The *Equinox* is my home," Kahli said without hesitation. "Rega-One has been trading on manipulation, fear and lies for far too long, increasing their egos and their lust for power to uncontrollable proportions. They are not my family. My family is here. It always has been."

Sentilla smiled slightly then opened her eyes wide in panic. "Wait. Are all of the Beta power cores connected?"

Kahli's answer was in her steely gaze. "I've made some calculations," she said, "and I do believe my core will be disconnected once we break orbit."

"You believe?"

"Until we know for certain, you will need to isolate me."

Sentilla looked at Kahli with concern. She didn't want to lose her. Not like this. "Is there any way to shut down the sequence?"

"No."

Sentilla's hand was across her mouth in shock. "How much time do we have?" she asked when she finally found the ability to speak again.

"A quartet, maybe two."

Sentilla stood motionless in contemplation. Then as if nothing mattered, curled her lips and said, "Then what are we waiting for? Let's get our home back where it belongs."

"I wish it were that easy," Kahli said, raining on Sentilla's excitement. "Unfortunately, DovenJadden gifted the ship with a virus. Unless we get the deactivation code, we'll be dead in the water."

Sentilla's smile grew even wider. "We don't need a code." She sprinted for the door, adding, "Get to the core."

"Sentilla." Kahli rolled her eyes. She knew what Sentilla was about to do, but the odds of it working were no more than eight percent — and that was pushing it. But right now, those were better odds than anything else she could do, especially if Tracey failed to get the code.

— 18 —

Tracey was on her feet before her awareness had completely returned. She looked around at the glass-covered floor and finally remembered what had happened — and that memory turned into a massive headache. As she relaxed her body against the chair, the gem glowed softly to help relieve the pain. When she finally felt ready to move, she rubbed her eyes to moisten them a bit and stumbled from the room.

She had no idea where she was going, so she allowed her instincts —

the gem

— to direct her in Jacquline's direction. Her speed picked up the longer she traveled until it was nearing the light jog of an average person in the middle of their normal cardio routine through the local park. Jacquline's presence grew sharper with each step. Eventually, she reached a stairwell billowing with smoke a few levels down. Breathing would have been impossible without the gem, and she wasn't willing to accept that much help from it right now. Whatever had happened would have to remain a mystery. Her only solace came from the belief that if Jacquline was in there, she must have made it out alive (or at the very least, was being protected), which until she was able to find another way past the smoke would have to be good enough.

She didn't make it very far back up the stairwell. Eyrixano covered the entire upper portion with his darkness. Tracey stood firm; she was far from afraid.

"Well, my child," Eyrixano hissed delightfully. "You've come back to me after all."

"I'm not here for you, Eyrixano," Tracey said fiercely.

Eyrixano laughed. "Your bravery will only get you so far, young one. Eventually, you will need to submit to your power."

"I will only submit when I'm dead."

"And indeed you will be... soon."

"What makes you think that?"

"You're not looking too well, child. With the cracks of your eyes and the yellowing of your skin, I would say you've expunged nearly every last drop of dominion you may have had over the gem."

Tracey didn't argue his point. The defenses she had erected had all but crumbled. It was only a matter of time. "Where's my family?" she said, avoiding his declaration.

"They are safe... for now. Give me your life and I will assure your family's protection."

"Get this through that dense little mind of yours, Eyrixano. I will never allow you to control me. I will not become a slave."

"So be it."

Tracey could feel the evil smirk under the light flames of his hood. "Touch her and the definition of torture will have nothing on what I will do to you."

Eyrixano laughed again. "Child, I don't wish any harm upon your sister. But you will be the one who kills her if you don't bow to me."

"I should kill you. Put an end to it all right now."

"Be my guest, child," Eyrixano said, spreading his arms out as wide as he could.

Tracey sneered. He knew doing that would ignite the gem. Whether she liked it or not, Eyrixano had the upper hand — and he always had. She stepped as close as she could and stared directly into the heat of his flames. "You will not win this," she said and grabbed his chest. In an instant, she was behind him, shoving him into the dark smoke below.

"I will protect you," she whispered to Jacquline and then headed up the stairs, her hand pressed firmly against the gem to try and alleviate the pain of her latest trick.

— 19 —

"Ship is prepped and ready," Jaenice said as DovenJadden walked onto the bridge.

"What about the others?"

"We were able to salvage six ships."

"How many Robots survived?"

"All ships have the required crew and are ready when we are."

"What about the girl?"

"I've asked her to stay in the brig for the time being," Jaenice said. "She's fine."

DovenJadden wasn't sure she believed her, but how could she not? It was clear Jacquline had helped Jaenice onto the ship, but if the program wasn't completed properly, there might be a few cracks that could be exploited.

"Fine," she finally said. "Once Eyrixano's on board, we go."

"Yes, ma'am."

— 20 —

Sentilla slid through the thinning corridors on the third level, leading her to a triangular dead-end. It was extremely hard to move her arms in any capacity, but it was enough to maneuver a panel off the wall. Inside, it was warm, but cool. There was a large physical screen with a double pane of glass stacked two inches apart just below. Sentilla waved her hand across the top pane of glass, lighting up the entire system. A holographic keyboard hovered above the second pane of glass, but it wasn't the one Sentilla needed. She started flipping through a series of keyboards until she came to one that included a lot of hieroglyphic characters with a handful of letters and numbers in the Lovient language, which even though she never expected to use it, her mother had forced her to remember.

Thanks mom, she thought as she typed in several lines of code. When they finally stopped, there was one line of code left at the top of the screen with a small blinking cursor sitting underneath.

"Here goes nothing," Sentilla whispered. She programmed like a possessed madman. Never before had Sentilla wished she had the capability to type as fast as Kahli. Luckily, for every line she entered, the computer would add two, which made her search for ground zero inside the maze of possibility a lot easier, even if it was taking much longer than she hoped. "Come on, baby, talk to me. Where is that little bitch?" Finally, she zeroed in on the location —

The weapons storage cache; *Damn it, DovenJadden, I should have known*

— and isolated the foreign code. She moved it up to the top pane of glass. After flipping through several keyboards again, Sentilla located the main activation unit and wrote a termination bomb inside the code. She then uploaded the entire thing back into the weapons storage cache and waited. Code ran across the screen faster than ever, the termination bug attaching itself like superglue to every important system.

"Come on... come on..." Sentilla repeated as the codes continued to fly by. Suddenly, the system froze and a massive box appeared in the center of the top pane.

EXECUTE?

"You bet your ass," Sentilla said and hit the button.

Everything went silent and dark.

Now it was up to Kahli to work her magic. Hopefully, the virus had been cleared, but they wouldn't know for sure until Kahli got the system rebooted. There was a chance Sentilla simply sped up the virus and caused the ship to completely shut down. If that were the case, Kahli wouldn't be able to do anything. But if she was right...

"Kahli," Sentilla whispered to herself. She then placed her hands to the wall on the ship and started to pet it. She closed her eyes. "Come on baby. Come back to me. You can fight this. It was just a little cold. You can do it baby, come on." Just then, there was a light click followed by a soft vibrating hum in the walls. Sentilla opened her eyes, extremely elated. She didn't want to get her hopes up, but when she saw the cursor flashing on the empty screen and the soft blue glow on the edges of the glass, she knew they were in business.

"Okay, okay, okay," she said to herself. "What do I do? What. Do. I. Do?" She took a breath. "Focus, Sentilla. Concentrate." The longer she stared at the screen, the more she did just that until her mind was clear. That was when she noticed a soft pattern inside the cursor. Sentilla stared into the cursor without blinking. With each new flash, a residual light remained, burned into her retinas. Eventually, she saw a tiny keypad with a code above and below it. She recognized it as the language of life, which every young mind on her planet was taught before they reached maturity. The statement read,

The code of the sun will ignite your life.

She smiled. If she knew anything, it was the *code of the sun.* Every night, her mother would tell her stories of the man who lived in the sun. Everyone wanted access to the sun's energy because they believed it held the secret to life, but not everyone deserved such information. The man who lived in the sun didn't allow anyone to enter his home without the proper code. Millions tried, some even attempted to break in, but all of their efforts were for not. Without the code, no entrance was possible. The man grew ever older and he feared that he would never find the man who would have the correct code. Then one day, a young, vibrant young creature stepped up to the old man and asked for access to the sun.

"What is the proper code?" the man who lived in the sun asked.

"Life eternal is a life without purpose," the creature said. "But a life with purpose is a life eternal."

The man smiled and granted her access, for he knew that she was not there to abuse the power of the sun. She was there to give her life purpose by granting him the chance to move on into the life eternal.

Sentilla rested one hand on the top pane and her other on the bottom. She repeated the creature's words and then removed her hands, leaving behind residue from her palms. She waited, afraid she had done it wrong, or that she had to actually write it out… perhaps her answer was wrong. Could her mother have told the story incorrectly?

Suddenly, lines of code buzzed across the screen faster than Sentilla was able to make out as words. It was all a blur, but with it came the return of the lights and a big sigh of relief. She folded her hands together and pressed them between her eyes.

Thanks again, mother. I couldn't have done it without you.

"Well done, Sentilla," Kahli said.

Sentilla lowered her hands. Kahli's head floated just off the wall in front of her.

"Thanks," Sentilla said.

"Meet me in command."

Sentilla nodded. "Yeah. Right away."

Kahli's head disappeared. Sentilla took another moment to honor her mother's memory and then replaced the panel.

It was time.

— 21 —

Leaving Eyrixano behind was at the forefront of DovenJadden's mind as she paced back and forth at the top of the ship's ramp. He had informed her quite some time ago that Kahli had set the timer for destroying Rega-One but never mentioned when that might happen. And except for Jaxxa Rakala, she had everything she needed to continue his work on her own. Giving up ultimate power would certainly be a sacrifice, but transferring her consciousness into Jaxxa Rakala would turn her into Eyrixano's slave. Immortality was a respectable trade-off for absolute power.

Her decision had been made. She walked to the wall and tore open the panel to close the ramp.

"I now see where your loyalties truly lie." The lingering smoke evaporated around Eyrixano's dark cloak. DovenJadden didn't say a word as he floated up to her and burned the flames of his hood into her eyes.

"Set a course for the *Equinox*," Eyrixano said.

"I'll send a couple of Regan ships —"

Eyrixano grabbed DovenJadden's throat. The pressure almost caused her to black out. "I will toss you off this ship right now if you don't do as I command," he hissed. He held her steady for several fluttered beats of DovenJadden's heart, then released his grip. "Set a course for the *Equinox*."

DovenJadden dropped to her knees. The return of oxygen to her lungs was extremely refreshing — and painful. "Why take the risk?" she sputtered out.

Eyrixano knelt down, his hood nearly touching the top of her brow. "I want to destroy them myself."

DovenJadden peered into the flames. For the first time, she thought she saw an actual pair of eyes staring back at her — black and full of intense depravity.

"Yes, sir," she said, barely audible.

Eyrixano pet DovenJadden's head gently. It was soothing and almost erotic. "What about the rest of the fleet?" she asked.

He stood. "Have them retrieve the remaining mind transfer components."

DovenJadden nodded.

Eyrixano stood. "I want to see her."

"She's in the brig." DovenJadden remained in her crouched position until she knew he had gone. She then took a few moments to make sure her legs were stable enough to rise and closed the ramp. After taking one more moment to breathe, she placed her hand on a metallic pad next to the panel. "Jaenice. Time to leave."

— 22 —

Ken fell from the grate. He wasn't sure if it was climbing around and running through the sewer or if the poison was beginning to work its way through his system, but he felt chilled, as if he was coming down with the flu. Not only that, but his joints were stiffening and every move he made caused a sharp pinch against his nerves. Clenching his teeth and sucking in thin waves of breath was all he could do to keep from constantly screaming. He tried to ease some of the pain by squirming across the ground, but there was no time for that, which Qah-Shekel so callously expressed after sliding from the grate. Lark was more compassionate (as he expected) and helped him to his feet. Qah-Shekel had already headed off into the desert.

"How much farther?" he said.

Lark didn't get a chance to answer. A loud explosion erupted behind them. They turned to watch Eyrixano's ship rise from under the ground. Six other ships followed and flew in the direction of the manufacturing plant. Ken couldn't care less about those ships. His eyes remained focused on Eyrixano's and the nightmare it induced.

"Ken," Lark yelled, knocking him back to reality. "Suck it up and get your ass moving."

Ken blinked repeatedly as he processed her words. When he finally acknowledged them, he started jogging as fast as his aging legs would allow him, Lark keeping her arms wrapped around him the whole way, making sure that if he did collapse, she'd be there to soften his fall. Just then, the engines of Eyrixano's ship lit up, shooting past them in the direction of the *Equinox*.

"Ah, hell," Lark said.

— 23 —

The rise of adrenaline to its absolute apex was Sentilla's addiction even before the gem. As she fell into the pilot seat and lit up her holocontrols, that rush burned a needle-like focus into her bloodstream. By the time Kahli had made her way to command and took her place at DovenJadden's station, all systems had been checked and flushed, or put on standby and repaired. Sentilla's baby — the child she was raised to protect and control — was primed for anything and everything she could think of.

"Have you located the others?" she said.

"We can't wait for them," Kahli returned. "Get this ship off the ground."

"We can't just leave them here."

"There's no guarantee they're alive. If we wait any longer, we all die."

Kahli flashed her hands across the holoscreen in front of her and pulled up the sensor readings indicating Eyrixano's ship heading in their direction.

"Are you…?" Sentilla muttered. She flipped on her navigation screen to verify the ship closing in. "Ah, hell."

— 24 —

Even though they all understood why, watching the *Equinox* fly away from them was disappointing to say the least. Ken let his legs go limp, causing Lark to trip over her feet and fall with him into the roasting sands of the desert.

"God, damn it, Ken," she said as she tried to get him to stand back up. "We have to keep moving."

"It's over," he said, and then even quieter, "It's over."

"No. No, I won't let you give up like that." She continued to try and drag Ken across the sand, but with the heat, her dry throat and the flames tearing a hole in her lungs, she couldn't handle it. She fell back and tried to catch her breath, the sun evaporating her sweat.

— 25 —

It didn't feel like a cell. The spherical room with its hue of dark grays that gave it the illusion of never-ending space was quite expansive with no bars or doors that she could see. It was more like floating about a black hole than anything else, but one with an invisible floor that could be seen only with touch. Jacquline sat on the edge of a padded rug that was as comfortable as anything she could imagine, relaxing her to the point of complete bliss. She was still slightly afraid of what might happen to her, but oddly enough, she felt far safer here with Jaenice and Eyrixano than she did with Tracey.

A loud click and snap reverberated through the room. It felt as if Jacquline was being forced to keep her head down as Eyrixano's cold presence entered. No matter how much she trusted him, there was no escaping the dread whenever he was close by. At least the hiss was growing quite familiar; it helped ease the doubt that haunted her still tainted memories. Deep down, something still felt amiss, as if her true feelings had been extracted and replaced with something she didn't recognize. But she couldn't fault the monster for this; she only had her own ignorance to blame.

The touch of Eyrixano's thin, almost bony, fingers were as soothing as her mother's hand brushing through her hair. She couldn't understand what he might be saying, but he was there to protect her. His only intention was to open her eyes to the truth and give her something to believe in; something to hold onto; something to live for. Jacquline no longer felt alone; she only felt comfort — enough to finally see the truth behind the fire of her savior.

His eyes matched his light, golden brown hair and his chiseled chin appeared soft upon the allure of his cheekbones hidden against his face with just the right touch of roundness and shadow. If she had to say, he was like a cross between Brad Pitt and Aiden Quinn, sensitive but commanding.

Jacquline smiled, matching Eyrixano's gentle smirk, which indicated his love and compassion for her. She took his hand with pride and blushed as he kissed it, though she didn't turn away, mesmerized by his stature and appearance. At this point, there was nothing she wouldn't do for him. He was her world; everyone else had been forgotten.

He pulled her to her feet. They walked from the cell, hand-in-hand.

— 26 —

"Eyrixano is closing," Kahli reported. "Ten delias. Nine."

Sentilla skimmed the ship across the desert, leaving a huge cloud of dust in her wake. She lit the engines up as hot as she could without fear of tearing the *Equinox* apart. "I can't push her any faster unless we climb." And they both knew if they did, they would lose their cover.

Much good it did.

"He's right on top of us," Kahli said.

"Where? I don't see him?"

Suddenly, an explosion blew a hole in the desert floor just in front of them. Sentilla almost flew into a second explosion as she maneuvered out of the original's path.

"He's firing on us," Kahli said.

"No shit," Sentilla roared back. "Send me the heat signatures of those missiles."

Kahli raced her fingers across the screen to bring up two windows, one with models of the *Equinox* in green and Eyrixano's ship in red, the other with a more complex blueprint of Eyrixano's ship, complete with highlights representing the electric conductors. She positioned one on top of the other and exported them to the right side of Sentilla's navigation screen. From just a glimpse, Sentilla could calculate when and where each electric bomb would be discharged, allowing her to outmaneuver several more shots. But without any defenses of their own, it was only a matter of time before Eyrixano changed tactics to find a new way to get the job done.

"We can't keep doing this," Kahli said, keeping an eye on the ship's integrity and the damage caused by the residue of the blasts.

"I know," Sentilla said. "How much time before the planet goes nova?"

"Half a quartet at the most."

"That's enough," Sentilla said, switching off the rear engines. At the same time, she flipped on the reverse thrusters, deadening their forward trajectory almost instantly. According to the radars, Eyrixano's ship flew right past them as expected. Without an ounce of hesitation, Sentilla switched the rear engines back on and made a sharp left turn, painting the desert with the side of the ship until she was back on course, heading directly for the city.

"What are you doing?" Kahli said.

"Trust me."

— 27 —

Lark was ready to pass out when she thought she saw Tracey racing up to them.

She blinked rapidly to try and moisturize her eyes, but all it did was blur them even further. When she finally cleared them, Tracey wasn't there. Lark chalked it up to a mirage, or maybe even a hallucination. That is until she heard Ken groan (or at least she thought). She curled around and sat up. Tracey was kneeling next to Ken with her hands wrapped around his throat. Her cheeks were white hot, as was the gem. Lark reached out to grab Tracey's arm but pulled away when the young girl looked at her with bright, sharp gray eyes. Several seconds later, Tracey let go of Ken's neck. The gem dimmed along with her cheeks. She fell backward, dizzy and exhausted. Lark reached out for her again. "Are you okay?"

Tracey nodded, but then again, it could have been a small seizure. "I'm fine," she said, the words forced and broken.

Lark wanted to object, but what would she be able to do or say that would help any? She looked to Ken. All of his wounds had been healed. "Will he be okay?" Lark asked as she swiped her hand through his hair.

Just then, Ken sat up sharply, gasping. It took a minute to bring his breathing under control, but once he had, he caught sight of Tracey, first with surprise and gratitude (and a great big hug, which wasn't easy with the cuffs), then with fear and anger (as he leaned back and held tightly to her wrist).

"What are you doing?" he said.

"She just saved your life, Ken."

He immediately grabbed his neck and didn't feel any wounds. He had to hug her again for that. "I'm sorry," he whispered in a much more calming tone. "I'm sorry. But what are you doing out here?"

"I followed DovenJadden to find Jacquline," Tracey said.

Ken lowered his head and rubbed his eyes. "Jacquline's…"

Tracey rested her hand on his shoulder. The pain in her chest was excruciating, but she hid it well. "You will get her back," she said.

Ken smiled, his eyes red and puffy. He nodded. "Not if the *Equinox* doesn't come back for us."

"I don't think that's going to be an issue." Tracey pointed behind him. Coming back toward them at an incredible speed was the *Equinox*.

Lark stood up. "Why is it going so fast?"

Before she could get an answer, the wind generated by the ship's speed blew her thirty yards away. Tracey held Ken to the ground until the wind died to a bearable speed.

"Lark," Ken called out as he scrambled to his feet to chase after her. Just then, an electrical spark snapped at the ground between them. Ken fell back to avoid the shock and then caught sight of the half a dozen Beta units closing in on them.

— 28 —

Sentilla settled the ship at the edge of the city. From her navigation screen, she saw frightened Regans running amuck while Beta units did their best to strike the ship with hockey pucks from their staffs.

"Yeah, keep dreaming," Sentilla said to herself, and then to Kahli: "Give me the outline of the city."

Within moments, a three-dimensional map sat hovering above her navigation screen. She quickly calculated a route in her mind.

"Eyrixano is approaching."

This is going to be fun.

Sentilla pushed the *Equinox* into the city, shimmying and shaking her way through the tapestry of buildings. Eyrixano's ship followed, but remained high above, firing down upon the ship. With each new flash of electricity, Sentilla shifted down a new street or squeezed into a new alley. The blasts toppled and destroyed building after building (and life after life). Smoke billowed along the streets, covering most of the flames in dark clouds. Within minutes, Sentilla had crafted a nice pattern throughout the city, making sure to cover as much of it in smoke as possible. When she felt she could cover no more ground, she slipped into the center of the city and halted all engines.

— 29 —

"I can't detect them," Jaenice said. She examined the scans on her console, but all she could see was an array of heat from the multitude of fires that now covered the city.

"They have to be down there somewhere," DovenJadden said. "Fire at will."

Jaenice obliged, firing shot after shot in a consecutive line across the center of the smoke. DovenJadden waited for any sign that they may have hit them, but it was useless to say the least.

"It's no good," Jaenice said. "We need to get out of here."

"Not until we confirm they've been destroyed."

"Odds are they won't know we've left. Let them get ripped to shreds by the planet."

"I'm not playing the odds. Get this ship down there."

"We won't be able to see anything."

"I don't care," DovenJadden yelled. "Get us the hell down there and find them."

"Delay that order," Eyrixano said. How long he had been on the bridge was beyond DovenJadden, but he seemed quite comfortable in his command chair with Jacquline standing by his side. "If we go hunt for them now, we might as well kill ourselves. Get us out of here. If they aren't caught in the blast, we'll tear them apart in space."

"And how do you plan on doing that?"

It wasn't clear, but DovenJadden felt a sinister smile grow within the flames.

— 30 —

"They're breaking away," Kahli said. If she wasn't an android, she might have felt as relieved as Sentilla, who wanted to jump and cheer but contained her excitement for later.

"We should wait to make sure they've left before we break cover," Sentilla said. *Then we pray the rest of our family is out there waiting.*

"I concur." Kahli spun a bit of information across the screen, then brought up a new window with readings that made her just a little bit nervous.

— 31 —

The simple wave of Tracey's hand was enough to send all of the Betas flying backward.

"Hurry," she said, urging Ken and Lark to retreat behind her. It felt extremely odd cowering behind his eight-year-old daughter, but his body hadn't yet healed, and trying to fight even one Beta unit right now would probably kill him. With the gem radiating a deep green glow alongside the soft white of her cheeks, Tracey was the most effective weapon he and Lark had. Ken wasn't sure he would ever get over that. "Stay behind me."

The Betas rose quickly enough and fanned out around them. Tracey spun around Lark and Ken, making sure to keep her eyes on every step each of the Betas made. No motion was too small to attract the gem's attention. If Lark didn't know any better, she would have sworn Tracey literally had eyes in the back of her head (or, better yet, a crown of eyes). When one of the Betas tried to take advantage of Ken and Lark's vulnerability, Tracey leaped backwards over Ken, landing on her hands just as the puck struck the gem, allowing it to absorb all of the electricity. She then finished the somersault to land a few feet from him. In the time it took for her to gain her composure, the Betas fired several more shots. Ken pushed Lark away from a couple of them, the force of which knocked him backwards to avoid yet another. Lark wasn't quite as lucky, as the edge of one of the pucks nipped her thigh, causing it to explode and sear a flurry of electrical current into it as if a twenty-pound bee suddenly stung her.

From that moment, Tracey jumped across the desert like the Flash on steroids, collecting every puck the Betas let loose. She eventually landed in between Ken and Lark with a fist pressed to the ground opposite her knee and her chin caressing the top of the gem. The Betas weren't sure what to make of her posture, so they waited to see if they had done enough damage. Ken scurried over to Lark and pressed his hands to her leg. She clenched her teeth, hissing the pain away (or doing her very best, anyway). Finally, one of the Beta units stepped to Ken and pressed her staff to his neck. He cautiously lifted his hands and was about to stand, but Tracey did it for him. All weapons returned to her as she slowly raised her head. For a long beat, Tracey just stared at the android in front of her. The Beta, unafraid and curious, stepped toward her. That's when Tracey opened her mouth and spewed every bit of energy she had collected back at each of the Beta units, melting every last bit of their skeletal structures. When it was all over, they were nothing more than a pile of goo that when cooled would be nothing more than oddly-shaped mounds of flesh covered balls of metal — that is until their cores detonated, sending shards of them all across the desert.

Tracey fell back to the ground.

"Tracey," Ken called out. He wanted to go to her, but didn't want to leave Lark.

"Go," Lark said. "I'm fine."

He checked her leg one last time (even though the wound had for the most part been cauterized already) and jumped to Tracey. Her gem was glowing brighter than he had ever seen it before and it frightened him more than words could describe. "Tracey," he said again, combing his fingers through her hair.

She opened her eyes ever so slightly. "The knife," she choked out, barely audible.

"The what? Tracey, what's happening?"

"The knife," Tracey said clearer and louder. She slapped at her leg, hoping it might clue Ken into what she was asking for. It did, but only after he noticed the edge of the sheath poke through the bottom of her pants.

"Press it against the edge of the gem," Tracey whispered.

Ken wasn't sure he understood.

"Hurry," Tracey said.

The gem glowed hotter now, the core having turned almost entirely white. He couldn't spend anymore time thinking; he had to start doing. He pulled her knife from the sheath and held it above the gem. It was like trying to push the repellent sides of two magnets together.

"It isn't working," Ken said.

Tracey grabbed his hand with both of hers and pulled it to the side, allowing the knife to rest on the very edge of the gem, lightly piercing her skin.

"I don't —"

Tracey pushed his hand a little harder, inserting the knife deeper into her chest.

"Tracey, I can't."

Tracey suddenly went limp. The entire gem was now white hot. Though he still wasn't sure if he was doing the right thing, or if what she was asking him to do would kill her, it was now or never. He pushed the knife as deep as it would go. A beam of light from the gem shot skyward, throwing Ken backward.

— 32 —

Sentilla spun her hands across the holocontrols, lifting the *Equinox* above the smoke engulfing the city.

"Where do you think the others might be?" Sentilla asked.

"We have no time to look," Kahli said, keeping tabs on a small timer she had brought up.

"We have to!"

"Sentilla, we are out of time." Kahli sent the timer to display fully on Sentilla's navigation screen. There was no denying it, and no further argument would persuade Kahli to track them down. Sentilla would just have to accept —

But did she? "What is that?" she said.

Kahli noticed the same outburst of energy, but as a set of unclear and fluctuating readings instead of the stunning visual Sentilla was looking at.

"Is the planet erupting?"

"No," Kahli said calmly. "This is something different; something organic."

"It's them," Sentilla said brightly. "It's Jaxxa Rakala."

"How can you be sure?"

"Trust me. I can feel it."

Kahli examined the readings even further but couldn't find anything that would be associated to Tracey, or anyone else for that matter. She tried to look at the surrounding area, but the energy from the light was so strong, it made it appear as if nothing else was there — almost as if everything surrounding the light had become a void.

"It's too dangerous," she said.

Sentilla pushed forward anyway, leading the *Equinox* toward the beacon.

— 33 —

Did he have to wait for the beam to stop firing at all cylinders before pulling the knife? What would happen if he pulled it out early? Would it trigger feedback in Tracey's system, causing her to explode into a hundred million pieces?

This was the dilemma Ken faced as his body grew soaked in fear. His hands still stung from the initial shock of the light escaping the gem. Even if he wanted to pull the knife out, he didn't know if he'd be able to grab hold of it, as hovering has hand even a foot away caused it to tremble with pain. And then there was Lark, who might have been nagging him about what to do had she not have been in serious agony herself. Or at least she was until the awe of what was happening to Tracey stole all of her attention. It was so brilliantly mesmerizing that she could hardly even think straight. Neither of them realized the *Equinox* had set down just a few yards away — not until the light vanished to reveal Sentilla rushing down the ramp.

"What happened?" she said as she dropped down next to Tracey. "Did she have another episode?" Of course she already knew the answer to that but she didn't know what else to say.

Ken looked at her quizzically for a moment until her presence finally made sense.

"*Another* episode?" he said. "This has happened before?"

Sentilla nodded, a little guilty for uncovering Tracey's secret. "She had one earlier when she was helping you hide from the Betas." Sentilla quickly pulled the knife from her chest.

Ken watched the wound heal (but only after an ounce of blood poured from it), shocked and a little ashamed. Had all of this been his fault? On the other hand, he was proud of her. It was stupid of her to keep this issue a secret, but damn was she brave for doing what she's been doing, knowing full well what might happen to her.

"We need to get her to medical."

"Take her," Ken said, referring to Lark. He had Tracey in his arms before Sentilla could object. After checking Lark's wound, she looked at her, terrified. "Where's Qah-Shekel?"

Lark shook her head. "I don't know. He took off ahead of us... I'm not sure. I'm sorry."

Sentilla looked back to the ship, hoping he would be standing there waiting for her. "He's alive," she stated, more to keep herself calm than needing a direct answer.

"Last I saw." Lark shifted her legs, clenching her teeth as she did.

"Come on," Sentilla finally said. She wrapped one of Lark's arms across her neck and escorted her back to the *Equinox*. Before heading up the ramp, she scanned the desert one last time. Qah-Shekel never emerged. With a low head, Sentilla hit the door closed. They were only feet away when Sentilla thought she heard Qah-Shekel yelling for them to open the hatch. It seemed at first to be a dream. The sound of his voice was too light; too distant. But then Lark spoke up.

"Is that...?"

Sentilla couldn't hold back her smile. Lark nodded and limped to the wall, where she carefully lowered her broken body to the ground. Sentilla rushed to the hatch and slammed her palm against the activation button. The ramp couldn't have lowered more slowly, but as it did, a rush of relief and excitement filled her body. She leapt into Qah-Shekel's arms before the ramp had completed its descent.

"Oh, thank the makers," she whispered.

"I'm fine." Qah-Shekel said. "But we need to leave."

Sentilla nodded and pulled him inside the ship. "Get her to medical."

Lark waved hello and then grabbed her leg with one more delicate hiss.

— 34 —

Believing there would be a series of minor explosions that would sequentially grow into the massive bomb that would rip the moon apart was clearly a false assumption on Sentilla's part. She failed to heed Kahli's warnings (even after she made her hasty exit to lock herself away in the brig to keep from damaging any major systems) and eased the ship through the atmosphere with unnecessary caution. Although the goal was to get the *Equinox* several thousands of miles from Rega-One before igniting the lightning core (which according to Kahli was the minimal safe distance to do so), Sentilla hadn't broken the edge of space when the explosion ripped through hundreds of miles of land in all directions, fracturing the moon's core — damage that would eventually force the moon to break from its rotation and collide with Rega, causing a chain reaction that would ultimately destroy the entire Rega system as it slowly collapsed into its sun over the next few revolutionary cycles. But Sentilla couldn't worry about inconsequential trifles at the moment. The blast sprayed a flurry of rock and dust toward the *Equinox* with extreme force. Sentilla did what she could to outmaneuver the initial debris field, but with the force of the shockwave negating everything she tried, it was only a matter of time before the ship was torn to pieces. Luckily, she had the sense of mind to shut everything down and ride it out.

After a few minutes elapsed, Sentilla rebooted her station to analyze the readings from the sensors still functioning along the outer hull. Most of them registered only light debris, and there were no residual signs of the shockwave, so Sentilla lit the interior of the ship back up and ignited the forward thrusters to ease their momentum. Once the *Equinox* had stopped hurtling freely through space and Sentilla had regained complete control of her baby, she tapped her fingers along her holopads to reawaken the main engines.

Nothing happened.

Sentilla didn't even try to troubleshoot the problem before opening a comm window to the brig. "Kahli. Are you there?" She knew if it took more than a few seconds, it wasn't good.

"I'm here," Kahli said.

Sentilla let out a breath of relief as Kahli's head appeared on the terminal behind her. "Good to hear."

"Report."

"Engines are off-line," she reported.

Kahli instantly ran a diagnostic, her eyes large and unblinking the whole time. "The lightning core is functioning properly," Kahli finally said.

"The debris must have damaged the power cells inside the engine housing," Sentilla said, trying everything she knew to back door a jump-start. "We're dead in the water."

— 35 —

Qah-Shekel lifted Lark onto the medical table and examined her leg.

Ken was near the back hovering over Tracey, who remained unconscious but alive. He turned to Lark, unwilling to let go of Tracey's hand. "How are you doing?"

"Oh, just peachy," Lark said and then screamed. Qah-Shekel had pressed his fingers into the wound and pulled out a small piece of bone that had been burnt off into her skin. After tossing it aside, he applied some soothing gel to her leg. Lark smiled, though the discomfort of his touch was hard to hide.

"Where is she?" Kahli exclaimed as she bounded into medical, locating Tracey almost immediately without an answer. She looked the child over before grabbing her medical glove.

"Kahli, what's wrong?" Qah-Shekel said.

"The engines have been disabled. I need Tracey to help repair them."

"Tracey can't help," Ken said aggressively.

Kahli ignored him as she wrapped her hand in place across the side of Tracey's head. It was hard to tell from her blank stare what Kahli was seeing in the small holoscreen, but Ken had to believe it would turn out okay. The gem would take care of her.

"I can't get any clear readings," Kahli said.

"What does that mean?"

"I cannot be certain. Her brain activity is all over the place, as if she has access to multiple minds at once." She moved the glove to her chest. After a moment, she shook her head. "The gem is somehow affecting the glove." She looked up to Ken. "I'm sorry. I'm not sure how to —"

Tracey sucked in a deep breath as she sat straight up, which shocked Ken into letting go of her hand and take a step away. Her eyes were wide but it wasn't clear if she was aware.

Ken hesitated to say anything, but he had to do something. "Tracey?"

She stared at Ken for several seconds. Without warning or reason, Tracey jumped off the table and flew out the door.

"Tracey," Ken called out and followed behind. Tracey was too fast for him, but not for Kahli, who reached the ladder just as Tracey disappeared into the upper deck.

"She's either heading to the engine room or command," Kahli said as she bounded up the ladder.

"Command," Ken yelled back with confidence. To her surprise, Ken was right. Tracey stood next to Sentilla staring at the half a dozen Regan ships on her navigation screen. Sitting directly in front of them was Eyrixano's ship.

"What's he doing?" Kahli asked as she sat at her station to start humming through a series of information.

"I don't know," Sentilla said. "He's been sitting there for ages staring at us like we're about to spontaneously combust."

"Between me and Rega, that doesn't seem to be all that far-fetched," Tracey said, shining a wink and a smile in Kahli's direction.

Kahli didn't think it to be very amusing. "This can't be," she whispered.

"What is it?" Sentilla said.

"Eyrixano," Tracey answered for her. "He's charging a weapon."

"So what? No weapon can be used in space."

"This one can," Tracey said with an eerie monotone.

"How is that possible?"

"Based on these readings," Kahli said, examining the details of the incomprehensible mechanism, "the Regans have somehow discovered a way to harness space dust into a compatible energy source that can travel and ignite through conditions of atmospheric emptiness. If they fire that weapon, we will be destroyed."

"Don't worry," Tracey said as if she had just taken a Xanax. She turned to face Sentilla and raised her hand. Sentilla backed away slightly, but felt safe at the same time, eventually allowing Tracey to rest her hand on her forehead.

"Stop," Tracey said as Ken entered command. He was nearly out of breath but the adrenaline masked the burn in his lungs. She didn't need to look at him for Ken to see the conviction radiating from her eyes. "Ever since the death of your mother," she said to Sentilla, "you've felt guilty about her death."

"Tracey," Ken squeaked out, but couldn't find anything further to say as he felt so weak and helpless, unable to understand how he could comprehend what Tracey was saying, even though she spoke in Sentilla's language. It was as if she was translating her words inside his head.

"The gem helped you rise above that guilt," she continued, "but I want to show you why." Tracey closed her eyes and the gem lit up. Sentilla's muscles constricted, but no matter how much Ken and Kahli wanted to stop her, they couldn't move. Sentilla sucked in an insane amount of air as Tracey removed her hand and took a step back. She waited for Sentilla to regain her senses —

and smile.

"As you witnessed inside the memory tablet," Tracey said, absorbing Sentilla's acknowledgment, "sacrifice is the greatest love there is because sacrifice helps you spread that love to all of those around you."

Sentilla was crying. "Thank you," she said.

Kahli hated to break the poignancy but: "Two quasers before the weapon is — wait."

Ken turned to Kahli, his face also flush with tears. "What is it?"

"Someone has just accessed the decompression chamber." Kahli quickly raised a comm window to medical. "Qah-Shekel. Lark. Are you there?"

Qah-Shekel's head appeared on the wall. "Yes. What is it?"

"Did either of you access the decompression chamber?"

"No. We haven't left medical."

"That can only mean one thing."

Kahli walked up to Tracey. Before Ken could yell for her to stop, she dropped her hand across Tracey's holographic projection. Sentilla sat back and covered her mouth with concern.

Ken couldn't believe his eyes, but now knew exactly what was happening. "God, no." He bolted from command as fast as his legs would allow, but it was no use. Tracey was already deep within the chamber. He pounded on the door and yelled out for her at the top of his lungs, even though he knew she wouldn't be able to hear him.

The thing was, she could hear him in her heart, which turned out to be a two-way transmission — one that pinched Ken's own heart like a vice.

"Tracey, please," Ken pleaded. "Don't do this. Please. We'll find another way."

The only words Ken heard —

I love you

— filled him with Stacey's soul, bonding them all together in one last existential hug.

Ken felt the tip of Tracey's lips on his and then — emptiness. "No," he screamed one last time before lowering his head with one last strike of his fists to the door.

— 36 —

Tracey hated to leave Ken that way, but it was for the best. He would understand why soon enough. For now, she had bigger fish to fry and she couldn't allow herself to be distracted. She used her steadfast determination to drive all of her attention into focusing the gem's power to her will. Even though she didn't have much time, every step was long and labored, as if she were wearing a pair of hundred pound metal boots. But it was a necessary concession to keep the gem from destroying her and everything around her.

— 37 —

"What is that?" Jacquline said as she walked up to the large, curved view screen focused on a small speck moving across the shell of the *Equinox*. DovenJadden stepped up alongside her, purring out what Jacquline believed to be an unintended translation.

"I am not detecting any anomalies," Jaenice said, running through several diagnostics at her command station.

"Zoom in on the ship," Eyrixano said.

Jaenice did as ordered, pushing in on the *Equinox* until Tracey filled the screen. Eyrixano floated up to it, burning with pleasure. He couldn't have asked for a better turn of events.

"What in the hell is she doing?" Jacquline whispered, holding her hand just above the glass.

"Ionizer's charged and ready."

"Fire," Eyrixano hissed.

— 38 —

Tracey was near the nose of the *Equinox* when Eyrixano's weapon expelled a blast of energy so bright, Tracey had to curl her eyes down to keep from going blind. That didn't stop her from locating the center of its mass and pulling it into the gem. She fought her body's unmitigated urge to rip apart as the force of the absorption slid her across the *Equinox*. When the blast had fully soaked into every vein of her body, Tracey knelt down and finally took a breath. A split second later, she looked directly at Eyrixano's ship, her eyes nearly glowing with pure white intensity. Slowly positioning her right foot behind her, Tracey lifted her body up slightly and then pushed off as hard as she could away from the *Equinox*.

— 39 —

"The blast has been neutralized," Kahli said.

"How is that possible?" Sentilla said, though with Tracey's hologram having dissipated just after Eyrixano fired the weapon, she already knew the answer.

Ken stumbled back into command a complete wreck. He could hardly walk much less speak, but was able to spit out, "I need to see her." Sentilla caught him as he fell to his knees. Her ability to look right into him was a universal language neither of them could deny.

"No," he eked out. "No. She's still out there. I want to see her." Ken desperately tried to reach the pilot seat, but Sentilla was too strong for him. During the struggle, Sentilla caught a glimpse of a small object floating toward Eyrixano's ship.

Could it possibly be?

She scurried back to her seat and pushed the holoscreen onto Tracey.

Ken was elated (and relieved to tears) to see her alive —

I knew it.

— but felt her grow more distant.

"Eyrixano is charging weapons," Kahli reported.

I love you, Ken said as loud as his mind would let him.

— 40 —

Jacquline stood in wonderment at the sight of her baby sister soaring like an eagle through the majestic sky. She pressed her hand to Tracey's cheek just as she stopped her forward motion, and then felt her love through the voice of her mother:

Beauty is a picture of the one I see,
Lying next to me, you will softly be,
Always loving, always kind,
Like the love I left behind.

You came from heaven, this I know,
Kind and free, you're pure and sweet.
You are that which love is built,
And in my heart you'll always be.

— 41 —

Floating in the direct center of the ships, Tracey relaxed every muscle in her body. Electricity crawled across her skin as she drew energy from every possible element up to a dozen light years away, mapping out the marks that were now painted along her entire physique. As the electric fingers buried themselves into the crescent moons to complete the luminous painting, Tracey spread her arms out at a forty-five degree angle and used her shoulders to put herself into a spin.

— 42 —

"What is she doing?" Ken said.

Kahli wanted to answer him, but she wasn't quite sure either. She examined every molecule surrounding Tracey for information and nothing made any sense. Lark and Qah-Shekel entered command just then to get their first glimpse at Tracey, who spun faster and faster with each passing second.

"Is that…?" Lark didn't need to finish. She simply took a hold of Ken's hands. He squeezed it tight.

"Kahli," Qah-Shekel said, hoping for answers. But she was in her own world, examining, calculating and learning. He kept his eyes on Tracey, who now appeared to be growing larger. Sentilla yelled something out and frantically buzzed through her own controls.

"My Karokil," Kahli muttered.

"What is it?" Lark said, tightening her grip on Ken's hands (if that was even possible).

"She's creating a black hole. And she's pulling us in."

— 43 —

"The gravitational force is too strong," Jaenice said. "If we push the engines any hotter, we'll destroy them."

"Fire the Ionizer," Eyrixano screamed.

"It isn't fully charged."

"Do it anyway."

"We fire prematurely, it could kick back onto the ship," DovenJadden said.

"I want them destroyed," Eyrixano fumed, the flames soaking the hood of his cloak.

Jacquline held her hand to the screen, smiling — fascinated.

— 44 —

By the time the *Equinox* and Eyrixano's ship were nearly ready to collide on top of Tracey, sparks of electricity tickled their hulls with anticipation. Tracey now spun so fast, she no longer appeared to be spinning and was able to look directly at both ships at the same time.

Power is an illusion. Don't let it control you. Find your way home.

There is another.

And with that, both ships vanished.

Seconds later, a dark cloud spilled from the center of the gem and enveloped Tracey. It tore the Regan ships from bow to stern, each piece becoming a part of her until they were nothing but particles of leftover dust. When there was nothing left worth consuming, Tracey was devoured into the depths of her creation.

— 45 —

The only one not thrown across the bridge was Eyrixano, who stared at the screen without any explanation for how every ship had just disappeared. "What happened to them?" he cried out over the wailing alarms.

Jaenice was quick to return to her station to assess the situation. "The ship has taken damage across the board, but nothing major."

"I don't care about the ship. Where is Jaxxa Rakala?"

If Jaenice could perspire, she would have been sweating profusely as she tried to find an answer — any answer — that wouldn't get her power core pulled. She finally caught sight of their current coordinates and had to double-check them to be absolutely sure. "They didn't disappear," she reported. "We did." She looked to Eyrixano, whose flames burned extra bright. "She sent us halfway across the galaxy."

"What do we do now?" DovenJadden said. Her knee hurt, but otherwise she was okay.

"We go after her," Jaenice said.

Jacquline wasn't sure she was conscious, but figured the pain in the back of her head was a good sign. She cracked her neck and massaged it generously as she sat up. When she finally looked at the others, she couldn't hear anything but Tracey's voice repeating the same phrase over and over.

Find your way home. There is another.

Jacquline sat still and silent for some time, feeling a soft, motherly instinct fill her soul. Finally, she said, "Tracey's dead."

Everyone turned to her. "How do you know that?" Jaenice asked, translating for Eyrixano.

"Trust me," Jacquline said. "She's gone and she took the gem with her."

The flames burned dark under Eyrixano's cloak. DovenJadden purred hysterically. She continually pointed at Jacquline. *Not* a good sign.

"There's another gem," Jacquline said. Jaenice had to translate several times before either Eyrixano or DovenJadden heard the claim DovenJadden stormed over to Jacquline and grabbed her throat. Jaenice was quick to stop her.

"How can there be another gem?"

Jacquline shook her head as she caught her breath. "All I know is a second gem exists. I can feel it."

"So what if there is?" Jaenice translated for DovenJadden. "Even if we were able to acquire it, we cannot use it."

"I may not be the Jaxxa Rakala," Jacquline said, poised and confident, "but I share her blood." It was a little white lie, but it kept her alive — for now.

"You think you can control the gem?"

"There's only one way to find out."

No one spoke for a long time after Jaenice finished her translation, and no one really had to. DovenJadden walked off the bridge as Jaenice slid back to her station. Jacquline could feel the pleasure emanate from under Eyrixano's hood.

"You better be right about this, baby Kel," Jaenice said, but with a wry smile.

— 46 —

Ken remained still against the wall, his eyes closed tightly. He didn't want to give away the image of Tracey he held so dear — her bright smile and warm, loving eyes.

Find your way home. There is another.

What did it mean? Ken didn't care. All he wanted was to remain in that moment. Not even Lark's gentle touch across his shoulders would keep him from it.

"Tracey saved us," Lark said. She kissed his temple.

He cried.

— 47 —

Qah-Shekel sat on his father's trunk in his living quarters, spinning the rock from his home world in his hand. He had spent the last couple of days helping Kahli rebuild the engines to working order, all the while nurturing an awkward silence between them. Neither was able to speak of what they chose to do, so Kahli's motivations for deciding to pull the trigger remained a secret. He was certain she'd tell him if he asked, but for some reason he didn't feel right about it. Yes, he had completed his quest for answers about his home world and all of its inhabitants, and he had received his vengeance against those who ultimately destroyed it. But it all seemed so hollow. He thought he would feel vindicated for avenging his parents and finally finding the strength to move on. Sadly, he didn't feel that way at all. In fact, he didn't really feel anything. Part of him regretted having been a part of such a genocidal act. The head of the snake had yet to be destroyed, and though his followers had seen their fates fulfilled, the majority of collateral damage was more than likely innocent of any crime — possibly even blind to the truth. For all he really knew, many of them may have turned against their own had they known. It was a decision that was fueled by emotion and one that he didn't think he'd ever be able to overcome. Not while Eyrixano was still out there, at least. His death probably wouldn't do much to satisfy his guilt, but at least it would bring him a modicum of peace; at least he would know that Eyrixano would never be able to manipulate so many into doing something so heinous ever again.

A soft red glow outlined the door of his quarters. He wasn't sure if he wanted to talk to anyone right now, but no matter how he felt, he still had to lead his team. He pressed his hand to the wall. The glow faded, allowing Kahli to enter.

"Engines have been fully repaired," she said immediately, "and the tracking device is still active."

"Thank you."

When he said nothing further, Kahli bowed slightly and turned to leave.

"Why did you decide to do it?" Qah-Shekel blurted out.

Kahli turned back to him. She had nothing to hide, but wanted to make sure she chose her words carefully so as not to upset him. "It was a necessary action," she said. "If we had done nothing, tens of thousands of innocent people would have been at risk, including us."

"I understand that. But you said it yourself. Who are we to decide the direction of fate?"

"Who are they to decide the direction of fate? Whether manipulated by Eyrixano or nourished by their own egos, the Regans had become far too dangerous. They believed in their ability to create, build, control and sustain life. For one community to have that type of power without restriction is dangerous and unethical to say the least. I didn't want to destroy the moon, nor did I intend to kill all of those innocent people. I admit I was more emotional than I could have properly prepared for and didn't gather enough information before executing my plan. Then again, I may have initiated the sequence, but Eyrixano did nothing to stop it. He ultimately killed them all, and he deserves to pay for his crimes."

"Perhaps. But I've come to realize... no amount of vengeance will make this better."

"Hunting Eyrixano is not vengeance, Qah-Shekel. It's justice."

Qah-Shekel knew she was right. Funnily enough, it didn't make him feel any better. That didn't change the fact that he was more than ready to do what was necessary to stop him from gaining any more power. They just had to track him down.

And the *Equinox* crew was well on their way to doing just that.

— 48 —

Ken stood against the wall with his head on his arm. The stars looked farther away and less vibrant than they ever had before. It might have been because his mind had been darkened. There wasn't a time he could remember that he felt so alone. He remembered the time when the cold hand of depression had sunk him into a black hole —

Black hole... Tracey!

— his soul hollowed and gutted so the only thing he felt was the consumption of his soul. He was alive but dead; his heart had been put to rest.

Now was different. He wasn't numb to his emotions, creating a dark state of anger and sorrow that scared him to his core. Stacey didn't feel as close anymore, either. Now that Tracey had destroyed the gem, his memory of her was fading quicker than he was ready for. It was now harder to deny the accusation that the depression he experienced with Stacey's abduction was only withdrawal symptoms and not based solely on his love for his beloved. Had the gem manipulated his love for her? Had she only been using him as a cover?

Did she ever really love me?

He couldn't wrap his head around the possibility, but the kernel of doubt was there, ready and waiting to be encouraged to grow. If the gem hadn't had such a hold on him, perhaps he would never have even thought about chasing after Stacey. At least then his daughters would both be alive — and with him — sharing their life together as an actual family — dysfunctional or otherwise.

He looked away from the stars; they only caused him pain. Although Jacquline was still alive, the distance between them felt further than two stars on opposite sides of the universe.

"Where are you?" he whispered.

He glanced up at Lark as she walked into the room. She was sweaty and full of filth but looked as hopeful, bright and energetic as ever. It made him sick.

"What happened?" he said as he turned back to the stripes of stars washing past the window.

Lark looked at her torn jacket and smiled. "Oh, I got snared on the corner of one of the engine beds. Nothing serious. We finally got the final engine up and running, so we should be able to jump into lightning five as soon as Kahli finishes all of her diagnostics."

Ken nodded. "Do we know where they're headed?"

"Unfortunately, the tracking device in the comm buds only registers distance. We'll know more once they slow down."

Ken didn't look satisfied with that answer. Lark wrapped her hands around his shoulders. "We'll get her back, Ken."

He nodded again, still unconvinced.

"Come on. Let's get something to eat."

"I'm not hungry."

"Then you can watch me eat. Have you ever done that? It's actually quite fascinating when you really concentrate on someone's lips as they chew their food." Lark chomped her lips together over and over, pressing them as close to his face as she could get.

Ken moved away angrily, but he couldn't help but absorb her infectious giggles.

"If anything, it'll get you out of here and take your mind off all the madness… for a little while at least."

"And if I don't want to take my mind off of it?"

"Then I'm going to have to club you in the head until you do."

Ken chuckled. "You'd probably do it, too, wouldn't you?"

"You damn well bet I would." Lark waited patiently for Ken to crack that winning smile of his. When he did, she raised hers and said, "Come on." She grabbed Ken's shoulder and pulled him toward the door.

Ken stopped a few feet before it and turned to Lark, who looked a little confused but patient. "Thank you."

Lark's smile became full of admiration. She rested her fingers gently on his cheek. "Always."

Ken nodded and left the room. Lark's smile suddenly faded as she curled her fingers together, lightly pressing them against her chest.

Always.

— 49 —

Sentilla sat at her station, constantly checking the navigation systems for any possible obstructions. She couldn't get the visual of Tracey spinning herself into a black hole from her mind. It wasn't only the bravest thing she had ever witnessed, it was the strangest thing she'd ever seen as well. And part of her felt sorry she was gone — her and the gem. Jaxxa Rakala had given her the ability to fight her weaknesses; she just wished she could have repaid her in some way, even if payment was a simple thank you.

 She was concentrating on the navigation systems so intently, she didn't hear Lark enter the bridge.

"Do you need a break?"

Sentilla jumped and growled slightly before realizing who it was and what she said. "Yeah," she said lethargically. She stood and squeezed Lark's shoulder tightly. Lark cupped her own hand around Sentilla's elbow and nodded with Sentilla in a sign of respect and honor. She then took her position as Sentilla left command for her living quarters, where a good long rest was waiting for her. And that wasn't all.

Qah-Shekel sat in the corridor outside of her door with a piece of rock in his hand. "I am a complete failure."

Sentilla sat down and wrapped her hand around his. "What makes you say that?"

"Every decision I've ever made has led to destruction."

"That's not true."

Qah-Shekel squeezed the rock so hard, he thought he might crack it.

"If this is about DovenJadden, she had us all fooled. Even Kahli."

"But it was my decision to bring her aboard. It was my decision to allow the humans to stay. It was my decision to…" Qah-Shekel turned away, dropping the rock to the ground.

Sentilla picked it up. She couldn't be certain where it had come from, but she had an idea. "How did you escape the purge?"

Qah-Shekel peered at the rock. He forced a smile that didn't last long. "I tried to feed my own ego. Sometimes I wonder if I hadn't have been so determined to break so many records, I might have been able to save them, maybe even stop it from happening."

"You couldn't have stopped it."

"Yeah." Qah-Shekel remained unconvinced.

"What records were you trying to break?"

"My rites of passage. Every young Krylexian must train for adulthood through the Kyilar. It's a series of tests that measure strength, fortitude, resilience and leadership. When my group was chosen to leave for Calicor, where the tests are conducted, I was so confident in my skills, I was in line to break every record ever recorded. Upon completion, I had passed every test at a higher level than anyone else but I was nowhere near the records. I refused to leave until I could train even further and try the tests once more. My mentor encouraged me, pushed me beyond what I thought I was capable of until I was able to do what I sought to do. But by the time I had, Krylex had been destroyed and all of my people — gone."

"It sounds to me your ego saved your life."

"And cost everyone else's theirs. And it's now cost the lives of thousands more."

"Qah-Shekel, none of that was your fault. There is no way you could have known any of this was going to happen."

"Maybe," he said.

Sentilla sat with him in silence for a few moments before she said, "There is something else to consider in all of this. If you had broken all of those records from the start, or failed to allow yourself to be better, we never would have met. You have a purpose, here, Qah-Shekel, as do I." Sentilla returned the rock to Qah-Shekel. "You can't let it haunt you."

"I thought finding out who killed my family would heal me. But it's only made it worse."

"It's hard. When my mother was killed, I thought I would never get over it. I was frightened, always trying to live up to her standards even though she wasn't here; always searching, keeping one eye open for the bastards who took her from me, hoping one day I might be able to return the favor. But Jaxxa Rakala showed me something that helped me finally understand why I was better for being able to let it go."

"What was that?"

Sentilla covered the other side of the rock with her hand. "That love will always exist. It never leaves you, nor will it ever disappear. All it does is transfer from one person to another, so long as you let it. If you don't, it will eat at you because you have no way to express it, which causes your other emotions to fight against each other. When I lost my mother, rather than trying to hold onto her love, I needed to notice it was all around me in the people that cared for me. Like Kahli, like Jaxxa Rakala; like you."

Sentilla leaned in and kissed Qah-Shekel. It was long and held all of the passion and love that he remembered from everyone he had ever cared for in his life and hers. It melted his body into a cloud that floated about Sentilla's lips, giving off a cool, soft breeze of a day lying on the rocks on his planet; the laugh of a friend as they wrestled along the sunny day of carefree playfulness. His mind was clear of any fear or anger he once had had; all he was was her, and she him, with their hearts burned together as one flesh.

When she removed her lips, Qah-Shekel caressed Sentilla's hair.

"I see your point," he said, "and I'll raise you one in turn." He kissed her again, and this time laid her back and enjoyed the love of their mutual partnership into the abyss of ecstasy.

— 50 —

A couple of months had gone by (or at least that's what it felt like before they finally started gaining ground on Eyrixano's ship) since leaving Rega-One to track down Jacquline. Ken spent most of that time keeping himself busy, helping Lark and Kahli with repairs where he could and studying up on all of the weapons DovenJadden had left behind, as well as all types of weapons that had been stored within the *Equinox* database. Sometimes Lark would help him when it came to translating certain accessories or uses, but mostly she would keep him company in silence as she continued to master Sentilla's language. He liked having her around for sure; that wasn't up for debate. But he also liked being alone when he could — it gave him the opportunity to think about his wife and daughter and relive some of their best moments together. He was coming to terms with the fact that they were gone, and chances of getting either of them back were slimmer than being struck by lightning after winning the lottery, but keeping them in his thoughts and prayers, and making sure to hold onto their memories, gave him comfort and reason to keep going. After all, Jacquline was still alive; Tracey wouldn't have saved Eyrixano's ship if she wasn't. She might have been brainwashed by Eyrixano's seduction, but he couldn't give up on her because of that. That could be reversed if they both fought hard enough to hold onto what remained of Jacquline's true spirit and remind her why he cares so much about her.

He was alone in the weapons storage unit reminiscing about an argument he once had with Stacey about gun control when Lark came rushing in, reddened with sweat and nearly out of breath. "Ken. Come quick."

"Why? What's wrong?"

"Nothing's wrong. We're approaching Eyrixano's position. Qah-Shekel wants us all in command."

Ken didn't have to be asked twice. The two of them hauled ass through the ship like a couple of little kids racing to meet their favorite pop star in the café before everyone found out they were there and scared them away. When they reached command, everyone was there with their eyes glued to the view screen. "You're just in time," Sentilla said and dropped the ship out of lightning speed. The screen was again littered with stars, but it wasn't until the *Equinox* sailed past a familiar looking object that Ken gasped in surprise. "Is that...?"

It took Lark a few seconds to register what Ken was seeing, but then she too had to do a double take. "Saturn?" she whispered.

As the ship continued to slow to a near crawl and Eyrixano's ship came into view just out of range of a large blue and green orb with a small moon sitting off to its side, Kahli walked up to them and smiled.

"Kenneth, Lark. Welcome home."

ABOUT THE AUTHOR

BRYAN CARON is a multi-talented, award-winning artist and creative director/owner of Phoenix Moirai, a company based out of Murrieta that serves as the creative genius behind all of your graphic design, writing and videography needs. Believing it was time to move on from the mundane routine of a nine-to-five job, Bryan pooled all of his talents to start the one-stop creative shop in 2014. As a fledging business owner, Bryan dove headfirst into a world he knew almost nothing about and, like any worthwhile endeavor in life, has learned on the fly, failing and succeeding with every new day. Ultimately, Bryan would like Phoenix Moirai to become not only a world-premiere creative agency for everything related to graphic design, writing and video, but a successful publishing company, capable of competing with the big boys while offering artists more creative freedom, giving them a chance where others wouldn't. *Memoirs of Keladrayia* is the first novel to be published under the Phoenix Moirai banner, and it certainly will not be the last.

On the artistic side, Bryan has published three additional novels and has written, produced and directed several short and feature films. He currently has several novels and screenplays in various stages of development and is always looking for that next big project he can sink his teeth into.

Bryan resides in Riverside County.

publishing.phoenixmoirai.com